ABYSS OF RUINS

The Protector Guild Book 5

GRAY HOLBORN

ISBN: 9798795353296

Cover: DamoroDesign

❀ Created with Vellum

❧ I ❧

DARIUS

"**W**ake the hell up, asshole."

The voice was gruff and filled with a sort of lingering pain, like uttering the sentence alone was a difficulty. But it was familiar nonetheless.

I peeled one eyelid open and glanced around the room. It was bright. The sort of sharp, piercing bright that could only be achieved by a cheap fluorescent lightbulb—the kind that didn't go away even when your lids closed. I caught sight of it dangling a few feet away from me, loose and wiry, like the kind of prop you'd find in a human's serial killer fantasy.

Where the hell was I? And how the fuck did I get here?

I tried to move my arm, but found out pretty damn quickly that I couldn't. Both of them were restrained above my head. I lifted my neck, groaning at the flash of pain that seemed to follow every single muscle movement, and caught sight of a set of thick chains.

Oddly enough, this wasn't the first time I'd found myself suspended from a ceiling. There'd been more pleasant versions of this very scenario in former bedrooms of mine.

But they never came with a heavy dose of confusion and disorientation. Almost never, anyway.

"Good, you're alive," the voice mumbled again from some-where behind me, like a grumpy fairy godmother or surly echo. I tried to crane my neck to get a good look, but I didn't have any luck. It felt like I'd been rammed by a train. Maybe even thirty trains. I hadn't felt this shitty since my days as a certified Guild lab rat. Not that those days were very far behind me. But still, there'd been some pleasantry—some hope—between then and now. "Now I can at least have the opportunity of killing you myself."

"Nash?" I asked, watching as my feet dangled a few centime-ters above a tiled floor, like I was a marionette doll without a puppeteer. The floor was the sort of grimy that told me this place hadn't been properly cleaned in at least a few years. Maybe even a decade. Then again, who bothered to keep a prison pris-tine if it was just going to be used as a torture chamber anyway? I certainly wouldn't bother. "What the hell did you do to me? You could give the protectors a run for their money with this sort of set up, you know."

I swallowed back a dry laugh, admiring the irony. I'd escaped one set of jailers, only to fall immediately into the den of another. Either I had the world's most rotten luck, or I made the worst choices imaginable. But I'd rather have a group of Guild researchers to contend with than Nash—Nash's imagination was a terrifying prospect.

"I didn't do this you mindless fuck. I'm locked up and in just as much pain as you are right now." He let out a frustrated grunt and I heard the rattle of his chains echo around the room as he made his point. I bit back a grin at the idea of him dangling there, as powerless as I was. "You've been in hell for a day and you've already gone and pissed off some pretty important players here. Color me shocked. I just wish you could've had the decency to leave me out of your shit for once. I should've known from the moment you walked into my territory that I wouldn't be so lucky."

I narrowed my eyes, studying the room with a renewed focus.

That didn't sound right. Nash—well, I was at least partially certain that he wouldn't *actually* kill me. And if he did, it would be a slow, drawn out sort of play-with-your-food kind of death. But if it wasn't him who'd locked me up, and if someone had gotten the slip on both of us....well, that didn't sit too well.

"What happened?" I hated the fact that I couldn't remember, hated that I had to rely on a mercy I was confident he wouldn't show. There were very few things about hell that I missed, but the old Nash, the one I grew up with, was one of them. Not that I'd ever voice that out loud. The prick had enough of an ego already.

"I should be asking you the same thing. I walked out of the warehouse and into an ambush. I don't know why I was surprised to discover you were at the heart of it. Who the fuck did you piss off?" He let out a humorless chuckle, his chains jangling like a ghost out of a Scrooge cartoon. "Easier question is probably who haven't you pissed off?"

I closed my eyes, as the memories started to jostle loose. Right. Ambush. Ratty wolves, a whole pack of them. Maybe even more than I'd ever seen in one go before, definitely more than I'd ever tried taking on, anyway.

I'd been stalking Nash, hoping to learn whatever secret he was so clearly keeping from me. Whether about what happened to his sister, Nika, or about where I might find Max's little incubus friend.

My breath lodged in my throat.

Max.

I shook my arms, trying to squeeze my wrists through the rings holding them in place. It was futile, especially while I was this weakened.

"The girl—" I blurt out, shocked by the terror even I could hear in my voice, "what happened to the girl? Did they take her? Have you seen her? Tell me she's fucking alive, Nash?"

Nash grunted and shook his chains again. The guy lived for drama. Normally, I'd find it amusing, but a fear unlike any I'd felt in a very long time was coursing its way through my veins. I held in my disgust with myself. Fear was a weakness, one I rarely allowed myself the agony of lingering in.

"Nash," I bit out again, my tone brokering no room for his games or grudges. I didn't so much as breath in the time it took him to answer me, my lungs suddenly deflated and empty, like a balloon with a puncture.

After pausing so long that my stomach tightened into a hard knot, he let out a low sigh. "I don't know. I haven't seen her. I tried taking down as many wolves as I could. I guess they thought I was with you—those assholes always seem to think that all vampires are aligned with each other. Ridiculous. If they'd only asked, I would've helped them kill you myself. Now, instead, I'm looped in with the enemy. I have my own shit to deal with, without adding your trash onto my pile."

He trailed off on some diatribe about wolf factions and me being a dickhead, but since it was clear that he wasn't going to tell me what I wanted to know, I was done listening. For now.

The wolves. We'd been attacked on the rooftop while spying on Nash. My lips tingled with the memory of Max's tongue sliding against mine. A shiver ran down my spine when I thought about how my body had responded to hers—a need the likes of which I hadn't felt in, well, maybe ever, if I was being honest with myself. What the hell was the little protector, and how was she able to twist up my mind and body with so little effort? It was almost like she was my m—

I shook my head, trying to refocus my thoughts. I could already feel the blood rushing to my dick, and that was just not where I needed it to go at the moment. Wolves. Max. I needed to get out of here, needed to find her.

The images rushed back in a flood, both of us surrounded. There had to be dozens. I was strong, way stronger than most. Taking on two or three werewolves was completely manageable for me on a good day. Hell, it was manageable on a bad day too. But I hadn't been properly feeding for the last half of a decade,

4

and there'd been way more than two or three wolves on that rooftop.

I remembered taking down half a dozen at least, and could still feel the sting of wolf venom lingering below my skin; but I'd heal, so I wasn't worried. My blood would burn it up in no time, the wounds most likely already closed over. How long had I been out?

Max's dark eyes flashed in my memory, the fear and confusion that widened her expression as she'd gone spilling over the rooftop. I'd tried fighting the wolves back to get to her, the rage and fear in my body more real than anything I'd felt in as long as I could remember. Something about that girl woke me up. And as annoying as it was, I wasn't ready for it to be over, for that part of me to disappear into a slumber again. At least not until I figured out what the fuck she was, why she affected me the way that she did.

It was a burning, all-consuming curiosity, nothing more.

She'd crawled her way back onto the roof, the look of fear replaced with one of vengeance. If I hadn't been so concerned in the moment, I'd have been turned on. The focus on her face, the power that seemed to encase her—it was mesmerizing. She was mesmerizing. Every chance I'd gotten, I glanced in her direction, just long enough to see that she was holding her own against the wolves.

When she'd tried hiding under a fallen body, I'd clawed my way desperately towards her, but the sheer multitude of the pack had made it impossible to reach her in time. There were too many. We didn't stand a chance. It didn't matter how strong we were, it wouldn't be enough.

But then there was fire—that peculiar flame that she'd suddenly started producing without any awareness. Another mystery added to the intriguing heap that was Max Bentley.

And then, nothing.

Just a swarm of gross furry bodies swallowing me beneath them as my body failed me, failed her.

My stomach dropped as I considered the fact that she wasn't here. The wolves had captured me alive. Nash as well.

The fact that we were both here was a bit of a marvel. It wasn't like the predators of this world to keep any semblance of a threat alive. And while I'd lost the battle, I'd taken out enough of them to make it abundantly clear I was absolutely a threat. There were many in this realm who would pay a heavy fee to do the honors of shutting me up permanently. I had a lot of enemies that I'd left behind—maybe I was a bargaining chip? A tool they could use to get out of here if they wanted? Had the wolves figured out who I was?

I shook my head. How would they have?

And Max wasn't here. If they were going to keep trophies, I'd imagine a girl who lit the world on fire would be a top-shelf prize. I slowed my breathing, trying to focus on her scent. The smell of her shampoo, vanilla and clean, had become so intoxicating that I could practically taste it along the surface of my tongue. It was the only scent other than blood that evoked that sort of muscle memory. I listened with every fiber of my being to whatever sounds were beyond this wall. But nothing. The only thing I could smell was my own blood, the lingering odors of whatever creature had last died in this room, and Nash's nasty stench. Nothing that even remotely smelled of Max.

Was it possible that she'd been killed?

My breath stuttered as the thought passed through me.

Possible? Yes. Probable? Also yes. But until I knew for certain, I couldn't let myself sink into that realization. Couldn't deal with the possibility of her no longer existing in the world. While she was in it, the world was actually interesting for once.

"Tell me everything," I said, the words little more than a whisper, but loud enough that I knew Nash could hear. I was done pandering to his childish grudges. There would be a time, a place, where he could hash out everything he needed to hash out —but right now was not that time, and this hovel was most certainly not that place. "I need to know who's taken us. What are the factions like now? Why would they keep us imprisoned, alive? How long have I been out—"

"Good," a thin, tall man stood framed in the doorway. His dark brown hair was shaggy and unkempt, his clothes so loose they were hanging off his shoulders like he was little more than skin stretched over a skeleton. The lingering scent of canine filled the air around me as he took a few steps closer to me. A wolf. "You're both awake."

"Who the fuck are you?" I asked, unable to keep the scowl of disgust from my face. It wasn't exactly good form to insult your captor, especially if you wanted to exploit them for information, but I was never known for my sound decisions. I took a deep breath, determined to play nice. "And where the fuck is the girl?"

Determined to play nic*er*, anyway.

He arched a thick brow, his lips tilting in a smirk so condescending that I'd have decapitated him instantly if I wasn't currently dangling like a carcass in a meat factory—*his* meat factory. "That's what I'm hoping you can tell me."

"I mean it you fu—" I cleared my throat as his words washed over me. "The girl I was with? You don't know where she is?"

"That's the only reason you're here," he said, his voice cold and dripping with disgust. "The only reason. You'll live for as long as it takes for you to lead us to her." He shrugged and awkwardly lifted a metal case as his eyes glistened with a slimy excitement. "And until you do, I've been given permission to have as much fun as I want, until death will seem like a great reward."

The wolf grinned, revealing a set of crooked, yellowing teeth. He opened the small case and pulled out a large, silver blade. The way he studied it, point at eye-level, was the way that I probably looked when confronted with a fresh tap of O-neg. Wolves weren't necessarily glorifiers of violence by nature; but this one in particular clearly had a sadistic bent that made even me a little queasy. And that was saying something.

I cocked an eyebrow. After years living in The Guild's

research lab, I was no stranger to torture. If anything, I'd come to count on it—pain was one of the few things for me to hold on to when boredom and monotony started to bubble. Pain was grounding. He wouldn't get what he wanted from carving me up, but let him try if he must.

In the meantime, he'd given me the one thing that I needed desperately—confirmation that Max was alive and not here in this hellhole with me and Nash. She'd gotten away somehow. He'd played his hand too quickly. Fucking blood-thirsty amateur. Wolves always were the most uninspiring creatures in this realm.

And while I was damn curious to hear the details about how she could slip away from a pack of werewolves without a single one of them able to track her down, I could live with that suspense for a while if I had to. Especially if it kept her safe. I couldn't be tortured to reveal information I didn't have.

"So," he said, drawing the word out as he closed the distance between us. Even his predatory crawl made my lip curl. "Who should we start with first?"

Nash exhaled behind me, almost as if he was bored with our creepy caretaker already. I suppressed a grin, wishing for a moment that I could see his face. This was the Nash I had almost fond memories of—the one with a penchant for violence that outweighed even mine. The one who would eat sleazes like this guy for breakfast, with relish.

"Look mate," he said, voice a lazy drawl like he was discussing Sunday brunch, "we don't know where she is. If you're going to kill us, just get it over with. I'd rather be dead than have to spend another minute in here with this prick."

I swallowed back my laugh. I knew Nash well—better than most. And while he was definitely exaggerating about choosing death over my company, I also knew that he wouldn't reveal any information, even if he had information to reveal. It was part of the code. There was a reason protectors had trouble breaking the monsters they captured. We didn't talk. And we didn't betray our people. It was the fundamental commonality between us all —a bone-deep promise of silence.

"You then," the wolf said, changing course and heading back to where I presumed Nash was hanging on an identical set of chains. "We'll start with you. Makes no difference to me, whose skin is split first."

There was a moment of quiet and then I heard Nash let out an almost imperceptible, pain-filled groan, the raspiness echoing around me, taunting me with a promise of my own agony. The scent of his blood coated my nostrils, until it was the only thing I could smell. Jesus, we were going to be in for a long night. While I could handle pain better than most, it didn't mean there weren't other things I'd rather be doing than acting as an art project for a skeezy, sadistic fuck. Vampires were difficult to kill, which meant that we were the perfect candidates for torture. As soon as someone went too far—cut a little too deep, or spilled a little too much blood—we'd heal right back up and they could do it all over again. And again. And again. We made Sisyphus look like a man with a happy, fulfilling life.

"The girl, who is she?" he asked, but Nash just groaned again, his agony turning into a hollow laugh, as the wolf dug deeper. "How many of you are there? And what were you doing in our territory."

"That's Nash Burns," a sultry voice whispered from the doorway and I snapped my eyes back open. She had long, dark hair and bright, intelligent eyes. Something about her was familiar, but I couldn't quite put my finger on it. It had been years since I'd been in hell, it was probably best if I expected constant deja vu. "He's a loner. You're not going to get your answers from him."

She sighed and walked further into the room, her boots clicking softly against the floor, sending echoes around the walls, until she was less than a foot away from me. The muscles in her face were still, unreadable, a blank canvas. There was a raw determination in her posture, and while her slimy friend looked like the type to run from an honest fight, she struck me as the complete opposite. That made her far more interesting, and far more lethal.

She tilted her head towards me. "This one, I haven't seen him before. And Jay swears that he was with the girl who took out Oliver yesterday."

Oliver? Jay? Who the fuck was this chick talking about? I hated when the villains of the story spoke in riddles. Just give me the information up-fucking-front and be done with it. I had daydreams to explore, fantasies with a very mesmerizing protector to get to.

"Then why was," he paused, "Nash, did you say? Why was he at the scene of the crime then?"

I bit back a grin. The guy sounded like a bad extra in a shitty TV show. His tone was sing-songy, taunting, but I could tell that he wasn't excited by the girl's interruption. This was his play-time. Probably the only contribution his pack really valued him for. I knew his type. Bloodthirsty, but he needed his conquests already knocked down a peg. Only way he stood a chance. Hell was a difficult place for creatures like him. He was lucky he'd found a pack that valued him at all. Most of his sort, powerless and desperate, died young or became mutilated, twisted toys for their superiors.

"Probably bad luck. Not everything is a giant conspiracy, you baboon, why is that so hard for everyone to understand? Besides," the girl said, her eyes were narrowed and studying me with a shrewd focus, "Jay said there was only one vamp when they were attacked. And the girl—whoever was with him, they couldn't get a read on what she was. Not a vamp, and not a wolf, but that's all they got." She arched her brow and leaned around me so that she could stare at Hannibal Lecter herself. "So that means they either picked Nash up after, or he has nothing to do with the altercation in the first place. Didn't you listen to the report when they brought them back in?"

The man grunted in response, and I had a feeling that if I could see him, he would resemble a shriveled up, scolded child.

"Jesus, kid, you're losing your touch," she muttered, disgust turning her lips down. "And your relevance. That's a dangerous rope to walk."

I let out a soft chuckle, the realization pouring over me like an ice-cold bath, once I set their interpersonal squabbling aside. Declan and I had taken out a few werewolves when we'd landed ourselves into hell in the first place. Apparently, they hadn't taken kindly to that. The ambush wasn't about Max then, it was just sweet, simple revenge. I almost peed myself with the relief of it. Max getting sucked into the rooftop soiree was just shit luck.

"Just so you know," I said, my voice lazy and calm, now that I knew that Max wasn't in danger. Or, at least, that she wasn't locked up somewhere in here where creepy could go hacking away at her smooth skin. "Your wolfpack attacked me and my friend first. That was a self-defense sort of situation. And now you've gone and kidnapped my innocent friend—" I ignored Nash's childish grunt, "and me, like good and proper villains. So, you know, karma and what not. Look out for it."

And it was the truth. I wasn't the sort to go picking fights in hell of all places, especially when so much had changed in my absence. I fancied my freedom and being alive to enjoy it now that I finally had it. Of course, 'had' was the operative word when it came to my freedom. The goal was to get in, rescue wolfy's baby brother, and get the fuck out. Making fresh enemies was more work than I had energy or time for.

The girl let out a soft, breathy laugh from behind me, but there was something almost sad in the sound. "I don't doubt that's the truth. But too bad for you both, it doesn't matter." She swiped a sharp nail down my back, tearing my shirt in the process. Keeping clothes intact in hell was proving almost as difficult as surviving. Who would've known? "Boss wants the girl. And you're not getting out of here until he gets her." I could hear her climbing on something, a ladder or steps, and then felt the soft whisper of her breath against the shell of my ear. "I can keep Mickey away from you, if you tell us where she is. I promise I'm more gentle than he is. And I only bite when asked."

Normally, that sort of thing would have my blood pumping and my dick hard. This girl's torture-kink approach was much more pleasant than her partner's. But right now, all I could focus on was Max. Where was she? And was she okay? What the hell was that girl doing to me?

"Why do you want her?" I asked, turning my head slightly to grin at her, laying the gravel in my voice thick. Women loved that shit. And I'd happily play into it if it got me the answers I needed.

"Jesus, nothing ever fucking changes," Nash mumbled behind me. Even though the room reeked of his blood, he still didn't sound particularly concerned or even interested in the situation he'd found himself in. If anything, he was treating this whole thing like it was nothing more than a minor traffic ticket on the way to the store, another inconvenience introduced by his dear friend, Darius.

I grinned in spite of myself, I forgot what it was like to have my kind around. Vampires were insufferable sometimes, but almost never boring.

"It's not every day that you run across a girl who can summon hellfire, least of all control it." She hopped down from whatever she was standing on and walked around me until I could see the curiosity written on every angle of her face.

Great so they'd seen Max light up like a Christmas tree.

Of course they had. It was pretty hard to miss when it happened. But that definitely complicated things. If the situation were reversed, and I ran into a creature like her in the wild, I'd want her too—more than I already did. She was like a rare, sparkly Pokemon. And that sort of power was a pretty hefty bargaining chip in a world that was filled with the sort of desperation that made Vegas look like kindergarten.

"Not to mention one who can control hellfire *and* teleport," the guy added, his voice trailing closer to us as he left Nash to dangle solo, the chains creaking softly as his weight shifted. "Heard about that part," he said, letting out a gruff breath of air with a smell so pungent, I almost wished I had human senses, "not that I'll believe it until I see it."

Teleport? My breath caught in my throat as his words registered. Had Max really teleported? That would explain how she escaped without leaving behind a trail for wolves to trace.

I snorted, musing over all the ways that girl managed to surprise me. Each time I thought I was close to figuring her out, she went and did something like this. What the hell was she?

My stomach dropped, surprise dropping into fear as I realized how much more valuable she was now—how much more difficult it would be to keep her safe. Especially in this realm. Not for the first time, I wished that I had just left her sniveling little incubus to rot away and stolen her off for my own safe keeping. Stockholm Syndrome was apparently a thing, so maybe it would've worked out in my favor. And she'd be safe. Saf*er*, anyway.

"That shit's unheard of, unless she's one of the ancients," the guy continued, desperate for the chance to talk, for people to listen to him. I almost felt bad that he had to resort to torture in order to garner an audience. He clicked his tongue loudly, like he was echoing a bad police procedural he'd seen one too many episodes of.

"She arrived from the human realm, so she's not," the girl responded, her words terse, as she rolled her eyes. I got the feeling she hated her friend—Mickey did she say? I didn't blame her, the guy was a creep. Even the air around him felt like it was oozing bad vibes. "Boss is sure of it. None of them fit her description. Which is why he's so keen on tracking her down." She grinned at me, her smile flirtatious and suggestive. "What do you say handsome, you want to play nice? We reward people here when they've earned it." She leaned in close again, "which explains why Mickey gets stuck with all the jobs nobody really wants."

"I'm a fucking werewolf," he said, his voice strained with rage, and though I couldn't see his face as he started pacing, I could picture it. "I can fucking hear you, you cunty bitch."

Cunty bitch? Who did this guy learn his social cues from? Even his insults were slimy and awkward.

He walked past me and tossed his metal box of instruments on the ground as he made his way to the door. "New girl thinks she's the shit just because she fucked the boss once or twice. Fucking ridiculous. You'll fall from that pedestal sweetie, just as they all do. Just you wait."

He left, mumbling about grabbing a drink and taking a piss before returning to the festivities, and the energy in the room shifted instantly. I could feel the girl's anger as she stared after him, like he'd left his phantom standing there, just to toy with her and piss her off.

This pack seemed to have some serious need of an HR firm to parse out their grumbling conflicts. Which was great news for me and Nash. If it meant getting us the fuck out of here, he might even be convinced to join me in my plan.

Conflict we could exploit. Maybe even turn this girl to our side. Something about the rigidity of her posture, the way she glanced at Mickey's discarded torture toolkit with a cool disregard told me that she wasn't too happy here, wasn't a huge fan of the whole violent culture that her packmate subscribed to.

"You sure you're properly appreciated here, princess?" I asked, winking at her in what I hoped was a suggestive gesture. It'd been so long since I'd flirted, or so much as had the opportunity for sex, that I wasn't even sure I still had my magical touch.

She rolled her eyes, the sharp green of her irises flashing with a reluctant amusement. "Of course I'm not appreciated here. You've met Mickey, haven't you? You were attacked by my pack unprovoked. Appreciation isn't exactly the vibe we go for."

I shrugged, or tried to shrug anyway. It wasn't exactly easy when my shoulders were being slowly dislocated. "Get us out of here and we'll make sure to demonstrate our appreciation. In tandem if it helps."

"Jesus fucking Christ, just kill me." Nash blew out a breath of bemusement behind me and I mentally punched him. He used to be an excellent wingman when we were kids. But now his misplaced aggression towards me was going to ruin our shot of getting out of here.

The girl leaned closer to me until I could feel the slight graze of her breasts against my lower stomach. "Appreciation isn't what I'm after. Appreciation doesn't help you survive. And out here, survival is paramount." She crossed her arms, disgust written plain as day across her face. "I might not exactly love every member of my pack, and I might not find the same glory in torture that Mickey does, but that doesn't mean that I'm on your side. Vampires are the fucking lowest form of existence. They've killed half my family."

Shit. This conversation was turning sour real fast. I knew my flirting was out of practice, but I didn't expect it to be received this poorly.

"Great, we got one with a personal vendetta. Just perfect," Nash muttered behind me. "Just so you know, princess, we aren't a monolith. We don't all kill just to kill."

"Yeah, not unlike you and your friend Mickey," I added, deciding to abandon my plan of seduction and go with Nash's much more pragmatic approach of reason. The girl seemed like she was smart, maybe we could logic her into letting us get the fuck out of here. I had a girl to find. And the knowledge that she was out there, alone, teleported to who knows where, had my skin crawling with a painful itch.

"Might be the case," she said, her brows narrowing in the center as her lip curled. She was a pretty girl, that sort of unchecked rage boiling beneath her skin didn't suit her. "But you killed my friend, asshole. So my first impression tells me you're one of the bad ones."

"Going to be honest," I said, throwing a casual wink at her, "that does sound like something I'd do. But in my defense, I've been locked up and tortured for years, so this sort of treatment only breeds more violence. You fuck with my brain and mess with my pain tolerance too much and there's no controlling who I may or may not kill. Break the cycle while you can."

"Jariss was the closest friend and ally I had in this pack. She saved my life," the girl added as she walked towards Mickey's discarded case. "And because of you, I'm left here with a bunch of dirtbags who care only about blood and power. Alone. You did that," she spat out, venom in her eyes as she glanced at me, "not Mickey."

Shit. Anger I could work with, exploit. Grief and isolation were a much harder bag of tricks to manipulate.

"Well," I said, drawing the word out as I watched her, "maybe Jaris shouldn't have tried to kill me and my friend first. Might still be alive if she'd left well enough alone. You could hardly expect us to just stand there and let her and the rest of your pack try to flay us alive. You know how things are here, you know how things work. Don't let a grudge ruin an opportunity."

She bent down and toyed slowly with the contents of the case, like she was choosing which flavor of ice cream she wanted, the sound of metal clashing against metal reverberating along the walls.

It was her own unusual form of torture, slowly selecting a tool to cut into us with, and I had to repress the urge to roll my eyes. Nash and I had experienced our fair share of violence, and I doubted anything this little girl was going to do would seriously affect me. And I didn't have the time to sit around while she figured that out. Max was out there somewhere, and I needed to find her before she got killed. Hell was no place to travel alone, especially for someone like her—powerful, but untrained; intelligent, but wildly naive. It was the sort of combination that would draw hellbeasts from miles around, curiosity peaked.

She pulled out a long scalpel-shaped object so covered in rust that I could hardly decipher its original shape and stood back up, a wistful grin on her face. Without so much as a single muscle forecasting her move before she made it, she flung the blade.

I inhaled sharply as it buried itself into my throat, gurgling around my blood as I tried to speak. I felt my blood quickly coat the front of my shirt. I couldn't get a word out. And if she didn't remove the obstruction, the wound wouldn't heal. The girl was well-trained, clever, I'd give her that. She had more than your average wolf's power. She had something just as valuable—skills with which to use that power. If given the chance to blossom, away from this fucked up pack, I had no doubt that she'd make something of herself, claim some of that power she so aimlessly served.

"Excellent shot," Nash muttered behind me, "but maybe next time, aim for the heart. I could do with some peace and quiet."

"I don't want to listen to your grievances," she said as she stared me down, her jaw clenched so tightly that I could tell every word she uttered was a struggle. There was anger, sure, but there was also fear. We'd taken away her person here, and that was a dangerous thing to do to a volatile wolf. Something about her seemed a little off too, like she was on the edge of something, ready to fall. If I didn't know any better, I'd think she was a new wolf, but it was extremely rare, hell, almost impossible, for a creature to transition in this realm. But a lot had changed since my last visit, so I wasn't throwing out any possibilities. New wolves weren't exactly known for calm and rational dispositions. And the grieving process took emotional mood swings and made them look like child's play.

She arched an expectant brow and I narrowed my eyes. If she was hoping I would respond or answer any questions she had, she was going to have to remove the little dart protruding from my neck first.

"Gotta say," Nash said, his words layered with amusement. There was no question that he was enjoying the prospect of watching me get tortured—even if it meant he would have to live through some pain himself. "My experience would be much more enjoyable if you left that thing right where it is. Listening to this asshole speak goes far beyond any torture your lot could dream up."

I rolled my eyes. Nash was always known for being particularly dramatic. But he was also my case in point about grief. Because of me, his sister was dead. And any fondness he'd felt towards me, any friendship we'd developed while growing up, was gone because of it. I had no doubt that if the girl in front of me didn't kill me, Nash would be more than happy to finish the job himself. Slowly, with the kind of drawn-out torture that would make Mickey look like a cartoon character.

"I want to know where the girl is," the wolf said, her voice suddenly devoid of all emotion, like she'd caged the wolf that had been leaking out of her pores. She was good at turning it on and off, I'd give her that. That was also a skill that took a lot of training. A lot of training or a lot of trauma—maybe a bit of both. "That kind of information could be invaluable, a way for me to leverage my way out of here, maybe even help me get out of here and find my friends."

Like she was the type to have friends.

Maybe it was a good thing I couldn't form any words beyond a gross choking sound. My smart mouth always had a way of landing me in deep shit.

"Wish I could help you, princess, really I do. What's your name?" Nash asked. "I know a lot of important people. A lot. I'm sure I could help you out if you give me the chance."

He almost sounded earnest, like the sympathy lacing his tone was real. But I knew Nash well enough to know that if he did survive this imprisonment, everyone who put him in here was as good as dead. He didn't take well to being one-upped. And capturing him and throwing him in with me was as embarrassing as things could get for him.

It didn't escape my notice that he'd adopted my nickname for the girl, so maybe I had a chance of folding him into my escape plan.

"At the very least, if you help me out of here, I won't take you down when I wipe out your pack," he said, the patience dissolving from his tone. He was usually much more level-headed, even in situations like this. Which meant one thing—he was in a hurry to get out of here, just as I was. And for a reason beyond his own well-being.

What the hell had he been doing in that warehouse, all alone? What shape had his life taken without me in it?

The wolf's lip curled, but she closed up the small case and eyed us both with a deep-seated disgust. She pulled her long hair back into one of those messy ponytails that girls always wore and thought looked cute, the movement pulling her shirt up high enough to reveal a toned abdomen.

Normally, she might even be my type—a little dark and twisty, but with a layer of intelligence that would be fun to play with. I wasn't really one to discriminate based on species. I'd had several wolves in my day, and they were always great fun when it came to getting physical. But nothing about her turned me on.

I knew Nash's type though, and the silence at my back was easy to read. Even if he hated her for keeping him here, I knew with absolute certainty that he was checking her out and liking what he saw. I tucked that realization away for later—I'd exploit his weaknesses when I got the chance as well.

"I told you," she said, her voice a low, sultry growl. "I don't trust vampires. And if you're as high up as you think you are, then I'm sure you know more about the girl I'm after than you're letting on. And if you don't...well, I guess that means you're not as high up on the food chain as you might think."

Smart woman. And I had to say, it was always good fun to watch someone treat Nash like he was lower than dirt—this girl was the first person not to kiss his feet that I'd met in a long time. Nika and I were the only ones who ever gave him any shit.

"Sarah, let's go," a feminine voice yelled down the hall, the echo reverberating along the walls. After a long pause, the woman grunted, probably because she realized that the girl—Sarah—wasn't moving with the desired haste. "Boss has a lead on a new group not far out from here. Wants them taken care of before they cross into our territory. Too many new faces in too short a time period. We gotta take care of it."

Without another word, she turned and left the room, leaving me alone with Nash and a gaping hole in my throat.

Which meant I had no way to annoy him or entertain myself. Great.

❧ 2 ❧
DECLAN

"She's gone." Eli's face was paler than I'd ever seen it as he glanced between me and Atlas, like one of us might have the answers he was looking for.

"What the hell do you mean she's gone?" I asked, annoyed at the way my heart rate picked up. Two fucking words should not have the power to change your body chemistry like that. This girl was messing with my mind in ways that I wasn't okay with. "I'm sure she's just in the bathroom or something. They don't all lie around waiting for you to return to bed, you know?"

I shook my head, trying to physically push the image of Eli and Max in a relaxed knot of limbs from my mind. I didn't have the time or energy to dissect that shit right now. And I most certainly didn't want to fall down the rabbit hole of why the thought of them together made it difficult to breathe. We were in hell; we had shit to do. Getting all twisty over a girl was not on my priority list.

"You don't think—" Eli ran his hands through his dark hair, his eyes wide with worry. "What if she heard what we were talking about?"

Generally, Eli was pretty calm and collected, and very few things caused him much anxiety. But the thought of Max overhearing our conversation about her was obviously one of those few things. The panic was practically tangible as he paced back and forth, fingers twitching. The girl had really done a number on him—I couldn't remember a time that he was this jittery after getting laid. It was like his whole world had gone and turned itself on its side.

And I didn't blame him. If she'd heard us, we were right and royally screwed. Not only had he confessed to taking her fucking DNA while making out with her long enough to distract her and extract it, but we'd also discussed the fact that we'd been lying to her since the night in the hotel.

That not only had we been essentially spying on her since her arrival at Guild Headquarters, but we'd lied about her powers. Pretended like she hadn't gone and torched a room full of vampires that were trying to kill Eli.

And honestly, thinking back on it now, I didn't know why we'd ever thought it was a good idea to keep her powers from her. She was too naive for her naivety to be an act. We'd been treating her like a suspect, rather than a scared girl who was thrust into the middle of a new world and complicated system of power. While we'd discussed the possibility of her being aware of her 'unusual qualities', I knew deep down in my gut that she wasn't. She was too desperate to fit in.

The desire to find her people and belong radiated from her like a damn beacon. I recognized it because I'd had the same desire buried in my bones before I'd stumbled onto my team.

If she'd really known how truly different she was, there'd be more angst there.

Why hadn't I trusted my gut? When had I stopped trusting my gut?

I held my breath as the answer came rushing into my mind— when Max showed up. Eli's life wasn't the only one that got twisted upside down with her arrival. Half the time when she walked into the room, my body didn't know whether it wanted to run towards her or away from her—she was like a magnet that constantly revolved between positive and negative, pushing and pulling until it became impossible to leave her orbit. And all that I was left with was an annoying churning in my stomach that felt disturbingly like butterflies.

"I'll try and check the bathrooms, you guys just keep an eye out," I glanced at Atlas, his posture rigid with tension. "See if you can sniff her out or something."

My voice and posture were calm, collected even, but the thought of her overhearing us sent an ice pick into my chest. If I were her and knew that the people masquerading as my friends had been keeping something so huge from me, I'd be done. Instantly. There was no coming back from that sort of betrayal—trust wasn't something that could just be re-earned like that. Not in our world, not when trusting the people you were with was literally a matter of life and death.

My nails dug into my palms, leaving small crescent-shaped indents, as I realized with a sharp clarity how much it would hurt.

Her hating me? Losing her trust forever?

And knowing that I was part of the cause of her pain?

No.

I might not understand my weird draw to Max, and half the time I was terrified as fuck of her, but I also wasn't ready for that to be gone. Her arrival hadn't made my life easier by any stretch of the imagination, but it reminded me of what it felt like to be alive again—like I could take a breath, even if it was painful and not quite deep enough.

If Eli was right and she'd heard us chatting, I wanted to make sure that I was the one to find her, to smooth things over and try to gauge her temperature towards us.

Atlas was consumed by his wolf and didn't exactly handle conversations with Max with much self awareness or tact. Ever. The guy was half in love with her, or at least his wolf was, but his stubbornness was ruining any chance he'd ever get with her. And I most definitely did not want to be around when the wolf realized that he was dangerously close to pushing her away for good —even as a friend.

And then there was Eli. I blew out a puff of air as I watched him comb the room she'd been sleeping in, lifting up random things here and there, like a full-grown woman would suddenly turn up underneath a cardboard box or pile of debris. He was insufferable when he was beside himself like this, anxiety leaking out of every pore. He didn't handle guilt well, and I knew that if Max really had heard what we'd said, the guilt he was feeling would be damn well warranted.

And that sort of guilt was the worst—the kind that was deserved. There was no escaping it, no valve to ease the pressure.

Part of me wanted him to linger in that pain, just for a moment. I wasn't sure if it was anger or something else seeping through my veins as I watched him. But I still couldn't believe he'd gone and fucked her after everything. The guy couldn't go two days without getting his dick wet. And Max—she was going through enough without having to add his ridiculous libido into the mix.

"I'll check down the hall," I said quietly, shaking myself back to the present. It was like we were all frozen in our panic, thoughts whirring wildly—we were standing together, but each of us was lost in our own mindfuck.

She was probably in the bathroom freshening up, she probably hadn't overheard anything. We'd find her, collect her, and decide how we'd proceed from there. And if that wasn't the case, surviving hell would trump harboring resentment towards us, at least for now. Max was a reasonably rational woman and she was just as devoted to finding and saving Wade as the rest of us were.

I unclenched my hands, trying to shed some of the tension coursing through me. All this angst—it needed to go. I couldn't see straight when it came to Max and lingering on that shit wasn't doing any of us any good.

Atlas nodded, and stormed out of the room, and I knew that his silence was partially due to his wolf. He always struggled with using his words, but it became damn near impossible when his wolf was this close to the surface. Usually their battle was a silent one, happening behind the curtains, but in moments like this, I'd get a peak of the turmoil behind his eyes. Deep down, I knew he was dealing with the sort of war neither of us was confident he would win. It was enough to draw chills every time I thought about it.

Another thing I didn't have time to worry about right now. The universe really needed to stop raining shit down on my to-do list. Type A or not, I could only take on so much.

I pushed into the hallway, trying to swallow my disgust at the state of the place. We'd crashed a wendigo's pad and the creature and her roommates hadn't exactly kept a clean home. There was trash all over the place and what looked suspiciously like random sets of bones, likely from discarded meals. I didn't look at them long enough to discern whether those bones belonged to a humanoid creature or an animal. I shivered at the thought of what could have happened to Max and Eli if Darius hadn't been around to take the twat-waffle out.

And then I shivered again at that realization. Feeling gratitude for a vampire was about as far from my comfort zone as I could get.

I shook my head. Now wasn't the time to dissect exactly how that fanghole had started slowly creeping his way under my skin like an unwanted infection. I hated him still, that much was certain, but I didn't want to spit fire every time I saw him anymore. He'd been useful, even if infuriating.

I pushed the complexities and discomfort down, locking them in a box I'd deal with later. Eventually. Maybe.

I wandered around for a few minutes, busting slowly into every room I passed. We'd swept through the place before we'd left Max and Eli, to go foraging for some supplies and food, so I wasn't expecting anything to jump out at me, but I probably couldn't be too safe.

We were in hell, after all.

And, speaking of hell, where the *hell* were the bathrooms in this place? I vaguely remembered one or two of them on this floor, but I couldn't place their exact location. Maybe she'd gone storming off to clean up after all of the fun she'd had with Eli. I'd seen enough of his girls tramping through the hallways after a roll in the covers with him to know that a hairbrush and shower were probably high on her to-do list.

My stomach tightened as I pictured her, sleepy and sated, and I tried again to push the thought of her and Eli together out of my head. But ever since walking in on them, tangled together in the throes of sleep, a heavy pit had positioned itself in my stomach: stubborn, solid, unmoving.

I knew, deep down, that Eli was partially right.

That I was jealous. Or that I was at least some less-gross cousin of jealous, maybe.

I stopped cold at the internal admission.

Accepting that I was jealous was enough to send white-hot rage flowing through my veins. Not least of all because Eli had to point it out to me. Out of everyone. The guy had an emotional range the size of an acorn. On a good day. The fact that he was more tuned into my feelings than I was, meant that I had some serious work to do.

Eventually. Ugh.

I sucked in a breath of air, trying to ignore the staleness of it. I missed home, missed the way things were a month ago, missed having the semblance of a strategy or plan and a routine. I had no right to be jealous. Max hadn't really shown that she was interested in women—other than one brief moment in that hotel suite, when I thought maybe, just maybe, she was.

Besides, Atlas's wolf was trying desperately to bond with her, and I wouldn't backstab my friend for anyone, even if he was being a stubborn ass about it. Wolves found their true mate bond on very rare occasions.

I think.

We didn't understand how mate bonds worked with any

supernatural creatures. Not really, anyway. Just that they were exceedingly rare these days and they were powerful. Demons kept those secrets guarded, like they were sacred, revealing very little, even under duress. If we were right, and Max really was his, I didn't know how long he could realistically hold out. Not unless he wanted his wolf to take the reins and run his life for him, because from the few glimpses I'd seen of the creature, I knew damned well that it was a possibility.

I wouldn't be the thing to stand between Atlas and a chance at happiness—I owed him everything. No stray feelings over a confusing girl would get between us.

I turned a corner and swung open the first door on my right. The second I stepped in, I had to swallow back bile.

I'd found the bathroom.

It must've been one of the ones the guys had cleared earlier, because I wouldn't have been able to forget a stench like that. Clearly the wendigos living here didn't know much about plumbing. That, or they just didn't care if their bathroom was overrun with shit. Literally.

I backed out immediately, not even bothering to check if Max was in there, freshening up after a fuck. No self-respecting person would spend more time in that room than absolutely necessary. Not when there were other options—hell, I'd have rather peed outside than suffer through that stench. The walls were caked in excrement, like a child had used its only resource to create elaborate finger paintings around the room.

After walking through a few more rooms, each just as disgusting as the last, I was desperate to find her. Not only because I wanted to make sure she was okay and clear the air about anything she may or may not have overheard, but because I wanted to get the fuck out of this place. Wendigos just might win the award for my least favorite creature in the realm—and that was a competitive category.

Soft footsteps echoed around me and I flexed my fingers around my blade, ready to unsheathe it.

"She's not here," Atlas said as he rounded the corner, each word crisp and short. I could tell from the wildness in his eyes, from the apathy in his tone, that he was pushing his wolf back. And that it was taking every ounce of strength he had, which was a considerable amount. "I can't scent her anywhere."

"Probably just because your nose can't work past all the trash and shit in this place," I said, my own stomach still reeling from that bathroom. His wolf was probably dying a slow, excruciating death. I would be if my senses were any more heightened than they already were.

He shook his head, his dark eyes flashing with threads of gold. It kind of made him look like a superhero when they did that, not that I'd ever go and tell him so. Neither of the guys needed an ego boost, that was for sure. "I'm telling you, she's not here."

His jaw was sharp and tense, and I glanced down at his hands. They were clenched into tight fists, knuckles white as bone.

Seeing him so worried only amplified my own concern. We had a habit of feeding off of each other. It had always been that way, ever since we were angsty teenagers. I guess that's what happened when you spent too much time with someone, especially in our line of work. Our anxieties were always heightened, always climbing and responding to each other. Sometimes it was a good thing, kept us on our toes, in sync. Sometimes it made us impulsive, got us hurt, put us in danger. "You think something got to her or do you think she ran?"

Neither option was good. Max was strong—stronger than any protector I'd ever encountered in her age bracket—but this was hell, and we had no idea what was out there waiting for us. Day one of our arrival and she was almost wiped out by a creepy, flesh-eating child-zombie thing. I didn't want to think about what she could run into out there by herself.

He shook his head, not offering any sort of conclusive

response, and I turned as soft, hurried footsteps made their way down the hall, the echoes a chaotic, uneven beat.

"Any luck?" Eli's face was clammy and pale when he rounded the corner and skidded to a halt in front of us. For once, the smug look in his eyes was nowhere in sight. He glanced between both of us, noticing that there was no Max, and shook his head. "I guess not. Should we keep looking? Which rooms and floors haven't been cleared? I can also double back, go through them all again. Maybe—"

I shook my head, cutting off his anxious rambling, and nodded towards Atlas. "He's got the world-class sniffer. She's not here."

Eli narrowed his eyes and studied Atlas. After a long moment, he started biting his lip—it was an old, nervous habit that I hadn't seen him fall back on in quite a while. "Like not in this building at all? Should we check the perimeter, maybe a few of the other dozen abandoned buildings around here? It's not like she just went poof," he smacked his hands together, "and disappeared, you know? She's got to be close by somewhere." He paused a beat, biting his fingernails now. "I mean, you don't think something got to her, do you? Like another wendigo." If there was any color in his face before, it was completely gone now. "Or something worse. We'd have heard something, right? If she was attacked or taken? It wouldn't just be radio silence."

I inhaled deeply, trying to recenter myself. One of my boys was turning into a babbling buffoon, the other was silent and dangerously close to being eclipsed by the monster lingering beneath his skin.

Which meant that I was going to have to take point on this. I could pretend to be calm, at least for a few minutes, while I developed a plan. I couldn't let myself sink into the panic that would come if Eli's darker suspicions were true. While I didn't know what to do with Max ninety percent of the time, I knew for certain that the thought of her not being around anymore made it difficult for me to breathe.

"I don't think she's been taken," I said slowly, trying to convince myself just as much as I was trying to calm the boys, "but if she was, she's strong. She's always been a great fighter—one of the best—and now with the whole fire thing she's got going on, I don't think we need to spiral into hysteria just yet. If something attacks her, she can fend for herself." I started walking back to the room we'd been speaking in before, confident that they would fall in line and follow me. The rustling footsteps behind me told me that they had. "So, we take our stuff, and go searching." I spoke up so that my words would carry as we wound through the halls. "Eli has a good point, she could have just gone to hide out in one of the other buildings. If she had been eavesdropping, I wouldn't blame her. I'd want some space from us too. We betrayed her. That's on us. It's possible she just needs a minute to collect her thoughts where she can get some privacy."

I swung the door open and grabbed Eli's pack. I shoved it into his chest, a little harder than necessary, and moved towards where I'd left mine. Apparently I was still a little annoyed about the fact that he went good on his rakish persona and screwed everything up. Not that I could vocally put that blame on him right now—I could see the guilt weighing heavily on his shoulders. He wasn't the best emotional regulator. And Max had him more twisted up than I'd ever seen.

"But this is hell," I continued, as I searched around for my stuff, noticing that her things were indeed no longer here in the process. I nodded at the empty blotch of ground where her things had been strewn about before, noting the absence to the boys. She definitely took off then. That should've been the first thing we looked for—assessed our surroundings. We were slipping. Our collective obsession over Max, the good and the bad, was clouding our judgment. "So I doubt she'd go far, no matter how pissed off she was. Atlas can help sniff her out, especially with his wolf so close to the surface. And hopefully we'll find her before dawn. Find a way to explain our side of things and hope that she can forgive us long enough to find Wade and then get us all the fuck out of here."

It was as good a speech as I was capable of giving, and I was damn proud of myself for keeping my own anxieties from filtering into my voice.

"Jesus, Dec," Eli said, his jaw loose and eyes wide. "You're worried. Like really, really worried." He ran his hand through his dark hair. "Fuck. You think something got her, don't you? Shit. Why are we such assholes? Why did we think it was okay to have a conversation like that when she was so close by?"

Alright, apparently I wasn't as good at hiding my feelings as I liked to think. At least not from the guys, anyway. Good to know. We all had things we could improve about ourselves, and I'd just spotted one of mine.

I chewed the inside of my cheeks, not even deigning to give the shithead a response. The problem wasn't just that we got caught, the problem was that we'd betrayed her in the first place.

Fucking men. What was the point of them?

"We should hurry, faster we go, faster we find her." Eli turned back towards the door and started jogging, patting Atlas on the shoulder as he passed him. "Come on Fido, let's put that fancy nose of yours to use."

If we'd been panicking before, after checking through four buildings with no lead on her scent, we were full on fucking beside ourselves now. None of us even bothered trying to hide the adrenaline and anxiety radiating from each of us as we searched, our movements growing more and more desperate with each moment that passed.

My heartbeat was going so hard, I could feel it pulsing in my neck, and I hadn't said a word since leaving the second building, for fear my emotions would just dump all over the place as soon as I opened my mouth.

"You don't think she'd straight up run away do you?" Eli asked. His hair was sticking up in every which direction because of how frequently he'd resorted to running his hands through it.

"I mean, yeah what I did was fucked. But not as fucked as getting eaten alive by a fucking hell demon. Max is smart, she wouldn't go traipsing off into hell by herself like that. Right?" He turned from me to Atlas, and back to me again. "Right?"

"I don't—" I cut off as I watched Atlas freeze every muscle in place, like a wave went over him, turning him full statue. During the last hour he'd uttered no more than a handful of words, most of them nothing more than a grunt-phrase hybrid. The stillness was new and judging by the dark set of his eyes, this version of new wasn't good. It was bad. Very, very bad.

"I've got something." He took a deep breath, frustration tightening the muscles in his back. "The vamp too." His voice was a low growl as he spun back towards me, his eyes gold and filled with a rage that had even me taking a few steps back from him. I didn't think Atlas's wolf would ever hurt me, not really, but that didn't mean I wanted to be within claw's reach when he had that look on his face. It was moments like this one when I realized how much the wolf had changed my friend—when I looked at him, it was like two creatures were looking back at me. One as familiar to me as myself, the other a stranger—and a dangerous stranger at that.

The vamp too.

Of-fucking-course. How had we not thought about him in all of our panic? The beast lived to sow discontent and chaos. He was the type to get high off of it.

"He came back here without letting us know? You think he found something? Went after her?" Eli asked, oblivious to the tension radiating from Atlas. He turned away from us and started pacing a worn path in the dirt.

The fanghole, Darius, had left us here hours ago. He'd told us he wanted to check up on some old friends, maybe get a lead on where Wade was being kept, but I hadn't been holding out any real hope that he'd save the day with any information he found. From what I could tell, everyone who knew him seemed to despise him just as much as we did. And from the way he'd been studying everything in this realm with a careful precision, something told me a lot had changed here in his absence. The hell we were in right now was not the same hell that he'd left behind all those years ago.

Part of me figured he was just using his errand as an excuse to ditch us here, to run away with his tail between his legs, confident that The Guild wouldn't be able to lure him back into captivity from here. Which, if I was being honest, was a win-win for us. The only reason we'd gotten him here in the first place was because Max promised that when we eventually got Wade back, she wouldn't come back to The Guild straight away.

Of course, we had no intention of letting her follow through on that promise, but still.

His obsession with the girl was peculiar. In all of my years with The Guild, I'd never seen anything like it—one of them taking such an...intimate interest in one of us. It grated against my nerves every time I noticed how closely he watched her, his expression filled half with curiosity, half with something that looked suspiciously like lust.

Suspiciously like the way that I occasionally caught Atlas or Eli looking at her, when they thought no one was paying any attention.

"Fuck," I whispered, dropping my hand against Eli's shoulder on one of his passes, to calm him down. His anxious energy was feeding my own and that was not what we needed right now. The pieces clicked in my mind, anger and fear lacing together to choke me. "Do you think he took her? Used this as his big opportunity?" I let go of Eli and gripped my hands together, trying to force them to stop shaking. "We were all distracted, and none of us was aware of the fact that he was back. It was the perfect chance for him to come charging in and get what he wanted. And he's only really wanted one thing. Her."

"Fuck," Eli yelled, the word long and drawn out and punctured with a harsh sound.

When I turned to him, he was shielding his hand against his

chest. Judging from the plaster falling away from the wall, he'd decided that smashing his hand into the side of the building we'd just finished checking was the best way to channel his own tumultuous emotions.

Like I said, fucking men. Useless.

"Well what the hell did you think was going to happen, you fuckwad" I muttered, unable to resist poking the bear as I watched blood drip over his hands as he reset one of his fingers back in the socket with a loud crack. I rolled my eyes at his scowl and the curl of his lip. "Don't be a baby, you'll heal in a few minutes."

When I turned back to Atlas to see if he thought my theory held any merit, I was staring instead at a pile of his discarded clothes. I glanced around looking for him, and met the bright golden eyes of his wolf.

He was tall, much taller and more muscular than the average wolf you'd find in the wild, with intelligent eyes that made it damn clear there was more than just an animal looking back at you. Dark brown hair rippled around him as he shook his head and turned away from us, nose pressed to the ground as he started to run.

My stomach dropped when I realized what this meant. Part of me had wanted Atlas to brush my theory aside, to say that Darius's scent went one way and Max's went another. Because if I was being honest, I wasn't sure the three of us stood much of a chance against the vamp if he had taken her. There was something off about him, and not just because The Guild had spent years messing with his mind and body. He was stronger than most vampires, as his battle royale with his brother made abundantly clear. It would be a hell of a lot easier tracking down one angry girl who didn't know her way around here and would probably be moving with careful, calculated steps. But when the vamp was thrown into the equation, our job became a lot more difficult.

Some might say impossible.

And if Atlas was in full on wolf-mode, that meant that the chances of him buying into my theory were high. Darius's scent traveled the same path as Max's.

Heat boiled through my blood as I clenched my jaw down hard and took off after Atlas. I could tell he wanted us to follow because otherwise he would have been going faster—too fast for a couple of protectors to keep up with. Generally when Atlas wolfed out, he tended to be more independent, didn't like to have us around too close, but was okay with us trailing at a distance. I think because, on some level, he was afraid that he didn't have control of his wolf. The wolf tolerated us, but he was still more feral in this form, less predictable. And if Atlas had been responsible for hurting one of us—well, I wasn't sure that was something he could come back from.

I felt, rather than heard, Eli running next to me, the two of us matching each other pace-for-pace as our steps pounded against the path. Atlas was taking us beyond the small cluster of long-abandoned buildings we'd been hunkering down in for the last few hours and deep into the woods where the trees were so thick that even if it were light out, none of it would have reached us on the ground. Instead, we were left clumsily traipsing after a wolf through a piercingly dark, bramble and root-filled forest.

Every step he took was with a hurried precision, and I could almost feel the focus radiating from his body, with every small turn he made to keep on the scent.

That focus balanced me and helped me center my own fears —hunting, having a clear goal, this was where we prospered as a group. It was a space to come together, to put all of the energy we couldn't understand to good use. It's why I loved my job as much as I did. The stakes were just a little more personal than usual this time.

We ran for what felt like hours, the sharp cramp in my side barely a blip on my radar. Eventually, even Eli was starting to get winded—something that happened almost never. Thankfully we'd found water when we went scavenging earlier in the day, so I dug in my pack hunting for the small bottle of it without breaking my stride. I drained about a quarter and tossed it without speaking to or looking at Eli, the sound of the water sloshing as he caught the bottle was the only confirmation I needed. We were a well-oiled machine, and I could predict his and Atlas's movements almost better than I could plot my own.

I refused to lose either of them on this journey, but I realized in that moment that I refused to lose Max too. I was done sacrificing the people I cared about like pawns in The Guild's war—a war that none of us truly understood, a reality that was becoming more and more apparent. She fit with us—maybe not in a way that we understood yet, but she did. We had to get her back.

"There's no way she could have made it this far, this quickly. Eli and I can barely keep up as it is," I said, my words coming out slightly winded as I leapt over a set of particularly gnarly tree roots. The woods in here felt so much more ominous than they did back home, like we were trekking through the sort of forest you'd read about in a dark fairytale. Everything seemed bigger, more dangerous and extreme than the types of terrain I was familiar with. Not to mention the fact that the environment shifted so much here—one second we were running through what looked and felt like a desert, the next we were on the outskirts of what seemed like an abandoned industrial town—that it felt like I'd been getting whiplash from trying to make sense of it. Part of me thought that this whole thing would've been easier if hell was just the monotonous fiery pit of despair that movies made it out to be. At least then it would be somewhat predictable. It would make sense. Instead, it was like a chaotic Disneyland of desolation.

"Yeah," Eli echoed, voice breathy and ragged, as he pulled in front of me, trying to close the distance between us and Atlas. "I'm close to my limit. Man, can you shift back, so we can talk and try to figure out what's up. We've been going for hours and the trail shows no sign of ending. We aren't familiar with this place at all, for all we know it could be a trap. Max is fast, but she's not vamp fast—" He stopped, placed both hands on his knees as he hunched over and tried to catch his breath. "Unless the fangfuck carried her, I guess. We don't know how long ago he took her ei—"

Eli doubled over even more, only this time I had a feeling it wasn't because he was winded.

A deep groan parted his lips as I watched a sharp gash appear along his arm, staining his skin red.

My head whipped to the right and then to the left as I scanned our surroundings for an attacker. But everything was silent, not so much as a leaf rustling in the distance.

Atlas's wolf walked slowly up to Eli, his steps sure, but careful, as if he was afraid he might frighten one of us. If I didn't have adrenaline pouring through my body, I'd roll my eyes at that. We'd been hunting with the wolf for months now, and while he was standoffish around us, it wasn't like there was any confusion about who or what he was.

Had someone shot an arrow? I looked at the wound again, noting the deep, severed line, and then another appeared. It almost looked like a claw mark, but each impression or nail was taking a moment to appear, like it was a ricochet of something we couldn't see.

Something invisible? Who knew what kind of monsters hell held in its depths. If anything had become obvious to me over these last few weeks—it was that The Guild knew next to nothing about the supernatural creatures it hunted. That, or it didn't share much with those of us who were in charge of the grunt work.

I'd deal with the anger that came with that realization some other time.

"That fucking vampire," Eli said, his teeth clenched and bared in pain as he poked at the phantom womb with a finger. "I'm getting really fucking sick of this shit. I was probably safer before he went and linked us with his blood." He grimaced as he pressed down on a new claw mark taking shape along his otherwise smooth skin. "In fact, I wouldn't be surprised if he linked us, just so he could kill me slowly. Probably more fun for him that way, watching me die by a thousand cuts."

Fuck. The bond. I'd almost forgotten about that. Eli had almost died a few days ago from an ambush of vamps. The only reason he'd survived was because Darius had fed him some of his blood, linking them for as long they lived.

If Eli died, so would Darius.

And vice versa.

As protectors, we knew next to nothing about the parameters of the bond, but the thought of Eli's life forever being controlled by a sadistic vamp did not settle well in my stomach. Once we found Wade and Max, breaking that bond would be moved to the top of my list.

"Shit," I said, holding my hands uselessly above the wounds, not wanting to make anything worse by touching them. We stood like that for a long stretch of breath, none of us knowing what to do, like we were just waiting for more bruises and cuts to appear. There was no defending against a ghost, which made me the things I loathed most: useless and defenseless. "Maybe you won't get the brunt of it this time."

The vamp and his friend, Khalida—or whatever her name was—didn't tell us much about blood bonds but they did say that they were unpredictable. It was an old, unstable sort of magic. Which meant that it was entirely possible that Darius could be attacked and Eli would remain untouched. Or his wounds could mirror the vamp's or even be worse. There was no way of knowing and there were too many contingencies. Did it matter how close they were? Was the chance of their wounds aligning higher if they were within the same vicinity as each other? If Darius was attacked in a way that would kill a protector, but not a vampire, would Eli die?

We knew next to nothing, which only made the wave of panic swallow me whole, even more than it had before.

"What do we do?" I started pacing back and forth, my hair a mess of knots as I ran my fingers through it. Atlas was torn, his wolf unable to decide between keeping an eye on Eli and continuing to track down Max. I could see the indecision in the set of his posture, feet dug in, ready to pounce, head shifting each way as if trying to decide on a direction.

It was like we were being hit from every direction, each of us dropping like flies. I knew hell would be dangerous, but I didn't expect it to divide and conquer—taking on Darius and Eli simultaneously, even though they were in completely separate locations.

"Max," I said, stopping cold, my eyes landing on Eli's and watching his brown orbs widen with a mirrored realization.

"Fuck," he yelled, through a groan as another stripe of blood appeared, this time bleeding through his shirt. "If the fanghole is being attacked, that means she probably is too."

The three of us froze, a helpless sort of terror rendering us all still. How did we fight this? How could we stop an attack that we weren't there for? We didn't even know where the hell they were right now.

I let out a deep groan, no longer able to hold the pressure inside of my chest.

Helplessness consumed me, a realization that led to a flare of anger. I was so fucking sick of the people I cared about getting attacked. By the time we all found Wade, there might not even be any of us left to rescue him.

Steely resolve cannibalized the panic on Eli's face, and I watched as he straightened his spine through the pain, every muscle tense as he tried to mask it. His gaze fell on Atlas and he nodded in the direction we'd been running. "Go. You're lightyears faster than either of us, even more so now that I'm dealing with the dickwad's beating. Go. Find her, we'll only hold you back. We should have told you to leave us behind ages ago."

I knew he was right, and I could tell by Atlas's posture that he knew it too. But separating was always a bad idea, and if Atlas left us now, it was entirely possible that by the time he found her and brought her back, Eli and I might be dealing with more bad luck than a few random claw marks. Neither of us had a supernatural beast lingering beneath our skin to come to our aid when we needed it. We were stronger with Atlas around.

Max had her strange fire magic that showed up every now and then and, when it didn't, a furry hellhound to watch over her. Hell, even the fanghole was a nice added layer of protection. And Atlas and Wade shared their bodies with monsters of their very own.

Who knew there would come a time when I was almost sorry that I was *only* a protector. Other than some seriously solid fighting skills and a bit of heightened strength, I didn't add much to our protective detail.

I clenched my jaw and nodded, knowing that I'd have to be the one to push Atlas over the cliff of this decision. I could keep me and Eli safe. I would have to. "Eli's right. We'll be fine. I've got food, water. We passed what looked like a small town not long ago. We can double back there and sit tight, wait for you to return and for Eli to heal and get through," I waved my hands uselessly at the lingering effects of the invisible attack, "you know, this."

His paws dug into the ground, like he was ready to spring, but the gold in his eyes tinted brown and I knew that Atlas was fighting for control, trying to process the decision with as much reason and logic as he could. Atlas wasn't impulsive, not in the way that his wolf was. He didn't rely on instincts or snap decisions—he was always focused, always so precise in every decision he made, like the weight of the world was constantly on his shoulders, ready to buckle him completely at the slightest opportunity. I had a feeling this was where the battle ground between him and his wolf would reach a peak—raw instinct was the wolf's greatest strength.

I shook my head at him and shoved him lightly, not even considering how wildly dense it was to goad a fucking werewolf. "Atlas, now. Go, don't think. If we don't get to them, it's possible it'll be too late—for Eli and for Max. You're our best hope. Go do your wolf thing and get the fuck out of here." I blew out a breath of frustration, swatting the air between us like I was trying to shoo away a fly and not a creature capable of ripping me limb from limb. "I'm a damn good protector. I can keep us safe in the meantime. And we'll hide out, we won't go looking for trouble or try chasing after you. We'll be okay, I promise."

As if that finally settled things, he nodded, his eyes filled with that creepy intelligence that made it clear-as-day that I was talking to far more than a wolf. With nothing more than a low whine, he turned his back to us and took off into the woods, his pace so fast that I lost sight of him after only a few seconds.

"Well," Eli said, with a cheeky grin, even though nothing about any of this was even remotely funny. We all had to deal with our stress somehow, I guess. Humor and sarcasm were always Eli's coping methods of choice. "Shall we go find a quiet place for me to die?"

⚜ 3 ⚜
MAX

One dark, almost black eye, and one golden-yellow eye peered at me with a leveled focus.

"Darius," I said as I ran over to him, my stomach tightening as I realized how excited I was to see a vampire. A lot had changed over the last few weeks, and I still had no idea how I felt about most of those changes. "You're okay?"

He arched an eyebrow as I closed the distance between us, shock shading his features as I wrapped my arms around him in what could only be considered by most people as a hug.

A hug. I'd advanced to straight up hugging a vampire now.

I cleared my throat and backed away, suddenly unable to look him in the eyes. What the hell was wrong with me? A few short weeks ago, this creature made my skin crawl as he watched me behind his cell window. And now...now I had no idea how to label the way being around him made me feel. Uncomfortable was definitely one of those feelings, but the rest were a strange muddled mess that I didn't want to dissect right now.

I glanced around the room, trying to figure out where we were. The walls were a strange mixture of gray and cream, the floor tiled but so grimey that what was once likely white, was now just an uneven yellow. A bright light bathed the room, so bright that for a brief moment, I thought we might be in a hospital. One no one had cleaned for a ridiculously long time. I looked up and saw a single bulb dangling from the ceiling, the wires looking loose and lazy. A serial killer's den then, maybe?

An involuntary shudder ran through me as I looked for a window, seeing nothing but a small sliver of one above us both. It was the sort of not-window you'd find in a basement underground. The air around us felt thick, filled with a murky humidity and a sharp, metallic scent.

No, not just metal. The scent of blood. It was the same cloying stench that lingered around a battlefield after the final body dropped and there was time to assess the situation, to suss out the damage. The smell of death.

I took a slow, deep breath, trying to ignore the premature panic surging through my body. It was strange. Half of my senses were poised for a fight, but my eyes and ears knew there was nothing in this room but us. I glanced at Darius, clocking a few cuts and bruises, but nothing too extreme. There was nothing exactly dire about his appearance, but something in the curve of his posture, the dampness of his brow, suggested that he wasn't quite himself. If he'd been hurt, I wouldn't really know it. Vampires healed extremely quickly; but that healing could drain a lot of energy. "Where are we, exactly?"

His brows bent in the middle, as if the question suddenly jostled something in his memory, shaking a trail of thoughts loose like spare change.

"I don't know," he said, the words slow and filled with curiosity as his gaze followed mine around the room. "How did we get here?"

He took a step back, rocking slightly. It almost seemed like he wasn't totally in control of his muscles. Something was off. Gone was the usual Darius that I was used to seeing: confident to the point of arrogance, aloof and difficult to predict, possessed with the kind of strength and apathy that had terrified me on more than one occasion. He seemed weaker, somehow. Exhausted.

This strange inability to trace my steps; this muddled confusion that lingered on the edge of my thoughts, like they were submerged in a thick liquid...

I knew this feeling.

I'd grown to almost crave it.

My heart skipped a beat and I glanced around again, with renewed vigor this time, looking for Wade. My mind felt giddy and hazy suddenly, the way that it did when I dream-walked with him. It was the only explanation for how we both ended up here, neither of us with any recollection, our previous steps stitched together in a puzzle that didn't yet make sense. This was an incubi's dreamscape. I felt certain of it, down to my bones.

And as soon as the realization manifested, some of the haziness started to disappear, to linger on the peripherals of my mind rather than in the center.

But Wade wasn't here—a revelation made incredibly obvious by how utterly filled with a *lack* this room was. There was no furniture, no decor. Nothing for Wade to hide behind. A set of what looked remarkably like old, rusted chains lined the ceiling, strands of metal cuffs dangling down above us like abrasive worms, but nothing else. Maybe we really were in a serial killer's murder den.

I needed to stop watching so much true crime. My real life was terrifying enough without the added imagery.

I ran to the door, but there was no visible handle. It was like we were on the inside of one of those giant walk-in refrigerators, with no emergency latch to escape if the door closed you in. My fingers dug into the seam where the door met the wall, desperate for enough purchase to pull or push the door open. But it was useless and all I was left with from the effort were a few nails bent back and bloodied, and a set of lungs that wouldn't quite fill with air all the way as light claustrophobia settled into my chest.

"Where the hell are we?" I asked again, my heart racing from the fear suddenly coursing through my veins. It was disorienting as fuck, waking up in a strange place with no idea how you got there.

Where was Wade? Was something wrong with him? Why wasn't he here? That creature—there'd been a cloaked man who'd pushed me from Wade's dream before. Had he gotten to him and trapped us here, in some creepy purgatory? Were we stuck in some dreamland until the cloaked figure released us?

I shook my head, unclenched my jaw, and tried to center myself.

I couldn't panic. I was Cyrus Bentley's daughter. I was raised to never panic when things went dark and unpredictable and the edges of the world blackened—those were the times when focus mattered the most. Focus more than anything else.

One heavy breath in and out, and then again. Cy always told me to come back to my breathwork, it was the foundation of our training. The room smelled faintly of stale air, so thick it was almost heavy with a putrid humidity. My gaze landed on Darius, and somehow his eyes drew me in, grounding me, if only for a moment.

One dark, almost black, one golden. Familiar.

Staring into his eyes, trying to dissect the transitions between gold and mottled brown, calmed me somehow.

I breathed again and felt my shoulders relax, just an inch, as I gathered myself in those eyes—they were unreadable, impassive, but still they called to me.

"What's the last thing you remember?" My voice came out low, but the edge of wildness was gone, control seeping back in. I closed my eyes, trying to focus, breaking the line of connection between us. I tried to dissect the images rolling through my head like a broken film.

Overhearing Eli and the rest of Six talk about their secrets.

Their distrust and disgust.

Claws.

Sitting around a fire with Darius.

Nash.

Fire. A different fire, stronger.

My hands wrapped around Darius.

Our lips crashing together with a fury that made my breath hitch in the present, just as it had in the past.

None of the scenes made sense, so I shoved them all away. Too much to deal with, too much to process. None of the visuals doing anything but adding more questions to an already high pile. I was so fucking sick of the neverending pile of questions.

I spun my head back towards Darius as he walked to the wall. His head leaned back and, slowly, like he wasn't fully capable of resisting gravity, he slid down until his butt landed on the ground. He looked exhausted, his eyes heavy and lidded as his focus left me. It was brief, as his thoughts turned inward, but it gave me chills to watch him engage and disengage, with less effort than a camera shutter.

He had a habit of doing that—of sinking into himself when things got serious or when he was worried. It made me think his usual interactions, the lazy indifference and snark he painted over every word and phrase, was nothing more than a disguise— a mask for whatever true demons he was wrestling with beneath the surface.

And part of me hoped I'd never come face-to-face with those demons, even if a smaller, much more annoying part of me was filled with a raging curiosity. In those moments, the reckless voice in my head taunted me to go to him, to reach into those soft moments of reflection and pull him out—to stare him in the eyes and linger there with him, with his demons, to greet them as my own. There'd been a frustrating but persistent piece of me that had been carving out a nook for Darius since the moment I laid eyes on him—a piece desperate to figure him out, to put him together until the puzzle pieces all made sense.

Would those puzzle pieces ever make sense? Or would they just paint a picture too gruesome for me to understand?

While I didn't know quite where that curiosity came from, I

knew with absolute certainty that it wasn't quite the sort of curiosity that a protector was supposed to have about vampire. I wasn't supposed to look at a vampire and want to unpack what happened to him in his past; I shouldn't look into his eyes and want to understand how his mind worked; I shouldn't have such an acute craving to comfort him, to glue him back together.

But here, in this room, in this dream, the curiosity that I could usually bury deep in a forgotten crevice of my thoughts, was back with a bleeding vengeance.

Without thinking, I followed him and sank down to my knees, my hand coming up to his cheek and resting against the smooth skin there. He was colder than most people, but not filled with the icy chill of a cadaver that most fictional vampire stories would have me believe. His skin was soft, and I tried to ignore the slight tingle that crept up my arm, emerging from where we touched, like a livewire. "Don't do that."

"Do what, little protector?" he asked, his words gruff, but still filled with the edge of teasing, like he was trying to climb back to me, but couldn't quite manage the effort. There was so much darkness in his eyes. I could see there was a storm brewing and, once it hit, we'd all be done for. That look held so much more than what I saw when I looked at any other vampire—and *that's* why he was so terrifying. That kind of raging whirlwind gobbling him up from the inside out was the sort of force I'd grown to identify as an intensely *human* pain.

The sort of pain that made men into beasts and made me realize that maybe the monsters I was trained to hunt weren't all of a supernatural bent. That maybe the distinction between monster and man was more tenuous than I was ready to fully admit.

"Disappear." I dropped my hand to my lap and stared at him, our bodies close enough that my knees kissed his. "We were fighting," I closed my eyes, willing myself to remember. I hated how this seemed to happen, how hours and days would some-times slip through my fingers when I was in one of these dream states. It was like trying to hold onto water. "I always seem to forget where I was after I've been fighting. Maybe I turned into a torch again. I imagine that's quite draining and disorienting."

I opened my eyes and looked around the room again, breathing slowly to keep the panic from clawing its way back. This feeling—it was like the way I felt when I slid into Wade's dreamscape. But there were differences too. I felt more in control, my body alive and hungry in a way that it wasn't usually. I felt a lingering power and alertness that felt new and intoxicating. My body tingled, giddy with anticipation, though I didn't know for what. "But Wade isn't here," I said, the words slow and more to myself than to the man sitting next to me. "He's always here."

"You're rambling," he said, and when I looked back up, his lips twitched into the shadow of a smile, until his eyes looked the way that they usually did, when his focus wasn't internalized and brooding. When he looked the part of a frustratingly coy vampire who enjoyed nothing more than watching the people around him unravel. He was a puppet master, eager to watch the world perform for him. I knew this Darius. I could handle him.

"You're always rambling," he continued, lips curving in a sad smile. "And I'm sorry to disappoint, but it's just me you're stuck with for now. The incubus isn't here. This isn't one of his dreams." A line formed between his brows as he considered. "It's possible this is just one of my regular dreams, nothing supernatural about it at all. Regular dreams do still exist, you know? They aren't all death and destruction." He pressed his palms to the cold ground and leaned his head back against the wall, studying me with a ravenous attention. "If it is just one of my dreams, there are much better ways I can think of spending it."

I swallowed at the heat that suddenly eclipsed his eyes. The vampire beneath was peaking through, but something told me that he was hungry for more than just my blood. And the thought of what he might really want from me had my heart galloping against my ribs, fast enough that I was sure he could hear it. Annoyingly, the thought of him noticing my panic just heightened it more.

I knew that I fascinated him, though I didn't exactly know why. And I wasn't at all sure what intentions lingered and braided together with that fascination.

My lips buzzed, like my body was remembering the feel of his kiss and begging me to continue what was so violently interrupted. My attraction to him was getting more and more difficult to fight and almost impossible to ignore. Something about being alone with him here, even in a room as creepy as this one, filled me with a sort of fear that had nothing to do with the kind of danger I'd usually associate with being in the presence of a monster.

And there was no mistaking it—Darius was a monster. He had that whole 'watch the world burn' vibe to him that went so far beyond simply being a vampire or a bad guy. He was a ball of unprocessed trauma, waiting to explode.

I glanced away, frustrated with the way a single look from him could fluster me so deeply. What the hell was wrong with me? "What makes you so sure this is your dream and not mine?"

His eyes narrowed with a teasing smile as his hand traced a long, languid line along my thigh. It was nothing but the ghost of a touch, his skin not quite meeting mine, but somehow the shadow of his presence had my thighs clenching, the air from my lungs escaping in a low, breathy gasp. "You saying you dream about me then, little protector? How interesting. Not that I'm surprised, of course. I can smell the desire you refuse to acknowledge."

Arrogant ass. His heavy gaze moved slowly around the room, my embarrassment adding to the confidence in his expression. The darkness and exhaustion that had consumed him was melting away, leaving a raw hunger in its place that I was just as ill-equipped to deal with.

He nodded up toward the heavy chains lining the ceiling. "This is the sort of landscape pretty common with some of my more exciting dreams. Are our proclivities the same, then, as well? Because if they are, that will make this all the more delicious."

The chains.

An image of being bound from the ceiling, dangling and vulnerable while Darius was in the room had my stomach dipping in a way that suggested it was more than fear sending shivers along my spine. The thought of having no control, alone in a room with a vampire, was terrifying. But the thought of Darius as that vampire was something else entirely.

I stood up, suddenly too aware of the fact that he was touching me, or nearly touching me. My head felt light, dizzy almost, and I suddenly desperately wanted him across the room, as far from me as he could get. But even the thought of speaking that desire out loud had my body freezing in protest, like it was at war with my mind. The sly grin told me he knew exactly what kind of effect he was having on me. When the hell did a vampire start making me feel like this? Why did the idea of him doing all sorts of untoward things to me send ripples of excitement and intrigue along my skin, like a lick of delicious fire?

As if sensing where my thoughts were going, no doubt because he suggested their course and cleared the path for them, he stood up too, stalking me with his eyes like the predator that he was, as I paced back and forth.

I felt trapped, suddenly, like I had no control over the situation. Despite not being strapped up in the creepy dungeon chains, I was as good as a fly caught in a spider's web. And as much as I hated to admit it, the adrenaline was morphing into something that felt more and more like a heated anticipation.

My body was betraying me, craving something that I couldn't give it. Something that I refused to give it.

I could feel his eyes as they peeled back the layers of my clothes, and I tried to shut my pounding heartbeat right the fuck up before I could hear nothing but its outrageous drumbeat, wild and intense like a battle call, as he took a step towards me, and then another, and then another.

"What are you—"

I swallowed my words as he pressed me against the wall, his palm splayed against my collarbone as he applied enough pressure to keep me still, but not enough to hurt or bruise. My breath hitched as he pinned me, the feel of his palm against the skin of my clavicle enough to pebble my flesh.

Those eyes—black and gold—all but hypnotizing me into compliance.

His hand lifted and fell with every heavy breath that scraped against my lungs, dipping lower and lower, until his thumb grazed the top of my right breast.

"Usually, when I dream about you, you're wearing something a bit—less," his other hand danced along my side as he touched my tattered leggings and tank top, "than this. Something a little strappier, a little more leather, maybe. But I have to say, this particular ensemble does add a bit more reality to the image. It's much more *you* than what I typically dream up. I'll have to make a note for future versions of this particular dream. I do so love to relive them, and in my weaker moments, even when I'm awake."

He pressed his hips against mine and I sucked in a deep breath as his hard length touched my stomach.

"You dream about me often, then?" I asked, suddenly emboldened by the realization that my presence was having a very real effect on him, too. I wasn't generally very forward, and I would never allow myself to actually mess around with a vampire.

Again.

But if this really was a dream—and not even mine, well...enjoying it a little didn't seem like the worst idea imaginable.

He bent his head down so that his lips pressed into the crook of my neck. I could feel him smile against my skin, the sensation sending a jolt through my core.

Fuck, did I hate that he had this effect on me, and with just the shadow of a touch, too. His breath tickled along my sensitive skin, sending a shiver through my body. It was somehow not enough sensation and too much all at once.

"You have no idea, little protector. Since the moment I met you, these little dreams of mine have been the very thing sustaining me. Curiosities at first, about you and your life." He pressed his teeth lightly against my skin, more sensual than predatory, and I inhaled sharply, unable to swallow my reaction, waiting with bated breath to see if he'd pierce his fangs into me. "But they morphed quickly into something hungrier." His breath on my neck sent a wave of heat down my body. "The very thought of tasting your blood against my tongue," he nipped playfully, not breaking skin "while I'm sheathed inside of you—" he let out a ragged chuckle, "you have no idea."

Suddenly I wanted him to bite me, wanted him to draw deep, hungry pulls from my veins, while I wallowed in the feel of him. A heavy heat lapped against my skin, like we were bathed in a bubble of lust.

A low, dark laugh told me that he knew exactly what I wanted too, that he knew what sort of shame filled me by acknowledging it—how even that shame morphed into something else, something hungry. Even here, even in a dream.

"It's just as frustrating for me, you know?" His lips pressed down against my pulse point, pulling a shallow moan from my lips as my body molded against his, practically desperate to touch him at every possible point of contact.

"What is?" I asked, my words little more than a breathy stammer. I needed to focus. Needed to push him away and figure out what the hell was going on. There were things we needed to do, that we needed to focus on. Important things. Life or death things.

"Wanting you, in this way. My kind—we don't normally fantasize about protectors. Especially not after we've been held captive by them for years." Another soft chuckle, empty of amusement, escaped from him, brushing a few strands of my hair against my collarbone. "But here we are. And I can't deny that it's more than your blood that I want. I recognize the same frustrated yearning in you too. On those rare moments when you allow it to push past your walls." He nipped playfully along my neck, his chest pressing flush against mine. Still, somehow, I wanted him closer. "One day," he said, his breath a delicious pur against the shell of my ear, "you'll want me to do more than tease you with my bite. And not in the cushion of my dreams, but in reality. In the flesh. You'll give into that heat, give into that desire. I can feel the thread growing, each time we get close—can't you? Tightening and thickening until it won't be broken. Until it can't be.

"You're more like me than you realize. It's why I can give into this now, if only for a moment. You're no protector, Max Bentley. You're a monster, just like me. And I'm just patiently waiting for you to embrace it." He inhaled deep, as his nose pressed against the sensitive column of my neck. "And I can be very, very patient," his words were a gravelly whisper that pebbled every inch of skin they touched. "Years of solitude will do that to a man. I know how to play a long game, when it matters."

My heart raced so hard that I grew dizzy from the feeling. I breathed in deep, trying to ground myself, but all that did was fill my senses with the smell of him—clean, warm, and that distinctly male spiciness that had me pressing closer against him, rather than pulling back.

I forced myself to look up, to study the predator caging me, with his strange eyes that seemed to see so much more than I ever could. Was he right? Did I have more in common with a vampire than I did with my own kind? Was I even a protector at all?

I wasn't sure.

One thing I knew, however, was that there'd been a draw, a strange allure that pulled me towards him, since the moment I'd met him. At first, it was fear—the slightly rabid vampire that studied me behind his cage, like I was the one imprisoned in a zoo. There'd been something about him that terrified me more than any creature I'd encountered before him. Like he was the sort of person who wanted to watch as the world crashed down around him, like he didn't at all care whether or not he was destroyed along with everyone else in the process, so long as he was amused.

But slowly, over the weeks, the fear grew into something else —curiosity—and then, something I couldn't quite name. He'd dug his way under my skin, slowly but surely, until he became a creature that I couldn't completely hate, couldn't quite bring myself to want to kill. And now—now, I wanted to do something so very far from killing him.

As if sensing the desire as soon as it made itself known to me, his eyes darkened and he brought his head down, slowly at first, until his lips crashed against mine.

It was a long moment, my lips pressed against his, each of us lingering in the feel of touching the other.

Too much.

My mind raced, outpacing even my heartbeat.

I shoved him away and slapped him across the cheek, the sound ringing around the room in a harsh echo. My breathing was ragged, like my lungs couldn't fill themselves properly while I tried to put some distance between us. A deep shame filled me, battling against the desire. He'd hurt people. Killed people.

I would never do something like that. Would I?

"You're wrong," I said, the words firm and hard as his eyes studied me with an edgy glee. I opened my mouth to say more, to tell him to stay away from me, that I was a protector and that I should've killed him the moment he was loose from the Guild lab, the very second I watched him snap a protector's neck like a twig. That I shouldn't have let him out in the first place, that I should have taken my shot when we'd sparred in front of my peers to end him instead of stun him. But nothing came out.

Instead, I closed the distance between us, pulled him towards me, and pressed my mouth against his.

It was not gentle, this kiss.

And before I could fully realize what was happening, I leaned into it, parting my lips and granting his tongue entry, just as desperate to taste him as he evidently was to taste me.

His hands cupped my ass and lifted me up, so that I could wrap my legs around his waist as he leaned me back against the hard wall. My body felt like it was a livewire, and I hardly even minded the hard stone-like texture against my back. If anything, it cooled down the heat blazing over my skin. All I could focus on was the taste of him and the feel of his erection pushing against my core.

My skin felt like it was tingling in a way that it never did in my dreams with Wade, like being with Darius was infusing me with something new. It didn't drain me, but sent a wave of power through my body instead. This wasn't just sex, this was a raw exchange of energy, a need to break out of—or into —something.

With quick hands, he lifted my tank top over my head, his movements so smooth that our lips only parted for the brief second needed to let the fabric pass between us.

I followed suit, clawing awkwardly at his shirt until he helped me pull it off, so that my skin was pressing against his. Unsurprisingly, he was covered in lean muscle, his skin soft as silk. I ran my hands over his chest, biting down gently on his lip, until he let out a low growl that I could practically feel reverberate in my own chest.

If he'd looked exhausted and drained moments ago, he was anything but right now. There was a wildness in his eyes, he radiated an excited energy that pulsed between us.

"What do you want, little protector?" he asked, though there was no teasing anymore. Instead, his tone was filled with a hungry need, a desperate desire for me to answer quickly.

What did I want?

I wanted more. Everything. Now.

His lips danced down my neck until it felt like electricity was flickering along my skin. For a long moment, I let myself float in the feeling, in the sensation.

Slowly, I unwrapped my legs, pulling them away from his body, even as my stomach clenched with the ache of removing his body from mine. With an electric focus, I studied him as my feet met the ground, watching his eyes with a heady focus. There was something in his expression that felt wild, unhinged maybe. The look of him standing there, above me, lust practically lapping against us, forcing us back together, was intoxicating.

He stepped back, sensing I wanted some space, though I could feel the strain as he did, like every single inch of him was desperate to get back to me, desperate for me to climb him like a ladder and continue what we'd started. His hands vibrated with the tension, with the anticipation.

I smiled, trying my best at a coy, sexy smile. The kind I always saw in movies. I got drunk on that power, on the feel of his eyes on me, on the knowledge that he wouldn't move an inch closer unless I allowed it. Until I demanded it.

Without breaking eye contact, I unlatched my bra, one hook at a time, until the fabric slid down my skin, getting caught briefly on the peaks of my nipples. His eyes took in every languid move, not so much as blinking as he stood above me, a tower of strength, violence, power.

His chest moved with each heavy breath as his eyes traced my torso. There was a darkness in his expression, a heat that told me he was imagining all of the different things he wanted to do to me, all of the different ways he'd had me in those so-called dreams of his. I wondered if this time would be different. If the version of me in those dreams was different from the version of me in this one. I hoped so.

I slid my hands down my sides until they reached where the hem of my pants met my hips. In a slow, teasing display, I pulled the fabric down, inch by excruciating inch until I could step out —first one leg, and then the other—kicking my shoes off with a semblance of grace still intact. I wasn't ashamed anymore of the heat radiating from my body, or the wetness forming between my legs.

I'd spent so long fighting whatever attraction was between us, denying it was there altogether, that for just this once, leaning into the desire made me feel giddy with anticipation.

If he'd been afraid I was ending whatever this was, the fear dissipated in an instant, replaced by a heat so searing I was certain he was the one with the power to control fire.

"I want you to take off your pants," I said, my voice low and sultry, surprising even me with the tenor of it. This. Whatever this was, was so far beyond my comfort zone. But the surge of energy I got from watching him fumble for his zipper, ripping his jeans in his haste to pull them down had my body humming with delight.

I could never have sex with a vampire. Not really. But I would let myself live out that fantasy in my dreams, even if just this once. I couldn't deny that there was a connection between me and Darius. And for once, I wanted to let myself explore it, free of risk and repercussion and judgment—even my own. Just one time, I'd let myself give in to my darkest desires, and push the shame of wanting more than one person, of wanting a vampire, as far into the recess of my mind as it could go.

His eyes narrowed with a teasing frustration as he kicked the dark denim away. He wasn't wearing any underwear. He cupped his length in his palm as he watched me—it was a test, an attempt to see if I was actually ready for him. If I really wanted him.

And I did. My eyes scraped along his body, taking in every delicious curve and hard edge, until I reached his waist.

He stroked himself slowly, and my body responded as if he was stroking me—like each sensation he felt was mapped across my skin as well.

"Done." The word was gravelly, filled with a heavy weight. And I knew that he was struggling to hold back—and that the struggle only served to heighten his desire. "What is it that you want now, little protector?" he asked, his brow arched in challenge as he leaned forward just a touch—enough to remind me that he was letting me control this little game, just this once, for now. But the tone of his voice, the way he framed the question, made it abundantly clear that I wasn't as much in control of this situation as I thought.

He was directing me, even as I directed him—a realization that made my mouth go dry and legs quake.

Done waiting, I dropped to my knees and took his length into my mouth, sliding my lips around him until he reached the back of my throat.

He groaned, leaning forward just a bit, his hands slapping against the wall to keep himself upright.

I grinned around him, at the way his body responded to me, pumping my mouth around him slowly at first, but then picking up the pace as the salt of his pre-cum hit my tongue.

One of his hands gripped the back of my head, fingers winding around my hair, directing me back and forth with the slightest of pressure.

Each throb of his dick made my stomach dip with anticipation, filling me with a swell of something I couldn't quite explain. I felt strong here, on my knees in this weird basement dream room. There was a certain sort of rush in making a creature as powerful as Darius respond to every muscle I moved with rapt attention.

I'd never done this before, but for once, I wasn't self-conscious. I let myself explore, lose myself in the sensations—reading his body and reactions as if they were an instructional guide.

My tongue circled the tip of his dick, and I pulled my lips back and away from him, in a long teasing beat, before taking him into my mouth again.

A low groan echoed above me, and I felt his pleasure to the bottom of my toes, like it surged right through me.

He pulled back, removing himself from my mouth altogether

and stood over me, caging me in. He pressed a single finger underneath my chin, forcing me to look up, into the murky depths of his gaze. With the mere suggestion of pressure as the pad of his finger pressed against my jaw, I climbed back up to my full height, as if my body was his to control. His eyes were wild with lust, the strange mixture of colors in them filled with a sort of mesmerizing beauty that I could easily float in forever.

His jaw clenched tight, the muscles tightening and releasing with every breath I took. He hovered so close that my chest brushed up against him when I inhaled, but I couldn't seem to break the moment as his arms imprisoned me against the wall from either side. The strange power I'd felt was gone, and now I suddenly felt how wrong I had been. He'd been the one in control the entire time.

But he wasn't any longer.

The vampire that lingered beneath his skin, the demon he battled in the quiet moments when he sank into himself, was at the surface now.

But I wasn't afraid.

Or, if I was, it wasn't the sort of fear I'd expected to feel when confronted with him. Anticipation and a desperate need clung to my skin as I stared into the heart of the monster, my body tingling with a desire I couldn't quite name.

I opened my mouth to break the silence, but before I could so much as utter the breath of a syllable, his lips were back on mine, punishing and furious.

His hand gripped my ass and pulled my legs up, in a fiercer echo of his earlier move. And just as my back went crashing against the wall with a delicious sting, he pushed into my core.

I inhaled sharply as he pumped once, then twice, as my body responded to his and adjusted to his size. I could feel each indentation of every pad of his fingers pressed into the skin of my ass —there was a bruising sort of possessiveness as he pulled me to him, like he couldn't get close enough, even as we merged.

The feel of my body around him sent a wave of pleasure all

the way to my toes, and I sank down onto him until his cock was completely sheathed inside of me.

I moaned into his mouth as he rode me into the wall, the mixture of pain and pleasure pushing my body in new ways. My teeth bit down hard on his bottom lip as a wave pulled through me, drawing blood. The taste of iron coated my tongue, surprisingly adding to the excitement of the whole thing. I was walking along the edge, not ready to come crashing down, desperate to extend the sensation as long as I could.

He pulled his face back a bit to watch my face, as his hands gripped my waist and pulled, impaling me again and again until I thought I would burst.

His eyes glistened with something that I couldn't quite place, blood from his lip slowly dripping down his skin. Strangely he'd never looked more like a vampire than he did right now, when my desire for him was at an all-time peak. And it was my doing, not his.

He swept his tongue and tasted his own blood, without breaking eye contact with me. I shivered at the sight of it, at the heat in his eyes—raw and possessive. Something in his expression screamed danger and the sort of power I hadn't seen in him before, but what scared me more was how excited I was by it— by finally seeing this version of him that I'd known was there all along. It was intoxicating being in his embrace, close enough to the fire to be burned, but desperate for more warmth, even still.

"You ought to be careful," he said, slamming me down onto him once more, the pace slow and teasing as it built to a climax. It was like he could read every muscle contraction in my body, every throb of my core. He kept me right there, panting for more, but refusing to give me the very thing I wanted—a realization that only made me want it more. "I can only control myself so far, little one."

"Who asked you to control yourself?" I challenged, the anticipation of feeling him ram into me again muddying my brain. I wasn't usually this girl—confident and seductive and open with my desire. But something in me was shifting as I slid down his shaft, controlling the momentum now. I wanted more, and suddenly, I knew that I could have it—here, in this dream, I could be as brazen as I wanted. There were no rules, only sensations. And right now, I wanted nothing more than to watch and feel Darius explode inside of me. The mere thought of him coming undone sent a surge of power and excitement through me, the longing in my body almost painful.

I ground against him so that my clit rubbed along his pelvis, the sensation enough to pull another moan from me—a moan that breathed against his lips as I followed suit and licked the remaining traces of blood in a slow, languid kiss.

For a second, he went completely still, and I was afraid I'd done something or said something wrong. Every muscle was frozen, except that I could feel the smooth pulse of his dick inside of me, the isolation of the movement teasing and intoxicating as I contracted around him. He held my waist so that I could no longer control the tempo, drawing a whimper from me as my fingers dug into his back. I wanted more, wanted him to take me all the way there. Now.

Eyes that were usually so arrogant, so unhinged, were suddenly open and filled with a heat that threatened to scorch me without apology. This was what a predator looked like. And if I wasn't currently fucking him, I'd be fucking terrified of him right now.

Maybe I was still a little terrified, even if turned on.

And maybe that terror turned me on even more.

With a wicked smile, his canines descended and I felt my body buzz with anticipation.

It was a dream. It was a dream. It was a dream.

And in this dream, I wanted to feel this, wanted to take this as far as it would go—just to see. Just to live out the fantasy I wouldn't let myself have in waking life. The one I wouldn't normally even let my thoughts linger on for longer than a breath.

As if sensing my excitement, he smirked one of those arrogant-as-fuck smirks of his. His head flashed to my neck before I fully understood what was happening, though my racing heart suggested my body knew, even if my mind couldn't quite catch up.

His teeth pierced the soft flesh of my neck just as he started to pump into me again, faster and faster, each thrust more demanding than the last.

I could feel the dizzying feeling as the blood left my body, a surprisingly erotic experience, to know that a part of me was inside him, just as he was inside of me. The pressure built and built until I felt like I was going to collapse from the sensations coursing through my veins.

"You're mine, Max Bentley," he whispered against my ear, his tongue licking up the traces of blood that lingered along my skin. "I suspected it from the moment I laid eyes on you, but now, now I know."

The feel of his tongue against my skin, cooling the sting, had me clenching around him until my body couldn't take it anymore. As if sensing how close I was, he brought one of his hands between us, his finger and thumb pinching my bundle of nerves.

"I want to watch you come," he growled, his gaze finding mine.

Instantly, I came apart, my body shaking against his, every muscle I had quaking with an exquisite pleasure.

He sped up, riding out my orgasm until he followed me over himself, his face buried into my neck as his teeth sank down again, muffling his groan in the bite.

For a moment, he held me there, both of us silent, but for the harsh shudders of our breaths, perfectly in sync. Slowly, he pulled me away from the wall and slid his back down until he was seated on the ground, me in his lap.

My head dropped to his shoulder, sated and satisfied, and unable to so much as utter a word.

I closed my eyes, letting myself linger in the feel of his skin against mine, in the taste of him still on my tongue, in the pleasant sting of my neck as each of his exhales blew against the wounds, like a soothing balm. In the strange feeling of rightness that cocooned me like a blanket. He was still inside me, both of us still convulsing with the delayed aftershocks of what we'd both experienced, in the most exquisite echo.

And then, all at once, he was gone.

❧ 4 ❧

MAX

A cold draft hit my body as I glanced around. I was no longer in the empty room of chains and serial killer vibes. Instead, I was alone in a room that seemed altogether unfamiliar and familiar at once. Like I'd left Darius's creepy dream dungeon, only to find myself in one of my very own.

It was a circular room that felt like the sort of Rapunzel-esque prison I might've read about in an old fairy tale—the walls covered with thick, dark stone held together by some sort of dried paste. The air wasn't as heavy as it had been in the dream, like I was somewhere near water or, at the very least, open fields. The scent of death was replaced instead by a salty brine. In the center of the small room sat a slab that looked like it was meant to be a bed of sorts, with tattered cloth that passed nominally as sheets and blankets, though it was a far cry from any bed I'd ever slept in.

The similarities came slowly at first, and then, all at once, I understood exactly where I was.

Wade.

This wasn't the exact room where I'd spent so many nights visiting him in my dreams. That room was burned into my memory, the edges crisp and clean, filled with fondness even with the dreary atmosphere. But this room was almost like a cousin to that one—a bit larger, the fabric covering the bed was a bit thicker, and the room wasn't quite as dark as I'd remembered his being, but otherwise it was the same.

The same feel of empty desolation, the same chilly air, the same gray on gray decor. It was like standing in a real-life black-and-white film, the whole backdrop devoid of color.

I stood up, slowly, my body aching like I'd just spent days on end sparring without a minute of rest. Every breath I took felt labored, and I could feel every muscle in my body working to keep me alive. It was a strange thing, to be so innately aware of how your body functioned, all the parts working together to keep the body whole.

I took a step towards the wall, and touched it. The cool stone against my palm was a strange balm, and I took a moment, trying to process where the fuck I was before trying to remember how exactly I'd gotten here. Since joining The Guild, I'd spent more minutes than I would've imagined feeling disoriented and lost, waiting for my brain to catch up to my body—a sensation that only heightened when I started meeting Wade, and now, Darius, in my dreams. Still, while I should be used to the dizzying experience by now, I wasn't. And I wasn't sure I ever would be, either.

The cold stones fit together with the grout like a lazy puzzle, mismatched and uneven. What kind of building was this place? And how long had it been here? I traced my hand along the wall, both so that I could try and find a seam, and because I needed the added support as I walked around. Even though I'd just woken up, it felt as if I hadn't slept in weeks— almost as it did when Wade first started pulling my energy in our dreams.

My fingers got used to the languid movement and feel as I walked: cool, smooth stone, rough, jagged grout, over and over, until it began to feel like a meditation.

GRAY HOLBORN

I made it all the way around the room and back to where I started. And then I repeated the circle again.

Like Wade's room, there was no door. No way out. Panic gripped my lungs, and I sucked in air, suddenly terrified by the thought of being alone in this altogether familiar-unfamiliar place. Panicked because I was alone, because while this room resembled Wade's, it was not.

"Wade," I whisper-yelled, like I could manifest him myself, if I just wished for it hard enough, half fearing that someone less friendly might hear me. In all of my visits with him, meeting in our dreams, we still had no idea who had taken him or why. Why wasn't he here with me? How was I here alone?

Eventually, that fear trickled into something deeper—the fear of being left here forever. No one knew where I was. I didn't even know where I was. How did I get here? Would anyone even know I was taken? Or would they just assume I was dead?

My breaths came quicker and quicker, until I walked from one side of the room to the other, like a door might suddenly appear if I just looked harder; if I could just manifest the sharp edges, the handle, the rush of fresh air, in my mind, maybe I could create it.

The concern about being overheard disappeared, and my screams for Wade started in earnest. I yelled and yelled and yelled. 'Wade' suddenly less his name and more the shape of my scream.

I banged my fists into the walls over and over, my fingers trying desperately to dig into the grout. I wasn't sure what I was trying to accomplish, where I was trying to dig through to exactly, but logic was a funny thing when anxiety hit. Panic had a way of all but erasing reason.

Growing up in the woods, feeling the open air all day long, I had no taste for confined places—and claustrophobia hit with the same force as Ro's fist on one of his good days.

My voice was hoarse, my throat scratchy, by the time I finally gave in and sat back on the bed, my limbs so heavy I didn't think

I would ever stand again. Every breath I took felt difficult, and my mind was still muddy while I tried to peel back the layers of how I'd gotten here.

Things were still fuzzy, but not nearly as muddled as they had been in that dream—the dream that had my body still tingling with a vibrant sensation of electricity. I shoved those thoughts away. My current reality was far more important than my annoying and thirsty as fuck libido.

Where was Darius? The rest of Six? Was anyone hurt?

I needed a plan, a set of actions I could take to make everything okay. I just needed a place to start—one step I could take, to guide my focus.

It had all seemed so simple, even if impossible: rescue Wade from hell, and then go home. Figure everything else out, all the turbulent emotions and betrayals, when we were all safe and sound.

But I was starting to realize that life in The Guild would never be safe and sound, whether we were stuck in hell or not. Entrance into the supernatural world came at a price, one paid in blood.

I closed my eyes, focusing on every inhale and exhale, willing some of the adrenaline to leave my body so that I could think and retrace my steps.

I was with Darius, we'd been staking out his frenemy, Nash, at the warehouse.

Things had started to get...heated.

Moving on.

And then the wolves.

The largest group of them I'd ever seen in one place. I knew that wolves operated in large packs, but there were never so many together in the human realm. At least not as far as any protectors were aware of. No single Guild team could ever stand a chance against a pack that large. Packs in the human realm were scattered, rarely ever more than a dozen. Unless the people in charge of The Guild lied about that too.

I needed to think, needed to understand.

More images flashed through my mind until I couldn't pull any two apart.

Until—

Darius under a pile of furry bodies as he worked to take them out. But there were too many. We didn't stand a chance. My chest tightened as I watched him fall, like some essential cord in me was snapping, a tendon ripping—quick and slow at once, painful all the same.

A flash of light, a wave of colors in reds and purples.

Bright and warm, and while it was terrifying, there was something comforting in the heat too, something familiar. I'd set myself on fire again. It hadn't hurt, hadn't burned me. Instead, it'd almost felt like—home, in a strange, impossible way.

And then, one moment I was there, finally gaining a bit of a control of the flames bursting from my skin like I was coated in gasoline. I was about to help Darius, to save him, to rescue him from the wolves he was drowning under—

Then, in the same moment, I was pushed into Wade's room, collapsed in a pathetic heap.

The images came rushing back into my memory with the force of a jackhammer—the swirling blade jutting out of Wade's stomach as he struggled to breath, to move. I knew that it took more to kill an incubus—decapitation or a blade to the heart— but something about that blade was otherworldly. It was like it was slowly pulling the life out of him, like it was sentient, power- ful. Ancient.

Where had it come from?

I squeezed my eyes together with more force, trying desper- ately to will the memories to the surface, to scatter away all the blurriness, all the confusion.

And then, there he was, clear as day—

The man in the shroud.

My eyes flew open as the memories came rushing back. The

same one who'd taken Wade's body the night he was attacked. The one who'd locked him here and shoved me from his dreams.

And now, apparently, he'd trapped me here too.

As if the mere thought of the creature summoned him, he appeared.

Tall and radiating a power so intense that the hair on my arms stood straight.

I couldn't see his eyes, but I knew with an unwavering certainty that they were boring into mine. Chills rippled down my skin, as unlike the chills Darius inspired as fire and ice. I struggled to stand up, to face him.

I didn't want him to know how weak I was, to see me as the pathetic shell I currently felt like. I slid my hand down my thigh, fingers aching to find my dagger. Not because I thought I could stand a chance against this creature with a fraction of my strength and a blade, but because I wanted the comfort, the familiarity.

My holster was empty.

The creature pulled back the cloak, revealing dark intelligent eyes and a jaw cut from granite. There was no emotion in his expression, save for the slight vestiges of a strangely amused boredom. I instantly wanted him to cover himself back up. There was a coldness about him, a power that tightened my stomach into a ball.

Without thinking, I took a step back. And then another, until I stopped myself. Cyrus didn't teach me to cower, to forecast my fear like a beacon.

The man was older than I was, maybe in his mid or late thirties, though I wasn't sure how I could tell. There were no wrinkles, no gray peppered throughout his thick black hair. It was as if he'd been sculpted from marble, not a single imperfection marring his skin.

But his eyes were filled with a strange, luminescent knowing —and I had a feeling that while he physically didn't look older than thirty-five, he'd probably been alive for much longer. Maybe even centuries, if such a thing were possible. I wasn't sure exactly what he was, but I knew with a sharp certainty that I'd never come across a creature like him before.

Just the image of him standing in front of me hit me with a wave of fear that I hadn't experienced when I'd encountered him before. Maybe because then, I was with Wade. I wasn't alone, left to deal with the mercies of this stranger on my own.

There was a cruel, hard edge as he studied me, like he was expecting something else and what he found instead was lacking. Without thinking, without him so much as moving a muscle, I flinched, fear suddenly dulling my curiosity.

He arched a brow, his lip curling slightly, like my terror both amused and disgusted him. He slid his hand into his pocket and withdrew my blade.

Silver-lined and sapphire-handled.

My heart squeezed at the sight of it, both with relief and with a peculiar sadness. Cyrus and Ro had given me a new set of blades for my birthday, days before I'd left them behind. To see one of them in the hands of my captor was an acute sting. But also, a strange comfort.

I needed to see them again—a need strong enough to rein-fuse my body with the determination and strength it was currently missing.

Without forecasting the move, the man tossed the dagger towards me. I reached up, plucking it from the air as I gripped it in my right hand, pleased that my instincts and abilities weren't completely washed away by his presence.

"W-why?" I asked, my voice still raw from the screaming. I wouldn't allow myself to look at the blade, to feel its comfort. I couldn't take my eyes off the creature standing in front of me. It was never wise to turn your back on a predator.

He shrugged as he crossed his arms in front of his chest. "It won't harm me, so there's no use in my keeping it from you. Especially if it shuts up your incessant screaming."

I knew with absolute certainty that he was right. There

would be no winning a fight against this man, not in the traditional sense. No amount of sparring could prepare me for this
fight. Not unless I somehow learned how to properly wield the
otherworldly fire that occasionally made its appearance when I
was in danger.

The image of lighting this man up in a blaze of flames would
have to do until I could make it a reality.

Cyrus, The Guild, nothing had prepared me to take on a
creature like him. Did they know that he existed, whoever—
whatever—he was?

"Where am I?" I squared my shoulders and tried to diminish
the shaking in my limbs. I wasn't nearly as drained as I'd been
when I'd first arrived here, but I also didn't have anything close
to my usual strength.

Still, I wouldn't sit back, withered like a broken, beaten
thing. Whatever this creature had planned for me, I would face
it—and him—head-on.

I let my mini pep talk flow through my veins and straightened my posture as I studied him.

His eyes narrowed slightly as he bent down. For the first
time, I noticed a small bag at his feet. He rummaged through it
for a moment, head ducked low and evidently not concerned
about me attacking him. I held my breath until he pulled out a
parcel and tossed it towards my chest.

My reflexes weren't as sharp as they usually were, but I
caught it all the same, just before it slid out of my reach. Hesitant, I unwrapped the fabric.

"Bread?" I asked. Though my stomach felt hollow, I wasn't
exactly sure this was safe to eat.

He grinned, but not with mirth. He grinned the way a
predator might, before devouring its prey, revealing a set of
straight, white teeth.

Apparently hell came with a good dental plan.

"It's not poisoned, girl, it's safe to eat." His eyes were cold
and calculating as he studied me, but something about the tone

felt like he was holding back from rolling his eyes. "If I wanted to kill you, it would be done."

It wasn't a threat, more just a statement. Rather than enhance my fear, his point diminished it. He was right. And if I was alive now, it was for a reason—worrying about him eventually offing me would just diminish energy that I didn't have to spare.

I needed to gain my strength back and then focus on developing a plan. Until then, the best I could do was try and learn everything that I could about where I was located, about who Creeper McGee was. And that meant taking every handout he was willing to give me—whether nourishment or information.

"What do you want with me?" I asked, surprising myself with the false bravado in my voice. I dug into the bread, pulling out a large handful that I unceremoniously shoved into my mouth, chewing as I watched him, waiting for him to pounce. I couldn't remember a time I'd been this hungry. It felt like I hadn't eaten in weeks. I sank down onto the bed, wincing at how firm it was, at how achey my body was, and finished off the loaf.

It was good, but I wanted more—I missed the unlimited buffets at The Guild something fierce. Hell, I'd even settle for the rewards of one of Darius's deer hunting sprees.

We studied each other as I chewed, neither of us breaking the silence.

Finally, I dropped my eyes from his and glanced down at my empty hands, wishing there was a nice steak or pile of fries in that mysterious bag he'd just shown up with. Or broccoli. God, I missed vegetables. Maybe if I stared hard enough, a five-course meal would appear in my lap. Weirder things had happened in my world.

And we were in hell—who knew what the limits of this world were. So far, I'd managed to basically self-combust here, so a steak didn't seem totally off balance.

"Your energy stores are low," he said, studying me with a cool objectivity, like I was a lab rat, a stepping stone to some larger, more important element in his grand plan. His brow arched slowly, and his expression flashed briefly with intrigue before all emotion dripped from his face. "Food will help, but I see you've already started pulling energy from another source."

I glanced up at him, confused. Partially because a loaf of bread hardly counted as 'food' in my book and partially because, "other source?"

"You don't know?" He grinned in that way of his that sent chills climbing up my spine and made it seem like he could end my life without so much as lifting a finger. "Of course you don't know. Protectors have always been very good at hiding their dirty secrets, at manipulating reality. Or simply ignoring it." He shook his head, amusement shining through in small, passing glimpses.

"Know what?" I asked, my voice harsh and cracked. I needed water. Bread was good, but hours of screaming had done damage that dry bread only highlighted.

His mouth carved into a cocky grin, drawing out the heavy moment until I felt like I might burst with anticipation. "You're a bit less intelligent than I'd have hoped for."

I narrowed my eyes as I waited for him to do his whole setting-the-pace-of-the-conversation power move. I hated when people knew something you didn't and deliberately tried to draw out your unknowing for as long as possible, and I wasn't going to make it easier on him by responding to his insult. Dick.

"You dream-walk. Semi-frequently from what I've gathered. You just woke up from a dream, of which I want no details, far more rested and energized than anyone else would be after what you just went through." He paused, staring at me with a pregnant expectation, waiting for me to finish his thought for him.

But I had no idea where this guy was going, so I shrugged, urging him to continue.

He exhaled dramatically, shaking his head just slightly as he pinched the bridge of his nose with long, strong fingers. "Demon's tit, girl. You're a succubus. Partially, anyway."

He shrugged, just dropping the statement there and leaving me with nothing to do but try and swallow it.

I wasn't entirely sure what I was expecting, but that was not it. I cleared my throat and sat in silence for a long moment, waiting for the creature in front of me to scream 'gotcha' or for Ashton Kutcher to show up and tell me that I was on a rebooted episode of Punk'd.

But all that I was left with was a cold, heavy silence that was somehow still deafening as the man watched me. Something about his stillness sent a bolt of irritation to my gut, strong enough to eclipse any lingering fear.

"I'm what now?" I asked, hoping he'd come up with a better story to weave. If I wasn't so hungry and, deep-down, incredibly terrified of the figure in front of me, I would've laughed my ass off. Me being a succubus made about as much sense as a screen door on a submarine. I'd had sex a grand total of once, and while that one time was most definitely mindblowing, even if the afterglow sucked, I didn't yield any supernatural lusty powers in the process. I'd been just normal, bumbling, awkward Max. "And I don't dream-walk. I mean, I've done it before, yes. But it wasn't my doing."

It was Wade's.

I froze, recalculating. In my most recent dream, Wade was most notably absent. As I sat with his sentence, lingered in it for a moment, my world started to stitch itself back together in a new pattern, the image somehow more clear than before as though the confusion was slowly slipping away into a heavy sort of realization.

Suddenly my dream with Darius came flaring back to life with perfect, vivid detail. It had been similar, felt similar, to my dreams with Wade, but I'd felt differently. I recalled that peculiar power that seemed to infuse my body with every touch and sensation, like I was feeling enough for the both of us. Like his lust was enhancing my own. While I'd told myself it was just any average dream, albeit one in which I got to explore a deep-seated desire that I'd never allow myself to act on in reality, it had felt anything but. I'd had...steamy dreams before, but never had they felt so all-consuming. So electric. So intoxicating. So...energizing.

And then there was the fact that Wade wasn't there. I'd traveled to Darius on my own.

"Please tell me you aren't as dense as you seem? I can never tell with those from your realm," the man said, as he looked down at me with distaste. He kicked the bag at his feet until it slid across the room, landing before mine. "There's water and another loaf in there. I won't be back here often, I'm a busy man. So you'll need to learn to ration it. I've seen how ravenously your kind can eat. Gluttonous buffoons, the lot of you."

I stared down at the brown bag, my chest suddenly hollow and head dizzy.

Succubus. I was part succubus.

As the word floated around, banging against my skull like a pinball, I felt the truth of it. I knew that I was different, always had. Ever since joining The Guild, I'd wanted nothing more than to belong—to fit perfectly with my community, my people. It suddenly made sense why I hadn't.

I didn't belong.

I wasn't one of them. And it wasn't like I had any idea who my real parents were. Maybe this was why.

Raw self-loathing filled my gut. Eli, Declan, and Atlas were right. I wasn't a protector. Or at least I wasn't *only* a protector. I was the very thing I was in training to hunt. The thing I'd spent a lifetime learning to kill. I gripped the brown bag, feeling my fingers break small holes into the paper. Did everyone know? Did Cyrus? Did Ro? Would I be banished from The Guild now —locked down in the lab, as people poked and prodded me, desperate for answers?

What if I hurt someone? Had I hurt Eli while we'd—done what we did? Maybe I deserved to be in the lab after all.

Wade.

As if his name alone could calm me, ground me, my shoulders dipped. I was like Wade. And incubus or not, Wade was the farthest thing from evil I could imagine. I'd spent days trying to convince him that he was worth saving—that he was no more evil than Ralph.

I wasn't alone, not in this. Hell, and then there was Atlas. Being part demon was starting to seem pretty par for the course for protectors, even if it was generally ignored or swept under the rug.

"Save the little pity-party for later," the man bit out, his words so crisp they sent a chill through me, "it's very tedious and cumbersome to witness and I'm a busy man. It's not particularly unique for protectors to have the blood of succubi running through their veins. I'd hazard a guess that a significant number of the vermin running through the halls of your so-called school have been fed on by an incubus or succubus in their lifetime."

"How?" I asked, even as I thought of Wade. Maybe he was right. And the idea that I wasn't a complete outcast soothed the panic turning my stomach to knots. I thought again of Darius. Had I drained him too much? Did he realize what was happening while it happened? Was he okay?

My chest flipped as I realized that what happened between us would be locked into his memory too—it wasn't just a smutty dream, hidden away in mine. Wasn't something that I could just brush off with the light of day. Because if it was true, if I really was a succubus, then it wasn't just a dream. Not in the traditional sense anyway.

Which means that Darius and I, that we'd—

And what if he regretted it? What if he'd had no sway against my powers, no way to resist? Vampires were powerful, him more than most, but they weren't immune to a succubus' draw.

I felt sick with the realization that I could have pulled from his energy without his consent.

The man exhaled and ran a hand through his dark, blue-black hair, in a gesture that seemed so human that I was hit with how very few of his mannerisms were. Something about him made vampires and werewolves seem friendly, tame. Simply being in the same room as him had my stranger-danger radar practically throwing a community-wide parade.

"Calm your panic, girl. You're actually quite weak as far as succubi go, and it's probably the least interesting thing about you. Your powers are infantile at best. They'll grow with time, if properly nurtured, but for now they are enough to help give you a bit of a recharge when you're in need. At least for as long as you are drawing from the energy of the hell realm." His dark eyes studied me, but they were unreadable. "Things are different here, than they are where you're from. Power is different here. If I'd known you'd go spinning into an existential life crisis, I would've saved the big reveal for when I wasn't here to witness it.

"Demons feed off protectors far more often than anyone in The Guild realizes. Powerful creatures prefer pulling from strong power sources. Protectors are weak by comparison to most beings that live in this realm, yes, but they offer significantly more juice than a measly human. And male protectors are often impulsive, reckless, constantly needing to prove themselves and demonstrate their worth. When you throw in the heightened sex drive that succubi bring, and a pretty face to boot, it's no surprise that their guards are lowered, that they fall to the temptation. Lust is a powerful drug, it has a way of blinding people."

I caged my arms around my head, blocking the man from my sight, and took a deep breath. Something about his rant felt personal, like he was justifying the reality as much to himself as to me. It was the most I'd heard him speak. And as much as it bristled my nerves, what he said made sense—protectors were stronger than humans, and in my very brief experience, it seemed that vampires preferred to feed from protectors when given the opportunity as well. So why not incubi and succubi?

But the puzzle pieces still didn't fit perfectly. If succubi frequently pulled power from protectors, I would've known, right? I'd heard almost nothing about any of the protectors on campus sharing bloodlines outside of our species. And lust demons were incredibly rare, with very few field teams ever even encountering, let alone capturing them.

"I've never met another protector hybrid at Headquarters," I whispered, more to myself than to him.

Lie.

I'd met Wade. And Atlas, too, though that was different since he was turned, not born.

The man's lips tightened, like he recognized the untruth, but couldn't be bothered calling me on it. We both knew that Wade was an incubus, and that he and I were well acquainted.

The hundreds of faces I'd encountered from my brief time at The Guild went rushing through my mind like sped-up film reel. Would I have known? Was there a tell? They all seemed to fit in with their world so perfectly, like they knew exactly where they belonged and what their roles in life were meant to be—and everyone was eager to fill them, like they were following a perfectly-tuned script.

A script I hadn't had a chance to rehearse for.

The man sighed, and I could feel his frustration coat the room, like a layer of impatient dust. "Let's get this over with so that we can move on to more important things, shall we? Protectors aren't actually aware of this. They meet succubi or incubi, fornicate, and then brush it off as a poor decision with a human. The unions almost never result in a child. Most women die during the pregnancy—hybrid births are very difficult things to survive, for mother and child both. But it's not completely impossible. I'm sure that you and your friend are not the only two demon-protectors born into existence." He glanced down, brows dipping in the middle in another shadow of a human gesture, though I didn't know him well enough to read the emotion that I glimpsed. Just as quickly as I saw the expression, it disappeared, and his face was hard, cold again. Impassive. "Protectors aren't exactly at the top of the hierarchy when it comes to intelligence. Throw in the promise of sex and some light power of suggestion and they ignore any signs of a demon that they might otherwise be hunting for. Lust has a way of doing that, of eclipsing your goal, of pushing you on a path away from your purpose."

I swallowed, thinking about how my own lust had screwed me over on multiple occasions. And very recently. Apparently my dream self was all about getting it on with a fucking vampire who'd killed who knew how many people. Having sex with Darius was about as far from my life's purpose as I could get.

"Still, I've never done...what I just did before," I said, ignoring the discomfort at acknowledging my sexy sleep time with a complete stranger. Maybe he was wrong. "I've never visited a dream to restore my own energy. The only time I've ever traveled to someone in my sleep was with Wade. And he's drained me, it's never been the other way around."

He exhaled, like he was growing tired of our conversation, but he answered anyway. "Succubi and Incubi are unlike most other demons. Their powers tend not to be activated until they are through the hell realm, at least not properly activated anyway. Something about the magic of this place is needed. Moving through dreams requires quite a bit of magical energy. The human realm does not quite offer the pull or the fuel. It's not something that is understood very well." He ran his fingers through the scruff on his face, filling the room with that scratchy sound of nails on beard. His brows bent in the middle, like he was lost in his own world, completely oblivious to the fact I was here with them—that, or ambiguous to my presence. I got the feeling that even he didn't understand the powers of lust demons very well. That he hated the fact that he didn't have all of the answers, that no one seemed to.

I wasn't exactly sure why he was taking the time to tell me all of this—there was something surreal about having my ancestry explained by a creature who rocked some serious supernatural serial-killer vibes.

He scratched the back of his neck, eyes darting around the

room. I had a feeling he wasn't entirely sure why he was being so forthright either. It wasn't that he looked awkward or uncomfortable, there was too much confidence and arrogance radiating from him for that to be possible; but there was something hesitant about the way he rambled, unsure.

"And until very recently, protectors haven't been known for making their way to this realm. If any others exist, the demon side will be latent until they do," he finished, tone cooling as if he recognized the strangeness of the moment, just as I did.

There was a long stretch of silence as we each eyed the other down. His eyes were so dark I was almost convinced they were pitch black. Whatever unidentifiable emotion he'd unintentionally leaked out during his speech was locked away, as if it wasn't ever really there in the first place.

He studied me too, and something about the lift in his chin, the occasional flare of his nose, told me that whatever he was looking for in me was severely lacking—like he'd captured the wrong girl by mistake and was too proud to admit fault.

Refusing to break eye contact, I let his explanation sink in. I thought back to Wade, and the way his powers seemed to emerge so quickly. We'd thought it was his human death that had triggered something, but maybe it was more than that. I didn't really begin having my dreams with him until he was taken to this realm. Had this stranger saved him, then? Pulled him into hell so that he could be reborn anew? Why? Why save him, just to lock him up, alone and scared for months on end?

But the thought of Wade filled me with a fresh wave of determination. I straightened my posture and narrowed my eyes, only flinching slightly at the steely focus I saw in his. Something about those dark orbs felt so familiar. They were impenetrable, like Khalida's, and spoke of another world, an awareness of things that I would never grasp.

Maybe they were both the same mysterious type of creature. No. Not the same, but adjacently related maybe.

I trusted Khali. Partially, anyway. But I did not trust a single hair on this man's head. There was a cruelty in his gaze, where there was only kindness in Khali's.

"What do you want with us?" I asked, abruptly changing the conversation to what really mattered. I'd deal with my own identity crisis later. Right now, I needed answers. And I needed to see Wade. Needed to know that he was still okay—still alive. "I want to see my friend. Now."

He let out a hollow chuckle, his eyes sparkling with mirth as he met my stare. For the first time since entering my humble little cell, his harsh facade cracked, even just slightly.

Rage coursed through my veins, and I hated that he found my sudden bravado so amusing. My fingers latched around the fabric I sat on, the scratchy fibers digging against my skin, grounding me.

He stood still, frozen so entirely that he made the Buckingham Palace Guards look like jittery dancers. So still that I couldn't even be sure if he was breathing. Did he even need to breathe at all?

What the hell was he?

"He's alive," he cleared his throat, but something told me it was a thing he did to appear more human, not something he actually needed to do. A mannerism that he'd adopted to soothe the anxieties of those around him. I supposed that was a good sign—that he'd studied how to put people at ease and put it to use. It suggested a shade of compassion, in some strange, twisted way. "For now, at least."

"That blade," I said, my words slow and steady as I tried to peel back the anger threatening to escape. I couldn't win against this man, I knew that. And if I wanted a chance at getting Wade out of here, I needed to make sure that I stayed far away from his bad side—as far as possible, anyway. I couldn't be brash, not here. It was more than my own life on the line. "What did it do to him?"

"It's unfortunate that I had to use it, I'll give you that. But it brought you here, which was my ultimate goal." He shrugged, as if to say that was that and there was no use unpacking anything more.

In the time it had taken me to process his words, he'd constructed a wall, repairing the small cracks that had led him to spill as much information as he already had. He turned to the wall, studying the exact space I'd been clawing at before with a cool disinterest. I hadn't made a dent, but there were small smears of blood from where I'd cracked my nails and fingertips against the hard surface.

I scrunched up my face and stared at him. He had a way of doing that thing I hated—talking in partial truths, like he got his kicks from keeping people in the shadows, from being the only one who saw how the puzzle fit together. "You going to elaborate on that, or are you enjoying this drawn-out, meandering process?"

So much for keeping on his good side.

But, honestly? I was hungry, I was scared, and I was in the middle of a seriously stomach-hollowing identity crisis. The guy was just going to have to cut me some slack if I was a little short with my kidnapper.

As if he could read my thoughts as they filtered through my mind, the side of his lips tipped up in what could only be described as an almost smile, like I amused him but only vaguely. The kind of smirk that came with a warning—that if I pushed too hard, I would regret it.

I had no doubts that this man would kill me if I gave him even the slightest reason to.

He took a step closer—just one, but it felt like he'd suddenly encroached on my space, like he'd bypassed an invisible boundary of sorts. His power grated against my skin with a force that would've buckled my knees if I wasn't already sitting.

"The blade is infused with my magic. And your magic is fused with the boy's. My blade, when put into contact with his blood, had the possibility of drawing you here. Of alerting you to his danger. It had a small probability of working, but in the end, my needs were met."

"What exactly are you?" I'd never heard of any such blade, nor had I ever seen the sort of swirly blue magic that surrounded the blade as it protruded from Wade's abdomen. Guild weapons were powerful, sure, but in the way that any blade was powerful: they stabbed and decapitated. They were never infused with magic. Magic wasn't some tangible life force that we could manipulate to our whims and fancies. "A stomach wound should not have harmed an incubus that badly. He looked," I shuddered, remembering the sweat coating Wade's skin, the pinch of his face as he floated in and out of consciousness, like the pain was too much to stay present for, "not good."

He shrugged. "It's not a normal blade. But, he didn't die, even though he could have, so maybe he's stronger than I gave him credit for. And he'll stay alive, so long as you cooperate."

Die? There was a possibility that a wound from that blade could have ended his life? And the man used it anyway?

"What is it exactly that you want from me?"

Silence. For a stretched moment, I watched that look of his that made it seem like he wanted to skin me alive, but in a way that was fun for him, not out of rage. In a way that would have made the wendigo look like a kitten.

"I want to see him," I tried again, standing and taking a step closer to him, crossing the invisible boundary between us on my own terms now, pushing back against his raw power with my raw determination.

Like most people, he was taller than me—significantly. But it wasn't his height that had my stomach flipping in fear. He hadn't laid a hand on me since entering this little medieval cave of his, but being in his presence had me almost wishing I was back on that roof, taking on a full pack of werewolves instead of simply standing in his presence.

His eyes flashed with something I couldn't quite decipher, though it had almost the edge of teasing—a resemblance to the sly, hungry darkness that eclipsed Darius on occasion. If Darius's teasing had a scarier, douchier older brother.

"If you want to see your little demon, figure it out yourself. You're capable of more than you realize. And I am interested in seeing exactly how far your capability can stretch. As I said before, I recommend rationing your supplies. I can't guarantee that I'll be back here every day. I'm a busy man." He turned his head, as if he was turning towards a door or an exit. Only there was no door, no exit. "There's a bucket in the corner."

I resisted the urge to point out that cylindrical rooms didn't have corners and followed his hand gesturing to the side instead. My stomach dropped at the sight of a dirty bucket, one that looked like it'd kept many prisoners company long before me. It hadn't been there before his arrival.

I took a step closer, my jaw tensing so hard that I'd need a dentist if I tried holding back my fury for much longer. "Just let—"

And then, with a small nod and low, taunting bow, he disappeared.

It happened so quickly that I was almost convinced that he was never here at all, that he was nothing more than a figment of my imagination that liked to pop up when the trauma was getting too intense to bear on my own. He'd become something like a nefarious fairy godmother in my imagination. Each time I'd encountered him felt more like a fever dream than anything grounded in reality.

I didn't remember seeing him disappear, the night that he stole Wade. So much of that battle lived in my head as distorted images and memories—the lingering grief and ache of losing Wade the only thing about it that felt concrete and grounded. His presence in Wade's dream had felt almost like a phantom memory, the feel of being ejected from the dungeon the only thing that still resonated.

And, just like that night, I was left alone, sinking into my fear and anger, with no way to push back against it.

I fell back on the bed and glanced around the room. How had Wade done it? How had he survived so many months alone in this small cave, with no company but for my occasional visits? A chill crept deep into my skin, tightening around my chest to keep my anxiety company, as I listened to the absolute silence surrounding me.

It was stifling.

🦋 5 🦋

ATLAS

My paws dug into the ground with each step, unleashing fresh plumes of dust into the air. I ran and ran for what felt like hours, maybe even days. Time was a finicky thing to track when things got like this, when the wolf and I merged and fought for control. Scenes flashed through my eyes in disconnected jarbles, patches of forest here replaced by dilapidated buildings there. It was impossible to piece everything together—both of us high on adrenaline and something that felt suspiciously like fear.

And, somehow, that fear was equal parts crippling and motivating.

Everything that wasn't Max's scent disappeared into the background, nothing more than white noise. There was one goal, one incentive pushing us forward. The driving need to find her, to make sure that she was okay.

Almost as soon as we'd left Declan and Eli, the wolf had taken full control, pushing me into the back seat in a way that he hadn't done since the very first day that he'd found Max.

I remembered very little from that night, a brief glimpse of a girl standing by a truck, dark hair and a hopeful, innocent expression plastered on her face. There was something so effortless and artless about her. She'd taken my breath away, even just that single glance, the way her smile seemed to light up from the inside, like she'd never experienced a moment of pain, never a single disappointment. The world had looked so beautiful through her expression, everything filled with an unfamiliar sort of hope. Her dark eyes were teeming with so much life, and as soon as I'd caught sight of them, I knew that I wanted to know her. That I needed to know her.

And then I saw that the reason for her radiating energy, the charge to that excitement that seemed to make the air around her buzz with electricity, was a fucking human. A perfectly average prick that had one hundred percent of her attention, like he was the center of her world. The moment that his lips touched hers, my wolf all but threw me to the back of the room, so that I barely got so much as a peek of her after that.

Rage, unlike anything I'd experienced, boiled in my veins and I fought to get back, to get control of my body, with a desperation so acute I could still feel it when I thought back to those moments, to that night.

That girl took my power away—her arrival in my life had ushered in the thing I'd been so terrified of since the moment the wolf had bitten me. When she was around, I lost my grip, lost control over myself. The fragile thread of control I had over my wolf was clipped.

It was terrifying, waking up hours later in the middle of the woods, with little to no recollection of what had happened. Of what I'd done. After, I'd eventually found my way home, my skin prickling with each mile of distance I put between me and the girl. As soon as I had access, I scoured the internet for days on end. Desperately checking every news source I could find for sightings of a wolf, for an attack, for some unexplained death in the area I'd stumbled upon.

Blacking out like I had meant that anything could have happened. I didn't trust the wolf, not completely, but especially not when I wasn't there holding his reins.

When Max was around, the wolf was unpredictable, which meant that when Max was around, I was dangerous—that the people around me were in danger. Including her. It wasn't her fault, and deep down I knew that, but I still couldn't bring myself to forgive her for that loss of power, that loss of control.

But this, now, this seething rage that seemed to grab hold of the wolf, made that night seem like a casual prank. While I hadn't been certain if the wolf was capable of killing someone back then, I knew with a sharp certainty that if the wrong person crossed my path now, there'd be no saving them.

He'd reached his point of no return, and then he kept going, long past it.

We landed, eventually, in a small area, scattered with old, dilapidated buildings. Most of the windows were busted and what looked like a once-clear path, was now reclaimed by nature, flowers and grass creeping up along the cracks and crevices. It was beautiful in a strange way, watching the environment take back what once belonged to it. I knew, in some strange, intuitive way, that the wolf preferred this sort of scene to the more urban places in our realm.

The scent of blood filled the air as we pressed our nose into the gravel, practically inhaling rocks in order to get to her scent, each hit of it leading to a frenzied need for the next. I could feel our heartbeat pounding as one, as my fear was amplified by the rabid, less contained fear of the wolf. For once, we were in sync, both of us focused on exactly one goal: finding Max and bringing her home.

Not that we were anywhere close to home. But, slowly, it was sinking in. That at least where my wolf was concerned, home would be wherever she was. That's all we needed. Her and the team. Everything else could be sorted out later.

It was an uncomfortable thing, sharing a body and mind with a creature who was singularly focused on the very creature I'd been trying desperately to keep my distance from. But now that she was gone, now that I was poised with the potential of losing her for good, I could almost understand his obsession.

Almost.

The scent seemed to be coming from one building, along the edge of the treeline. It was only a few stories, so we reached the top in no time. The second we stepped onto the roof, panic settled over us, collecting and sticking like a horrible snow storm —until it was almost too heavy to bear.

We found bodies, so many bodies. Many of them burnt to a crisp, the stench of charred flesh filling the air with a perfume so strong that it all but drowned out everything else.

Her blood was here, on the ground.

Quite a bit of it, too, mixed with the blood of the creatures who attacked her. The second it reached us, a heavy stillness settled over us both, a stillness filled with a nameless terror that turned our thoughts inside out until all we could see was red.

It took a long, breath-shattering moment for us to realize that while her blood was here, she wasn't. Bodies littered the flat rooftop, so many that only patches of the ground could be seen, peeking out here and there between gruesome splotches of blood and fur-lined carcasses.

My thoughts flittered, the wolf fighting me for the front seat as we both tried to process the scene in front of us. I dug in, trying to claw my way back. It was so much more difficult than it usually was. The last few months, I'd had much less control over the wolf, but the turbulence of our relationship was only getting worse. I could feel him digging in, ready to grind me down to dust if that was the only way for him to emerge. He was growing tired of my resistance, I could feel his impatience lap against every inch of my skin.

I screamed as the transformation pulled through my body, so much more painful than usual, like the wolf was exerting half of our energy to fight me, even on this.

Our bones cracked and shattered, only to reshape themselves new, each sensation crawling through our body with a sharp, elongated agony. I'd long stopped expecting the shifts to get easier, to dull some of the pain through repetition and muscle memory. Each transformation hurt as badly as the one before it; if anything, they were getting worse.

It took only a few minutes, but it felt like hours, until, halfway through the excruciating battle, I could feel myself tipping the scales. Until I sat in a pile of ash and bones, naked, furless, and covered in sweat.

"Fuck," I croaked, my body shivering with exhaustion and adrenaline as I dug my fingers into the ground, my palms snapping a dry bone as I pushed myself up. I sucked in air as I scrutinized the scene around me, my mind lagging as it clawed fiendishly to take back control from the wolf. It took me a moment to understand where I was, what I was looking for.

The push back into being a man was always a disorienting one, but never quite so much as it was now. Maybe that fucking parasite was right—maybe the wolf really was splitting me in half, slowly blotting out the pieces of me that were mine and mine alone.

The look on the vamp's face when he'd studied me, in those moments when the wolf was clawing his way to the surface, I knew that he could see it, could see the war being fought beneath my skin. He was able to see, to understand, in a way that no one else had. The monster that lingered just below the surface in his eyes saw the monster that lingered below mine and understood with a clarity that even I couldn't seem to obtain. That I was in a constantly escalating battle over my own body.

And I was losing.

My hands dug into my hips as I desperately sucked air into my lungs, willing my body to function again, to remember how to exist in the strangely-uncomfortable and rigid human form it was so desperately trying to reject. I studied the graveyard around me, trying to assess the surroundings with the sort of cold, objective observation I would use on any other mission.

We'd been combing over the surface of this rooftop, circling the small block over and over. But Max's scent just—disappeared.

I stared at each body on the ground, terrified that the next set of eyes I'd find cold and lifeless on the ground would be hers. But she wasn't here—a realization that filled me with both fear and relief. If she wasn't here, she could still be alive.

But if she wasn't here, and her scent carried no further trail, where the hell was she and how would I find her?

I ran my fingers over my eyes, trying to keep the sweat from blurring my vision. What the fuck had happened here?

The remnants of the fire pointed to Max. She was the only person I'd ever come across who could straight up light themselves on fire like that. It was like she could tap into the exhilarating energy that made her radiate like the sun, the energy that seemed to draw and pull at us all, and make it tangible. Make it as fierce and powerful as she was.

The fact that half of the bodies up here were barbecued suggested that little skill of hers had saved her skin once again.

But did it?

Where the fuck was she? I took another lap around the roof, slowly this time, taking in every detail with as much focus and clarity as I could muster. And then I did it again, and again, and again, until my approach grew more careless, more unforgiving. I threw bodies over the edge, not even blinking as the skin on my feet was torn over and over by haphazardly crunching on the dry, brittle bones that littered the ground. There were so many bodies that it felt like I was standing in the middle of some ancient burial ground, a gruesome mix of ash, bone, meat. Had Max and the vamp really taken on all of these creatures alone?

For just two people, they'd certainly taken out a disturbing number of wolves, more than should be possible.

For a moment, I thought about finding my way back to Dec and Eli. We could regroup, Dec could work her magic and calm me down, and we could formulate a plan. There were too many

loose ends, each pulling me in different directions like an excruciating tug-of-war that would leave me drawn and quartered.

I wasn't sure where to go from here, which trail to chase. Eli
hadn't looked great when I left, a lingering concern that I
wouldn't let my mind focus on for more than a few seconds at a
time, pulling back each moment that fear turned disturbingly
close to grief, as if deep down I knew there was a very real possibility that he might not be there when I returned.

There were too many obstacles, too many ways for all of our
hard work to go to shit. And Wade—we hadn't gotten any closer
to finding him. I hadn't gotten so much as a whiff of his scent
since dropping into this literal hellhole.

Everything was all loose ends and gnarled knots and I didn't
know how to tether my team back together. Where the fuck was
I supposed to start?

A frustrated sob wracked my body, and I found myself
suddenly grateful that there wasn't a soul around to witness it, to
watch me crumble to pieces while everything I cared about, one-
by-one, was taken from me.

I choked on my breath, trying to fill my lungs and clear my
mind—I needed to focus, I just didn't know what to focus on.

The vamp. He wasn't here either.

Rage billowed beneath my skin as the vestiges of his scent
prickled at my nose, toying with me even in his absence. The
wolf was pushing back again. He'd been satisfied to sit on the
sidelines for a few minutes, more than fine with giving me some
small semblance of control while I tried to make sense of this
strange reality that felt more like a neverending nightmare. But
the second that my brain focused on the parasite's scent, it was
over.

I could feel him looking out through my eyes, could feel him
beneath my skin, like a phantom limb. Could feel as he transitioned from shadow to something more solid, more tangible,
more permanent.

This was all the vampire's fault.

He'd taken her out from under our protection, dragged her across the plains of hell, and pulled her right into the middle of an ambush. He should've protected her. And now—now, where the hell was she? I had no idea how to find her from here. No trail to follow, no map of hell to instigate a search. Nothing.

Just her loud, deafening absence, and the heavy, cloying fear her absence left in its wake.

What if she was killed? How did someone straight up disappear, every trace just vanished on a spot? I kicked a decapitated head from the roof, listening as it landed with a dull thud, and bent over. My hands gripped my hair as I took slow, deep breaths to calm myself down, trying desperately to approach the situation more rationally, to hold onto myself. To stay.

But that wasn't the wolf's way.

My blood flooded with an anger so acute that I felt like I might turn into a living flame myself. My knees hit the ledge of the roof as my body fought with itself—fought to stay here, to stay in control. My fingernails lined with blood as I dug them into the concrete, trying to push all of my strength into holding on, staying present.

Until I froze, every muscle in my body still as I realized the truth, logic laced with venom.

I couldn't find Max. I didn't know where to go from here, there were no options or strategies to deploy. There was no real thing for me to do other than chase myself in circles, falling into a fit of molten anger every time I came up to the same dead end. I was out of options. No Wade, no Max—no sign of either.

But what I could do was track down the vamp. His scent lingered, his blood mixed with the blood of the pack he'd tried to take out.

There were too many of them, dozens. Even with the strange power he possessed, he couldn't take on this many wolves. Not on his own.

They'd taken him, and Max disappeared, and I wanted to know why.

Why hadn't they killed him, ripped him limb from limb?

Especially after he'd massacred so many of them. I'd find him, and when I did, if he didn't point me to Max or my brother, I'd kill him myself. I wouldn't give the wolves the satisfaction of doing it themselves.

Once I'd gone through every last wolf of that pack, picked them off and bent them individually until they broke and fractured, I'd have a lead—I'd find her. Then, we'd find Wade. And then I'd get Dec and Eli, and the five of us together, we'd find a way home.

Logic, focus, control—the things I'd spent a lifetime cultivating didn't matter anymore. They were useless to me. All that mattered was finding my team—my pack.

And I didn't care who I'd have to go through to get to them.

For once, I wasn't going to fight back. I couldn't keep trying to feed the wolf's strength and power into my own goals and plans. If it meant finding Max, or killing the man responsible for her death, it would be worth it.

I fell back, let the steely fear bleed and morph into a focused determination, a rage that made every one of my muscles tense.

And then, I gave in.

I let the wolf take over.

❦ 6 ❧

MAX

S taring. That's all that there was to do in this small cell—
stare at the wall and hope for something to happen. I'd
memorized every groove of stone, every inch of porous
grout, and no matter how much I tried to will myself to sleep,
sleep wouldn't come.

I wasn't sure how much time had passed since my captor had
disappeared, leaving me in this icebox alone. Despite all of the
information he'd dumped on me, I was only left with more questions. I pulled the tattered fabrics scattered around my bed
close, trying to stifle my shivering as much as possible.

Where the hell was that damn fire trick when I needed it? I
took a deep breath in and tried to visualize that strange swirl of
fire—the orange and red, mixed with purple and blue—to feel
the peculiar tingle that crept along my skin when I lit up like an
inferno.

But nothing.

And why the hell was hell so freaking cold in the first place? I
watched with lingering amusement as my breath turned into
smoky clouds, wafting around me like it was alive. So much for
fire and brimstone; this place had more of a medieval apocalyptic vibe than anything I'd imagined in my head.

The fairytales got so many things right about demons and monsters and magic, but they got a wild amount wrong too. Hell was nothing like I'd imagined it to be. Then again, I was starting to realize that the demons I'd been training my whole life to hunt weren't how I'd imagined them to be either. Nothing made sense anymore and I wasn't sure what to believe.

Somehow my old life seemed so far away now—The Guild, my family. It hadn't even been that long since I was walking Guild halls, but it felt like a lifetime ago. Everything in my mind was morphing and rearranging itself into before hell and after.

Everything was different now. I was different now.

I stared at the stone walls long enough that I was almost convinced that they were the only thing that really existed. Each time my stomach tightened with fear, each time I thought I'd scream from being trapped alone in this room for another moment, I'd focus on the wall and I'd think of Wade. He might not be in this exact room with me, but I knew he was somewhere in this strange building, waiting, just like I was—trapped behind walls just like mine. And I'd get to him if it was the last thing I did.

We were so close, the giddiness of that realization enough to cause a vibration of anticipation to go rippling through my body. The mission had seemed so impossible, such a wild stretch of the imagination, but here we were.

And I'd come too far to get shot down in the final stretch. After everything, I'd made my way to him. It wasn't exactly the grand rescue mission I'd imagined in my head. I didn't come in all blades of glory, ready to hack away at a trove of monsters until I reached the prince at the top of the tower. Instead, I'd gotten myself in the exact same predicament I was trying to save him from.

So no, I wasn't exactly a hero of the story. Not yet, anyway.

But right now, all that mattered was that he was alive. I hadn't learned much, and I was trying not to pick at some of the information I had gleaned in these walls. In fact, I was adamantly ignoring the whole succubus thing for now. A girl could only handle so much trauma in one go. But I believed the creature when he told me that Wade was alive. For some reason, one that I couldn't quite explain or understand, I knew that I'd *know* if he wasn't.

On some ethereal level, Wade and I were on the same wavelength, like I was constantly aware of his presence. Even when he'd disappeared that night, I knew that he wasn't gone, not really. I could feel it in my bones, and spent all of my time and energy searching for him in my dreams—until I found him.

Or until he found me, I wasn't really sure.

And what about the others? I had a feeling that Darius was, at the very least, alive. Otherwise I wouldn't have been able to feed from him—an event that I was also going to ignore for the time being. If I survived this, I'd have to deal with those consequences eventually, but for now, I could only devote so much energy to dissecting what happened. And drowning in the fear of what might happen in the future would lead me nowhere good.

But where exactly was Darius? The dream room we'd been in was empty and terrifying, the sort of room that acted as a backdrop in those creepy Saw movies. That hadn't stopped us from...enjoying the space, sure, but still. If he wasn't killed by the swarming pack of wolves, then they must've taken him.

Why, though? What the hell would they want with a sarcastic, unpredictable vampire? What was with this realm and kidnapping people?

Supernatural creatures acted nothing like how I thought they would. Something big was going down in this world, the air was almost heavy with the electricity of it, like the whole place was just waiting for the shoe to drop, the calm before the storm. I hoped like hell that we'd all be out of here before the downpour started. Something told me that we'd get swept up in the hurricane if we lingered in this realm much longer. And whatever battle was brewing, one thing was certain—it was not ours. And it would most definitely be best if we weren't around to see it all unfold.

I closed my eyes, my brain occasionally cycling through the images of *that* dream, my skin lighting up with a much more pleasant shiver with each memory of Darius's touch, every trail of his tongue.

And his teeth. The memory of his fangs puncturing my skin sent a pulse through my body. I'd been bitten by a vampire before, but it hadn't felt like that—

No. I gripped my hair and slammed my eyes closed, trying to push the images, the sensations, down as far as they would go.

That was the succubus talking. Now that I was aware of her, and now that I had nothing to do but dissect my own thoughts and feelings, I could identify where my desires ended and hers began. Sort of. That's what I was telling myself anyway.

Either way, my sex drive was so far from fucking important right now.

And that fucking word. It wouldn't stop ringing in my head.

Succubus.

I shot up from bed, as the sound of it floated through my mind again, like an agonizing taunt that wouldn't be hushed. No matter how many times I tried to redirect my thoughts, that word always came fighting its way to center attention again with a heady vengeance, like a handful of glitter that refused to be swept away with one pass. Or two. Or a hundred.

I looked at my hands, my fingers dancing in front of my eyes, and tried to see it—tried to rectify that term with the body I'd occupied my whole life. I was awkward and bumbling, always rambling about nonsensical things. I spent all of my free time eating mountains of food and sweating in a gym while I tried to perfect my fighting tactics. My experience with romance was all but nonexistent, just fantasies constructed in my imagination from a lifetime of movie-watching and book-consuming.

I was so far from the sort of girl who oozed sex. Hell, I

barely had any traditional sex appeal, let alone the sort of sex appeal amplified by the supernatural.

I'd met exactly one succubus in my life, Darius's friend, Villette, and she'd fit the bill to a T—she'd practically radiated sex, every syllable a purr of seduction. Simply being in her presence was like a crash course in libido.

Try as I might, I couldn't align that visual of her power, of her presence, with my own. But if the man was right, and I really was like her, even a diluted version, I needed to learn to get a grip on those powers.

Before I hurt somebody.

Before I *killed* somebody.

A chill ran through my body, not at all related to the temperature. It was a strange thing, feeling like you didn't recognize yourself—that you shared yourself with someone, or something, else. For the first time, I was afraid of being alone with my thoughts, afraid of being in my own skin.

My stomach tightened as the knot that was becoming all too familiar settled low in my belly.

I closed my eyes, trying to block out the fear, until I remembered what it meant to be a succubus. Maybe I didn't have to be alone, not truly.

The blood of a demon might run through my veins, but that meant the power of a demon did too. And if I couldn't escape this room in body, maybe...well, maybe I could in mind.

I fell back down, my head dropping uncomfortably on the hard bed where no pillow sat, and closed my eyes. For what felt like hours, I tried desperately to fall asleep, until frustration bled into anger, and anger into fear.

I swept my fingers over my cheeks and pulled them away.

They were wet. I'd been crying. And for long enough that my eyes felt swollen with a heavy exhaustion, but still no sleep came. I fucking hated that I was feeling...this. I was supposed to be a capital-P protector, a girl with the blood of angels running through her veins, a goddamn badass who kept the world, and the people in it, safe. Instead, I was falling apart.

Deeper than my own self-pity lay a tremor of pity for Wade. I was the only one who'd been able to reach his dreams across the realms. Save those few visits, he'd been completely, irrevocably alone. I at least knew that he was here, that no matter how alone I felt, he was probably just down the hall, locked up in his own personal torment.

What would that do to a man, over the span of weeks? Months? He'd gone all this time by himself, in a new place, coming to terms with the fact that he was the very thing he'd been trained to kill. And while the disappearing man seemed to almost enjoy dropping those big reveals on me, had he been as forthcoming with Wade? Or had he simply left him there, to wither away, alone with his thoughts, with nothing to do but to sink into the fear and anger?

I shook my head and inhaled slowly, trying to dispel the tightness gripping my chest like an iron vise. I didn't want to linger there, to let the panic overtake my mind. There'd be no returning from that sort of battle, not in this place.

I took a deep breath again, in and out, focusing on the air as it inflated my lungs, only to be met with the atmosphere once more as I let go.

The important thing was that Wade was alive. I said it over and over again in my head, until it was all but carved across my skull.

And judging by my X-rated dream, Darius was alive too. Which meant that Eli was okay—well, alive at least. Their bond would complicate things, but at least for now, it functioned as a tracker of sorts. If one was alive, the other was too. It was all I had to go on. But for now, it was enough.

I pressed the pads of my fingers into the groove of the wall, where one stone met another. I'd spent hours running my hands along the cool stone, digging into the grout, bloodying my hands, waiting for them to heal, and then doing it all over again, like a strange, soothing routine. There was nothing else to do here, and the subtle, lingering pain provided a way to ground my thoughts, the illusion of actually doing something to get out of here.

Where were the others? I hadn't let my thoughts roam too freely on the members of Six. That wound was still too raw for me to walk around pouring a canister of salt all over it.

They'd lied. About so many things.

I couldn't even think about Eli, beyond simply acknowledging the fact that he wasn't dead. Any time my thoughts started to drift to him, heat clawed at my body, sinking me back into that moment with him. It had felt so right, being with him like that. The feel of his skin, the taste of his tongue as it slid against mine.

Only to be ruined as soon as I woke back up. Not only had he lied to me, but he'd stolen my DNA and given it to Seamus. He'd used me. He used my attraction to him to get what he wanted, as if I was nothing more than a puppet.

My heartbeat picked up as I realized what that meant—once those test results, of whatever test he was running, came back, that would be it. Even if I survived this place, even if I found some miraculous way to escape from hell, the truth hit me like a bulldozer until I felt so hollow I might as well fade into nothing.

I'd never be welcomed back to The Guild. Or, if I was, it would only be to trade my place as an apprentice for that of a prisoner.

I could never go home.

I OPENED MY EYES AND WAS NO LONGER IN THE DIM dungeons of hell. Clothes were scattered around the room, shirts draped across an old armchair, denim tossed over a lampshade, like the person dwelling here hadn't been bothered by the thought of laundry or cleaning for weeks. If the tornado-like quality of the room hadn't felt so familiar, I would have thought it was a deliberate design choice—shabby chic with an edge towards chaos.

I took a step forward, cringing as the sound of metal hitting metal echoed through the room. I bent over, picking up a pair of daggers I'd jostled, examining their familiar handles, pricking my finger on the sharp tip of one. It was a welcome sort of pain, a pain that brought back hours upon hours of sparring—those hours filled with the promise that we were working towards something big, that we'd be helping people.

I wasn't so sure that was the case anymore.

"You've never been one to take such terrible care of your weapons," I said, my words low, tentative, like I'd burst the bubble of this moment, of this scene, if I spoke them too loudly. "They've always been cleaned, polished, and set back in their proper place." I set the blades down on a small dresser that was covered with water bottles and half-empty glasses, all drained to various levels. Some were starting to look a little suspicious, like the early layers of mold were starting to form.

He was never exactly the tidiest person in the world, but I'd never once seen his living space quite like this.

"It's you," his voice was ragged, filled with a rawness that made my stomach hurt.

Slowly, I glanced up at him, terrified that any quick movement might bring the dream crashing down, dissolving the room until I was left alone again. Dream-walking was still so new, and in this particular moment, it was a gift. So I held onto it with a soft grip, afraid of destroying it.

"Hey Ro," I said, my eyes blurring over with liquid as I closed the distance between us, losing all patience with preserving the moment. A girl could only swallow so much emotion in one go. I collapsed against him, my body shaking softly as I breathed in that scent—fresh soap and a light musty fragrance. I used to make fun of him for wearing cologne when we spent all of our time sparring in the woods. But now, that somehow soft and sharp scent smelled like home. It had only been a few days, maybe a week or two since I'd last seen him, but it felt like it had been years, like I'd lived a lifetime since the last moment we were together.

I felt myself crack a little around the edges, the desperation to be back with him suddenly the only thing I wanted in the world.

His arms pulled me to him, rough enough to bruise. He dug his face into my hair, and hugged me with as much force as he could muster. We stood like that, suspended in the moment, breathing in the familiarity of home.

Because that's what Ro was. Home.

"You're alive, please tell me that you're still alive," he said, the words like a desperate chant, liquid and filled with a hollow sadness that made my knees weak. "You're okay, I mean, you are okay? Right? I mean, you're here. Why did you take so long? I thought you'd visit me sooner. After Izzy—"

With another squeeze, I pulled back, needing to see him, to make sure that he was okay too. His normally bright blue eyes that always looked at me with such warmth, were dimmer than I'd ever remembered them being. His face looked a little hollow, his cheeks more pronounced than I'd ever noticed before, the bags under his eyes more prominent, like they were carving out a permanent spot. There was a hardness about his features that hadn't been there back in the cabin. It was almost like he'd lived just as much life in the last few days as I had, like he'd experienced just as much pain. Just as much disappointment.

"What happened?" I asked, the words more a croak than anything, like the echo of my screams had followed me into this dream. "Are you okay? Cy—"

He shook his head and gripped my hand in his before he fell back down on the bed, like he couldn't bear to hold his weight up for another moment.

I sat down next to him, welcoming the feeling of sinking into a proper bed.

"I'm okay, Cy's okay," he ran a hand roughly over his face, like he was trying to rub it out of existence, "but Max, you have to tell me everything. What the fuck were you thinking? Where are you? How are you here now? When are you coming back?"

He looked around the room, like he was trying to unearth something—or someone. I knew instantly that Izzy had told him, had explained how I was able to visit her in a dream with Wade. But that was before—before I knew that I was a demon too, that the power to visit them had always lingered under my skin, latent and waiting for the opportunity to rise.

I dropped my eyes from his and tried to rehearse a script in my head. How could I tell Ro that I was one of the very creatures he'd spent a lifetime learning to hate, learning to kill? Would he look at me differently, now that I was more than just some bumbling girl he grew up with? Could he love a demon?

My hand wrapped around my stomach in an echo of a hug, like the soft pressure could stop me from dissolving into a puddle all around us. I scrambled for something else, a way out of this conversation.

"I know that it was reckless," I started, my gaze focused on a pile of books, each opened to a random page, like the moment he got mildly bored with one, he just dove right into another. His small, stiff penmanship littered the margins. What was he researching so heavily? "It's just that Wade came to me, and I knew he was alive. Once we realized the truth, we couldn't wait. And you—you were gone, on that mission with Ten. If I'd known it would have all become so complicated, so—" I broke off and shook my head. "I need to know that you're okay. What's been happening while I've been gone?"

He stilled, pulling my attention away from the mini library. His jaw was clenched, nostrils flaring just slightly. I could tell from his deep breathing that he was trying to swallow back his anger.

My breath hitched—I'd never been on the receiving end of

Ro's ire. For small things, sure, like stealing the last piece of pizza or accidentally breaking his Playstation. But not like this.

"How the hell do you think I've been, Max? I left to go on a mission, one you were forbidden from going on because Cy wanted you to stay on campus where you'd be safe, and when I came back, you were gone. Literally the only thing you were asked to do was stay put, just for a day or two. And instead—" he let out a humorless laugh and shook his head. "How the fuck would you be if things were reversed? If I'd gone traipsing off to hell with a vampire and a werewolf, with little more than a goodbye note. How the fuck do you think I am?"

Guilt was a bitch, and even more so because he was right. If Ro had been the one to ditch me for a *beyond* dangerous mission, I'd be livid. And I'd probably look as starved for rest and sleep as he currently did. But it wasn't like—

I stilled, eyes snapping to him as my brain stumbled over his words, reciting them over again. Izzy told him about hell, that wasn't what tripped me up. It took a moment of focus, but then —werewolf. "You know about Atlas?"

He shook his head and stood up, cracking his neck from side to side. "I was there the night that thing killed Wade. Or knocked him out or whatever the hell happened. Atlas turned into a wolf after I reached him and the rest of Six. Not the sort of thing that I'd easily forget."

"You never told me you knew." For some reason, that pierced, cutting into my lungs with an unexpected fury. Ro told me every-thing. I was the first person he came out to, the first one he'd confessed to about scratching Cy's truck. "This whole time you knew what he was, and you never thought to mention it?"

"Get off your damn high horse, Max," he said, brow arched and jaw tensed, "you didn't exactly go sharing that bit of infor-mation with me either. And after speaking to Cyrus, we just figu—"

"Cyrus knows too?" I stood up, any semblance at preserving the peace long gone. I locked my eyes on Ro, noticing the tears in his black band T, a reddish tint to his skin, like he'd been covered in blood and not bothered properly wiping it away. "What hap—"

He laughed again, but one of those infuriating laughs that was more of a dig. "Of course Cyrus knows. I told him that night. You were sharing a roof with a fucking werewolf, Max. That was something he needed to know. And I needed to make sure you were safe. It's my job. And you were so bent up after that night, I wasn't sure if you even knew about Atlas. I didn't want to add more to your plate, and since you moved in with us, and he left with his team, it didn't seem like it was worth digging all that back up."

I bit the insides of my cheek and started pacing. The room was small and so cluttered that my pacing was more like a strained step from one side of the small gray rug to the other. He'd gone behind my back. How often did he and Cy have conversations about me without me being present?

My vision blurred as I focused on the old Dead Kennedys poster tacked on his wall. The placement was uneven, the poster worn with the sort of wrinkles that warped the image and made it difficult to fully decipher. Ro didn't even listen to the band, but he'd found it in a small yard sale in town when we were kids and kept it like it was some strange, buried treasure. It had become the defining piece of his bedroom growing up—always there, always a part of our home. "You told Cy."

"You would have done the same if you were in my position. Seamus and Cyrus aren't dense, Max. They both already knew, but Cy assured me that Atlas wasn't a problem, wasn't a threat to you, and to leave it. So I did. It was difficult as fuck to do, especially when he came back into town. I knew it was only a matter of time before he pulled you back into something dangerous— Six always seems to do that where you're concerned," he shook his head, body vibrating with anger as his eyes pierced me. I dropped my gaze, unable to bear the weight of that glare. "But yeah, your weird band of monsters isn't as stealthy as it thinks it is. Seamus has known the truth since the very first time Atlas turned. He's been keeping an eye on it, making sure that Atlas is in control. They're convinced that he won't hurt anyone, that he's retaining his sense of self, whatever the fuck that means."

Seamus and Cyrus knew, but they hadn't done anything about it—they hadn't reported to Alleva or had Atlas locked up. They were protecting him even though it went against everything The Guild stood for, against every rule the system had in place. Why?

My head spun as I tried desperately to fold all the pieces together, to figure out how everything worked, to understand the endgame. There were too many competing forces here and I wasn't sure what Seamus and Cyrus were after anymore. They'd protected me when I let Darius out. Twice. They'd had a plan in place to get Ralph out of the lab, despite the fact that the higher ups, whoever they were, wanted him dead.

And even before then, Seamus had begged Cy to come back to The Guild, for years. But Cy only took him up on the offer after Atlas showed up in our woods. Nothing made sense, but clearly they weren't toeing the party line anymore. There was something larger at play here. And clearly they had a plan of their own.

I desperately wanted to know what it was.

"Did you know what I am?" I asked, accusation dripping from my tone, as the words fell from my lips like a busted dam. "Have you all known all along that I'm part succubus too? Did you come up with some secret agreement to keep me in the dark about that as well?"

It was the first time I'd uttered it out loud—admitted to more than myself what I was. I wrapped my fingers around the worn, wooden bed post at the bottom of Ro's bed and steadied myself. I forced my eyes from my feet and looked up at Ro.

He glanced away, eyes shifty and tense, but I saw what I was afraid I'd find lingering there in that brief flash of blue: guilt.

My chest tightened, and I struggled to breathe, like he'd knocked the wind from my body with just that momentary look.

It felt like my chest had been punctured, a wound no amount of rest or supernatural healing could mend. "You did."

The words fell so softly from my lips that I wasn't sure I'd even breathed them into existence. He'd known. The one person in the world who I trusted beyond a shadow of a doubt. The one person who was always in my corner, who fought for me, protected me, helped me understand what it meant to have a home, to have a person.

He'd known and he hadn't said anything.

Suddenly, the walls felt like they were closing in, until I was hit with a suffocating claustrophobia that made my prison cell feel like a mansion. I wanted out, wanted out of this dream. I'd rather be locked alone in my tiny dungeon in hell than deal with this betrayal, this open, weeping wound.

Because all I could feel in this moment was absolute loneliness, like the final thing tethering me to my life was snapped for good.

"How long? How long have you known?" My breathing was rapid now, my head growing dizzy as I looked around the room, suddenly desperate for an escape. I sucked in air, trying to fill lungs that wouldn't inflate, my eyes catching detached images of books, dirty socks, old plates. "How fucking c-could you?"

My fingers dug harder into the bedpost, until the rough feel of splintered wood was the only thing I could focus on.

Heavy hands clasped my shoulders, and when I looked back up, round, sad eyes were mere inches from mine. For the first time in my life, those eyes felt strange, unfamiliar to me.

He exhaled, his breath cooling the tears across my cheeks. "Max, it's not what you think. This hasn't been something I've kept from you. I always suspected that you were a little different. Cy's always devoted so much of his energy to monitoring you, to keeping you safe. But after your visit with Izzy, I sort of put two and two together. I haven't discussed it with Cy, haven't said anything to anyone, but I'm certain he knows."

"What do you mean?" I asked, my voice even and calm, until I couldn't recognize myself in it.

Ro's grip on my shoulders was tight, bruising, but necessary —like he was the only thing holding me upright, like if he let go, I'd float away. "I mean that you dream-walked with another incubus. That's not how that kind of magic works, it's not a ride you can just hitch. The fact that you traveled to Izzy—Max, you did that. Not Wade."

Slowly, I glanced up at him, afraid that the look on his face would carve a scar so deep, I'd never be able to repair it. Instead, I saw warmth, the icy blue melting into fear. His lips were pressed tight, small lines forming around his mouth, the tension in his jaw making his face look more angular than it usually did.

"You said that you've always known I was different," I whispered, like raising my voice a decibel would distort his features, harden his expression, bring me back to that feeling of complete isolation. For now, he was looking at me like he always did when I was hurt or scared or reckless. Protective. "What did you mean?"

He exhaled softly, his brows lifting as he squeezed my shoulders and guided me back to the bed. As if dealing with a child, he helped me sit, before joining me—our sides pressed together like a zipper, his arm wrapped around my shoulder, pulling me to him.

In that moment, the warmth and pressure of his body was a glue that kept me whole.

"I mean that I always knew that there was more to your story than Cyrus ever let on. Cy," he shook his head, the breath of his words blowing a few hairs around my face in a strange, ethereal dance, "he's not really the type of guy to just casually adopt a baby, you know? Think about it. Why the hell would he disappear from society—actively sever every tie to his people he had —live in a secluded cabin, and then go adopt a child? It never made any sense. It always came back to you—you were the reason he left. He wanted to hide you, to protect you."

"He adopted you too though," I said, a strange lightness brewing in my chest. If I was a monster and Cy knew it, maybe Ro was like me, maybe we still fit, still operated as two peas in a pod. Slightly different, but similar in that difference. "Do you think—"

He dropped his arm from my back, folding both of his hands in his lap. The sudden lack of his comfort felt chillier than my dungeon in hell ever had. For a long moment he sat like that, hunched over and staring at his fingers, like they held every answer if he could just learn to look hard enough.

Despite being so close, he'd never felt so far away from me.

"I think that Cy knew my parents," he said finally. "I don't know much about their deaths, but I've been doing some research since we arrived on campus, and I think they got involved in a really sticky situation."

I held my breath and waited. Ro rarely spoke about his life before me and Cy. And I never pressed him. Part of me selfishly feared that he preferred that life to the one he made with me and Cy.

He let out a hollow laugh and straightened his spine, picking at his fingernails as he studied the wall, small flakes of enamel floating to the ground like small sheets of mica. "No one will talk about them. No one has heard of them. It's not normal, Max." He turned to me, his blue eyes creased in the corner and I felt the exhaustion that plagued him as clearly as if it was my own. "I think Cy knows more than he's letting on, but anytime I bring it up, anytime I mention them, he brushes me off and tells me to leave the past in the past. But that doesn't matter—the point is that there are things going on in The Guild that are so fucking far above our pay grade. And when my parents were killed, Cy heard about it and found out where I was living. And he brought me back to you both."

I grabbed his hand in mine, rescuing his nail beds, and squeezed softly. "We'll figure it out, Ro."

Suddenly, I felt sick that I'd been so angry with him, guilty that I thought for even a moment that Ro would betray me. He'd been holding all of this, for all of this time—all on his own.

He dropped his gaze, his hand falling limp in mine. "Max, I know what you're thinking, but I'm not like you. I'm not part demon, don't have any special powers. That's not why Cy took me in. He adopted me *for* you. To give you the semblance of a life, of a family."

My face scrunched as I stared at him, and I opened my mouth to tell him how ridiculous he was being, but he pressed on.

"Don't get me wrong, he cares about us both. I know that. As much as someone like him is capable of caring. But I think he knew that you needed companionship, more than an old, grumpy, retired protector, if you were to have any sort of a life at all. I think he took you in to protect you. That's why we grew up in the middle of fucking nowhere in a tiny cabin—no school, no friends, no attachments. No threat." He stood up and stretched, his back cracking loudly, the echo strange as I processed his words.

When we were young, we made up all kinds of reasons for why Cy adopted us—but I'd never once thought that he lived the way that he did for a reason beyond his own antisocial tendencies. The self isolation had always made sense with his personality, he'd never shown interest in anyone in town, never expressed a desire to be around anyone other than us.

"Cy loves you, Ro," I said, my stomach tightening at the realization that he might not know that, that he might have gone most of his life thinking he was nothing more than a plus one.

He shook his head and kicked aside a pile of books with his foot, his toe popping through a small worn hole in his sock. "I know that. He loves us both as much as he's capable. But that's not the point. He's keeping things from us, and he's been keeping you from...someone. I don't know who or why, but I promise you that we'll figure it out. That we'll do it together. You just have to come back—"

His voice broke slightly, a small crack for a rare show of emotion to leak out. Guilt at leaving him flared through my body again. I could've waited, could've found a way to have him meet us in Seattle. I should have checked in. I'd have been gutted if the situation was reversed, if he'd done to me what I did to him.

And as difficult as the pieces of his budding theory were to hear, they rang true. Since we were kids Cyrus had told next to nothing about his life in The Guild. He'd trained us, made sure that we could take care of ourselves if we were ever attacked by vampires or werewolves. Hell, our entire lives revolved around training and honing our bodies to be the best weapons they could be, to the point that our muscle memory when it came to sparring was practically perfectly programmed.

And then, after a run in with Atlas's wolf, he moved us to The Guild, dropping all pretenses about preferring life in seclusion, despite the fact that he clearly didn't want to be back at Guild Headquarters, didn't want to fall back into this life that he'd left.

Since the moment we arrived at Headquarters, I knew something was off; could all but see Cy slowly pulling away from us, keeping us out of the loop more than usual, giving little away about how he was spending his time or who he was spending it with.

"Max, the thing is, Cy was right. He knew what he was doing, putting us together. I will always be your family. I will always protect you. You will always be my biggest priority."

I wasn't sure how long I'd been off in my own world, falling over each of my thoughts like I was jumping from stone to stone, desperate to keep up with some phantom realization that I couldn't quite catch no matter how quickly I moved.

"No matter what," he said, his voice sure and strong.

Like a boulder, it hit me all at once, how much he'd changed since we'd arrived on campus. Ro was always the more serious of the two of us, always calmer, more rational and careful. When it came to siblings, there was always one who was always a little bit more the child, not just because of age, because it was how the relationship worked, the give and take. Ro was always the adult.

But I'd never felt that cavern between us more acutely than now. I saw it there in his face—the determination, the strength. He'd grown harder over our time working with The Guild, more cynical.

And while I'd grown and changed my fair share over the months, I'd never stopped to think about how Ro was handling everything. Maybe that lack of curiosity was what made me the child.

I sucked in a breath and focused my eyes on the Dead Kennedys poster. I didn't want that space between us to deepen and lengthen. So I needed to do the work to mend it, to fix the small fractures and pull us back together again. I had to trust him implicitly, to hope that no matter what I said or what I was, that he wouldn't look at me like I was a monster.

"The thing is Ro, it's more than the succubus thing. I've been lighting up like a christmas tree, magically healing people with my fingers, and I recently even managed to teleport like I'm a fucking psychic Pokemon," I said, the words tumbling one after the other until my confession morphed into one long word rather than anything intelligible. It was the only way that I could get it all out, the only way I could muster the bravery—to let loose and let the pieces fall.

I felt his muscles stiffen next to mine, but I couldn't bring myself to look at him. My eyes refused to move from the poster where a corner was torn and taped, refused to confront the fear or anger that I was certain I'd find in his expression.

"I don't know what's happening to me," I continued, my voice thick and cracking as the emotion started to rise up in my chest, until it was all but choking me. "I'm stuck in some creepy hell dungeon with a guy who's got some serious Thanos vibes, Six has been lying to me, keeping these weird abilities from me and manipulating me into thinking they care long enough to get the information they need, I had mind-blowing sex in a grimy wendigo nest, and I—" I let out a soft sob, "I think I'm starting to feel things for a fucking vampire. And he's not even the one I had sex with."

Strong arms pulled me in, hands pressing my head against a chest that had comforted me for half of my life. The sudden stillness of my body, caught in the vise of Ro, was the final thread. Sobs pulled through my body until I wasn't even sure what one thing I was crying about—was it because I was confused? Because I was turning into some demon even The Guild didn't know about? Or the fact that I had feelings for more than one person? Maybe it was everything, all of the brambles and loose ends hanging limply from my hands while I tried to figure out what to do, where to go from here.

Ro ran his thick hands through my hair, snagging on a few tangles, but I didn't care. The sting was soothing in a strange way, just knowing that he was trying to calm me.

And that's when it hit me, the thing that hurt most, more than all the existential identity bullshit and distrust between me and Six—I wanted to go home.

I missed my family. I missed my brother.

It came with the crippling fear that I might never be welcomed back. I wasn't a protector—the sudden realization ramming me with enough force to steal my breath. Cyrus probably knew all along. He'd let me have hope that I might fit in at The Guild, might find my place there with his people. But maybe that was the problem, maybe I didn't have a place. Maybe his people weren't mine.

"It's okay," he whispered, breath whispering against my hair, voice calm and soothing in a way that only Ro's gravely timber could be. For a moment, I let myself sink into it, hardly letting myself breathe for fear that he might push me away, disgust in his eyes. "We'll figure everything out. It'll be okay. You'll be okay. I promise you that, Max. I won't rest until it's true."

My chest squeezed and I flung my arms around him, holding

him to me with enough force to bruise his ribs, but he didn't push me away. Instead, he just pulled me closer.

"You're not afraid of me? You don't think I'm evil?"

A soft chuckle, like music to my ears, filled the space around us. "Max, you're no more evil than Ralph. Or Atlas. Or Wade." He pulled back a few inches, creating space between us. His thumb tilted my chin up until my eyes met his. Even through my blurred vision, I could see the warmth radiating from his expression in that swirl of soft blue—brows furrowed, smile kind, eyes wide. Ro. "Don't you get it? Things in The Guild aren't what they seem. We were naive to think that the lines of good and evil were so clear and distinct. We've only ever heard one side of a very complicated story—the side The Guild wanted us to hear. And I think there's a reason Cy wanted to keep us away from that conflict for as long as he could. There's something bigger at play here. And we'll get to the bottom of it. But I know with absolute certainty that you, Max Bentley, are as far from evil as a person can get." He ran his hands along my cheeks, wiping away a few tears carving trails down my face. It was rare, me crying, and Ro always hated the sight when I did. "All the other stuff will fall away. None of that matters right now. All that matters is that we'll figure out how to keep you safe when you get back. But first, we have to get you back."

I grinned at him, the metal knot that had been lurking in the pit of my stomach unraveling, even if just a bit. Ro didn't hate me. How could I have ever thought that was a possibility?

"I don't exactly know how to get out of the medieval prison I'm currently sitting in. But while I figure it out, maybe you could talk to Cy—and if he won't give you any information, maybe hit The Guild Library to figure out what kind of hybrid monster I am. I've never heard of a demon having this particular assortment of abilities before." I paused, my shoulders sinking. "But something about the way Six was talking about me...I don't think it's common."

I shook my head, cataloging the small holes in his shirt again, the drawn look on his face. He'd made me feel better about the clusterfuck that was my life, but I still felt unsettled about his own. "What's been going on here, Ro? You look exhausted. Been getting visits from an incubus?" My small attempt at humor fell flat, but it was enough to lift the corner of his mouth into a semblance of a smile, an echo of the grin that could fill a room with mirth.

He brushed my hands away as my fingers reached for what looked like a recently-healed cut along his forearm. "Things here are just amplifying a bit is all. The attacks are getting worse, all over the world. It's like the world is a balloon that keeps expanding, but it's at that moment right before it's filled too much, ready to pop," he muttered, before quickly adding, "But that's all background noise. It doesn't matter right now. What matters is you getting back safe. I'm going to spend as much time as I can digging. And I'll try getting Cy to talk. Maybe the two of us together can find a way to get to you. How'd you get into hell anyway?"

My stomach dropped at that and I shook my head so sharply I almost gave myself whiplash. "No, Ro. You have to promise me." I gripped the edges of his shirt to get him to focus, to hear me. "You trying to get to me won't solve anything, just keep yourself safe and see what you can learn in the meantime."

His features sharpened and then softened and I knew in that brief transition what was going through his mind. He'd made a decision, one I didn't agree with.

"Fuck, Ro. I mean it. Do not under any circumstances try to come after—"

I let out a sharp yell, dropping Ro's shirt and doubling over. There was a fiery pain pulsing through my body, so strong and present it was all I could focus on.

Suddenly, try as I might, my lungs wouldn't fill with air and I couldn't speak. What the hell was happening?

I saw more than felt Ro grip the sides of my face in his hands, saw his mouth shaping words, but I couldn't hear or comprehend anything beyond the sharp panic in his eyes and the feeling that a large metal spatula was scraping out my insides. I closed my eyes, willing my brain to focus, to work past the pain. It was like there was a strange thread caught in a tug, like a string pulled taught, ready to splinter. Like some essential part of myself was about to break off.

And when I opened my eyes again, all I saw was red.

❧ 7 ❧
ELI

"Y ou know," I mumbled as my head rolled against Dec's shoulder, "part of me wonders if the fanghole's endgame with giving me his blood was to draw out my misery. He has a bit of sadist energy about him."

She blew out a puff of air, her eyes scanning the horizon for some unknowable threat. Atlas had been gone for an hour or so and while I'd only received one or two fresh wounds, the ones I had weren't showing any signs of slowing down in terms of blood loss. I was growing dizzier and dizzier by the moment.

"Wouldn't put it past him. The guy's a creepy fuck. I've heard stories about him, about his years in the lab. He wigs out most of the researchers down there." Her voice was hushed, like she was afraid someone or something was going to overhear.

"Seriously, you know," I winced as my foot caught on a gnarled branch, unable to keep my voice as level as hers, "you'd think that being bonded to a vampire would come with some perks. Maybe some added strength or my very own Twilight fan club. *Something* mildly beneficial anyway." I blinked, eyes burning, as sweat or blood—I couldn't really distinguish between the two anymore—blurred my vision. "Doesn't seem fair really. Atlas is a werewolf and now Wade's an incubus. Me? I'm like a supernatural piñata for all of that asshole's enemies. I mean, at the rate he pisses people off, I'm sort of shocked I'm not six feet under already."

"Yeah, well" she said, and I could hear the tight smile in her voice, even if I couldn't see it, "while the fangfuck is clearly unpopular, he also seems pretty decent at staying alive. So that bodes well for you. And if it makes you feel any better, I'm still just a run-of-the-mill protector. No special powers to boast about."

"You're a hot badass with an Irish accent, Dec. That makes you more enviable than some added supernatural juice any day. I mean, hell, you're probably my biggest competition when it comes to flexing my sex appeal—of which there is a lot—around campus—" I coughed, the sound thick enough that I knew I was coughing up blood, "well, you would be my biggest competition, if you actually had any interest in utilizing your god-given talents anyway. Tell you what," I added, wiping my lips with the back of my hand, wincing when a dark liquid smeared over my skin. That couldn't be a good sign. "I officially bequeath my fun drawer to you. My toys ought to go to someone who stands a chance of putting them to use."

"Shut up, you ass," she said, her words laced with a sadness that I'd heard all too often in my years of living with her. Dec harbored more grief and boiled-down anger than most retired protectors. It pierced my stomach every time she let some of it escape in her voice, in her actions. The girl deserved some small sliver of happiness. More than any of us did. "You're going to be fine. I'm sure Atlas has found them by now. And that vamp is too stubborn to die. He won't be your ticket out of here. Not yet anyway. We just need to lie low for a bit and stem your bleeding."

She let out a heavy sigh and readjusted my body against hers. She'd been carrying more of my weight than I'd realized over the last couple of miles. I tried to pull back a bit, to straighten my posture and stand on my own, but my body only collapsed against her like a dead weight in response.

"I hate being fucking useless," I whispered, annoyed that I couldn't even muster the strength to punch a tree or stomp around. I had no outlet. Nothing to do but just wither away and wait for our discount Edward Cullen to stop getting the shit kicked out of him. "Just drop me here and then go after Atlas—he might need help. Max might—"

Another coughing fit took over, and a sharp pain bolted through my neck. I opened my mouth to finish my sentence, but all that came out was a fucking disgusting gurgle and some awkward croaks as blood spilled between my lips.

I was going to kill that vamp next time I saw him.

Well, I guess not really, since I couldn't kill him without taking myself out too. Bit of a Catch-22.

If I was being honest, that was the real travesty. We couldn't lay a hand on him, not if it meant I'd get the brunt of it. Which meant that the vamp was never going to get what was coming to him. By tying me to him, he'd basically ensured that none of us would touch him. He'd get through this all, free as a bird.

Part of me wanted the agony to just end, to fall over and sink into the nothingness. Added bonus was that if I was out of the picture, it meant the fanghole was too. Silver linings and all that shit.

Declan's eyes pinched in the middle as she stared at me, like she could watch my thoughts unfurl before her. She winced, her fingers pausing a few inches short of my neck, like what she saw there was bad enough that she didn't want to make it worse. "Don't talk. For once in your life. Don't worry about your biting commentary. I know you're witty and hilarious, I don't need more proof. Just try and relax. I can take a little more of your weight, so just lean against me." She readjusted again, lifting me a bit as if to prove her point. "The town we passed earlier is just through this brush. I think."

I opened my mouth to fight her on it, to push back against, but all I managed to do was trip over my own feet until we were both stumbling forward. She groaned as she scooted me up against her side and I tried not to whimper as the movement sent a fresh wave of agony piercing through my body.

Helplessness was not a good look on me. And I was getting really fucking tired of being the weak link in the group, constantly on the brink of death because of that asswipe.

I'd worked my whole life to make sure I was never in this position, that I was never the one holding my friends or my team back. I'd promised myself long ago that I'd do everything in my power to never be the reason one of my friends didn't make it back. And Dec was too goddamn loyal for her own good.

She was hitching her ride to mine, but it was increasingly looking like I was heading downhill towards a cliff. Fast.

I closed my eyes for a few moments, head dizzy and lolling as Dec guided us towards safety. When my eyelids fluttered open again, we were standing outside of a dilapidated building, a wash of gray and what looked like chipped concrete littered the ground around it. So much of hell looked like it belonged in an abandoned industrial city. It was nothing like I'd expected it to be—just a sadder, more desolate version of home. Somehow both alike and not.

"We'll stay here for awhile," Dec muttered, her voice softer than it usually was. Fucking pity. It made my skin crawl. I didn't deserve it. I glanced to the side and saw her face pinched in concern. "Atlas will be back soon, so we'll wait out...whatever is happening to you. Once you're able, we'll come up with our next plan. It'll be okay. We'll be home soon."

In all my years of knowing her, Dec had never been one for soft edges and false promises—the fact that she was coddling me now hit harder than my phantom injuries did. She was scared. Like really scared.

She didn't say it, but I knew she was thinking it. Things weren't looking good for me, and Dec wouldn't be able to stay cooped up in a warehouse with me for days on end, waiting for me to heal up from injuries protectors didn't survive. Sitting around with me was fruitless and a waste of her time.

Hell wasn't a quiet place; we'd encountered nothing but unfriendlies since the moment we went through that portal. And now, without Atlas around to round out our group, we were screwed if any of the beasties caught our scent and decided to come party. We couldn't afford to stay still in one place, waiting for that to happen.

She needed to get Wade, find Max and Atlas, and get the fuck out of this realm before she ended up as screwed as I was.

"Dec," I croaked, her name barely decipherable on my lips "just lea—"

She shook her head, a swath of her dark hair brushing against my face from the sharpness of the movement. "Just shut up, you asshat. I'm not leaving you. Period. So get that out of your head and focus on resting up. You're annoying as fuck, but you're also a tough son of a bitch. If anyone is going to be stubborn enough to keep death-by-vampire-bond at bay, it'll be you. So put that annoying obstinance to good use—it's about time you make that particular character trait work in our favor."

My throat tightened, eyes going glassy at the depth of her sentiment. Dec always had a way with words. And she was loyal to a fault.

Without waiting for my attempt at a response, she pushed open the door to the nearest building and leaned me against the wall. Her hands rested on my shoulders as I tried to balance myself, to stay upright on my own.

I slid down the wall slowly, her hands guiding me gently to keep me from landing with too much of an impact on the cold, hard ground.

She knelt down so that her eyes were level with mine, the depth of her concern dulling their usually vivid color. Still, even in the dim light, I could see the fear shadowing them. And the dip of her lips and small tremor in her hand told me that whatever was wrong with me was worse than even I realized.

The pain wasn't too bad anymore, almost just a dull ache that was slowly flattening. That was never a good sign.

I reached my fingers forward, to smooth the line forming between her brows, but the movement was too heavy, required too much strength, so I dropped my hand down again.

In that moment, I hated myself for being the cause of that look in her eye. I was so fucking sick of letting down the people I cared about.

And Dec, well, she didn't deal with losing people very well. Not that anyone did, really, but for her, grief was like a tidal wave —big and angry and all encompassing. In the rare moments when she went under, it was almost impossible to bring her out.

"Stay put, I'll be just a moment," she whispered as her hands slid quietly for her blade and she stood up.

I watched as she walked from the room, her steps careful and silent, every muscle somehow both tensed for a fight and relaxed at the same time. She was always in mission mode. It would serve her well in hell, at least. But I hoped that she would get the chance to relax again, to settle in and actually live her life, without constantly worrying about protecting herself and those around her.

In our line of work, the odds of her actually getting that life were about as close to zero as they could get. Sometimes our world was a cruel one. And I promised myself then and there that if I miraculously survived this literal hellhole, that I'd do two things: never lie to Max again, and teach Dec how to actually kick back and enjoy her life for once. It was possible to be a good protector and have fun at the same time, I was living proof of that.

I wasn't sure how long I sat like that, floating in and out of consciousness while she scanned the building to make sure we were safe. As safe as we could be in this realm, anyway.

Dec wasn't exactly the most maternal person I'd ever met, and half the time she kicked my ass as much as she tried saving it, but something about her presence, about her focus and desperate need to keep her friends safe, coated me with the same kind of warmth that I imagined a mother's love might provide.

Even with my phantom injuries from the fangfuck and the fact that we had no concrete plan to get back home in one piece, I felt safe almost, at least for now.

The room I was in was cold and dark, but didn't smell quite as bad as the wendigo nest had, despite being littered with just as much abandoned junk. Hellions seemed to universally have a hoarding problem. That, or they just didn't give a fuck about chore charts. Maybe that came with the territory of living in a world that was constantly trying to kill you—tidiness sort slipped out of the picture when desperation hit.

With a heavy thud that was far less graceful than I wanted it to be, my head slipped to the ground, the cold, dirt-laden floor cooling my skin. I could feel a sheen of sweat coating my body, which meant that I probably had a fever—a rare accomplishment for protectors. Whatever that asshat was going through had to be pretty bad.

So long as he didn't meet an adversary as strong as his brother, I might stand a semblance of a chance at surviving the night, but that small spark of hope was starting to dim, until it was little more than a dull quiver in the darkness.

Max. God I hoped that she was okay, that she was far away from whatever the fuck was going on with the vampire. He could withstand a lot, vamps were difficult creatures to kill. But Max—

I closed my eyes and pushed away the visual of her defeat, of the way her eyes might look as the light left them. Instead, I let myself linger, briefly, on the feel of her skin on mine. On the way that my lips felt like a goddamn livewire when she pressed hers to mine. My chest tightened as I felt the shadow pressure of her head resting against my chest, our limbs tangled together in an impossibly comfortable knot.

I'd never get to apologize. I'd never get to tell her how sorry I was for betraying her—for lying to her.

Why, of everything, did that seem to matter so damn much?

"Eli," a quiet voice echoed around me, but I couldn't quite locate the source. My focus was still on Max, on her dark brown eyes, the way her face scrunched up in frustration or curiosity, the smooth feel of my fingers running through her hair. "Damn it, Eli, wake the fuck up."

Dec? I groaned in response, and tried to open my eyes to calm the panic I could hear brewing in her voice.

"Fuck, fuck, fuck," there was a soft *click-clack* sound, like she was pacing back and forth. I wanted to reach out to her, to calm her down before she had one of her attacks. There was almost nothing more heartbreaking in the world than watching Dec spiral. But my limbs wouldn't move, my arm nothing more than a stationary log attached to my body. "I swear to god, Eli Bentley, if you leave me now, I'm going to rip you out of the afterlife, just to kill you all over again myself."

Her voice trailed off into a series of rushed babbles, but it grew more and more distant, like she was disappearing down an echoey hallway, or like I was floating away.

For what felt like forever, I tried to climb after her, to chase after her voice and cling to it with the sort of ferocity she deserved. As much as I liked to piss her off, Dec was always like a grumpy big sister to me. The thought that I was causing her pain—that I was the reason for that tremor in her voice...

It didn't sit well with me, that much was for sure.

Eventually, despite all of my efforts, her voice turned into nothing but a whimper, and then a breeze, and then it was just gone. Clinging to consciousness was no longer possible. All I could do was sink into the tide and let the wave of darkness swallow me whole.

"ELI, WHAT THE HELL HAPPENED TO YOU?" A QUIET, SOOTHING voice whispered as a soft, cool hand pressed gently against my forehead. "Fuck. Where are you? What happened?"

Something about that voice brought me back to the surface, my heart stuttering back to life, like it hadn't been used in years and was eager for practice. Slowly, I opened my eyes, the hazy light of the room somehow still blinding. What time was it? Where was I?

I glanced around my surroundings, expecting my room back in the cabin, but getting something far from it instead—everything was a washed-out gray, like the color had been zapped from the world. Dust, so thick I could see it where the soft light from the window shone through, caked the room. The floor was barely visible, covered instead with papers and leaves and all sorts of debris. Despite being so full of clutter, the room felt empty, with no recognizable furniture or order.

My body felt stiff, like it didn't quite remember how to work properly, and I rolled my head from side to side, trying to breathe movement back into my limbs.

Memories of the last few hours flittered back through my thoughts and searched the room with renewed energy. Where was Dec? Was she okay? Was she still here or had she left to find Atlas, as I'd wanted her to?

Finally, my gaze landed on a pair of dark eyes—wide, mesmerizing, and filled with worry. Dark hair flowed in waves over her shoulders, the ends of the strands tickling the skin along my neck. The soft light seemed to surround her, to light her up like she was a goddamn angel.

It nearly stole my breath, just the sight.

I felt my lips pull into a lopsided grin.

"This is a good hallucination," I muttered, my voice cracked and dry, but I didn't care. She was here. If I was going to die, to float off into whatever lay beyond, I wanted to do it while looking at Max, even if it was just a phantom of her.

"It's not a hallucination you buffoon," she said, her tone harsh, but unconvincing with the small smile that lifted the corners of her mouth. It was adorable how even as she tried to hold onto her anger, every atom in her body seemed bent towards the positive, resisting the pull into darkness. "What the hell happened to you? Are the others—is everyone okay?"

Her eyebrows bent in concern and she trailed her fingers slowly from my forehead to my neck.

The feel of her skin grazing over mine sent shivers down my body. How could such a simple touch undo me like that?

"Where are you?" I asked, not even bothered by how ridiculous it was to ask a figment of my imagination a question. Death meant there was no need to be self-conscious, to give a fuck about how absurd and needy I sounded. "I-I'm sorry."

For kissing you. For tricking you. For lying to you. For fucking you without coming clean about all the other stuff first. For making you feel like you didn't matter when you were one of the only things in my life that did.

For wanting you at all when I knew I shouldn't, when I knew I wasn't good for you.

For falling for you anyway.

She exhaled sharply, the hair around her face dancing in the fabricated wind. "We'll deal with apologies later, Eli."

There was a dejectedness about her that squeezed my chest, and I felt in that moment that she might never forgive me, even this phantom version of her. The thought of dying with that look on her face the last thing I saw—and the fact that I put it there —downright stabbed me to the core.

Her mouth dipped as she studied me, some of the guardedness falling away into something softer. "You're injured. Badly. What the hell happened?"

My stomach soared at the worried hitch of her voice—worry was good, worry meant that she cared whether I lived or I died.

I opened my mouth to explain, to beg, but no words would come. Just a mind-numbing ache in my lungs, like I'd been breathing in ice-cold water.

Her fingers dug into my chest, like she was trying to identify and isolate the pain, her eyes bent in focus.

She swept her hair over her shoulders, framing her face, as she concentrated all of her focus on me. Slowly, the dark brown eyes I was becoming obsessed with started to transform, black bleeding into the brown, until the original color was eclipsed completely.

"What a—" I choked on the word as a sharp tingling sensation crawled along my skin, like there was electricity zapping around inside me. It wasn't unpleasant, just strange, so I let myself sink into the sensation, studying her with far more interest and hope than I had any right to.

"I-I don't really know if I'm doing this right," she muttered, as a heavy wind swept up around us, swirling around like we were in a budding fall storm. Where the hell had that come from? "Khalida walked me through it last time, and this is in a dreamwalk so who even knows if it will work at all. But I'm here and it's worth a try."

She was babbling, her words little more than a mumble as she clawed at my chest with her slim fingers, digging them in until the pressure made it difficult to breathe. I didn't care. Didn't care what she was going on about. She was here. And for now that was enough.

"Shit," I yelled as my chest jerked towards her. There was a pain so sharp that I couldn't bear it another moment longer, a pain so acute that it felt like my body was being shredded into tiny pieces, so sharp and unwavering that all I could see was black—and then, nothing.

I inhaled sharply, the air sweet and pure, and feeling like I'd never breathed properly before in all of my years. Suddenly, I was looking at Max with fresh eyes, like she was a part of me, like we were one.

The rest of the room—all the grime and clutter and gray—disappeared completely. The pain that had been swimming through my veins was just a memory.

Her skin was clammy, duller than it'd been a minute before, but she moved her hands up, pebbling every inch of skin she touched, until she reached my neck. Her brows pinched in focus, her hands static with a strange energy that sent little shocks through my body, somewhere between pain and pleasure, or maybe both. It was too much sensation, my nerves practically bleeding from it, but the last thing I wanted was for her to stop touching me, to stop whatever the hell it was that she was doing.

"Max," I said, voice low and soft. I could speak again, my throat dull and achy, but not nearly as bad as it was before.

Was this what dying felt like? Like being reborn again?

Why did she suddenly look so exhausted, like she hadn't gotten a proper night of sleep in weeks? The image of her in front of me, drawn and worn, was such a heavy contrast with the visual of her from just a moment ago, it was like my brain was experiencing whiplash, trying to rectify the two versions.

"Max," I said again, pulling her hands away from my neck. I dropped them instantly, like I'd been burned. When I looked down at her smooth, narrow hands, they almost glowed—not bright, not with a light, but with a sort of strange shadow. "Max," I said again, harsher this time as my heart beat out a hard rhythm. I kneeled forward and gripped her shoulders, staring into the black abyss of her eyes.

It was like she wasn't there, not really. Her eyes were so dark, so unreadable, that I couldn't tell if she was even hearing me or seeing me—all I got from her was my own panicked expression reflected back in them. My chest felt hollow.

"What the fuck is happening? Max, snap out of it." I shook her shoulders, gently at first, but when she still showed no sign of recognition, I shook her harder.

Nothing.

Instantly, I recalled that moment in Claude's house—it felt so disconnected from everything that had happened, like it had been months or years ago, even though I knew it'd only been a few days at most.

I wasn't awake then, wasn't fully present when it happened, but the girl—Khalida—and Max, they'd healed me. Somehow.

And I remembered the fear in Dec's voice as she recounted the experience to me later, even though she'd glossed over most of the story, I knew that it had cost Max a lot. That the healing was another power that she didn't quite have control of—a dangerous sort of power that had almost harmed her. Like she'd given too much of her life force in trying to restore mine.

Had she done that again? Sacrificed a part of herself to keep me alive? Even after everything I'd done?

My breath was coming in and out so fast that my body didn't have enough time to actually use any of the oxygen.

"Max," I said again, the name sharp and loud this time. I almost couldn't recognize my own voice, the fear lacing it amplified by the echoes around the room.

Still, nothing. It was like she was trapped somewhere inside of herself, and something about that vacant look in her eyes had me desperate to bring her back. To pull her back to me, before she drifted away into a place I couldn't reach her.

"Fuck it," I whispered, before crashing my lips down on hers. My mouth paused on hers, and I waited a beat to see if she'd respond, like I was some damn prince in a fairytale with magical lips to bring her back to life. If only.

Just as I was about to pull away, a rush of heat flooding my cheeks with embarrassment, I felt her lips press back against mine. It was gentle, almost completely impossible to register at first, but then, slowly, she started to respond with a spark of heat.

My tongue met hers in a teasing clash, barely touching, like we were both only able to handle a taste. I slid my hands over her neck until they tangled into her hair at the base of her head.

My lungs were filtering air so quickly, it was like I'd been running miles. How was just one taste of her able to undo me so quickly? Why was she so goddamn addicting?

The memory of her lips against mine was nothing like the reality. I deepened the kiss, my dick throbbing as she responded with a small moan that set every nerve in my body on edge.

She gripped my shirt in her hands and pulled me closer, like she was just as starved for my touch as I was for hers.

I slid my hand under her ass and lifted her up, placing her

down on my lap so that she could feel just how much I wanted her—my need slowly spinning into a heady desperation.

Her hands slid underneath my shirt, the graze of her fingers against my abdomen, slow and teasing. She pulled my shirt off, breaking our kiss for only as long as it took for the material to move between us, every inch of my skin on fire as the material grazed me. Just a fucking cotton t-shirt. How could it feel so good?

It'd been less than a day since we'd been together, less than a day since I'd been inside of her, but it was too long—my body shivered beneath every touch, the mere feel of her hair sweeping against my chest enough to create electricity.

There'd be no other girls after her. She'd ruined them all for me.

Fuck I was screwed.

I made quick work of her shirt, while she unbuttoned my pants, creating enough space for her hand to slide inside.

The moment her hand gripped me, I groaned into her mouth, like I was a teenager and this was my first time being touched by a woman. Her teeth playfully nipped at my bottom lip as she stroked me, each up and down motion in perfect time with her tongue sliding against mine.

With a hurried maneuver, I pulled off her pants, far less gracefully than I'd usually manage. My heart was racing so hard, my body hungry for her like it'd spent a lifetime experiencing starvation. It was a hot, desperate need that I'd never felt before, not like this.

My fingers slid along the seam of her underwear, teasing, but not making any direct contact with her clit. Her cotton underwear was soaked, her breath coming out in heavy pants that glanced along my neck, until the hair on my arms was standing on end from the anticipation. My thumb gently stroked her clit through her underwear as she pressed against me.

"More," she said, her voice nothing but a desperate, breathy beg as she ground her core against my dick.

Unable to wait another moment, I pushed her underwear aside and slid two fingers into her cunt, pumping in and out, laboriously slow, as she continued to work my dick through her fingers.

She seemed to glow from the feeling, her eyes no longer black as they'd been moments ago, but glistening with a strange depth, like there was a rippling of lights swirling through her dark irises.

Her lips were parted slightly, her teeth grazing her full bottom lip.

Suddenly, hands and fingers weren't enough. I needed to be inside her, like a drowning man in the desert, who'd come upon a raging rapid of fresh water.

I shifted my pants down out of the way and lifted her onto me, the feel of her warmth enough to push me over the edge almost immediately. What was it about this girl that made me feel like this?

Her fingernails gripped into my shoulders and drew jagged lines down my back as she moved up and down, riding me as her head bent slightly back. The pressure built up between us, as our muscles tensed in time with each other, like everything I felt was mirrored in her.

I watched her. It was all I could do. Stare, mesmerized, at the girl in front of me. I inhaled sharply, my breath coming rapidly now as I pulled her hips down onto me. I needed more— couldn't do the teasing for another second. My tastes were usually a bit more...involved, but I didn't have the patience for toys and drawn-out, edging orgasms right now.

Something was happening. Something big that didn't make any sense.

It was like, suddenly, there was some invisible string tying me to this girl, reworking my world so that I saw it through her— wanted to make it better for her.

Her pace matched mine as her lips crashed against my mouth again. She let out a small whimper as she reached her climax, tightening around my dick as she rode it out. I followed her over the edge, my body suddenly drained and exhausted. I came hard, like I hadn't had sex in months, the sensation of releasing inside of her somehow heightening it all.

I leaned my forehead against her shoulder as I tried to steady my breath, to pull myself from the euphoria of a goddamn perfect afterglow.

When I pulled back and looked at her face, her eyes were closed, her features smoothed out and soft, her skin looked so fucking flawless that it was like she was being lit up from the inside.

The dullness from before was erased, and she looked more energized, alive, and just...more.

Instead of slowing, as it usually did after a solid orgasm, my heart only raced faster, the more I looked at her. Why did it do that? Why did sex with her always leave me wanting more? I'd never had this feeling before—like no matter how many times I'd have her, I'd never get her out of my system. Like even though I'd *just* had her, I was already desperate to have her again.

And was it just sex that I wanted? Or something more—

I inhaled sharply, dragging my hand down my face, my fingers pressing down on my eyelids as they closed. No, I was not going to go there. Not with Max, not with anybody. That was against all of my rules, and those rules were there for good reason.

This—whatever this was, it couldn't happen. Not now, and not ever. I needed to set boundaries before I was too far past them to matter.

"Max, I—"

She opened her eyes and they found mine instantly, the shadows in them clearing just a bit as she focused on me. Whatever expression was on my face seemed to startle her.

"Oh my god," she said, hands ruffling through her hair as she lifted herself off of me. "What am I doing? I can't be doing this. That wasn't supposed to happen. I'm so sorry. Fuck, fuck, fuck. I could've killed you."

I narrowed my eyes and smirked at her confidence. Sex with her was good—fucking fantastic, really, but I wouldn't call it particularly dangerous or dark. Not yet anyway. And I'd had sex many times while recovering from injuries—protectors were never *not* recovering from injuries—so it wasn't a risk I wasn't accustomed to.

Still, my ego took a bit of a hit. I wasn't a fragile flower that she needed to handle with delicate kid gloves. Did she not enjoy herself? Was her orgasm not mind-shattering, world-melting like mine had been?

My stomach dipped with the possibility that I wasn't enough. And that only made me angrier. I did not do insecure. That was as far from my MO as it got. Who the hell did this girl think she was? What was she doing to me?

If I got a chance, back home, when we weren't dealing with the dangers of hell and a mission that got more complicated by the moment, I could take it to the next level, pull her to the edge of her desires and dangle her over the cliff, watching with heated anticipation as I dropped her right over. Until all she could focus on was me.

No.

I forced the images away. No more sex, not with her. Things were getting way too complicated, way too messy.

Like she was suddenly unable to look me in the eyes, she started shoving one leg into her pants and then the other, hopping around like a drunken sailor as she cursed under her breath, her chest lifting and dropping in shallow breaths.

Shallow breaths, I realized, that mimicked mine, like we were still physically linked, bodies mirrored.

Why did I care so much? Why did it matter that she clearly wanted nothing more to do with me, that she was constructing a wall between us that would have had any contractor impressed with the speed and sturdiness.

On some level, that was what I fucking wanted. For both of

us to move on—for me to go back to casual sex with friends and strangers.

There were so many fucking girls. When we got back home, I'd basically have my pick of whoever I wanted.

So why did the visual of her putting as much distance as possible between us hurt worse than getting my skin peeled off one layer at a time by a wendigo?

"Max—" I started again, but stopped at the hollowness in my voice. I sounded like a pathetic, broken little thing. I refused to let her see how her rejection was affecting me. She was right to want distance—after what I did. If I was her, I'd want the same. "I'm sorry," I said, settling for the fewest words I could muster, but the most important words all the same.

"I'm the one who's sorry, Eli," she was pacing now, eyes narrowed in focus, like she was trying to bend a spoon with her mind. "I shouldn't be here. I shouldn't be doing this. This," she paused, swiping her hand between us, "it can't happen again. Not ever. Okay?"

I stood up and reached for her, but the second my skin made contact with hers, she was gone—vanished, as if she was never here to begin with.

I was alone.

I looked around the empty warehouse that had seemed so bright, so filled with possibility just a few moments ago. It took me a few minutes to breathe through the strange ache building in my chest. The pressure was building until I was certain that this was it—that death was around the corner for real this time.

And that—that was the last I'd ever see of her.

I screamed, unable to contain the pit in my stomach for another moment, and looked down at my right hand, the knuckles bloodied and battered.

My eyes scoured the walls until I found a small hole, a hole wide enough to fit my fist.

I really needed to get a grip on the whole punching-unusu-ally-hard-objects thing.

It took what felt like forever—forever that consisted of nothing but me trying to ignore my labored breathing while watching the cuts on my hand begin to heal—before I realized one thing.

I wasn't on the edge of death. I could speak, could breathe, could walk around punching things. Whatever injuries I'd incurred from the fanghole's bad people skills were almost completely healed, like months-old injuries now instead of the death sentence they should've been.

Max had healed me.

Again.

And the realization that I'd betrayed her, that she wanted nothing more to do with me, created a crater in my chest that no mysterious, magical dream girl could fix.

8

DECLAN

Hours. It'd been hours—so many that I'd lost track—since Eli slipped into a sleep so deep that I was almost certain that—

I shook my head and placed two of my fingers, nails worn down from hours of biting, onto his pulse point again. For a long, impossibly infinite moment, I focused on feeling the familiar thrum of his heartbeat, but the movement beneath his skin was so faint I wasn't sure whether or not I was imagining it, or if it was just my own pulse in the first place.

I stood up, hands sweeping roughly through my hair. It was so knotted at this point that my fingers barely moved through two inches of strands before getting caught in the tangles. I hadn't thought about coming to hell with a bottle of a detangler. Next time, maybe.

"Fuck, fuck, fuck," I whisper-yelled at his lifeless body, my stomach a mess of knots that made my hair look tame, "if you die on me Eli Bentley, I swear to god, I'm going to murder you."

Nausea rolled over me. I was not prepared to handle this situation, and I was most definitely not prepared to handle it alone. There'd been no sign of movement in the area, so I figured it was best to just lay low until Atlas showed up. But it'd been ages and there were still no signs of him or his wolf showing up to save the day.

Which meant that I was alone.

For the first few hours, I cleared the area, tried to make Eli a bed out of our change of clothes and the few scraps I found lying around in a few of the rooms. We appeared to be in what must have once been a small motel or apartment set up. It was weird thinking of monsters as having use for something that just seemed so...human. Did they travel around and visit each other? Was there tourism and recreation in hell?

And if they did use motels, why was this one in such shit shape? There weren't even any mattresses in most of the rooms I'd checked—and in the few that had them, they were so filthy that I had to hold my breath to block the stench.

Nothing about this place made any sense—literally every single building we'd come across since walking through that portal was either abandoned or inhabited by mystical squatters. It was like hell had experienced an apocalypse, but we never got the memo earth-side.

A shiver ran down my spine as the wendigo came floating back through my mind. I'd have nightmares about her peeling the skin off my friends for months, maybe even the rest of my life. Vampires were gross, and I hated them more than I could put into words. But something about that creature, hearing about how it toyed with Eli and Max, seeing the way that it lived, just made my skin crawl. I might've found my new least favorite brand of demon.

Who knows what would've happened to Max and Eli if that fanghole wasn't there to—

Ugh. Feeling gratitude for a vampire's presence was enough to send a wave of revulsion down my back, like nails on a chalkboard.

"You flirt with death like you flirt with women," I said, glancing down at Eli while I resumed walking back and forth on the same three-foot patch of hall I'd been pacing on for hours. If

I squinted, I could almost see where the old, decrepit carpet was starting to wear from my path. "Nauseatingly and way too frequently for your own good."

Eli was one of the best protectors I'd ever encountered, it was why I'd always wanted him on our team, even when he drove me so wild I wanted to flay him alive myself. He was smart, ridiculously skilled at fighting, a whiz when it came to basic field medics, and an excellent reader of people. Including me, though that particular ability frustrated me even as it impressed me. To see him dancing so close to death's door, like a drunk man on a tightrope, had my stomach so hollow that it hurt to breathe.

"Please just pull through this." I'd been repeating the same thing over and over again, until it started to feel like a strange prayer on my lips, whispered to an entity that I didn't even believe in. "I swear on my life that I'll do anything if you just open your damn eyes. Literally anything. I'll even wingwoman you for a lifetime, without complaining once. I'll take all the gross jobs on our missions, I'll cover for you with Atlas when you've been out all night and skipped patrol. I'll actually be nice to the girls you bring over. Or act like a jealous girlfriend when you want them to leave."

I walked over to him again, sliding along the wall until I was sitting on the corner of his makeshift bed, my legs stretched out in front of me.

His dark hair was curling over his brow, his skin clammy with sweat. I knew with a certainty that made my skin crawl that he was fighting for his life. I felt so powerless, unable to do more than simply watch him struggle through it. We were at an impasse, and there was nothing I could do but wait. And in situations like this, sometimes waiting felt like the most difficult task in the world. Fighting and kicking ass, I could handle. It was the whole 'doing nothing while someone I loved fought their own battles' thing that chipped away at my insides with the fury of a rabid ice pick.

What the hell was happening to Darius? And how far beyond

those of a typical protector were Eli's limits, now that he was tied to a vampire? Could he survive injuries he normally wouldn't? Or was he just doubly-screwed now that he had to watch his own back *and* the back of a creature who pissed off everyone he came into contact with?

I moved a few lazy waves of hair away from his eyes and studied the smooth expression on his face.

His skin was still marred with blues and purples from phantom bruises, his throat caked in layers of crusted blood. In sleep, there was something almost child-like about him; like it was the one place where he let the usual mask he wore slip away, no longer able to wrestle with it as he moved through his dreams, languid and peaceful.

Even as a child, he'd always been this way—all hard edges and bad choices on the outside, but a vulnerable mess underneath it all. A mess that was visible if you worked hard enough to uncover it, to peel it back and understand him.

It's why I loved and hated him in equal parts—so much of him, his expressions, his actions, felt like a refracted mirror of my own mess. We migrated through the world in different ways, but there were so many similarities tying us together. As much as he frustrated me, I understood him. And part of my frustration came from the fact that he understood me too.

The thought of waking up tomorrow and not having him down the hall, ready with burnt coffee and a wisecrack, made my stomach clench so tightly that all I could taste was bile.

I found myself stuck between trying to remain optimistic, to believe that he could pull through whatever the hell was happening to him, and to not give myself hope. Because if I had hope, and he pulled it away in one fell swoop, I wasn't sure how I would move past it. I wasn't sure I could.

My nails dug into my palms as I watched the almost-invisible rise and drop of Eli's chest. It was almost like seeing the air wave through a heavy heat—I stared so long, wished so desperately for his lungs to fill with air, that I couldn't tell whether or not I was imagining the minimal movement I saw.

Why the fuck had we thought that jumping into hell for some grand rescue mission was a good idea in the first place? Now, not only was Wade still stuck in some creepy room, trying to come to terms with the fact that he fed off lust, but Eli was lingering dangerously close to the afterlife. And who even knew where Max and Atlas were—or, if they were even okay?

Clearly the vampire was fucked up pretty bad. And if something in this world could take him down in less than a day, what chance did any of us have? Was Max still with him? Was she still even al—

No.

I wasn't going there. I took a deep breath and stood up again, back to pacing as I studied the cluttered room, rife with dust and debris. What was I going to do if Atlas never showed back up? I wasn't a werewolf, so tracking him would be damn near impossible. And I didn't know the landscape in hell at all. The fanghole twins didn't exactly bother supplying us with a map for our mission.

I scratched at my throat as it started to tighten; the familiar pain in my stomach that was part pressure, part nausea was building again; and my breaths were coming so quick and shallow, that it was like my lungs thought they'd just run a double marathon, despite the fact that I'd done little more than stand like a hovering mother hen all day.

I dug my fingers into my thighs, trying to focus on the slight pinch from my nails, to ground myself in the small points of pressure. I couldn't lose it, not here, not right now.

The only thing standing between Eli and all the creatures hell-bent on killing us all was me. He needed me strong if he was going to survive this. We both did.

I sucked in a quick breath and stared around the room, clocking the grimy windows that hadn't been cleaned in years, the walls that were that peculiar shade of yellow that was clearly once white, the small patches of carpet that were so dusty and worn that I didn't even want to think about the number of microorganisms that were living in the threading.

My breathing calmed slightly, and while the panic attack was slowly ebbing, the lingering nausea and fear still coated my insides like sticky molasses. Because the truth of the matter was that, no matter how I tried to dress our current situation up with optimism, I was alone and didn't have the slightest idea what to do next. I could do nothing but wait for Eli to hopefully wake up; and if he didn't, I—

No. My thoughts needed to stop circling in that direction. I wasn't much of a believer in the whole manifestation thing, but in times like this, it couldn't hurt. So I walked back to Eli and tried to visualize his eyes opening. If I closed my eyes, I could almost perfectly imagine that snarky ass smile that always drove me nuts, could almost hear his voice uttering a suggestive comment about me hovering over him while he slept. Could almost see the unreleased laugh lingering in those auburn eyes.

But when I opened my eyes and stared at his face, nothing had changed. He was still lying there, looking so lifeless and helpless that my fingers desperately searched for his pulse again as my stomach turned over in fear. The steady thrum was easier to find this time, and I couldn't be certain whether it was my imagination or not, but it almost seemed stronger, more insistent.

My lips cracked into a smile as I clung to his wrist, letting the steady pulse wash over me until it felt like we were in sync; like he was just as alive as I was, simply enjoying a long nap.

Eli was a stubborn asshole, and something about the idea of him fighting back, even against death, warmed me for the first time in days.

Maybe Darius was okay? And maybe, somehow, since Darius was healing, Eli was healing too? The magic of the blood bonds was new to us, but it had to be a good sign that his body was fighting, that he wasn't slipping off into a place I could no longer reach him.

How long would it take, before I knew either way? The unknowing, the lack of certainty and direction, was eating me alive.

I wanted so desperately to be anyone else—to have the sunny, naive energy that Max radiated; to treat everything as a long nihilistic joke, like Eli; to have Wade's calming compassion or Atlas's stubborn control.

I took a deep, steadying breath and let the optimism flow through me—he would be okay, he would fight off whatever it was he needed to fight off, and then he'd wake up. When he did, we'd come up with a plan. Together.

We'd find Atlas, or he'd track us down, and then the three of us would go after Max and Wade. Hell, I'd even be happy to see the damn fanghole at this point, if it meant that him walking around happy and alive meant that Eli was too. We'd figure it out —all of it.

I could get through damn near anything if I had my team to hel—

The echo of a snapping twig sounded outside.

And then another, from a different direction.

My heart stopped and I held my breath, listening, as I dug quickly through my bag, fingers reaching for that familiar prick of my blade. My hands were numb with anticipation, but I was able to wrap my fingers around my dagger with enough control to pull it out, legs crouched in a low lunge so that I could spring to action at a moment's notice.

For a long moment, all I did was stand there, awkwardly hovering over Eli, while I waited for something to happen. The atmosphere felt so still, so silent. And I'd been on enough field missions to know that no good ever came from that sort of silen—

A loud crash echoed from a room or two over, the familiar sound of splintering wood as a door was pulled off its hinges.

For a brief moment that had my pulse racing in excitement, I thought it might be Atlas. Or even Darius and Max. But just as soon as the thought emerged, it vanished. None of them would be so careless. They wouldn't cause such a racket.

Which meant that whoever put into motion the domino of sounds was not a friendly. And whoever they were, judging by the heaviness in the air that was filled with an almost tangible anticipation, they weren't alone.

A loud, high pitched, crinkling crash sounded.

Shards of glass started to rain down around us. I glanced down at Eli to make sure that he wasn't cut anywhere, only to remember that his body was already a mess of lacerations. When I looked up, I saw a giant werewolf land on the ground a few feet away, coat white and thick. It shook it's fur, the way that wet dogs had a habit of doing, sending a spray of finely ground glass into the air.

I put my forearm before my face to try and guard my eyes, but I couldn't turn away.

Two more followed the first one, both just as large, both with hackles raised. A low growl emanated throughout the room, the vibration of it piercing me.

As much as I loved Atlas, I fucking hated werewolves. There was something so alarming about the intelligence in their eyes— something so human, while at the same time so wild and raw.

I stood in front of Eli, dagger gripped loosely in my right hand. There was absolutely zero chance that I'd be able to carry him out of here and make a run for it, which would be the ideal scenario. I couldn't take on three wolves solo, not even on my best day. And there was even less of a chance that I'd abandon Eli here by himself, defenseless and fighting for his life.

Maybe the vampire wasn't going to be the death of us after all.

With one, deep breath, I dug my toes into the carpet for purchase, thankful that I still had my boots on so that I wouldn't shred my feet on broken glass, and leapt at the first wolf. The momentum of my body destabilized it slightly, so that we both went crashing to the ground in a heap of fur and skin. The beast's weight made movement difficult, so I dug my blade into its stomach, unable to get the angle right for a shot to the heart.

Not ideal, but the low whine emanating from the wolf meant that I'd done a little damage. That was good. But it wasn't enough.

One of the wolf's pals joined in on our tumble, a set of claws digging into my shoulder blade as I kept my hand at the first wolf's throat, trying to prevent a bite with my arm outstretched.

The smell of blood was already clogging my focus, which meant that my back was probably fucked, even if the adrenaline kept me from lingering in the pain for the moment.

I maneuvered myself so that the wounded wolf was on top of me, as a sort of shield, the thick fur tickling my nose and making it difficult to breathe. My arm was shaking with exertion as the creature snapped at me, trying to break out of my grip and rip my face off.

A loud crash sounded from my right as the door burst open, a giant plume of unsettled dust from the commotion lacing my nostrils. I choked back the debris, my lungs already working overtime from the weight of the wolf on my chest, and glanced towards the door.

At least three more wolves crowded through the doorway, heads ducked low and teeth bared as their unmistakably yellow eyes landed on me—all of their attention in my direction at once.

Fuck, fuck, fuck.

How the hell was I going to get us out of this? Six wolves? I was so thoroughly screwed that I might as well be a pornstar.

I ripped the blade from the first wolf and with more precision and elbow room this time, I was able to shove the dagger underneath the wolf's deep rib cage and into its heart. My blade slid in like butter, all the way to the hilt.

The creature fell loose against me as the life left its body in low sigh and brief shudder. I removed the blade as warm blood slowly coated my hand and arm, loosening my grip on my weapon. My free hand reached for the wolf, its fur sliding between my fingers. With a heavy shove, I tossed it aside. It was enough to push it a few inches off me, but it didn't go far.

My breaths were ragged as I tried to steady myself and catch my bearings. Just as I recentered myself, ready to turn and face the second wolf without my makeshift shield, it shoved behind me. Claws that felt more like a newly-sharpened set of butcher knives dug into my back and my hand holding the dagger fell limp—as did the arm attached to that hand.

With a soft clatter that landed like a boulder in my stomach, my blade fell to the ground.

"Fuck." I groaned, my eyes clouding over with a layer of frustrated tears that pissed me off just as much as dealing with a pack of rabid wolves in an abandoned hotel in the pit of hell did. The wolf that had been attacking me while I was fighting off its friend, clearly did more damage to my shoulder and arm than I thought. I glanced down, pleased enough to find that the arm was still attached to me, so it hadn't ripped it clean off at least. Hopefully it was an injury I could recover from. "Why do you fuckers keep coming after us? We were just sitting here minding our own damn business," I muttered as I tried to move my body away from the wolf, this one black and gray, and just as large as the first. "Now I'm pissed right fucking off."

Using all the force I had left, I elbowed it in the jaw, satisfied when I heard a crack and a low whine, and slid away, digging my feet into the worn carpet as soon as I could find purchase.

I stood, hands held in front of me like I could ward off the remaining wolves with nothing but some nonexistent air magic. The wolves that hadn't attacked me yet seemed happy enough to watch their friends, but now that I'd killed one and injured another, I knew that would change—they'd underestimated me, but that wouldn't continue.

I saw the moment the glint in their eyes turned from vague

amusement to a feral rage, like dominoes until each angry wolf was focused on me.

"If I were going to miraculously turn into a special supernatural creature like the rest of my team, now would really be the fucking time," I muttered as I glanced between the window and the door—and then down to Eli.

He was just as still as he'd been before the wolves attacked, his body now partially covered by the wolf carcass I'd shoved aside, like he was wearing a strange fur coat covered in gore. He almost looked like the love child of Sleeping Beauty and Cruella.

Hopefully we'd survive long enough for me to tell him so. He'd find that amusing.

I took a breath, as we all stood, suspended briefly. It was like the wolves were toying with me now, like they were playing with their food while I tried to think up my next attempt at escape. There was something malicious in the way they studied me, each taking a slow, taunting step forward, to close me into the half circle they'd created. My back was to the wall and they were just enjoying the hunt now, confident that they'd cornered their prey.

At least their focus was on me and not Eli.

For now, anyway.

Had the wolves noticed him yet? Or were they just not threatened by his presence, given the fact that he was already on the edge of death? Maybe they didn't even register that he was there, his heartbeat had been so faint that I had to focus all of my attention on finding it earlier.

Or, maybe while I was struggling with my own fight, he'd lost his.

No. No, I didn't believe that, wouldn't believe that. He was alive. He'd stay alive as long as I was here to watch over him, to help him.

Once I was taken down though, I knew they'd sweep the room and go after him—wolves were smart, they attacked and guarded against the thing that posed the greatest threat first. Right now that was me, but once I was dead, it would be him.

I stood no chance against these wolves on my own, which meant that Eli—alone, unconscious, weak—was for sure a goner once I was down for the count.

My nostrils flared slightly with the weight of my decision as I looked down at Eli, hoping like hell that this wouldn't be the last time I saw his annoying face, but knowing with a hollow certainty that it probably was.

I felt each muscle flex as I forced my eyes away and reached for my discarded blade, the movement fast and sure as I carved through the path I'd already outlined in my head. I shoulder checked the wolf closest to me with my good side as I made my way out of the circle, hitting it with as much force as I could, while still maintaining my balance.

"You fuckers want a fight?" I asked as I moved towards the window without breaking my stride, every muscle in my body working overtime to give me the speed I needed to reach it before they reached me. I hopped onto the ledge, my hand sliced to hell from a broken shard of glass as I pulled myself out. "Then come get it."

Without looking back, I dropped down, snagging my side against the narrow window and ripping my shirt. My body rolled to the ground with less control than I would've liked. I'd lost more blood than I'd realized. The drop was only a few feet, but right now I had to focus more on speed than precision if I wanted to lead them away from Eli, so it wasn't as graceful a move as I would normally be able to pull off. I was usually decently agile when it came to improvising on scene.

A fresh cloud of dirt surrounded me as I rolled down the slight incline, until a thick tree stopped me cold, my limbs wrapping around it at a less-than-desirable angle.

I didn't wait.

In less time than it took for me to take an orienting breath, I peeled myself back up until I was standing with most of my weight on my right foot, and took off, my pace as quick as I could manage with a slight limp. I wasn't sure whether I'd rolled my ankle in the fight or the jump, but I ground my teeth together as I pushed the injury to its limits and kept moving. It wouldn't matter in twenty minutes whether I died with a fucked up leg or a really fucked up leg.

With a sinking realization, that somehow brought clarity and focus, rather than fear, I understood the reality of the situation. There was no point preserving my body for the long game at this point—I just needed to get them away from Eli as quickly as I could, for as long as I could.

It was the direction and purpose I needed, the guidance I'd been so desperate for since we sent Atlas off.

There were worse ways to die, than trying to save someone you cared about—or at least buying them time for a miracle.

The sound of harmonized growls echoed around me—that, coupled with a series of soft thuds told me all that I needed to know.

They were following me. And judging from the cloddy noises, none of them stayed behind with Eli. It was working.

My lips split into a grin as I took off into the woods, my path zig-zagging every which way in the hope that any change in direction would slow them down, requiring time for them to process.

I wasn't nearly as fast as a wolf, but I wasn't completely useless. I was on Team Six for a reason, and I'd spent years filtering every ounce of willpower into pushing my body to its limits. I'd even learned to enjoy the pain that came with a partic-ularly brutal beating, to crave it.

Just as I moved into a small clearing with diverging paths, I took a nanosecond too long to decide which direction to go.

A nanosecond that cost me.

A heavy thrust shoved me into the ground, my fingers digging into the mud to try and stabilize me as my body went crashing. It was only a matter of time before they caught up to me, I knew that. Knew that they were so much faster than me on a good day, let alone now when my body was battered and broken.

I took one moment to center myself, to try and wrap my head around how I was going to get out from underneath one wolf and run from the others that I knew were probably forming a circle around us, each preparing to assist in ripping me limb from limb.

I had a feeling that they wouldn't play with their prey this time—not after I used the extra beats of time back in the building to create a shoddy escape plan.

I threw my elbow back, catching the wolf…somewhere, though I couldn't tell where exactly my left elbow hit it.

My right arm was still relatively useless, so I kept it pinned close to my chest, out of my way, as I pulled myself back up. Apparently my elbow game wasn't exactly strong, because the wolf was already mid-lunge, ready to attack again.

A moment before it reached me, I thrust my left arm forward, burying the dagger with as much force as I could muster.

Unfortunately, it wasn't much.

The blade dangled awkwardly, positioned between two of the wolf's ribs. Which meant that all I'd done was piss the creature off even more than it already was.

And, what's worse, the angry canine backed away from me, taking my one and only weapon with it.

Fuck.

They were all closing in now, so without thinking, I ran towards one of them, closing the two-foot distance between me and the nearest tree in our circle of doom.

There was a low-hanging branch that I tried to grab with my good arm, using the momentum from my feet scaling the trunk to push me closer to it.

But it wasn't enough. My fingers closed around the top of the branch, but I didn't have enough purchase to pull my body weight up. I could already feel my fingertips slipping, digit by digit as I rocked my body like a pendulum, desperate for some momentum.

This was it, this was how I was going to die. Dangling from a tree like a barrel of monkeys toy.

Something sharp dug into my calf, and I could feel the weight of a wolf pulling me down. A loud noise burst through my lips, half scream of anguish, half battle cry as I tried to kick the creature off of me.

My right arm was fucked, but it was functioning enough that I could just barely lift it up to the branch if I ignored every nerve ending screaming through my body. The balance from both of my arms helped to stabilize me and I used the last of my energy stores to heave myself up.

My legs wrapped around the base of the branch as soon as they were high enough and helped me from overcorrecting and falling over to the other side.

The entire right side of my body was screaming in agony as I lowered my center of gravity and clung to the branch like a damn sloth.

The bark dug into my fingers as I gripped it, but I didn't mind—this tree was my last ditch effort and I'd happily trade the skin on my palms for a moment of reprieve. My heart raced as I watched the wolves trying to jump up after me.

But they weren't in human form, and my precarious branch was perched about a foot higher than any of them were able to reach on their own.

I sucked in air, my lungs so tight that it felt like I was trying to breathe underwater. They were all there—all circling my tree like a pack of dogs waiting for a squirrel. Only the look in their eyes was filled with a vitriol so strong that it could melt metal.

Still, I let out a soft laugh, my body flattening to the branch as my breathing slowed to a more normal pace. Somehow, against all odds, I'd been given the gift of a moment—a literal pause-button for me to slow down and figure out a way to get us out of this, or at the very least to give Eli as much time as possible.

But now that I was still, I could feel how dizzy the blood loss had made me. And while I was successful in pulling their attention away from Eli for a little while, what good would that do in the long term?

My one weapon was buried in a wolf and I was up here with no supplies, no back up, and a body that was pushed far past its limit.

I wasn't sure how long I was suspended like that, my eyes dancing with bright lights as I tried to hold onto consciousness. If I passed out, it was over. But still, the allure to close my eyes, just for a moment, was hypnotizing. Maybe if I just let myself fall into a quick sleep, I could wake up refreshed and rebooted, ready to come up with a plan?

At least I'd taken down one of them. All things considered, surviving as long as I had and taking one out was pretty damn impressive. I wasn't used to fighting these demons without my team, without Atlas at my back. Not that anyone back home would know about it. My glory would die with me, while I was lodged in a tree and leaking my O-neg all over the dusty grounds of hell.

The wolves were growling and yipping, but the ringing in my ears helped drown them out until all I could hear was the pounding of my heartbeat.

Maybe Eli would wake up—maybe I bought him enough time to escape before the wolves came back for him. I could've sworn that his pulse was strengthening, that his skin had even looked brighter than it had in hours, just before we were rudely interrupted by the pack.

I exhaled, grip loosening just slightly as the idea solidified until it became reality, as if he really was already safe and far away from this place.

Yes. He'd be okay. It was worth it. It would all be worth it.

He'd wake up, find Max and the others, and return back to Headquarters. They'd all be okay. That's all that I needed.

A series of cracks sounded below, jostling my daydream, and I lifted one eyelid, an act that required far more energy than it should have. I'd never been aware of how many muscles it took to blink.

The scene below me was like one out of a horror novel.

The wolves' limbs were bending and cracking, the hair receding back and back and back, until all that was left was smooth skin in all different tones. The beasts went from standing on all fours, to rising on two legs. It was like watching evolution speed up—animal to man.

And there were more, more wolves emerging from the path we'd carved through the woods in my pseudo-escape. Where did they come from? Why didn't they attack all at once? Did they really just enjoy slowly playing with their prey—like I was nothing more than a toy, an evening's amusement to them? There had to be ten, maybe even a dozen now. All in various stages of a shift.

They were like pros compared to Atlas. I'd only seen him transition a handful of times, but it looked like hell each and every single time, the anguish and agony clear in every break of his bones.

The creatures below me, moved like a practiced unit, their shifts powerful and intentional. Maybe this was the true differ-ence between born wolves and turned; it seemed so effortless, so routine, like their two halves were really one. Maybe with time, Atlas's transitions would become just as seamless, just as natural. I watched a few of them change in awe, unable to identify the precise moment when the wolf disappeared and the humanoid emerged.

Was the boundary between Atlas and his wolf just as ambigu-ous? If so, did that make him like them—wild and dangerous and evil—or did that mean that they were not completely unlike us?

Could I reason with them? Beg them to take me and leave Eli be?

Werewolves in human form always terrified me more than when they were covered in fur. When they looked just like people, it was hard to remember that they weren't, it was easier to fall prey to their manipulations and strategies—the boundaries between us and them blending and bleeding unpleasantly.

And then I realized what this meant. Now that they were shifting back, my tree was no longer a temporary safe haven; a semi-peaceful ledge on which I could spend the last few moments of my life withering away in self pity while a pack of dogs circled below me.

One of the tall men bent his knees, prepared to lunge—his features were shadowed, but I could see the predatory gleam, the yellow weaving throughout his dark irises. He wanted to be the one—the one to cut into me and stop my beating heart.

Was it his friend, the wolf I'd killed? Had he been the one to claw into my back and fuck up my arm?

If so, I could almost understand. If the situation was reversed, and he'd taken a member of my team from me, I'd be just as hungry for blood and vengeance as he was. When it came to family, the lines between good and bad blurred, even more than they already were.

All the lines that I'd lived by seemed permanently blurred these days—no clear direction, no clear good to strive for.

The man's eyes locked on mine, and I saw emotion there, familiar emotion, *human* emotion—rage, pain, anticipation, victory.

The world was just a goddamn mess both here and back home. Nothing made sense anymore.

Maybe it never did.

Belatedly, I realized that they'd been toying with me, were toying with me still—a few feet up a tree was nothing for a wolf. I'd seen them in action, seen Atlas in action. They'd been letting me think I was safe, letting the fear dissipate a bit, just to watch it come back in a rush.

Even now, as the man watched me with that quiet, furious gaze of his, I knew that they were still just playing with their food.

I just didn't know if I had the energy to care anymore...

"Stop. Leave her be," a quiet but confident voice echoed through the trees, strong and clear and like a whisper from the gods. A voice that was achingly familiar.

I tried lifting my head, but could only manage an inch or two. A woman, tall, lean, and naked walked into the small clearing. Each of the wolves around her parted to let her pass. Her steps were graceful, sure, as she moved among the creatures. Like she belonged with them.

I closed my eyes and opened them again, trying to see past the blinking lights of unconsciousness threatening to pull me under, convinced that I was seeing things.

Dark, long hair. Greenish-blue eyes. Full lips that knew how to twist a blade with each word. That cocky arch of a brow that showed up with every smirk.

How was it possible?

Maybe this was what death was—a final mirage you got to share with the people you loved and lost, there to send you off into whatever came after.

"Sarah," I muttered, though no sound left my lips.

And then, my eyes drifted closed, the last sensation a lurch in my stomach as I fell from the tree.

❦ 9 ❦
MAX

I opened my eyes and discovered I was right back where I had been before: stuck in a mother-fucking dungeon in the middle of hell. It felt like the worst version of Groundhog's Day imaginable. Only I didn't have Bill Murray's humor to keep me optimistic.

How had so much happened in the last few hours, or however long it had taken me to dream-walk between worlds, and yet nothing had changed?

Someone needed to make a manual that explained all the rules for us newbie demons, because I didn't have a goddamn clue.

The walls were still made of the same cold, gray stones that were somehow both rugged and smooth, the air was still crisp and laced with an icy chill. My bed of rags was still lumpy and uncomfortable.

I sat up, half-expecting the cloaked man to be here again, watching me like the creep that he was, but I was alone. Completely and utterly alone.

Leaning over, I reached for the small bag he'd left. There didn't appear to be any new provisions, which I took to mean that he hadn't come to visit while I slept. Good. I had enough things to worry about without having to deal with a creep watching me sleep and have sex dreams.

My skin pebbled at the memory of Eli's touch, like his phantom fingers were somehow grazing my skin miles away.

I stood up, took a long breath in, and breathed it all out in one loud hum—like I was doing some of Cy's yoga breathwork that he always tried to drill into us.

I was not going to let myself linger there. Not going to think about what happened with Eli when the rational part of my brain turned off. Apparently, Dream Max thought only with her vagina.

Did my body just completely forget about the fact that he'd been lying to me? Spying on me and using my attraction to him as a way to get information about my past? That wasn't the sort of thing I could forgive. And I most certainly did not want to be with someone who was using my lady bits for intel.

My feet wore a familiar path as I started pacing around my cell, trying to shove the sudden heat flooding my body at the memory of his touch into something closer to repulsion.

It wasn't working.

I paused, examining my frustration from another angle.

In the last few hours, I'd learned that I was, in fact, a demon. That Eli had a perfectly rational reason for his undercover seduction. And that maybe Six had been right, keeping track of me and maintaining their distance and suspicion. That whole 'keep your enemies closer' saying had some pragmatic value to it. Would I have done the same if Seamus or another of the senior protectors had told me to keep my eye on a suspicious person infiltrating The Guild?

I wasn't sure. I most definitely would not have gone the particular route Eli had chosen to tread, that was for damn sure.

Still, if they really were charged by Seamus to keep tabs on me, I much preferred Atlas's brand of coldness. Which was a big shock. He'd always kept me at a distance, his suspicion of me constantly raging and clear, like a damn neon sign. I knew where

I stood when it came to Atlas: on the outside of his team, held back by more than arm's length. Maybe that was preferable?

But Eli.

I shook my head and went digging through the bag, suddenly ravenous and desperate to translate my anger into something else.

Eli had played with my emotions, used my need for human connection against me. And he was supposed to be someone I could trust—he was related to Cyrus for crying out loud. The first friendly face I'd met at The Guild.

I should've listened to Ro—he'd warned me the very night I met Eli about guys like him. But I chose to learn that lesson the hard way. I was never going to be that stubborn again.

At least I would try not to be, anyway. Dream Max had a mind of her own.

I shoved a piece of dry bread, far too big for me to chew gracefully, into my mouth, the rough edges of the crust scraping uncomfortably against my gums. I needed water. And a lot more than the two bottles good old Cloaky had left me with.

Looking at the provisions, I couldn't tell how long he'd planned between his visits. Based on my normal appetite, this wasn't enough food to count as a snack. But it was enough to keep me alive for days. Weeks, even, if I portioned it out properly and didn't exert too much energy.

After choking down the first piece, I shoved one more bite in, anger chewing as I tried like hell to avoid any more thoughts of Eli.

Instead, I just got a layer of rage that boiled like lava in my belly. Annoyingly, it was directed more at myself than at him. What had I been thinking? Having sex with him in a dream? It was like the moment I was there and he was okay enough to hold a conversation, I was eating him up the way I normally would a heaping plate of steak and potatoes.

The emerging succubus was a thirsty bitch and I needed to get her under control before I killed somebody.

Then again, maybe Eli deserved it.

I exhaled, the air from my lungs making my flyaways dance around my face. My own sarcasm was about the only thing I had to keep me company in this room.

I tried to focus on the fact that, for now at least, Eli was okay. He'd been in rough shape when I'd first dream-walked to him, but clearly that had changed quickly enough. I just had to hope that wherever he, Declan, and Atlas were, they were okay. I couldn't let myself linger in the fear that they were anything but safe.

Because the truth was, if I didn't direct my frustration at Eli, I was left with something worse.

Fear. Anger. Shame.

None of which I was particularly excited to sit with while locked up in a dungeon. In the middle of hell. Alone.

All the information I'd learned since landing in this cell was clawing at my brain, demanding my attention. Between the cloaked man, Ro, Cyrus, and Eli, I was spiraling into a pit of doom. And I did not have time for that fucking shit right now. Did not have time to linger in the betrayal of the realization that everyone around me had been lying to me, about one thing or another. Did not have time to get lost in my own drama when Wade needed my help.

Maybe later. If I rescued Wade, got us back Earthside, and survived. Then and only then, would I let myself focus on figuring out who the fuck I was supposed to trust and how I was going to deal with the demon lingering beneath my skin.

I convulsed at the thought, my skin itchy with the realization that I was sharing my body with a creature I didn't know or understand, a creature my people were taught to despise and hunt. A creature *I* was taught to kill.

Self-hatred was a bitch and I was not eager to parse that steaming pile of shit into something more manageable.

Later. I'd deal with that later.

Right now, I needed to focus. So that's what I did. For hours.

Stared into space and tried to come up with a plan for getting us out of here.

Only problem? The walls were impenetrable, there was no door, and I had no way to communicate with anyone outside of unpredictable dream-walks. It wasn't the first time that I found myself wishing that hell had cell service.

As it was, my starting point options weren't exactly inspiring much ingenuity.

And even if I got out of this room, what then? It wasn't like I had a map of hell printed on the front page of my Big Book of Quests. I had no idea where I was, how I'd find the others, or where we'd find a portal without Darius or Claude to help us through it. There was a reason that portals were so finicky and difficult to locate—the creatures in hell were literally trapped in hell. If they struggled finding a way out, what chance did we have? Each step came with a thousand new problems, like the sort of books that answered one question, only to throw three thousand more at you, just to keep you on your toes. Only problem was, even with my toes dancing to an outrageously fast tap number, I still couldn't keep up.

I finished the first bottle of water, so refreshing that I half worked myself up to another orgasm, just from the thought of it. I wanted more. Apparently my succubus wasn't the only thirsty one in this body.

My eyes landed on the bucket that I'd moved as far from my makeshift bed as I possibly could. It still wasn't far enough. But it was another problem and looking at the small pail had me wishing I'd saved some of that water for later. My lip curled at the thought of using it.

Being held prisoner in some mythical realm wasn't nearly as glamorous as novels and movies led me to believe. Instead, the experience was overshadowed by boredom, hunger, thirst, and the gross ick factor of having nowhere to dispose of your shit when you solved two of those three problems.

Like a ton of bricks, the last thing Cloaky said to me

pummeled into my mind: if you want to see your friend, figure it out.

The only reason I even found myself in this building the first time was because I teleported like an amateur X-men character. And if that neat little trick was anything like my human torch affliction, I could probably do it more than once.

Which meant...

No doors?

No problem.

I'd just pop my ass to the other side and hunt Wade down myself.

I stood up and rubbed my hands together as the start of a new plan began to stitch itself together.

But then I deflated, my shoulders sagging as I looked down at my body. How exactly did I flip the teleportation switch on?

I stared at the wall, imagining myself running through it to the other side, like my body was made of nothing but air...er, the sort of air that could pass through walls. My hands clenched into fists at my sides, and my forehead started to get sore from all the furrowing my brows were doing as I focused all of my concentration on simply existing on the other side of the wall.

Nothing.

How had I even done it the first time? If I didn't know how I initially tapped into the power, I was basically going to be starting from zero to replicate the process. Again, a manual would be really fucking fantastic right about now.

Hell, I'd even settle for a grumpy-ass mentor.

I paced back and forth, trying to remember the mental and physical state I'd been in, each time one of my convenient new powers decided to show up.

The healing thing? Eli was on death's doorstep. Both the first time, when Khali helped me tap into my own energy source, and during my dream-walk.

The dream seduction with Darius and Eli? My energy stores

were depleted and my body was entering dangerous levels of fatigue.

The tingly fire that consumed my hands? Both times, I'd been in the middle of a battle that logic swore we stood no chance at winning.

Meaning, *I* was on death's doorstep.

Teleporting to Dracula's lair? Wade was dying and the cloaked man explicitly used my connection to him—whatever that meant—to lure my body here.

So...if I wanted to escape my chilly prison, I needed to be on the verge of death. Or I needed someone I cared about to be on the verge of death.

Not exactly a great way to start a rescue mission—by inciting the need for rescuing.

I took a deep, centering breath and closed my eyes. Maybe I could trick my body into thinking I was in more danger than I really was. Currently, anyway. Being trapped in hell was already dangerous, of course, but not quite the same thing as having a literal pack of wolves trying to devour you piece by piece.

Artificial adrenaline was a difficult thing to muster, but I lingered in the feel of each of those battles. Let my body breathe into that swath of fear as I pressed my palms against Eli, willing him back to life with every atom in my body; played back memories of a pack of wolves piling on top of Darius; forced my mind to focus on the image of Eli trying to fend off a group of vampires hellbent on vengeance; held my hand up before me, like I was the one lodging a magical blade into Wade's abdomen to lure me here.

My heartbeat perked up at the memory, and the added claustrophobia of being trapped in a small, circular room, helped amplify the anxiety building in my body.

But after what felt like an hour of lingering in the gore of those moments, of trying to internalize and heighten that fear again, I started to get frustrated. Not only because I'd gone exactly nowhere in my teleportation attempts, but also because these boys seemed to flirt with death the way that Eli flirted with anything possessing boobs and a vagina. They were, collectively, going to be the death of me.

At least Declan and Atlas seemed to like being alive enough to stay that way.

I paused, realizing another, more frustrating truth: as pissed off as they made me, the fact that my body responded as it did, going all Phoenix and what not, meant that I cared.

More than I really wanted to. Especially when it came to Six and the way they'd used and lied to me. And I didn't even want to start unpacking what it meant to care about the wellbeing of a vampire—and one whom I'd watched kill someone.

Being around them made me stronger, helped me dig into myself and awaken whatever demons lingered beneath.

It was infuriating.

But it was a start.

So, instead of only focusing on myself, I focused on them, and the tingly feeling under my skin that showed up whenever I was around one of them. That feeling that seemed to emerge in each of those moments.

I held onto that feeling as I let frustration wash over me. Frustration with everything—with Eli and my traitorous body's strange desire for him, despite him being an asshat, with the fact that Wade was taken from us all and we were on a doomed mission to bring him back, with my kidnapper and the brutal reality that I was left chained and helpless.

The images and feelings flashed in my mind like I was watching a sped-up film, until I couldn't tell where one memory ended and another began—until I couldn't separate my emotions, the images, and my thoughts. Until everything became a hot ball of blinding rage and fear.

I opened my eyes, looked down, and jumped. I was on fire. And it took me a long breath of a moment to realize that I couldn't stop, drop, and roll this fire away, couldn't escape it no matter how many times I flapped my arms around like an injured bird. Because it was coming from me. I controlled it.

As the initial panic subsided slightly, my lips turned up in a small grin.

Holy shit. I was on fire. And not in a burny way that would lead to a painful death.

I held my hands in front of me, careful not to get too close to my face. Could I burn myself? I wasn't sure. But I didn't want to add singed eyebrows to my long list of grievances at the moment. The swirls of blue, orange, red, and purple were hypnotizing, each flame licking my skin with a powerful fury.

It was almost as if the fire had an agency all its own, an almost imperceptible urge to be put to use, to come alive. How long had it been buried inside of me, trapped behind some locked door until I was able to set it free?

This wasn't the power that I'd wanted to summon, but now that I had, I focused on the way it felt, willing my heartbeat to slow down just a bit, to not panic at the fact that I was literally on fire.

I was okay, this fire came from me, and while I realized that, it was still difficult to convince myself not to fear it, even just a little bit.

I took a few calming breaths, letting myself almost enjoy the liquid heat—warm and soothing, but not hot enough to burn— to feel the tingling energy dance down my body like a feathered, barely-there touch. Rage was still flowing through my veins, my muscles still achingly tense with it like my body was poised for a fight, but it slowly started to dissipate, to fold itself into a steady control.

My hands were curled into fists, so I unfurled them, imagining the fire slowly receding, crawling back into my skin and disappearing from sight until I needed to call upon it again. Shoving it back into its room and shutting the door, but not locking it away with a key.

And, to my surprise, that's exactly what it did.

And, perhaps more importantly, I now knew exactly where that door inside of me was located. I could hopefully access it again.

I felt my face crack into a big smile as the tension that was coursing through my body slowly ran out until it was just a soft hum.

I did it.

I didn't really understand how I did it exactly, and I probably couldn't replicate the sensation at the drop of a hat. I doubted any attacker would let me pause for hours while I situated my body and brain into the perfect harmony I needed to call up the fire—but it was a start.

The first piece fastened together in a new plan—hope, even if just a small dose.

Shoulders relaxed and eyes focused with renewed determination, I stared at the walls surrounding me. They didn't quite feel like they were closing in anymore. Instead, when I looked at them, I saw the possibility of escaping.

I closed my eyes and tried to imagine the sensations that ran through my body as I was transported from the roof with Darius, to the dungeon cell with Wade. It was painful, exhausting, and had left my body feeling more broken and fractured than I could ever remember it feeling before. There had been a sort of heaviness in my bones, like my body wanted to sink into a never-ending sleep just to dull out the pain and exhaustion. But I wasn't afraid to linger in that pain, not anymore.

Not if it meant getting out of here, finding Wade, and going back home to Ro and Cyrus and Izzy.

My biggest concern was trying to gauge the depth, to visualize exactly where I wanted to end up if I wasn't actually familiar with my surroundings and where I hoped to land. I'd read enough fantasy novels to know the horrors of accidentally teleporting yourself into a wall instead of outside of it; of moving your body from one location to another, but leaving a few limbs behind.

So I focused on all of me, every inch of my skin, on every muscle and bone, the way that I tried to do when I sparred—and thought longingly of the other side of the wall.

I wasn't sure how much time had passed. Minutes? Hours? Days?

A heavy exhaustion coated my limbs, an exhaustion I could feel down to the marrow. Until, suddenly, the exhaustion doubled, and then tripled, and my legs gave out and my ass landed on the floor with a dull, heavy thud.

My breathing was labored, my forehead clammy with sweat. I felt like I'd been hit by a truck—or five—and contracted the flu all at once. I could almost feel the process as my body tried and failed to mend itself together again.

But then, even though it took more effort than it should have, I opened my eyes.

The walls were still made of stone, the atmosphere still lifeless and cold. But the floor stretched wide and long, a series of torches lighting a path along the walls.

New walls. The area around me was suddenly longer and more narrow. I'd stared at the stone wall in my circular room long enough to know that these were new stones, with unfamiliar dips and grooves.

I let out a breathy chuckle as the reality of what just happened settled over me. I'd teleported. Probably only a few feet, but I'd done it all the same.

My fingers trailed over my body in quick, hurried movements, as I tried to make sure that all of me made it through. Nothing more awkward than leaving a boob or something behind.

A groan pulled from my lips as my body aches doubled with the small movement. But achiness and exhaustion aside, I was in one piece. And the acute pain was slowly dissipating as I gained more control over my body. Slowly, I stood up, one hand pressed against the wall as my head swam.

Still, even with the less-than-ideal side effects, a wave of pure, unbridled joy swept down to my feet.

My lungs filled with fresh air as I studied the strange decor. It was neither hall nor room, but some sort of strange combination of the two.

There were two diverging paths and I didn't have a single clue where either actually led. I felt like Lara Croft, exploring an ancient, not-altogether welcoming terrain.

The first step had simply been teleporting out of my small holding cell. Now came the equally impossible task of locating Wade and getting out of here before good old Cloaky intervened and sent me back to level one.

But how the hell was I supposed to do that in some demonic dungeon? I had no idea how large this place was or what sort of creatures lingered between the walls. Were they all prisoners, like me and Wade? If so, I might be able to convince them to help—a little inmate uprising.

A certain chill in the air that had the hair on my arms standing to attention told me no—that if I encountered a creature on my path, the odds of it being friendly would be slim to none.

I just had to push all of my hope into the fact that none of them would be quite as menacing as the cloaked man—something told me that his wrath was not something that I could survive.

Then again, it had almost seemed like he'd wanted me to escape, to go find Wade on my own. To flex my powers and learn to use them, like teleporting was nothing more than working a new muscle. A very weak new muscle.

And honestly, maybe that was true. I felt drained. More drained than a day of non-stop sparring or battling supernatural creatures had ever made me feel. It was a sort of weariness, like my body wasn't totally mine, like it was still stitching itself back together, molecule by molecule. I was whole, but not yet in control of myself in the way I was used to, not yet me.

Despite the exhaustion, I wasn't at the level I'd been when I first arrived here. Maybe it took more energy to go long distances. I wasn't sure how far this prison was from where I'd been on that roof with Darius, but it was certainly a longer journey than moving from one side of a wall to another.

Plus, I'd had a couple of sex dreams to restore me. It had been subtle, but waking up after being with Darius, and then again after being with Eli, was refreshing in a strange, new way.

I cringed, thinking about the demon lingering in my body, feeding on the people in my life with little-to-know effort or control on my part.

A problem for another day.

My chest felt odd, a sort of tightness that was unfamiliar, but not altogether uncomfortable. There was almost a warm pull, like the hint of suggestion or deja vu which told me to go left instead of right. It was the same feeling I'd had when I led Darius to the wendigo nest Eli was being kept in.

Seeing as I had nothing else to go on, and it had worked in my favor before, I followed that not-quite intuition and turned left.

The hall was filled with a strange heaviness, the torches so dim that I could only really see a few feet ahead of where I was walking, the path unraveling like a suspenseful video game. Only this time, if I lost a life, there wouldn't be a do-over.

There were no doors, no signs, no signs of life, just these unusual flames. Each one was a swirl of colors, no two the same, and while they appeared to be fire, it didn't look like the sort of fire you'd see on Earth. Maybe hell's elements were slightly different? Like the magic distorted and infused them somehow.

I paused, my body clenching with a sudden familiarity, that deja vu feeling sending my nerves on end. The firelight familiar in its strangeness. The orange, red, blue, purple, all swirling together—

I stared at the nearest torch, no more than a few inches from me. There was something revitalizing about the warmth it projected.

Just as I reached for it, not quite to touch it but to feel the heat more closely against my skin, the flame seemed to stretch, closing the distance between us. As it licked against my skin, just barely, I realized that it was the same sort of flame that I produced.

I spun around and stared in the direction I'd just come. The lights that had previously guided my path were dim now, the torches burning low and, if I squinted and looked further into the distance, extinguished altogether.

When I turned back in the direction I was going, the lights were brighter, more vivid and urgent, like they were calling me forward, guiding me.

Was the fire coming from me?

Momentarily mesmerized, I held my hand back up to the flame, my fingers more sure this time, submerging into the flames like they were made of liquid. But it didn't burn. Instead, the fire burned brighter, like it was enveloping my hand in a strange hug.

I shook my head and tried to focus. There'd be time for questions later and, hopefully, more chances to explore the boundaries of these new powers. For now though, I needed to find Wade and get the hell out of here.

Ignoring my exhaustion, I took off at a slow jog, my feet landing softly as I tried to make as little noise as possible. Luckily, Cy's training helped a lot with that. He was all about nimbleness and grace when it came to the battlefield, which was part of the reason he sent us on nightly runs through the woods.

Ro and I used to make a game of it, playing hide and seek while running as fast as we could. Whoever snapped a twig or rustled too many leaves was always out.

The halls seemed never-ending, with diverging paths and winding stairs every few minutes. I didn't think. I took the paths my gut seemed to hint at without question. If I didn't find Wade, I'd come back and retrace my steps more systematically.

But right now, for the first time, I was allowing myself to run purely on instinct, like there was a strange invisible thread pulling me to Wade.

The building was strange. Sometimes it seemed like the entire place was comprised of cylinders, like the circular room I was kept in. Other sections appeared more traditional, with clear right angles. Maybe Dracula's castle wasn't too far off of a descriptor.

After what felt like twenty minutes of exploring the dungeon, I skidded to a halt. There was nothing but a thick stone wall in front of me. A dead end. It was the first I'd come across since leaving my prison, like the entire building was an infinite labyrinth. Until now.

A low growl sounded behind me, the sound menacing enough to send a chill down my spine.

My body froze. Slowly, my fingers gripped my knife, the one that Cloaky had let me keep. It was a power move, letting me know that no simple blade could cause him harm, like he was leaving a puppy with a chew toy, nothing more.

I closed my eyes and took a breath in, hoping like hell that whatever I'd see when I turned around wouldn't find the image of me with a dagger so humorous.

I turned around slowly, hoping not to startle the creature into an attack, and found myself less than two feet from a large beast covered in black fur.

My heart stuttered as I studied it. Dark hair that was thick and wiry, eyes an unusual, unearthly blue. From one angle they'd look bright and crystal clear, but from another, they seemed almost indigo and dark as a night sky. There was a sort of knowing in those eyes, and it felt not unlike looking a werewolf in the eyes—like the beast lingering beneath the fur was filled with an intelligence that could strip you bare. Sharp, white teeth were bared as it lowered its large head and slowly prowled towards me, movements smooth and precise.

A hellhound.

Where my hellhound, Ralph, looked and acted more like a puppy, this one had the energy of something more menacing. There was a threatening glint in its eyes that had my blood pumping at an impossibly fast pace.

I raised my hands in front of me in a sign of surrender, trying to slow the rapid beating of my heart. I remembered what Khalida, Claude, and the others had said. That most hellhounds were wild and powerful. That they took little to no interest in befriending other creatures, let alone protectors.

Ralph was the exception. He'd bonded to me, for a reason no one quite understood. Something about the narrowed eyes and the rumbling coming from this creature's chest, told me that I wouldn't be quite so lucky with this one.

For once, I understood how most people saw Ralph, why his presence inspired so much fear in them, when it only filled me with warmth. Nothing about the creature in front of me made me feel safe, cozy, watched over. I felt like a slab of raw meat dangling in front of a lion.

I realized suddenly, too, how small Ralph was in comparison. Where Ralph was significantly larger than a dog, and probably weighed close to two-hundred pounds, the creature in front of me looked heavier and more muscular. There was an edge about him too, that suggested he'd had a rough life. This hellhound was like the rabid guard dog you'd find at old junk yards, while Ralph was the golden retriever puppy you got to play with your children.

"I don't want to hurt you," I whispered, hoping that the animal in front of me could understand me the way that Ralph seemed able to. And I meant it. Something about harming a hellhound didn't sit right with me, not that I thought I'd stand a chance against a full-grown one like this anyway. "I'm just trying to find my friend. That's all."

The hellhound continued to growl, every muscle in its body tensed and ready to pounce.

I shuffled my feet forward just a bit, because there was nowhere for me to go but towards the creature, and something in its posture told me it had no plans of moving from its current position.

"I'm a fan of hellhounds," I said, my voice wavering strangely in the echo of the halls. "I mean, I even have a hellhound friend, myself. His name is Ralph. Maybe you know him? I don't know how many of your kind there are, so maybe that's like someone in Europe hearing I'm from the U.S. and asking if I've ever met their cousin in Delaware." The creature let out a low grunt, his breath strong enough to lift some of the stray hairs around my face. It's posture shifted slightly, studying me with a focus that made me pause. Whether it was amused by my rambling or wanted to lob my head off, I wasn't sure, but I shuffled forward again, the sound of my movements quiet, but not completely silent in the hollow hall. "But my point is that I don't want to hurt you. I'm just going to squeeze past, and then I'll be on my way to find my friend."

I felt ridiculous, talking to a hellhound that had me cornered in a hell dungeon. But I wasn't exactly certain what else I could do. Carefully, I slid my dagger back into the sheath around my leg, placing my empty hands palm out again. "See, no weapons."

Not that a single blade and a partial succubus could stand a chance against a full-grown hellhound. And as I got closer to the creature, it's entire body moving with each inhale and exhale, I tried picturing Ralph instead. It was almost as if I was looking at a completely different species. Hell, maybe there were multiple kinds of hellhounds. We weren't exactly taught about them in classes.

My body stilled as I came within two feet of the creature. It's head was ducked low, so that its eyes were leveled with mine—clear as the ocean and brimming with intelligence.

I tried to blot those eyes out of my vision, recalling Ralph's warm amber peepers instead.

My panic ebbed slightly as I closed my eyes and let the image of him fill my mind—dark hair, gray patch around one ear, paws bumbling and awkward as he ran through the forest.

With a deep breath, I opened my eyes again. This time, when I saw the imposing face in front of me, I was almost tempted to reach a hand forward and pat the good boy on his head. Something told me this creature wouldn't be as fond of ear scratches as Ralph was.

"So here's the thing. I'm going to walk past you. I need to. And when I do, I'd really, *really* appreciate it if you didn't decide to take a chomp. Sound good?"

The hound's chest made that gurgle sound again, somewhere between a growl and what seemed almost like a laugh. A gust of warm breath washed over my face as he flared his nostrils. His nose pressed closer towards me until it was almost touching my face.

Every muscle in my body was flexed, but unmoving, as I stood there and let the beast get his fill of sniffs. Mostly, I was just proud of myself for not peeing my pants.

With a small huff and shake of his head, the hound backed away a few inches. I wasn't sure what he caught in my scent, other than the obvious fact that I was in desperate need of a long, luxurious bath, but he hadn't decapitated me, so I was taking it as a win.

Or, at the very least, a temporary truce.

Standing so close, and now that I was reasonably certain that I wasn't about to be served up as dinner, I suddenly missed Ralph something fierce. I clenched my fingers into fists, physically restraining myself from running my hands through the thick fur that looked simultaneously rough and soft. Of all the beasts I'd encountered, hellhounds pulled at my heartstrings in a way that other demons hadn't. Maybe it was because Ralph had always seemed like an overgrown Labrador, or maybe because he'd found a way to come to my rescue over and over again.

My association with the species was only positive, so I couldn't help but transfer some of that goodwill to the beast in front of me, even if not all hellhounds were like mine—even if the fully grown ones were as dangerous and unpredictable as everyone had warned.

As if we understood each other, the beast tilted his head slightly, studying me again, but with less scrutiny and intensity as before—he seemed curious now, less convinced I was a threat.

With a long, steady breath, I moved slightly to the side, until my arm was flush against the wall and started to slowly make my way around the hound. My eyes never left his, even as his head craned to the side to watch me pass him.

No bared teeth. And I wasn't dead yet. So I was taking it as a sign that my friendly rant had worked.

Working against every instinct in my body, I turned my head so that my back was facing the beast, and made my way out of the small alcove I'd found myself in.

My heart beat hard against my chest, until it was the only sound I could hear, as I took a step forward, then another, until I came to a fork in the path. Slowly, afraid to make any sudden movements, I turned back to the creature.

Blue, piercing eyes watched my every move, but he hadn't moved an inch, or repositioned himself like he would need to if he wanted to come after me or attack. If anything, he almost seemed surprised by my actions, amused even.

"When I get my friend," I whispered, not entirely sure why I insisted on carrying on a conversation with a hellhound who could snap me in two with little-to-no effort, "we're going to find a way out of here. I-I don't know if you can actually understand me, or if you're being held here against your will. But when we do leave, you can come with us." My hand rested on the corner of the wall, as I peered back at him. "If you want. Just find me before we go. I'm sure Ralph would love a friend."

Not bothering to wait another second longer, I disappeared around the corner and resumed my slow jog. The air was chillier than it had been a few moments ago, and it took me a few seconds to realize that the flames burning in the torches were almost nonexistent. Was I losing energy? Was the fire finite or in need of a charge?

Again, a rule book would've been nice.

Turn upon turn, hall upon hall, I was starting to think that I'd been going in circles—that trying to make my way out of this maze of stone was more impossible than escaping my doorless cell had been.

Another path, another fork. I stopped, hands sweeping through my hair as I looked at the options. On an exhale, I closed my eyes, trying to reconnect with that strange intuition I'd felt earlier. Since leaving the hellhound, I'd been wandering aimlessly. I'd even tried doubling back, wondering if I went back to where I'd found him, if he might help me find my friend. He hadn't killed me when he could have, so maybe he would've helped.

But when I reached where I thought the dead end had been, there was nothing there but more paths, each direction seemingly empty of life.

"I need Ro," I mumbled, as I tried to slow my breathing. He was always so much better at tracking than I was. Even back home, I often got myself turned around in the woods—the same woods that I'd spent a lifetime combing through. A strange, mystical building in a new realm? I didn't stand a chance at navigation.

I tried to calm the panic building in my gut. I hated that feeling, like there was a swarm of bees rattling around in my stomach, climbing around my ribs, some even reaching as far as my throat. My palm stung, and when I looked down at my hands, I saw a series of crescent-shaped cuts lining the soft flesh. My fingers were so tight from fisting them that they felt almost painfully numb, like the feeling you got when trying to hold too many plastic grocery bags in one hand.

I looked at the stone walls, desperate for a sign, as if there'd be an invisible map that would reveal itself if I looked closer, a sign that said 'Wade: two steps forward, and then a left,' if I just wished for one hard enough.

But all I saw was more lifeless gray, and the dull whimpering of a single torch just out of my reach, the flame dimming with each passing moment until I was left in a small orb of light, like a character on stage.

A sudden wave of warmth coated me, that familiar tingling sensation of something trying to get out, beating just as persistently as my heart against my ribs. When I glanced back down, my hands and forearms were coated in a thin layer of flame. I waved them about, trying to pull the fire back inside, to shove it back into the cave from which it'd emerged, but it was stuck like glue.

Desperate, I dropped to the ground and did the whole stop-drop-and-roll thing just in case, but no luck. The flames grew thicker and higher, the more tense my body got, as if they were feeding off of my anxiety.

Unfortunately, the thing about anxiety was, the more anxious you were about it, the more heightened it became.

"Damn it," I whispered, or at least I thought I whispered, but the echoing reverberation around me sounded like a chorus, my panic refracted back to me over and over again until it felt like I was drowning in a sea of apprehension.

A deep, soft chuckle reverberated around the walls, marrying together with my curse like a macabre lullaby.

That chuckle did not belong to me.

My blood ran cold as I turned around, desperately searching for its source.

A man sat against a small ridge built into the wall, his legs crossed at the ankle, back leaning against the wall. Dark hair swept over his brows, making his stormy blue eyes stand out, even in the dim lighting.

"Who are you?" I asked, straightening my posture as I corrected the grip on my dagger.

"Are you supposed to be wandering the halls, little girl?" His voice was deep, but smooth like velvet. "Although I have to admit, I always do *so* love when they talk to themselves. This maze is known for twisting its inhabitants upside down until they go wild with the frustration of it. It's one of its many charms."

"Who are you?" I repeated, injecting as much steel into my voice as I could. Out of the corner of my eyes, I clocked the two paths I could take if the man decided to attack. One, the direction I'd just come from, and the second dark and impossible to gauge, since no torchlight illuminated it yet.

"Who I am isn't important. He doesn't like when his pets try making a run for it, you know," the man arched a brow and stood up. He took a step closer, and then another, until he was less than a few feet from me.

He was tall. Probably only a few inches past six feet, but everyone felt like a giant compared to me. I was used to it, and I'd had more than enough practice taking on people twice my size.

I glanced down at my hands, ready to brandish the flames in front of him, only to find that the fire had already dispersed in my distraction.

Old school then. I raised my dagger a few inches, and relaxed my shoulders as I parted my feet a few inches to get into a better stance—fight or flight, I'd be ready for either.

"How exactly did you get out of your cell in the first place?" he asked, closing the distance between us, one step at a time. "Can't say that happens every day."

"My friend," I said, voice wavering only slightly. "I'm looking for my friend. Wade. He's an incubus, do you know where he is? Where he's being kept?"

The man's cocky smile and narrowed eyes were his only response.

"You can either tell me or get the fuck out of my way. Those are your only two options."

That soft chuckle again, low and syrupy. "I'm sure I can think of a few more options than just those. Besides, he doesn't keep his prisoners long if they are of no use to him. If your friend is still alive, it'll be because he's needed for something. And if he's needed, you'll stand no chance of getting him out." The man shrugged, his posture lazy, like he was having a relaxed chat over brunch. It stung a little that he didn't seem at all intimidated by me. "I've learned the hard way to stay out of things that aren't my business."

"Who exactly is *he*?" I asked. While I was certain that he was referring to the cloaked man, I wasn't entirely sure. I still had no idea who that man was, who was in charge, or why he'd captured me and Wade. "And what does he want with us?"

The man crossed his arms over his chest and shrugged, eyes dancing with an annoying amusement that made my lip curl. "I've learned over the years not to question his reasons, but I'm sure I'd be rewarded for taking you back to your room."

As soon as he took another step closer to me, I lit up like a kid on Christmas morning, flames licking furiously along my hands and arms. "Stay the fuck back," I said, jaw tense and words clipped."

To my surprise, the man broke out in a deep laughter that sent chills down my spine. Instead of moving away from the flames, he wrapped his fingers around my wrist. There wasn't a single ounce of pain on his face as my flames lapped around his hand. If anything, he seemed amused. There was a darkness in his eyes that I couldn't read, but it unsettled me all the same.

A creature that was immune to the very same flames that had taken down a pile of vamps and wolves? Yeah, not good.

My free arm drew back quickly and I used the momentum to lodge my dagger into his neck.

The shock of my attack loosened his grip on me, but his lips curved into a thin grin as his eyes met mine. There was a challenge in their swirling depths, one that I wasn't sure I could meet.

While I had the element of surprise, I took off, my feet pounding into the hard ground so fast that the rest of my body struggled to keep up with them. I took off down the dark hall I hadn't explored yet, my blood running cold as I heard a steady tapping behind me. He was following me and, judging by the increase in volume, he was fast—fast enough that I knew he'd catch up to me in no time.

I raced down the hall, using every ounce of energy I had, barely aware of the fact that my arms were still operating as torches, lighting my way as I passed by one fork and then another—I turned left and then right, not even thinking or planning, just trying desperately to lose my tail.

That tight, tingling feeling was back again, mixing with a fresh layer of panic as the man's taunting chuckle echoed around me like I was in a haunted fun house. My legs were moving so fast that they were turning to jelly, the sound of my feet and his pounding against the ground kept perfect time with my racing heartbeat.

I could try to fight him. Turn around, stop the chase, and try to take him on. Clearly my fire didn't inspire any fear, but I could try something else.

My dagger. He'd moved away from me before I'd had time to pull it from his neck. Which meant I was weaponless.

I pushed myself further. Darius said that I had more speed than an average protector, I just needed to tap into that power. But it didn't help that I'd used most of my energy stores hopping to the other side of my prison wall. My chest felt heavy, my breaths coming out in stilted waves as the tingling tightness flowed through my body.

A wave of air blew against my neck and I knew that he was

close now, that he'd be within reaching distance in another moment if I didn't think of something.

I closed my eyes, taking as deep of a breath as I could.

My lungs caught on the inhale until it felt like I would suffocate, my head suddenly so heavy with pressure that I was certain it would pop. The ground disappeared from beneath my feet and when I opened my eyes again, my knees buckled.

I fell on my ass, but the blue-eyed man was no longer on my heels. Instead, I was in a small room. A room that I'd been in before.

My stomach dipped with a desperate hope as I spun around, too afraid that the familiar bed wouldn't be behind me when my eyes reached it.

But there it was—a flat slab covered in tattered fabrics.

And sitting on top of it was a man with blue eyes that made me stutter with relief, not fear.

"Wade."

✣ 10 ✣

ELI

The room was fucking chaos embodied. Even more so than it had been before I'd passed out.

I tried to sit, but something heavy was weighing me down. When I went to shove whatever it was off my lap, I almost jumped out of my skin. A fucking werewolf.

Napping under a dead monster wasn't a very good look for me.

My heartbeat picked up as I studied the carcass, satisfied from its stillness that it was, in fact, dead.

I brushed my hands lazily along my neck, my sides, quickly making sure that I hadn't been chomped on while I was in dreamland.

What a way to get turned into a werewolf—dozing through the whole thing.

But I seemed to be okay.

I scanned the room, desperate to put together the story of what happened While I Was Sleeping. Something told me it wasn't as wholesome of a story as the romcom would suggest.

There was splintered wood and broken glass all over the place.

I seemed to be the only person in here, like the lone person emerging from an apocalyptic landscape. Only person breathing anyway.

I patted the wolf on its haunches. Poor guy didn't seem as lucky.

Where the fuck was Dec?

I shoved the beast off of me, less jumpy this time, and stood up. My bones were achy and my legs felt weaker than usual, but it wasn't the sort of lingering pain that signaled distress. It was the way I often felt after a long afternoon sparring with my team. The kind of ache that made my body sing, the kind of ache I didn't mind lingering in for an afternoon. It meant time well spent. My fingers scratched along my neck as dried flakes of blood cascaded down, like a bad case of violent dandruff. But there was no open wound.

"Dec," I whispered, my throat still a bit scratchy from wear, but again, nothing to write home about.

I flexed the muscles in my arms and legs, testing each as I continued surveying the room. How long had I been out? I pinched the bridge of my nose, trying to remember what the fuck had happened.

Atlas had run off in a desperate flurry to find Max. Did he make it back? Had he found her?

Dec brought me here, on the brink of death. Each breath had been a struggle, my eyes weighted down like the lids were attached to anchors. My neck—the blood. That fucking vampire fuck. God was I getting sick of this shit.

A dream, a wildly real, exhilarating dream with Max. I shoved that particular little wet dream away. Now was not the time to linger in the stomach of knots that girl created. Dream or not, I'd come to an important conclusion. From here on out, I was putting up a big fat stinking wall—a metal one—between her and me.

The feel of her fingers as they went through my hair, the taste of her tongue as it slid against mine, the feeling after we finished...peace and raging terror.

Nope. Not going there. I didn't do sex and feelings. I did sex. Just sex. Fun and feral and meant for escape.

Focus, Eli. For once in your life, fucking focus. The room was a mess, clearly from an ambush of sorts; I'd been on the brink of death before drifting to sleep.

And yet, somehow...I was okay?

I thought so anyway. My body felt fine, for the most part.

My gaze caught on a large puddle of blood, and then as I scanned the grimey-ass floor, another.

The window was busted, blood crusting along a jagged piece of glass like the room was a backdrop for a shitty horror film.

My stomach tightened as I noticed Dec's bag on the ground —the bag in which she kept most of her weapons. The bag was here, but she wasn't. Had she been chased out? Taken? Killed?

And, judging by the level of disarray the room was in, this was no small pack that had crashed our pad. Had Dec taken them on solo or was Atlas back? Max?

Hope lit my veins until a crystal lake of fear pooled in my belly. If they were back, if they'd taken on the pack and won, they wouldn't have left me here. Which meant—

With a feverish hurry, I tore through my own bag, grabbing a pair of blades and slipping on a pair of shoes so I wouldn't bust my feet up on all the shit layering the floor.

Without a backward glance, I ran from the room, ears desperately searching for a sound. Any at all.

How was I alive? If there were multiple wolves, why did they leave me? It would've taken little to no effort to bite into my neck while I lay there, completely vulnerable. Maybe they didn't see me as a threat. I was on death's door anyway. I tried not to take it as an affront.

My thoughts worked furiously, trying to piece together some version of events that made sense, until—

Dec.

She must've hidden me and drawn them away. Just the sort of sanctimonious shit she would do. Now, I'd owe her one. Majorly.

Assuming I found her.

"Fuck." I ran through the hall, breathing heavily as I glanced briefly in each room, hoping each time that I'd find a pair of familiar green eyes teasing me in the distance, lying in wait to scare me.

A knot the size of an anchor had formed itself in my stomach by the time I reached the door to outside. Dec was in trouble. I knew it with every fiber of my being. If she wasn't, she would've come back for me.

That girl better not have fucking died on me—left me to rot in hell all alone. I needed her. She was fucking family. And I was done losing my family one member at a time.

Maybe this was what hell did—the true nightmare of it.

Split us up, leave us to fend for ourselves, bleeding and scraping our way back to each other as fear suffocated us slowly, overwhelmingly. Fuck it, I was ready to be done.

The dirt-laden path was covered in prints, a swath of paws, but also a familiar boot print carved right alongside them. I followed, running as fast as my injuries would let me, pushing as hard as I could. The path veered into a winding patch of trees, clumped together so tightly that almost no light illuminated the ground. Apparently this was the 'creepy forest' part of hell. Occasionally, this realm lived up to its stereotype.

I followed. The path was uneven, twisting and turning in unpredictable patterns. If Dec was dead by the time I found her, I was going to fucking kill her.

A low growl reverberated around me, joined by another, and then another, until it was like a terrifying symphony in the middle of the woods.

My feet skid to a halt as a large, brown wolf emerged onto the sort-of-not-really trail, blocking my path. A smaller, gray wolf appeared just behind it.

Fuck.

I exhaled, squaring my shoulders. Fuck it. If this was how I was going out, I'd make it one hell of a mess—painting the ground in as much red as I could draw.

I gripped a blade in each hand, bent my knees slightly, debated which one to go for first.

And then, I sprang, landing on the smaller of the wolves, figuring that was my best shot of doing any damage.

The beast growled, the sound so deep that I felt the vibration as my arms gripped around its chest. I dug one of my blades into the only spot I could reach—low in the belly—hoping that the injury would slow it's response time.

Sharp, angry teeth snapped less than an inch from my face, the dog's breath coating my nostrils. What a terrible last smell to breathe in.

Pulling my left hand back, I prepared to strike with my other blade, the first little more than a diversion. Hopefully this time, I'd hit where it mattered.

"No! Eli, stop," a deep, feminine voice echoed around us, just as my blade buried into the wolf—deep enough to elicit a howl, not to kill—as hurried footsteps thudded in our direction.

Mindlessly, I did just as the voice asked, instinct and familiarity stopping me short of ending the gray wolf. The voice was familiar, but it didn't sound like Dec. There was no slight Irish lilt in the sound, less anger and gravel than I was used to hearing from my friend.

The wolves deepened their growls as I backed away, scurrying with my ass on the ground as I searched for whoever had spoken. I stood, watching as the wolves' claws dug into the dirt, ready to pounce, to resume the skirmish, but they didn't. I could see the indecision playing out in their strange yellow eyes, like part of them wanted to ignore the order and attack.

But then a slim figure emerged in the distance. Long dark hair and an hourglass silhouette. As the woman moved closer, a pair of blueish eyes I'd seen almost every day growing up came into view.

"No," I said, dropping one of my blades onto the dirt, dust from the impact coating my feet, as I stared, my brain not believing what my eyes were seeing. How? How was this possible? Was this some twisted magic in this realm, playing mind games with me?

The figure was running, not even bothering to slow as it neared, until the resemblance was impossible to ignore.

The girl collided into me, arms wrapping around my torso, pinning my limp arms to my sides as a familiar scent, clean and floral, tickled my nose.

"You're still alive," she whispered, words broken with a loud, cracked laugh, like she couldn't quite believe it herself. "I knew you wouldn't be far, not if Dec was here."

"Sarah?" The word came out heavy, diluted with disbelief as I pulled back, needing to see her again. While I grew up learning about the supernatural, ghosts weren't a thing. I was pretty sure they weren't, anyway. My brain and my vision couldn't quite parse through the reality of what was happening.

She let me put a few inches of distance between us as I studied her. She was a bit leaner than I'd remembered, her muscles more toned and features more angular. And her eyes—there was that chaotic yellow that I'd seen fighting in Atlas's expression, mingling with the threads of blue and green—but they were the same. Somehow both cold and warm at once, open enough to see what she wanted you to see, but still barricaded enough to hide what she didn't. The same shit-eating grin and 'fuck-off' expression she always wore like a mask, softened a bit by her excitement.

"You're alive?" I asked, as my fingers pinched the soft skin of my side, just in case I was stuck in another overly realistic dream. Then again, judging by my most recent dream, I was pretty sure that the whole 'you can't feel anything in dreams' thing was a load of shit. "How are you here? How are you alive? Is this a trick? Are you a ghost?"

Her eyes glassed over in a rare enough show of emotion that I was almost certain that this was a trick, that this wasn't my dead teammate back in the flesh, but she shoved my shoulder the way she always used to and let out a watery laugh. "I'm alive, jackass. Turned," her eyes dropped at that, a rare vulnerability leaking out, "but alive."

I nodded, trying to follow along. The wolves approached on either side of her, like a private sentinel as she studied me. Their eyes were still boring into me, the hair on their backs raised like they were prepared to lunge at the slightest suggestion.

"These belong to you, then?"

She glanced down at the wolves, her posture growing more rigid as her glance met mine again. There was a whirlwind of emotions playing out in her expression, which in itself was strange. Sarah was always so composed, good at hiding things she didn't want seen. Hard edges just like her cousin.

"Part of my pack, but no wolf belongs to another," she said, like she was reciting a spiritual chant. "That's one of the first things they make sure we learn."

"Dec—" I started, panic seizing me, as well as hope. If Sarah was here, if she got to her in time before the rest of the wolves tore into her. If she stopped them, like she did just now—I shook my head, trying to erase the image of the room from my memory, the blood and the broken glass scattered around like an exploded snow globe. If Sarah was here then that meant there was a chance that Dec was—

"She's alive," Sarah said, her face cracking into a smile. "In bad shape, but she's alive. I left her with a friend to keep an eye on her vitals. I knew she wouldn't be alone out here and wanted to find you all before any of my pack—" she shook her head, her hair flowing around her shoulders, "before you were seriously hurt. Where's Wade ? And Atlas?"

Her face lit up, as her eyes searched behind me, like they'd both suddenly appear at her mention, ready to join in on this strange as fuck reunion. Hell. At least the place wasn't boring, I guess.

My shoulders sank in relief, a strangled laugh pulling from my lips as I fell to my knees and sucked in a deep, heaving breath, all the anxiety releasing from my body. Some of it anyway. Dec was alive. She hadn't gone and gotten herself killed while I was out like an ass, fucking Max in my dreams, unable to have her back. My body hummed with adrenaline as I held onto that fact. I didn't lose another one. She was alive. Dec could be insufferable sometimes, and seemed to make it a life mission to get on every last one of my nerves, but she was family. And family—the family that stayed anyway—was everything.

"I need to see her." I looked up at Sarah. "I need to see her for myself."

She nodded once, and I saw a deep understanding in her eyes as she reached for my hand and pulled me up. Her grip was stronger than it had been before, making it abundantly clear that a wolf lingered beneath her skin. It was the same when Atlas turned—little changes here and there, his body and instincts altering in ways he had to learn to mask. Sarah didn't have to hide her new nature though, not here. As she turned, guiding me in the direction from which she came, I studied her silently, trying like hell not to sink my blade into the gray-furred wolf walking behind me, far too close for comfort.

These assholes had just tried to kill me, so it was hard trusting them not to finish the job, even with Sarah at my side. Something in the way the wolf occasionally brushed up against me, close but not quite touching, told me that it wanted revenge for the pain I'd inflicted, that this wasn't finished simply because Sarah was here. It was a pause, not game over.

But I knew that if they wanted me dead, there would be very little I could do about it. I was beyond outnumbered, so the best I could do was go along for the ride, observe, and prepare for whatever the hell was next.

Sarah was alive. And she was a wolf. Did she grapple with the demon beneath her skin with as much ferocity as Atlas? More importantly, was she winning that battle?

Was Atlas?

She'd saved me, or at least saved me from expending my last vestiges of energy on the two assholes following us. And she was relieved to see me—she stopped them from killing me. So while it was strange to think of her as part of a pack, as part of a team that wasn't ours, I trusted her.

Enough.

For now.

But I still didn't know what this meant in the long term —was she with them or was she with us? Because I had a feeling that trying to plant a foot in both camps wasn't going to be a realistic option for her. Wolves were hungry for the blood of protectors. There was no denying that fact. The truce she had instigated was temporary. As the low, reverberating growls from her packmates made abundantly clear.

"Atlas and Wade," she muttered, glancing at me from the side of her eyes. She was tense, and I wasn't sure if it was because she was worried about her companions attacking or because she didn't know how to act around me now that she was...well, a wolf. While she didn't broadcast her anxiety, I could tell in the stiffness of her walk that she was actively trying to keep her composure, to iron out the adrenaline I knew was flowing through her body.

I knew what she was asking, but I didn't know how to answer, how much information I should give her, how much I could trust her with. She'd loved them both—Atlas especially.

They were bonded. Did that connection still exist between realms? After turning? After they'd all changed so much?

The Guild really needed to develop a rule book or manual for this sort of shit—none of us had any idea how it worked once boundaries started getting blurred.

If so many members of my team were secretly more than protectors, I was starting to wonder how many more demon-hybrids lived within the walls of The Guild. How many were hiding a buried part of themselves, fearing that they'd be killed or captured, preventing them from challenging the bullshit structures that kept everything as it was.

A silent chuckle escaped my lips. All three of them were now part-demon. Almost like that bond of theirs was soaked in bad luck. And a selfish, horrible part of me wondered if they all reconnected, if Wade and Atlas refocused their attention on Sarah, if I'd have a better chance with Max. I knew they both wanted her too, that her dreams with Wade especially had transitioned into a beyond-friendship sort of thing.

It was an annoying desire, one that made my skin crawl with self-loathing, because I knew that truthfully, I needed to stay away from Max, needed to build those walls up as fast as I possibly could. This life was not one that benefitted from close ties beyond those that tethered teams, no matter what The Guild tried to push in terms of bonding.

"They're not here," I answered, settling on the bare minimum of the truth while nodding back at her two friends. I didn't want to say too much in front of them. I trusted Sarah for the most part, but that connection didn't extend to her new family of canines. "They're in hell too...which is such a weird sentence to say. But we were split up. He went after Max."

Her brows bent in question. Of course Sarah hadn't met Max, but my world had changed so dramatically since she'd walked into our lives, that it seemed wild to have to explain her existence to someone, to think back to a time before she'd come barging in like a storm. So many of my thoughts and actions seemed to revolve around that girl.

"She's a girl," I continued, the descriptor tasting flat on my tongue. She was so much more than a girl. And that, honestly, was part of the problem. "Uncle Cy adopted her. He's back too, at Headquarters. It's a long story. And she's...I don't know, it's complicated. She's...just a girl."

How did I explain everything that Max was? Especially when I didn't fully understand it myself? Because deep down, I wanted her to be *just* a girl. Not the fucking force that confused and complicated my perception of this world. I didn't want my heart-rate to start quickening at the mere thought of her. Didn't want this pit of anxiety permanently knotted in my stomach whenever I didn't know where she was, if she was safe. I wanted to go back to my old life. Killing monsters, fucking random girls, rinse and repeat. No feelings, no complications, just work and fun.

That's what I wanted: things back to normal.

Didn't I?

Sarah arched a brow, lips curved in that smirk that always pissed me right the fuck off. The girl made my teasing sarcasm look tame, sweet even. I was so happy to see her though, that it only brought out my own in response.

"Just a girl, eh?" She nudged my shoulder with hers, an echo of our history buried in the gesture. Sarah was my team member—we shared a lifetime of friendship and antagonism, but things were different now. And while I knew we both wanted to traverse that divide, to find a way to navigate around the edges without falling into the abyss, neither of us knew how to do it. Things were so fucked up. But maybe all that mattered was the fact that we both were reaching for each other—that we wanted to connect, even if we didn't know how to do it. Maybe that was enough. "I dare say there's a light blush coating your delicate cheeks, Eli Bentley. I've never known a girl to fluster you by just mention of name alone."

I shook my head and threaded my arm through hers, basking in the warmth of her skin against mine. Sarah and I had never had an easy relationship, not compared to the others. We were too much alike, grated against each other's nerves, pushed each other's buttons at every opportunity. But seeing her now, it was like finding out a sister had come back from the dead. My body buzzed with excitement, a lightness settling over my chest for the first time in a long time.

"So," I said, stretching the word out, "you live in hell now. How's that? Care to elaborate on what I've missed?"

Her head shook slightly, so slightly it was almost just a

twitch, and her eyes seemed to scream 'later' at me, even though her expression remained the same.

Interesting. She didn't want to reveal too much in front of her new friends either.

We entered a small clearing and I saw a body crumpled at the base of a tree.

"Shit." I jogged over the tree and studied Declan. She was unconscious, but I could see her chest rise and fall with each breath. Her skin and clothes were covered in blood, but it was impossible to tell how much of it was hers, and how much belonged to the others.

But she was alive. She'd taken on a pack of wolves, kept me safe, and managed to still be breathing. Tough son of a bitch. But there were no surprises there.

"Her pulse is steady." Sarah stood above us, tall and imposing, surrounded by more wolves hovering in the nearby shadows. "Jasper has been monitoring her, I'll have him carry her back."

She didn't say where 'back' was, but something in her voice told me that we didn't have a choice about going or not.

I shook my head, picking her up myself. I swallowed the groan as I straightened up, the fresh reminder that I wasn't back to one-hundred suddenly painfully clear. "I've got her."

I adjusted my arms, shifting Dec's weight slightly.

"What exactly happened to you?" she asked, eyeing the crusted blood along my neck and the stains that had soaked through my shirt. I probably looked like an extra from a horror film. "You look like you've come back from the dead. And not because of the wolves."

Protectors generally healed fast from injuries, far faster than humans. But I knew that the sort of healing I'd done in the last few hours was so far beyond what my body would be capable of on its own. That the dream I'd had with Max was probably way more than just a dream. I didn't want to talk about Max though —didn't want to announce her strange powers without talking to my team first.

I shrugged, cocking my eyebrow. "Maybe you're not the only one who's changed these last few months, Sarah." At her questioning glance, I let out a forced chuckle. "It looks way worse than it is. Vamps are asses, as you're well aware. Er," I nodded back to her friends with a wink, "if you still think that anyway? I'm not really sure if you're just pro-wolf right now or if that extends to all the beasties in hell, now that you're one of them."

She rolled her eyes and nudged her shoulder into mine. "Vamps are still sick fucks I'm happy to decapitate. They mostly keep away from us though. The factions in hell are pretty divided—" she paused as the wolf to my left growled, like it was warning her not to divulge too much information. "The details don't really matter. But you guys shouldn't be here, shouldn't be wandering around on your own, without the protection of one of the powerhouses. You might as well be hopping around, begging someone to show you to your gravestone."

Powerhouses? Factions?

Claude and Khali had made it clear that hell was a difficult, undesirable place to be. And when Sarah spoke, her eyes were filled with something I'd almost never seen in them before: fear. Life here was clearly difficult, complicated. Would she come back with us if we offered her a way out? Did *we* even have a way out?

A shiver ran down my spine at the thought of being stuck here forever. Dependent on the kindness of werewolves to keep us alive, assuming we survived long enough to be taken in by one of the factions.

That wouldn't be the worst of it though, kissing the feet of the creatures I'd been sworn to kill. The worst would be leaving behind my father—no explanation, no goodbye. He'd be destroyed.

We walked in silence for a few moments after that, the atmosphere filled with an unspoken question. Neither of us knew where we stood with the other anymore, what to say or ask, how much information to divulge.

Declan's breathing was ragged and shallow, and she'd done little more than mutter a nonsensical word here and there. Neither Sarah nor I discussed her, both of us too worried by what might happen if she didn't start showing signs of improvement soon. Protectors healed quickly, but some things there was no healing from.

"Was she bitten?" I asked, after the quiet started eating away at my skin like a piranha. We'd been walking for what felt like hours, and my arms were starting to feel numb with Dec's weight. After a long stretch of silence I glanced at Sarah, noting the small ridge between her brows as she stared at the ground. "Not that it's a problem if she is," I rushed out, embarrassment making my voice warbly, "there are worse things than becoming a wolf. I just want to make sure she's okay, that she survives the shift." I glanced down, weighing the decision for a moment. "Atlas—he was turned too, you know?"

Sarah's eyes flew to mine in a rush. They were filled with a sad worry, but also with a lingering hope that pulled at my chest. Suddenly she looked so alone—the loneliness only amplified by the glimmer of hope that it might end, that she might share her fate with someone else. Someone she loved. "He turned?"

I nodded, not sure how much was really my place to say about him or the constant war he fought with the new demon half of himself. She seemed to have a much better grasp on the creature beneath her skin, like they were partners—one and the same. Would Atlas have had less trouble if he'd had other wolves there to help him through it? My stomach dipped as I glanced down at Declan, the sweat keeping her hair stuck to her face like it was coated in resin. If I had to do it all over again—help a friend through that—I'd do it better than I had. It wasn't enough, us simply trying to ignore Atlas's demon half, hide him. I exhaled slowly, feeling the weight of everything buckle my knees. "Yeah, it happened the night you—"

I cleared my throat, not knowing how to finish the sentence. Wade and Atlas had only been there that night because Sarah followed some intel and rushed into a mission without proper precautions and protocol. They went after her and, well...

She nodded, lips pulling down in the corners until her face brightened suddenly. The small glimmer of hope I'd seen before was now like the sun—bright, unwavering, difficult to look at. "The Guild's okay with—"

I shook my head, cutting her off. That's why she hadn't returned. She didn't think there'd be a place for her—didn't think we'd be there for her. The Guild wouldn't have been, of course, but it stung to know that she didn't think we would've helped her through it if she came to us. How had we had so much of this wrong? "No one knows. Just us. We've been able to keep it secret, to protect him."

Of course that was becoming increasingly difficult now that half of our team was part demon and included one Max Bentley who was...well, who the fuck knew what the hell she was? Maybe it would be better if we got stuck here. There'd be no hiding all of the changes drifting through my team—we'd all be hunted. I didn't trust The Guild anymore, not enough to put my friends' lives in its hands.

"That night," Sarah started, as she pulled back a thick branch for me to duck under, the dry leaves crinkling as they swept across my forehead, "it was my fault. I shouldn't have been there. He'll probably never forgive me for it. But I—" the words evaporated from her tongue, drifting into a heavy silence.

We both knew who the 'he' in that statement was. She was bonded to Atlas and Wade, but she'd been in love with Atlas since we were kids. Being responsible for his transition, that was an impossibly heavy burden to carry.

"I don't think he blames you." My foot stepped on a twig, the snap creating a loud echo around us. Sarah and the wolves flinched at the noise, their necks craning, like they were expecting someone to rush us. It was strange, being the weakest, least graceful in the group. I was alarmingly aware of how much quieter Sarah and the wolves were, like they were ghosts moving through the forest. Maybe that was why hell was so silent. Not because it was empty, but because silence was necessary if you wanted to stay alive. "And he and Wade—they didn't need to go after you. That was their choice, not yours. You shouldn't carry the burden of their decisions."

Her lips tightened as she considered my words, and I could tell that she was at war with herself. Maybe not with her wolf, but with her own actions and choices.

"And what about you?" Her eyes pierced mine, those blue-green shields that were always so coy and guarded, suddenly vulnerable. She was different, since I'd last seen her. Harder somehow, wiser even. Like she'd lived through a lifetime of experiences since we'd last met. She probably had. "Do you blame me?"

"You made a mistake, Sarah. I'm not going to sit here and tell you it was a good decision." I exhaled, wiping some sweat from my forehead as I readjusted Dec slightly. Sarah gestured for me to pass her over, but I shook my head. Dec had watched over me, had kept me safe and stayed with me. I'd do the same for her. "I make about a million bad choices a week. It's kind of my M.O. So no, I don't blame you for Atlas's transition. I'm just glad that you're okay. That you're alive." I paused, considering her for a moment, opening my mouth and closing it, unsure how to ask the next question.

"Spit it out, Bentley," she said, her voice taunting, "you look like a damn puppy when you make that face."

I narrowed my eyes, secretly pleased with the return to her usual dickish self. Teasing Sarah, I could handle. The guilty, burdened version was out of my wheelhouse. "It's just, why are you here? Why didn't you come home? Instead, you just let us all think you were dead. I know you probably have been going through some serious shit, I just wish that you'd trusted us with it. We could've helped." I glanced down at Dec, at the small pout that somehow still remained despite the fact that she was unconscious, like she couldn't soften and relax ever, not even in sleep.

Declan had been all hard edges and metal walls from the moment I met her, so it shouldn't surprise me that she remained so, even now. Somehow though, it did. She didn't deserve the pain she'd had in her life, shouldn't have had to feel like the only way she could survive was by keeping the world out. "They took it really hard. Dec—"

Sarah nodded, her eyes glazing over slightly, but I saw the tension in her jaw as she clenched it, the way she gripped her hands into tight fists, ready to fight an invisible enemy. "I couldn't—" she took a deep breath before glancing back at the wolves. I got the feeling that even though they were following her lead, even though they were letting us live because she'd asked them to, things weren't all rose petals and daisies with her new crew. Hell didn't seem like the sort of place where true trust and friendship could blossom. Instead, it was the sort of environment that sucked all hope from the world, survival the main and only goal. "They've been taking female protectors, bringing them back here. They're looking for someone, all the factions are, and while it was clear I wasn't her, I turned. So they brought me here," she scratched the back of her neck, her hair falling forward like a screen over her face. "Hell isn't an easy place to leave, Eli. And I have debts to pay."

Debts? What the hell kind of debts? "But still—"

"We can talk about this later." There was a finality to the statement, no question or room for argument. Sarah was always confident and authoritative, even while playful. That hadn't changed in her transition.

I nodded, unable to do much else. "How much farther until we get," I glanced around at the never-ending, dark forest. Sarah and the wolves carved a sure path, turning and directing as one, without so much as a word, but the path we followed wasn't exactly clear or defined—the ground nothing but knotted roots and brambles, "er, wherever it is that we're going?"

"Just through this clearing," she gestured with her head straight forward. "It's why we were after you in the first place.

You were in our territory, so base isn't too far out from where we found you. We're nearly there."

I didn't miss the way she said base—it wasn't with the same kind of fondness she'd always had when referring to Headquarters. This 'base' wasn't home for her. I could almost feel the walls building themselves up around her the closer we got, like she had to shed the final vestiges of herself before entering wherever it was we were entering. And though I didn't know them, the wolves seemed to be doing the same, their postures more rigid, their occasional playful hops and nips, abandoned.

And well, I didn't want to complain, since thanks to Sarah, I was still alive, but something told me that wherever it was she was taking us, we weren't going to be welcome. I was also pretty damn sure, judging by the tight formation of wolves behind us, and who knew how many were tailing us from out of sight, that we also didn't have the option of dipping out altogether, of trying to forge our way on our own, Sarah in tow.

"We could go find Atlas," I whispered, words so low that they almost weren't words at all. "And Wade and Max. You can leave this place."

She didn't say anything in response, the only sign that she heard me, the flex of muscles in her shoulder blades and the thin line of her lips, pressed so tightly together that it looked like she was trying to force whatever words she wanted to let slip back down, where they wouldn't escape.

Instead, we walked in silence, buffered only by the occasional warning growls of her packmates, until we came to a large wall of thick, overgrown, bushes.

Rather than turn down the veering path to the left, she walked up to the wall of green and shoved her arm through, pulling enough of the vines and leaves back to create a small hole. "This is it," she said, her tone hollow and monotonous. "Just through here."

Two of the wolves hopped into the leaves, ignoring her small opening. Like that was the signal for most of the ones in hiding to follow, they appeared as if out of nowhere, each puncturing a small hole in the wall and disappearing from sight once more, far more lithe and graceful than I could ever be. I had a feeling they were going to warn whoever was in charge that they weren't coming back alone, that Sarah was bringing potentially unwanted guests back to their territory.

An even deeper feeling told me that most of the pack would take issue with that; that this temporary life extension Sarah had given us was exactly that. Temporary.

Suddenly I was profoundly happy that Max and Atlas weren't here. Hopefully he'd found her by now; hopefully wherever they were, they were safe.

I took a slow, deep breath, tilting Dec's body in my arms so that her face was guarded by my chest and went to step through the opening.

Sarah laid a firm hand on my shoulder, stopping me as I put one foot in the twiggy hedge, one still on the overgrown path. Her eyes pierced mine, wild, wide, and filled with so much that I couldn't read. Not for the first time, I wished that I'd known her better, that we hadn't had such a surface relationship. Maybe then, I'd know what to do or say, or what it was she was trying to convey with all that heaviness in her gaze.

"I don't know how you will be received," she whispered, her voice little more than a breath. "It might not have been a good idea to bring you here, but I didn't know what else to do. If I left you, my pack might have— " she broke off, her eyes glancing around like she was afraid the leaves were eavesdropping. "Just try and follow my lead and say as little as you possibly can. For once in your life, bottle that obnoxious Eli charm. Protectors are not thought of kindly here. They'll be interested in how you got here though, and will likely take an interest in Dec especially. I'll try and keep you alive through the next few hours and then sneak you out tonight. I'll find a way."

My blood turned cold. And while I wanted to be angry, I knew that if things were reversed, that if Sarah brought a couple of werewolves to Guild Headquarters, that those creatures would be locked up at best, killed at worst. No questions asked.

It was, after all, why we were keeping Atlas's transition a secret.

But what would happen to her if Dec and I disappeared in the middle of the night? It would be ridiculously obvious that it was because she'd helped us.

Which meant that I had to convince her to come with us.

So, instead of fighting her on it, I just gave her my signature wink. "You finally admitting to yourself that I'm charming, Connolly?"

DECLAN WAS RESTING ON A SMALL BED, HER BREATHING SLOW and steady, body hooked up to a makeshift saline drip to keep her hydrated. It was the most that I could do for her, other than monitor her like a hawk.

I dressed the wounds on her back, deep enough to make my stomach turn, and a particularly marled one on her leg. The gashes were inconsistent and swollen, like both spots had been hacked at multiple times in a row. While my field med skills were the best on the team, I was no true healer. It was difficult to tell whether I was looking at claw marks or shallow bites. Suddenly, I found myself desperately wishing that we were back at Head- quarters, that Dec was in the hands of our favorite nurse, Greta.

Her back was torn to shreds in a way that made it seem like they were most likely claw tracks. The muscle was seriously damaged and, from the amount of blood loss and the fact that the wound was still open after our long trek here, I had a feeling they were deep. Down to the bone, even. Dec's reflexes while I worked were also pretty unresponsive, but there was nothing I could do but wait. These were things a protector could theoreti- cally heal from, it would just take time—and time was a thing that we didn't have in this place.

I didn't have enough supplies to do the sort of assessment I usually would.

We were working with outdated, slightly unfamiliar equipment, whether because that was all they had or because that was all they deemed her worthy of, I wasn't sure.

When we'd first arrived, I'd ignored the angry emo stares trailing after us, focused completely on getting Dec the medical care she needed. It had been like walking through the halls in those human high school movies—the scenes when you knew that everyone was just discussing the main character in an unfavorable light. Only way more terrifying because these were not moody adolescents we were dealing with.

All eyes had been on us, the place filled with a sort of silence that wasn't natural. My instinct to get us the fuck out of here as soon as possible had been on full blast and hadn't quieted.

I'd trusted Sarah to have our backs as much as possible as she'd led us to the small room we were stuck in now. It hadn't escaped my attention that while the room had a pair of single beds that looked as fresh as anything had looked since crash-landing in hell, the room didn't lock from the inside.

Instead, I'd heard the distinct clink of a lock on the outside of the door as soon as the three of us were inside. This wasn't just a room to rest in, it was a prison.

"We'll be back to get you in a few minutes, Sarah," a gruff voice echoed through the crack at the bottom of the door. "Boss is mighty interested to see why the fuck you thought it was a good idea to bring protector scum into our base. We're all mighty interested, if I'm being honest with you. Wouldn't be surprised if your welcome back is less warm than you might be hoping. Your pussy only grants you so much favor here."

Sarah's face flushed as her gaze dropped to the ground.

I forced my fingers into a hard fist, freezing my tongue in place so that I didn't lash out at the asshole. I'd only get her in more trouble.

The dickwad left, the distinctly high, scratchy sound of my

blade scraping along the walls, acting as a background tune to each footstep.

Unsurprisingly, they'd confiscated mine and Declan's weapons the second we turned up. But the fact that he was mistreating the weapon that had saved my life countless times—countless times, but not this time—felt like the pack was pouring salt on an already gaping wound. Weapons were sacred to my people.

"Try not to worry," Sarah whispered, though the tense lines in her forehead and the way she was fidgeting with her fingers told me that she wasn't following her own advice. It was rare to see her like this—generally I was used to her being so unshakeable. "I'm having a friend bring some medical supplies. I trust them," she paused, lips tightening, "for the most part. Not everyone here is a monster."

That had been hours ago—the friend who brought the supplies exchanging them for Sarah's company. When she'd left the room, her eyes were dim, jaw clenched. I'd watched with a small prick of pride as she straightened her posture and nodded to me. Then she'd left to go encounter her fate—leaving Dec's to me.

I wasn't great with waiting around at the best of times, but it was especially grating while I was locked down in enemy territory, while the baddies decided what to do with me. I'd been trained from birth to act, to protect. Waiting in enemy quarters made my skin crawl.

How had all of this gotten so completely fucked?

My team was split up, Max was who knew where with the world's most obnoxious vampire, and we had no concrete plan to get out of here—no real direction about how to get home.

Not to mention that we all seemed to be taking turns dancing with death since arriving through the portal.

At least I knew that Max was still alive. Probably.

That dream hadn't felt like just a dream, especially since I woke up with my injuries having slowly sewn themselves back together until I was mostly right as rain.

She'd healed me one before, I just didn't know how it had been possible for her to do it again when we weren't even in the same room.

And on top of all of that, our formerly dead teammate went and got zombied with a mysterious resurrection.

I was happy as hell to see her, but I couldn't lie that her sudden appearance back in our lives complicated things. Her buddies had been trading off keeping guard outside our cell, yelling taunts that would normally make me laugh, but today had only made my blood boil. Most of them had never seen a protector in the flesh, and their curiosity was palpable. The foot traffic outside had been Times Square levels since Sarah ditched, their abrasive faces pressed to the small barred window in our door.

I felt like a damn zoo animal. And honestly, for the first time, I sort of understood why our resident fanghole was such a dick. I was ready to bash some heads in after a couple of hours. Who knew what a couple of years of that sort of treatment would do to a dude?

"Hey." Familiar eyes replaced the beady black ones between the bars.

"You're okay," I said, my body sinking with relief at the flash of blue-green. I hadn't realized how worried I'd been about her until that worry started to leak away at her arrival. She looked okay, no new cuts or abrasions. And while she wasn't exactly smiling, it didn't look like she was suffering through a world of hurt, either. Maybe her pack wasn't completely upset with her for bringing us here. Maybe they'd even let us go.

"Unlock this, Mickey," she said nodding to the short guy who'd been standing guard for the last hour or so, his face grimey as all get out like he'd never heard of the concept of hygiene. He'd been fiddling with a rusty knife, staring at us like he wanted to peel back our skin, layer by layer. Maybe he was a wendigo and not a wolf after all. "Boss wants to see the girl as soon as she's awake, thinks there's a chance she might be the one. Something about a balance shift since she came through the portal."

The one?

I opened my mouth to ask, but Sarah's sharp gaze locked on mine with a slow, almost imperceptible shake of her head.

Not here.

Not in front of him.

Understood.

The man grunted, his nostrils flaring with a silent rage as he shot a dark glare in her direction.

Mickey wasn't one of the ones she considered a friend then, that much was ragingly obvious. Thank god too, because the guy gave me the heebies. Would've hated having to pretend to like him for fear of offending her new bestie.

"Figures," he grumbled, as the sound of a key clanking into a metal lock reverberated on the other side of the door, my heart lifting at the sound of the mechanism shifting. Since when was I claustrophobic? My body was practically screaming at me to grab Dec and burst through that door, the second it was opened. Then run as far and fast as we could. "You go do the unspeakable, bring trash onto our compound, and get nothing but a damn pat on the shoulder. Fucking predictable."

Ignoring him, Sarah shoved into the small room and moved towards where Dec's head rested on an absurdly thin pillow—so thin I was almost certain it was simply a pillowcase with no stuffing at all. Hell wasn't exactly known for creature comforts. My bed back in the cabin sounded like pure bliss right about now.

"Whatever," Mickey grumbled again, his gaze bouncing from Sarah to me, like as far as he was concerned, she was just as much an enemy as I was. "Time I got back to the vamps anyway. Neither of them has said anything useful—I think boss is finally going to give me the okay to kill 'em. Nice and slow. Especially the one with the smart ass mouth."

He gave me one last glare, his lip curled in disgust like I was the grody one, and then walked away.

Vamps?

Was this the same group that had been lingering on the outskirts of Guild grounds? Vampires and werewolves working together was always thought to be impossible. Recently, that had been disproven. Was this the group we'd been chasing for months?

"Any improvement?" Sarah asked, her voice soft and monotonous, like she was fighting back all emotion, terrified of letting even one escape.

"Not really," I leaned against the wall and closed my eyes as exhaustion rolled over me, the wave thick and heavy enough that I could've drowned in it. I'd been so hyper-vigilant since getting here. Having Sarah back here, someone I was used to trusting, was enough permission for some of the adrenaline to leak from my body. But when it did, I was left feeling so drained that I just wanted to collapse and not open my eyes for at least two days. "I'm generally good with getting my team stable until we can get back to Headquarters, but I'm no real medic, as you know, and this equipment isn't exactly the top of the line stuff I'm used to. She's good for now, but I think it's going to be like it always is with these attacks—wait to see if her body heals from the blood loss and trauma. That and I can't tell if she's been—"

My voice trailed off as I glanced at Sarah, my stomach lurching at the realization that she'd gone through this too. Only she hadn't had her team there to keep her safe, to watch over and protect her. She'd been alone, away from people who cared whether she lived or died.

"That and wait to see if she was bitten," she exhaled, blowing a few strands of hair from her face, "and if she was, if her body will fight off the venom or internalize it."

I nodded, unsure of what else to say. Wolf bites were unpredictable. If the wound wasn't too bad, protectors healed over time. But sometimes the venom killed them, and sometimes, on rare occasions, it turned them.

The fact that Sarah and Atlas had both been turned was a wild coincidence. That, or The Guild kept the true facts and figures about transitions and death rates a close-guarded secret. Or maybe transitions used to be rare, but weren't anymore, for some unknown reason. There were too many variables, too many uncertainties and dead ends to make sense of anything anymore.

"Are you in a lot of trouble?" I took a step closer to her and rested a hand awkwardly on her shoulder, trying to provide the small comfort I could, even if it was belated. She looked stronger than she had before she disappeared, but more haunted too. I wasn't sure how to reach her, how to help. I wanted to know as much as she was willing to tell me, but we had more pressing things to focus on. My gut instinct told me that if we didn't get out of here soon, Dec and I didn't stand a chance of surviving until morning. And I wasn't so certain what Sarah's chances of survival in this pack were either—there was a feral quality to the wolves here, like it was a tooth and nail pack with little room for stepping out of line. "Why does your boss want Dec? What do they think—"

My words dropped off on a loud gasp as a sharp pain carved its way through my abdomen.

Sarah's nostrils flared, like she smelled the blood before she saw it. She gripped my hand in hers and watched, eyes wide as a fresh line of blood bled through my shirt. "What—"

"Fuck," I yelled, ripping my arm away and pressing my hand against the cut, trying to stem the blood flow. "You've got to be fucking kidding me. Part of me just wants this fucker to die already. I've generally been one to like being surprised, but these are the worst surprises in the world. Reckless fucking asshole. Doesn't he have a single goddamn friend in hell? Just one person that doesn't want to bleed him dry?"

"Eli—" Sarah stood in front of me, placed her hands on my shoulders to keep me still, eyes wide with worry. I'd been pacing, whispering to myself as I imagined all the ways I wanted to rip that asswipe limb from limb, pull out his teeth, one by one— fantasies that would have to stay just that if I wanted to keep my own body intact. "What the hell is going on?"

I took a deep breath and grinned down at her, embracing the absurd, clusterfuck of deadly dominoes that was life in hell. "Did I forget to tell you? I'm blood-bonded to a fucking fanghole now. And the most annoying leech in existence too, since the fates have the worst sense of humor in the world." I looked up at the ceiling, ignoring the unidentifiable dark stains, and pinched my nose. "I must've been a dictator in a previous life to deserve this shit."

"Vampire? Blood-bonded?" Her focus went from my phantom cut to the door, like she half-expected the guy who did it to be standing there.

I understood her confusion. It was a strange magic to get used to. Even here.

"Yeah, he's the one who brought us here. Appears you and Atlas aren't the only ones to tip Team Six into demonic territory." I doubled over, as blood spilled from my lips, laughing because what the hell else was there for me to do?

This was hell. We were just going to get fucked over and over again—each breath of fresh air tarnished by some new, unforeseen annoyance. At this point, I wouldn't even be surprised if the next hurdle was a fire-breathing unicorn that had a hankering for protector kidneys.

Sarah's eyes met mine, wide with a realization I was too annoyed to follow. "The vamp who brought you here...you've got to be kidding me." Her face went ashen as she glanced towards the door. "Fuck. Fuck. Fuck."

She gripped my hand in hers and tore from the room, ignoring the scattered shouts of the wolves ricocheting down the hall, as well as my protests about leaving Dec unprotected.

11

WADE

I blinked.

And then I blinked again. And then I rubbed my eyes, just in case I was seeing things.

"I don't remember falling asleep," I whispered, as I stared at the girl in front of me—dark clothes a mess with rips and what looked suspiciously like blood, wide eyes, crooked grin twisted in surprise.

"Wade," she said again, the word almost like a prayer on her lips.

"Did you just appear out of nowhere," I gripped the edges of my bed, trying to hold myself back from pouncing on her, "or have I been here so goddamn long that I'm starting to full-on hallucinate now?"

"Yes," she said as she stood up and moved towards me. Her legs were shaky, like simply holding herself up was exhausting.

Seeing her like that, skin clammy with sweat, face so washed out she looked like a ghost, lodged a rock in my stomach. Max was always so filled with life; even after getting attacked by a vampire, she still had energy and her usual spirit, as soon as her eyes opened.

"Yes to the hallucinations or to the appearing from

nowhere?" I gripped the bedding harder. Was this another trick? Another tool my captor had up his sleeve to slowly break my mind? I pinched myself, but all that accomplished was to give me the early tinge of a bruise. Had I fallen asleep? I'd gotten so much better at lucid dreaming, at focusing when I was dream-walking and recognizing the particular feeling of the incubus beneath my skin creeping to life when he met with Max.

This, whatever this was, it didn't feel like that. Was she an apparition?

She closed the distance between us and placed my face in her hands. Her eyes were glazed over with liquid as she studied me, almost like she couldn't believe that I was here, in the same room I'd been in, every time we'd visited in our dreams.

Her face split in a watery smile that made my breath stutter. "Yes I appeared, no you aren't hallucinating. And no," she shook her head and I watched, every muscle frozen, as a single tear made its way down her cheek, "you're not dreaming. I'm here. Like *here* here. I did it. I found you."

I studied every inch of her face as her words washed over me, my chest tightening until I realized that I'd stopped breathing. I opened my mouth to say something else, and then shut it again, probably looking like a fish. Part of me still didn't want to believe it, to believe that she was here.

Because if she wasn't, if this turned out to be a trick, it was the sort of devastation that would chip away at the few remaining vestiges of control I had left. I couldn't fall apart completely, not here.

And part of me didn't want it to be true because if she was here—well, then she was in a hell of a lot of danger. Not only would that mean that she'd really found a way into hell, but that she'd somehow dragged herself into the mess I was suffocating in —she'd literally come traipsing into my kidnapper's little den.

Her skin was so pale, such a stark difference from the usually-vibrant olive tone I was used to seeing. And her eyes, there was a dimness there that I didn't remember. But even through the exhaustion, ignoring the purple bags under her eyes, she was still filled with a sort of energy that seemed to sing—like one look into her eyes could straight out rip my heart from my chest and throw it on the ground.

There were patches of dirt all over her face and arms, and my hands started roaming over the crusted blood, searching for wounds. Was she hurt? Flakes of dried blood fell to the floor, but I didn't see any lingering injuries beneath. Maybe this wasn't her blood, and if it was, maybe her wounds were healed.

She didn't look to be in pain, just like her energy had been zapped.

"Wade," she said again, her hands coming back up to my face to focus my attention back on her eyes. "I'm okay. And you're okay. I'm here. We're going to find a way out of this. I promise you."

"H-how?" I asked, my voice cracked and gravelly from weeks of little to no use. "Max, how are you here?" I stood up, and her hands fell from my face. I needed distance, needed to do something with the sudden rush of energy flowing through my body and settling like a hive of bees in my stomach. I paced back and forth, right at home on the small patch of stone floor that I'd walked over so many times that it was almost shiny from wear. "You need to get out of here. Th-this," my hands swept through my hair, and I put pressure on my skull, trying to stem the panic rising in me, "this place isn't safe. You're going to get yourself killed. If he sees, if he knows—" I shook my head, eyes pressed tightly shut as I tried to force the images of him torturing her away from my mind, "you need to get out of here. Go back home."

Small hands gripped my biceps and gently pulled my hands away from where they were rubbing into my eyes, like I'd been trying to literally erase the last few moments of joy that had imperceptibly spilled into me from seeing her again. How would I go back to surviving in this fucking hellhole alone?

"Wade," she said, her breathy exhale tickling the skin of my arms and sending my lower stomach into a dip. God I'd missed her; missed hearing the sound of my name on her lips. It wasn't the same—dream-walking. Seeing her here, smelling her vanilla scent, faint but present; feeling the smoothness of her hands on me—the dreams were simply pale images of reality. "It's okay. The cloaked man knows that I'm here. He's the one who brought me here."

My head snapped down and I took at her small face, determination spilling back into those striking eyes of hers. Her posture was hunched slightly, like she hardly had the energy to remain standing. Gripping her elbow softly, I led her back to my bed, pressing her shoulders down gently until she sat.

I tried to see this place through her eyes. I was sure it probably didn't smell great, nor did I, after weeks or months of living here—I wasn't even sure anymore. Time had long ago lost all meaning. My days were measured by seeing Max and then not, nothing else seemed to matter. I just needed one thing to hold onto—and she was it.

My skin was grimy from lack of a shower, the fabric on my makeshift bed coated in layers of sweat, lingering evidence of the nightmares and panic attacks that crept into my daily ritual since finding myself here. I fluffed the extra padding I used as a pillow, and swept my hands lightly over the rest of the fabric, as if I could simply erase the debris by my touch alone.

Max grabbed my hands to hers and held them to her chest, her eyes pressed closed as she took deep, slow breaths. Small tears wove around her lashes, and I found myself mesmerized by each tiny droplet. It took all of my focus not to pull my hands from hers and press my fingers to her eyes, to wipe away any of the negative emotion in the rigid lines of her face.

"You're okay," she whispered, eyes still closed. "And I made it. We're together. We can figure the rest out in time."

Time. That word again. We simultaneously had all the time in the world and none of it. All at once. This place, this realm— it didn't operate by the same laws and rules that ours did.

She was here, but she was alone. Did that mean—

"Max, how are you here? Where are the others? Please don't tell me they—"

My voice broke and her eyes snapped open.

"They're all okay, Wade." Her brows bent in focus as she tugged on my arms, guiding me to sit next to her. "At least, I think they're okay. They were doing just fine when Darius and I left them."

I didn't miss the bitterness in her voice, but my attention focused on that name. "The vampire?"

Her lips tightened as her thumb moved in small, soothing circles against the pad of my palm. "He's helping us. He's the one who brought us here—" she shook her head as if trying to unjumble her thoughts, "well, he's sort of the one who brought us here." She let out a heavy, soul-weary sigh and straightened her posture. "The details don't really matter. Let's just say it's been a complicated few days."

Unable to stand it for another moment longer, I brought my palm to her cheek and closed the distance between us until my lips were pressed against hers.

She gasped in surprise, and I swallowed the small breath of air like it was a prayer or communion. It was a small kiss, chaste even, in comparison to the stolen moments we'd had in our dreams. But feeling her lips against mine made all those other moments feel like movies or paintings—imitations of the art, but not the art itself.

After a long moment, I battled with my desire. I was stuck between wanting to take her here and now, and a desperate need to know more information. With a sigh, I pulled away, my eyes latched onto the dark brown of hers—I could see my restraint reflected there in those orbs.

"Max," I whispered, breath glancing along her skin as I tried to maintain a few inches of separation between us. I wasn't sure if it was just because I was an incubus or what, but the pull to her was stronger than ever, until it sank in my belly, a permanent and heavy anchor of need. "Why did you leave the others?"

She stood up, creating a chasm of space between us and began pacing. I found I already missed her touch, and had to physically keep myself from going to her and folding her into my arms, breathing in the scent at her neck and lulling myself into a calm—a calm I so desperately wanted. Needed, even.

"They lied to me," she said, the words so soft that I had to strain to hear them. Her eyes moved from the ground to mine, and I almost had to look away at the emotion pooling in those depths. "Did you know?"

I stood, reaching for her, but she stepped back, signal clear. I swallowed the disappointment and sat back down. "Know what?"

"That I'm not a protector. Not just a protector anyway." She walked over to the far side of the room and leaned her shoulders against the stone wall. Something about her looked so fragile in that moment, on the cusp of shattering into a pile of ragged pieces. The bags under her eyes were more visible suddenly, as was the sallowness of her skin. "Were you aware that Six was charged with keeping an eye on me, with digging up information?"

My stomach dipped, a wash of metal lingering in my mouth. It took me a moment to realize that I'd bitten my tongue, the soft lap of blood bringing me back to the present moment. "Yes, Seamus and Cyrus asked us to watch over you. After the attack outside of the club. And Atlas—" I shook my head, running my fingers through the new growth of hair on my face. "He was suspicious. Didn't fully trust you or Cyrus—he wanted more information. So he asked us to dig up any information we could, while maintaining a healthy distance from you at the same time." I looked at the ground, unable to meet her eyes, until her words settled into focus. "Max, what do you mean you're not just a protector?"

"And have you also been messing around with me to get

closer and manipulate information out of me?" she asked, arms crossed and posture rigid. There was a vulnerability in her eyes that I wasn't used to though, and I could see a world of hurt behind those lashes that cut like a knife to the stomach.

No longer able to stand that look on her face, afraid that I was a part of the reason it was there in the first place, I moved towards her until my hands were gripping both of her arms gently. "Max, I would never do anything like that. Ever." I shook my head, as a wave of anger swallowed me whole. Had one of my team members used sex to get closer to her? I thought back to one of our last dream-walks, when we visited Eli—the wave of lust that slammed into me the moment he saw her standing there. Would he? "Look, if anything, Atlas has been telling us all to keep our distance, to not pursue anything romantic or physical with you. I—well, I just haven't been able to follow that order. But not because I wanted something nefarious from those moments—because I wanted you so much more than I wanted to obey orders not to."

Her body was shivering slightly, while her eyes bore into mine.

I stood still, not wanting to scare her off and hoping like hell that she could see the truth to my statement. What the fuck had Eli done while I'd been locked up in here? That asshole was always on the prowl to sever every emotional and romantic connection he'd ever had, but for some reason, I thought his approach with Max would be different. I was certain he'd felt the same connection to her as I had—would he fuck that up?

I swallowed my sigh, of course he fucking would. Eli was terrified of vulnerability, of giving a shit.

"Look," I started, voice low like I was trying to keep a skittish pet's attention, "I don't know what's happened while I've been gone. And something tells me that Eli's probably stepped in it as he so often manages to do. But we all—" I gripped her shoulder softly, trying to tread carefully, "we all feel drawn to you. And some of us, well, some of us are better at handling that than the others. But if he's hurt you, I can promise it wasn't intentional or about you. He's just got his own shit, and a habit of dodging it."

Her eyes cut to mine at that, like I'd had her convinced until I tried to make excuses for Eli.

I dropped my hands and started to pick at the fraying fabric of my sweatpants. "Okay, let's not talk about Eli," I tried instead, wanting that look on her face to disappear completely. Something about seeing her frustration directed towards me made my skin crawl. "I won't try to make excuses for my team. I have no idea what's been happening while I've been here. But I can promise you that while we were ordered to keep an eye on you and to protect you, I never once entered into that obligation with any sort of manipulative intent. But Max, I need to know what you're talking about—what do you mean you aren't just a protector? What the hell has been happening while I've been, you know," I pointed my finger around aimlessly, "here?"

Her lips lifted at the corners at my awkwardness and my stomach tightened at the sight of it. How could a partial grin have my body twisting into knots, desperate to keep that grin there for even just a single moment longer?

She ran a tired hand over her face, dropping it to her hip as she looked around the room. Her jaw was clenched tightly while she came to whatever decision she was coming to. And then she looked back into my eyes, with a leveled determination and focus, like the vulnerability that was there a moment before had dissolved right in front of my eyes.

She shrugged. "So, turns out you're not the only sex demon in the group." A small, humorless chuckle pulled from her lips, but the look of understanding that flashed in her eyes told me everything I needed to know—she was like me.

A selfish, horrible part of me surged at the revelation. I wasn't alone. I wasn't the only outcast of the group—and maybe, if Max was like me, she wouldn't care that I was a demon, wouldn't let that stand in the way of us being together. If we actually survived this ordeal anyway. We could leave The Guild behind, find a new path out of this miserable war.

But then I caught the way her eyes dipped to the ground, the way her hand fell loose by her side. She looked so dejected. So scared.

And I realized a moment too late why. Like me, she would never be welcome among our people again. Her brother, Cyrus— who knew how they would take the news if they weren't aware of it already. She was going through the same sense of confusion and grief that I'd been battling through since the moment I woke up in this hellhole. The thought that I'd been even momentarily excited by this news made me taste bile.

I closed the distance and folded her into my arms, breathing in the scent of her hair as I held her to me. "I'm sorry, Max. I know from experience how difficult that is to process. But if it helps," I whispered against the soft skin of her neck, "this incredible girl I know told me that I can be an incubus and a good person—that I wasn't evil. And once I let that settle in, once I let myself really, truly believe it, it changed everything."

Her fingers gripped into my shoulder blades and I felt her shake a little against my chest while she processed those words. She pulled away a few inches and looked at me with another one of those earth-shattering, watery smiles. "Also, my arms turn into living torches sometimes and I teleport now. You experiencing any of that or is my hunch that I'm not just a protector-succubus-hybrid, probably an accurate one?"

I opened my mouth and closed it again, quickly running through every text I'd ever read about the hell realm and the creatures that lived here. I'd never once come across a single being that could do either of those things in my research. And I'd spent more time hitting the books than most of the people on campus.

While her tone was flippant and I could see that she was pulling herself back together, one thread at a time, that vulnerability was still projecting out of her eyes—almost like she thought I'd reject her once she unveiled the truth.

I shrugged, grabbing her hand in mine. "Seems like those could be some really useful tools for getting you out of here."

All at once, the walls that she'd been slowly constructing since her revelation seemed to tumble to the ground—she wasn't yet her usual light and cheery self, but I could see the steely determination in her eyes working to get that version of herself back.

She walked back towards my bed and sat back down—the exhaustion that had been so evident before suddenly on full display. What had they been doing to her in here? She looked so rundown, like she could desperately use a solid night's sleep—or fifty.

"I don't fully have control of it," she said, staring at her hands, like the answers were mapped across her skin. "I'm getting a bit better. I think. Almost like each power is a muscle that I have to strengthen." Her brows bent in focus and she went quiet.

"How did—"

A quick glare from her dried the words in my mouth and I stared, focusing on every inch of her face—from her full, pink lips, to her dark, striking eyes—while she sat in concentration.

After a few long moments, I jumped back.

"Holy shit." I walked towards her, my eyes almost blinded from the flames coating her hands. After all of this time sitting in this dark cell, the bright light was almost painful to look at.

I reached a hand forward, mesmerized by the swirling colors lapping against her skin like waves—the triumphant curve of her lips enough to tell me all I needed to know, that these flames didn't cause her any pain.

"No, stop." She pulled her hands away from mine, just as my skin would've made contact, the flames extinguishing just as suddenly as they'd come.

"Sorry." I stared at my outstretched hand and pulled it back.

Something about that fire had pulled me in, drawn me to her like a literal moth to a flame. But while Max didn't seem affected by the strange blaze, I had a feeling I wasn't so lucky. "I wasn't thinking." I looked back up at her face, her eyes darker, pupils blown wide. "That was amazing."

Her lips curved again as her smile deepened. "It's getting a bit easier each time, and doesn't seem to be draining me quite as much, the more I summon it. But the teleporting is still unpredictable and exhausting as fuck." She leaned back against her elbows and stared at the ceiling. "I don't know how to control it. Or what the limits of the power are."

I sat next to her, like my body couldn't stand even the minute distance between us that she had created. Was it the fact that she was part succubus and I was part incubus? The draw when I first met her wasn't nearly this strong, but it was there; almost like an undercurrent waiting to pull me in, lingering just beyond reach—my magic unconsciously reaching for hers. But now, it was like every fiber of my being was aware of every inch of her, desperate to be as close as possible.

Like she was home.

I cleared my throat, and looked at her—I'd deal with my own lust issues later. "I think the best thing for you to do is to work on developing the powers more. Secretly, while you're in whichever room you're being kept in." Her face paled at the thought of going back to wherever she'd escaped from. It was a fear and anxiety that I knew too well. She was out—walking around the prison with a modicum of freedom. It would be hard to give that up, to return to her cell, nothing to comfort her but loneliness and fear. "Just for a little while. They keep us fed here, if a little weak. Build your energy and flex those muscles. And then, eventually, you can escape. This is a war—between protectors and other supernatural creatures. I used to think it was between good and evil, heaven and hell; I used to buy into the idea that protectors were descended from angels, representing heaven's arsenal of sorts, even if I've never believed in such a place. But now, I know it's so much more complicated than that—and messy, as wars always are—and you need to find a way to stay safe. There is no good and evil anymore, just everything in between."

Her jaw tensed as she crossed her arms over her chest. "Are you suggesting it's just me escaping? Wade," the pitch of her voice heightened, "if you think there's even a fraction of a chance that I'd peace out of this place without your ass in tow, you haven't been listening. We've spent all of our energy, pinned all of our hope, on coming to rescue—" she paused, like she was tripping over the use of 'we.' I needed to know what happened between her and my team, but I had a feeling that was information I wouldn't be able to pull out at any pace but her own. "I'm not leaving without you."

"Max—"

"There's no argument here. But I do think that learning to harness my fire and teleporting skills will help us both out. The man who brought you here—"

I arched a brow in question, trying to follow the excitement flowing through her voice. It was difficult to be excited in a place like this and I could almost see the early embers of a plan begin to emerge behind her eyes.

"He teleported *with* you. It's how he brought you here in the first place—just poofed away with you cradled in his arms. So maybe if I work on it enough, I can do the same." A slow, crooked grin appeared on her face as her hands reached for mine, grip tight and vibrating with the anticipation in her body. "Maybe I can even find a way to teleport us all back home," her voice dipped low, eyes down, as if she was talking to herself now, my presence nothing more than a formality, "since we never actually had a plan for getting out of here. We weren't exactly well-organized, with the urgency of the mission and our defiance of The Guild. And who knows where Darius is, or if he's even alive to help us find a portal. But he damn well better be, because Eli—"

"Max—"

"No," her eyes snapped to mine, the dark brown momentarily bleeding into that strange blackness I thought I was imagining when she burst into flames, "this isn't a discussion, Wade. This is the plan. You can either get on board and help, or leave me to my own devices. Either way, I'm dragging your ass with me."

Was she always this fucking stubborn? I wasn't sure what I wanted more: to follow her every whim and fancy or toss her over my shoulder and protect from her own bad ideas.

Still, I recognized the heat in her eyes, the almost invisible wall of steel that seemed to encase her entire being. After growing up with Atlas, I knew this look well enough to know that I stood no chance at getting her to give a little. As much as they liked to pretend that they hated each other, they were a lot alike.

Her mind was made up, there would be no argument.

I sighed, ran my hands over my eyes, like I could massage away the exhaustion and grief of living in this cell—one moment to collapse into myself, and then I was back. I straightened my posture and turned towards her, ready to be given my assignment, like this was nothing but another Six mission, like she was channeling Seamus—albeit Seamus never made my stomach rattle with nervous energy and need. "How can I help?"

The corners of her lips twitched, the swell of her victory too much to completely contain. "What have you learned since being locked up in here? What can you tell me about the cloaked man?"

I didn't know much, but I told her all that I could remember —how frequently, or, rather, infrequently he seemed to stop by, the brief mention of my mother and the fact that he knew her. The occasional aside that I knew little of Guild history, of the intricate war of angels, or creation of hell. He spoke in riddles, never giving me information I could use. It wasn't a detailed report, because I knew in the depth of my being that the cloaked man had brought me here for one purpose, and one purpose only. That purpose was suddenly bright as a headlight, staring me dead on.

"Max." My fingers tightened around hers, pulling her closer, "I think he's after you."

She pulled her hands away and cracked her knuckles, the snaps ricocheting around us like a macabre applause. "Yeah, I got that feeling, I just don't understand what he wants with me."

I folded my hands in my lap to keep from pulling her close— something about seeing her distressed was like feeling a vice around my own lungs. "Well," I smiled, trying to lighten the tension, "I'm going to take a guess and say it has something to do with the fact that you can flambé your enemies and hop around country-to-country without the use of a motorized vehicle."

She rolled her eyes, but the corners of them softened a bit. With a deep breath, she straightened her posture. She was always doing that, breathing deeply before she went on one of her ramblings or when she was coming to a big decision. They weren't quite yoga breaths, but something close. I had a feeling Cy was responsible. Seamus was always talking about things coming back to breath work.

"Okay, so we know that we're dealing with Cloaky—"

"Cloaky?"

"Do you have a better name for the man in the cloak? Cloaky makes him sound less intimidating, more defeatable. The bad guy who successfully ends the world? His name would never be Cloaky." She arched her brow in defiance, but when I only shrugged, she continued, "Right, so Cloaky, one hellhound who deliberately chose not to have me for dinner, and a creepy man who has some serious Cloaky vibes. Maybe they're the same sort of demon? Or similar anyway. Have you encountered anyone else?"

"No, I've only had the pleasure of an introduction with Cloaky. But if the other dude and the hellhound are working for him, we should get you back to your cell before they sound any alarms."

Her face was relaxed, impassive, but I could see her thoughts going a mile a minute, despite the projected calm. "No, I think he wants me to develop my powers. I'm not sure why, but something tells me he needs them. So as long as I don't make a run for it, I don't think it will matter if I take a small hop here and there —it's almost like he doesn't trust that I'll be able to escape, like I don't have the strength yet to do a big jump on my own. And after everything, I think he knows that I won't leave you. You're part of his leverage."

I paused for a moment, studying her, once again taking in the clammy, dull skin, the darkness beneath her eyes. I tried ignoring the throb of guilt at her last point. Max was right, I couldn't make decisions for her. Arguing with her to leave me behind wouldn't achieve anything if her mind was set. "You do seem to be draining a lot of your energy, so he might be right. How did you heal back up from your first jump here?"

Her cheeks reddened as she looked to the ground, "the—er succubus powers came in handy. I wasn't aware I was using them," she rushed out, and I could almost see the guilt weighing her down, "I thought it was just a normal dream with Darius, and then, later, with Eli, things got carried away."

My body tightened, my gut sinking like I'd been punched. I wasn't usually a jealous person. But when it came to Max, it was like all restraints and decorum were cut loose. The thought of that fucking vampire feeding her...in that way. I stood, trying to process the information.

It would be her choice. If she chose a vampire or Eli, after all of this was over, if we were still alive, I'd step aside.

But I would put up a fight and throw my cup into the ring until the moment she told me not to.

"Wade, I'm sorry. I know this is awkward—"

I swallowed her words as my mouth pressed to hers, hard and insistent. Her lips were smooth, but firm as she responded to my kiss, and when my tongue met hers, she let out a small moan that sent all of my blood rushing to my dick.

As I deepened the kiss, my fingers ghosting down her sides to the hem of her shirt, I felt a weird weighty lightness seep in. Like the incubus was rearing its head, clouding my typical reservations and insecurities and pushing me to the edge.

Usually, I tried to bury those moments when I felt myself merge with the incubus, when the power would slowly start to burn at the edges of my mind, but for once, I wanted nothing more than to let myself cling to it, to embrace that flame until every last ounce of me was turned into ash.

"You need your energy, Max, so let's make sure you leave this room sated," I whispered against her lips, letting my breath cool her skin before I pressed my mouth against hers once more. If she needed power, I wanted to make damn sure I was the one to give it to her. I couldn't be the only one between us who felt this connection, who felt the way our bodies aligned like they were designed for each other.

I wasn't exactly sure what would happen when two lust demons fucked, but the incubus lingering at the surface desperately wanted to find out—even more than it wanted to escape this place or survive.

She groaned as my tongue swept along hers, the tip teasing hers with each thrust inside. I felt her melt against me like butter as I dug my fingers into her hips.

I gripped her ass and pressed her down onto my bed, momentarily mesmerized by the vision of her hair splayed out along the scraps of fabric that had functioned as my pillow for so many sleepless nights. My fingers dug deep indentations into her smooth skin, as I watched her arch and writhe against me.

With a quick flip of my wrists, I ripped her shirt up over her head, my lips and tongue working their way down her neck. I pushed her bra to the side and sucked her nipple into my mouth, teething it gently as she let out a breathy moan. My dick pulsed with each small whimper that I pulled from her lips, until I was throbbing hard, each moment of anticipation an exercise in restraint.

My pants were straining against my cock, so I removed hers and then my own, until the tip of my dick met the skin above her clit. I couldn't remember ever wanting somebody as badly as I wanted her right now—every molecule of my body was humming with desire.

"Wade," she moaned, as her hands gripped my hair and her lips pressed against mine, smooth and soft, with a desperate need to create more points of contact between us.

I pulled back, using every ounce of willpower I had and rubbed the tip of my dick up and down her pussy, teasing the entrance and then her bundle of nerves. With one single pass, I was soaked—she was just as ready and aching for me as I was for her. That realization made me feel more powerful than anything in the world.

When my eyes met hers, I saw my own lust mirrored there, but it was the swirling waves of black that kept my focus. Whatever magic had awakened in her was boiling on the surface—there was power there, in her eyes, but also a gentleness. My chest squeezed, until I couldn't breathe, until all I could think about was fucking her, and only her, for every waking minute that I had. My dreams with Max had been amazing, the best sex I'd ever had and it wasn't even taking place on a physical plane, but in person, like this, every last inch of my body was lit on fire. Whatever connection or draw I'd had to her seemed amplified somehow, like each caress solidified it just a little more—my body developing an addiction I wasn't sure I'd ever want to kick.

Unable to wait a moment longer, I sheathed myself inside of her, the warmth and wetness from just one thrust almost enough to make me come instantly. I could feel her tightening around me, encouraging me to keep going, to ram into her until we both forgot where we were and everything that had happened in the last few months—until everything disappeared except for this moment, between the two of us.

My lust was feeding off of hers, and vice versa, as my incubus and her succubus greeted each other the best way they knew how.

I went slowly, teasing her with each thrust forward, keeping my pacing erratic and unpredictable, so that she was forced to dance on the edge, responding to my every whim. Her claws dug trenches down my back as she writhed below me, the slight tingles of pain only amplifying the pleasure. She'd drawn blood and, surprisingly, I liked it.

In a move so quick I almost couldn't trace it, she wrapped her legs around my hip and spun until I was below her. It was a move she'd used many times in sparring sessions, but I'd never been as fond of it as I was now.

With a teasing grin and arched brow, she hovered above me so that just my tip rested at her entrance—she held that position for a long moment, with the kind of restraint that I would never have, teasing and enjoying the power exchange, before slowly allowing her weight to fall on top of me, one centimeter at a time. Gravity was a sadistically slow and subtle bitch.

A low groan pulled from my chest. The torture was exquisite.

I tried sitting up, to move so that more of my skin was touching hers, but she shoved me back down, palm splayed against my chest as she rode me, slowly building the pace while I watched.

She was magnificent, and in this moment, I didn't care if she fucked every member of my team and every supernatural creature in hell, so long as I could see her like this—wild and untamed and filled with the sort of desire that had the murky boundaries between me and the incubus blacking out everything around us.

My fingers stroked up her thigh and gripped her ass, as I took over the pacing and pulled her up and down on top of me.

For a moment, she resisted, trying to take the reins herself, but then I moved my thumb to her clit, rubbing in slow, teasing circles, and she stilled, letting go completely. Her head fell back in ecstasy, lips parted in a delicious and silent moan as I pinched her clit between my thumb and forefinger.

The pressure she was using to keep me down was long forgotten, so I sat up and nipped at her neck, swirling my tongue along her pulse point as I flipped us around so that I could get a better angle. She didn't fight being on the bottom this time, her body pliant and light as it built up for release. I positioned her bent right leg over my shoulder, lifted her ass up so that she was at an angle, and rammed into her. Again and again and again.

"I want to feel you spasm around me" I said, stroking my finger in slow circles around her clit.

As if that was all she needed, she let go, her body spasming around my dick as her teeth sank into my shoulder to muffle her screams.

"Good girl," I whispered into her hair.

Quickly, I pulled out and followed her over, the warmth of my cum coating us both as my strength gave out and I sank down on top of her.

For a long moment, we both lay there, cocooned in the energy of our lust as it pulsed around us. I felt more alive and powerful than I ever had, as if in giving her energy, my own somehow had doubled.

Her chest was rising and falling in heavy bursts, her skin coated in sweat as she studied me. Eyes that were usually warm and brown, were a tumultuous flurry of black. While she seemed as exhausted and spent from our collision, the energy I felt seemed to radiate and suffuse her as well, like we were both drinking from a well and taking our fill.

The bags under her eyes were all but invisible now, her skin plump and filled with a lustrous glow that radiated around her in a soft caress.

She opened her mouth, her full lips parting on a gasp and then she closed them again, like she didn't know what to say or how to say it.

"Let's just lie here." I pressed a finger to her lips, afraid that she'd burst whatever bubble of bliss we'd just created with her reason and rationality. I wasn't ready to come back to the real world yet. Whatever we'd just done—it was like being born into something new.

It felt so right, holding her in my arms, like this was how it was always supposed to be—me and her. I wasn't sure I'd ever outgrow this feeling, that I'd ever stop wanting her. If anything, I only wanted her more now. I'd been bonded before, knew what the shadow of that connection could be.

This. This was next level.

The energy I was slowly starting to recognize as the incubus, lingered on the edges, clawing against my skin with greed, ready to initiate round two, to claim her permanently. But I pushed it back, locking the incubus down as far as he would go. Neither of us understood the limits of the demons we harbored, and until we did, the less we relied on their presence, the better. They were a part of us, but they weren't nefarious in the way we'd been taught creatures of hell were—I'd watched Max come alive with the power and joy of it. It was beautiful.

I folded her in my arms, pressing my forehead against hers as I regulated my breathing with hers—both of us drawing long breaths in and out as we slowly came back to earth, together.

Well, hell, I guess.

The jealousy and feverish need that had taken over was tucked away with my demon, but I couldn't resist pressing my lips against hers once more as I studied the emotions raging behind her glassy eyes. There was so much going on behind them, though her face remained impassive. I couldn't get a read on what she was feeling or thinking, which was strange.

Max always wore everything on her sleeve, never having needed the social skills to hide her thoughts before moving to Headquarters. It was one of the things I loved about her—how open and free she always seemed to be. Her time at The Guild, and in hell, had created the need for depth there, the need for disguise and question.

Amongst protectors, vulnerability was seen as a weakness, and I could see her closing up before me, guilt and satisfaction, and so many other things swirling together before she locked them out of sight.

"You look stronger," I said, my stomach dipping at the crater carving its way between us.

Silence. Her eyes were unblinking, whether looking at or through me, I couldn't be sure. There was a storm inside of her, like she was on the edge of something big, but she wouldn't let me stand on that cliff beside her.

"I'm sorry if that, if you reg—"

She pressed a finger to my mouth, the spark of her skin pressing against my still-swollen lips like a live-wire running through my body.

"I feel stronger," she whispered, her eyes closed tight, like she was trying to look inside of herself, to locate the energy and dissect it. "It's...it's just a lot. And somehow both new and familiar. If that makes sense."

My stomach dipped at the fear and hollowness in her voice. I opened my mouth to ask which specific bit she was talking about, before I realized that was part of the problem.

In the past few months, this girl had moved away from her isolated, protected home, moved to a community woven together with secrets, been attacked on multiple accounts, traveled to hell, found out she was part demon—

The 'it' was everything.

"You should get back," I said, pulling a few inches away from her, giving her space even though every fiber of my being seemed to fight me on it. I'd known I'd wanted Max since the moment I'd laid eyes on her. But I'd understand if she needed time to figure out the shit-storm that was thrown at her, and time without me there to tarnish any clarity. She deserved more. More than I—

"You want me to leave?" her brows dipped in the middle as her eyes widened, some of the vulnerability leaking out.

I shook my head, gripping her arm gently as I nudged her to look in my eyes. "I don't want you to leave. I never want you to leave. But you should get back. Before your absence is noticed. You have more strength now, you can go back and practice. Exercise those new badass supernatural muscles of yours. And maybe soon, you can come back. Having someone here, having *you* here—it helped quell some of the loneliness, helped remind me why it's so important to get out."

Her lips curled up a bit, the movement barely perceptible, and she nodded. "Okay."

She slid back a few inches, creating a clean line of separation between us. Her eyes closed, face scrunched up in concentration, fists clenched like she was fighting an invisible foe.

And she stayed exactly like that, sweat slowly coating her forehead, for what felt like twenty minutes. I could feel the frustration radiating off of her as she tried desperately to tap into a power that she didn't understand.

I recognized the frustration so acutely because I'd felt it myself. And Max had been the one to provide some calm, some clarity. Her steady presence was what helped me finally figure out how to tap into the outer edge of dream-walking, to pull it closer.

My chest pinched watching her go through the same cycle of frustration and failure.

Tentatively, so as not to startle her, I reached my fingers forward, covering her small fist in mine. "Max, just breathe. One big breath in and one big breath out."

Her eyes sprang open, nose flaring softly as she tried to swallow the suggestion and follow it. I understood. When frustration was high, it was always annoying to hear someone tell you to just take a breath. And even more annoying was the fact that, so often, a breath was all that was needed.

"You'll get there," I said, my voice barely a whisper, "just try to remember the feeling of what happened before. Were you thinking about something specific? Were you doing something that might have triggered it?"

Her brows bent in the middle as her eyes danced between each of mine, like a hypnotic pendulum. "I was running," she closed her eyes, pulling herself back into that moment, and I let go of her hands, "that man, the one almost as terrifying as Cloaky, was chasing me as I ran. And right as he reached for me, I reached for you, my body a tangle of nerves and desperation, and then," she opened her eyes, sharp brown that seemed to carve into me each time I looked at them, "then I was here, with you."

I nodded, not needing to say anymore. The exchange was clear, she knew what she needed to tap into.

Her mouth tightened into a tight line as she stood from the bed, silently putting her clothes back on. Soft pink highlighted her cheeks, like she'd completely forgotten she wasn't wearing clothes and wasn't sure how to feel about being naked in my presence.

I turned my head, trying to give her the privacy and the distance that she seemed to need right now.

There was a long moment of silence that tore away at me, like a flesh-eating virus. There were so many things that I wanted to tell her, that I wanted to protect her from, that I wanted her to understand.

I didn't want this distance between us, and I hated that the gulf seemed to grow only after we were finally together again, after all of this time.

"Maybe," I started as I turned back towards her, an idea crossing my mind.

But she was gone.

And I was alone again, sitting in a puddle of pride and fear.

12

DARIUS

"Two hundred thousand one bottles of beer on the wall," I sang, my voice echoing around the room as I hung, content as a clam. My voice was a little pitchy, but I'd listened to worse music during my years in the human realm.

"For the love of god, man, please fucking shut your mouth for two seconds. I can't even hear myself think at this point."

It was the first thing Nash had said to me in over three hours. The annoyance layered in his voice only made my grin widen. Not that he could see it.

He'd been tight lipped ever since I'd regained consciousness, body lithe and happy after that dream with Max.

My little protector really was part succubus. Point to me for early guesswork.

It was hard to decipher at first, the subtle pull of energy, the intoxicating flow of power. Sex was always about power of course —about exchanging it and lingering in the drawn out transfer of it between bodies—but succubi took it to the next level. I knew what to expect from a succubus. But damn—Max was a fire-cracker when the demon came out to play. For such a typically bumbling and awkward girl, she'd turned me into a puddle of goo, all but begging for each caress she deigned to give. And I wasn't completely convinced she even realized what she was doing—every move she made seemed effortless, artless.

I wanted more.

I could still feel the shadow of her blood on my lips. I'd never bitten a lust demon, never consumed blood through a dream.

It wasn't quite the same as it was in person, but her blood had helped to stabilize me as she pulled my energy, helped me maintain some of the power and control. But no. It was nowhere near how it would've been if I'd bitten her in person.

My mouth watered at the thought of it—she'd tasted sweet, but there was an unexpected level of depth, like a fine wine aged to perfection. I'd give my left testicle for just one drop of her in real life.

But where other lust demons had simply drained my energy stores in the past, she'd helped heal me right up at the same time, stitching me back together, inch-by-inch, with her magical vagina.

I knew she was pulling from the same power source she'd tapped into with Khali, back at my asshat of a brother's place. I didn't know how she managed to draw from it in a dream. I'd never heard of such a thing before. Khali could heal, but it was always in small doses and almost always took more from her than she was able to comfortably give. Dream-walking at the same time? How the fuck had Max done it? And why did it seem like it came so naturally to her? That sort of magic took serious time and patience to master.

Hell, Khali still didn't have that much control over her healing powers.

I closed my eyes, breathing deeply as I tried to force my focus back on the current situation. The dream had been delightful, but all it had done was solidify my interest in the peculiar protector even more. She was a mystery that kept throwing me for loop after loop.

And while her powers were impressive—and far more developed than I'd imagined possible at this point—that only made me worry more. She'd be a valuable prize in this place. I needed to find her before someone else did.

Strangely, I found myself wanting to preserve her naivety, to shield her from the harsh reality of this world—and her own.

I wasn't sure I'd ever desperately wanted to protect someone, to watch from front-row seats as their life unfolded. I didn't want to miss a second of Max Bentley's future if I could help it. Something told me it was going to be one hell of a show.

And me? There was no question anymore—I was all in with her. From the moment I saw her, all of my focus had pointed in exactly one direction. I was ready to stop ignoring that pull. It was far too alluring to fight. Even if it meant having to deal with a sanctimonious band of protectors and misfits in the process.

The sniveling shifter had come in a few more times, slicing and dicing as he saw fit, but for the most part, the boost of energy Max had given me healed most of the more egregious injuries. And, most importantly I'd gotten my voice back—something Nash had been on the receiving end of for hours.

While I was slightly concerned about my current predicament, the shifters weren't my biggest liability.

But, surprisingly, the protector hadn't been killed yet either. He'd managed to keep himself alive in hell, for more than an hour without my protection, so perhaps he wasn't completely useless after all.

Either way, I was alive, had the best wet dream ever dreamt, and Max was still breathing, I just didn't know where. All things considered, this was definitely not the worst torture session I'd been on the receiving end of.

"You know more than you're letting on," Nash whispered behind me. It was the first not-insult he'd directed at me since I'd woken up in this asscrack of a doghouse. I'd almost forgotten he was here, but now I could feel his eyes drilling holes in the back of my head. My skin was crawling with the feel of his judgment. "About the girl—" there was curiosity in his voice—too much curiosity for my taste. My fingers tightened around the metal chains, sending a low groan echoing through the room, but I tried to keep my composure. I didn't want him to know he'd hit a nerve. Nash was an important player in this realm and, like all of us with that kind of power, he was willing to do anything to make sure that he kept it. I didn't want Max to become anyone's prize but mine. "What is she?"

Silence

"Where is she?"

I clenched my jaw.

"What do you want with her?"

I wasn't sure I could answer that question if I wanted to.

"What do you know, Darius?"

I cleared my throat, tilting my head from side to side to loosen up a muscle cramp. "I'll tell you what I know," I paused, drawing out the moment and wishing like hell I could see his face, "two-hundred thousand bottles of beer on the wall, two-hundred-thousand bottles of beer." My voice bounced around the room in loud waves. I was man enough to admit that I couldn't carry a tune to save my life.

"Insufferable."

"Take one down, pass it around."

The door opened on a loud creak, punctuating my verse.

"One hund—ah. A newcomer." A grin split my face. I was so happy to see someone other than Mickey that I didn't care if they were here to carve ugly pictures into my skin.

Happy for the distraction, I waved a few of my fingers at the tall figure, the only part of my hands that had any mobility after being suspended from the chains for who knew how long. One thing I'd learned about captivity: it was best not to count time. In fact, it was best to pretend that time simply didn't exist. Hours, days, months, years—they all just rang with a resounding disappointment when counted with no clear end in sight.

"Is Mickey tired with us already? Sending in some fresh blood?" I took an exaggerated breath in as the wolf framed by the doorway took a few confident steps into the room, "you smell a little withered, a bit foul. But don't worry, I'm hungry and an avid member of the Clean Plate Club, so I won't let that get in the way of my appetite."

Second thing I'd learned: deliberately pissing your captors off was never a good choice, but often a fun one. Sometimes it was even worth the beating afterwards, just to see that familiar, achingly delightful jaw tic.

But this wolf was harder to piss off than the last. He simply cocked an eyebrow, head tilting slightly as he studied me and then dipped his gaze behind me towards Nash, as if I wasn't interesting enough to hold his attention. "When they said there was a pair of mouthy vampires refusing to cooperate, I should've known it would be you two. Not the first time you've been the base of one of my headaches." He took a step closer as his dark eyes bounced back to me, narrowing with the familiar edge of disgust.

There it was! Ah how I loved inspiring that expression. Truly an art form, really. I should run a Master Class.

"Last I'd heard you were on the other side." His dark eyes pierced mine, something in the narrowed expression ringing familiar.

"I was, but I'm back now. Good of you to keep up with my travels," I said, trying but failing to make my disinterest sound genuine. "Sorry, I don't mean to be rude, dog breath, but have we met?"

"You don't remember me?" His voice was cool, clipped. Spoken with the leveled monotony of strength and the confidence that came with power. He was as unlike my new friend Mickey as a wolf could get: tall, imposing, corded with muscle. His dark hair was swept back with precision, his clothes neat and pressed, despite the fact that we were standing in the armpit of hell. "The pair of you were always a couple of raging pricks."

"Excellent," I grinned, nodding my head back towards Nash. "See that, Nash, I thought so—this gentleman does know us."

"Fucking hell, just kill me already." Nash's tone was filled with the boredom of one who'd spent an afternoon crunching numbers, head bent over a desk, not one who'd been tortured for hours on end in the belly of an enemy's den.

"I wish that I could." The man's nostrils flared slightly as he took a few steps forward, not stopping until my foot was less than a few inches away from him. "I'm sure there are few things that would give me more pleasure; and I don't doubt the world would benefit from the peace left in your absence."

"Brave man, you're within striking distance." I wiggled my foot and mimed kicking him, only letting the toe of my shoe brush against the fabric of his pants.

"Even when you're tied up with no means of protecting yourself, you're still an arrogant asshole." He shoved my foot back, the room ringing with the groan of my chains as my body bobbed about like a straining punching bag for a long moment. "No more games. The girl. Where is she?"

"This again. I've already told your sniveling sidekick. I don't know. Sounds like she's got the power to disappear completely if she really wanted to." I paused, basking in the chips of armor falling away as the man's apathy made way for the early tremors of rage. People were so fun to toy with.

The man's nostrils flared almost imperceptibly, but it was enough to confirm that hot, liquid anger was bubbling under his skin. Judging by the daggers his eyes were throwing and the constraint keeping his body in place, I assumed if he wasn't going to kill either of us, that it was because he knew exactly who we were.

"Jameson?" Nash said, chuckling softly. "Holy shit you look different."

Jameson? The name tumbled around, rattling a few memories loose, until the image of a pale, thin boy stood out from the rest.

"You're shitting me?" I could feel the grin carve across my face. "You filled out."

I tried to parse the image of the man in front of me, radiating a frustratingly stuck-up power, but power nonetheless. He'd been so gangly as a kid. We'd run into him a few times back when we were younger. He'd flitted from pack to pack, never quite settling into any specific place in the world. There was something about him that had always seemed so...lost.

"Talk about a glow up. Look at you, finally having a play at top dog. Gotta say, I'm impressed." If my hands were free, I would've patted him on the back. I loved when things—and people—didn't turn out the way I'd expected them to. Made life much more entertaining.

His posture was stiff, like he had to use every muscle in his body to keep himself still. When I looked into his eyes, surprisingly I found no fear. He knew who we were, but he didn't fear us. Interesting.

There was no such thing as a true alpha in a wolf pack, not in the way humans thought of them in their silly books. But it was undeniable that Jameson was the leader of this pack. The man in charge.

His eyes darted quickly to the discarded box of tools Mickey had left. His lip curled as he surveyed what he had to work with. Most of the metal was rusted and coated with blood.

A true artist learned to care for his tools. Mickey was no artist.

Something told me the same could not be said for Jameson.

Jameson pinched his pants as he bent down, the muscles in his thigh straining against the fabric, and reached for a particularly gnarly looking blade. He studied it with a careful focus, eyes narrowed and assessing. And then, in one smooth motion, he stood and bent his arm at the elbow, throwing the blade with the same effortless guile only a skilled dart-player could manage.

"Ouch." I drew the word out slow and taunting as I looked down at my torso. I couldn't see too well from this angle, but he'd met his mark if the small tingle of pain was any sign. The blade stuck out of my abdomen, though it hadn't hit anything particularly important, buried to the hilt.

Something told me Jameson had never fully gotten over being the underdog, that he didn't quite like being poked like a bear.

Excellent. That meant good ol' Nash and I had found a chink in his armor. The more of those we collected during our visit, the more leverage we'd have during our escape. And, more importantly, the more fuel we'd have for vengeance.

A clumsy cadence of footsteps echoed down the hall, but Jameson seemed uninterested as he studied the blood pooling at the waist of my pants. With a quirk of his lips, he dove through Mickey's toy box, searching for his next choice.

Good for him. He'd grown a spine since we'd last seen each other. No wonder he'd survived as long as he had.

"I want to know where the girl is," he mumbled, his voice buried in the sound of metal scraping against metal.

"As do I," I said, my smile faltering slightly as a fresh, unwelcome wave of fear carved a path through my gut. Not fear of whatever the hell Jamey was going to do to us. But Max was wandering through hell, alone and scared, with powers that she didn't understand. It was a recipe for disaster. And the sooner I got out of here, the better. She needed me.

It was weird feeling—being needed. And even stranger was the fierce need to protect that seemed to roll over me wherever and whenever she was concerned. I'd managed to go most of my life keeping people at a distance, neither caring nor concerning myself with whether or not they survived. But something about this girl had me...invested; invested on a deep enough level that I was starting to grow almost concerned with my new obsessiveness.

Vampires were a possessive sort, that was nothing new. We didn't share our things, didn't like it when other people played with them—or even looked at them. I'd felt territorial before, but never...this. Whatever 'this' was, anyway. Since the moment I laid eyes on the girl, she'd become like a stubborn craving, subtle and intriguing at first, but now every cell in my body seemed desperate to find her, to keep her close, to keep her safe. Like she was mine. Almost as if she were my true mate—the way the stories painted that bond, sentimental and consuming.

My heartbeat stilled as the realization flooded my system. Weakness. She'd become my biggest weakness. And if Jameson— or anyone—needed to find a way to get to me, they'd learn quickly that the way to do it would be through her.

The blood in my veins went cold as I listened to the soft clangs as Jameson took his time sorting through the tools.

A piercing, loud howl and jangle of metal sounded down the hall—some angry wolf had been raging in its puppy cage for hours. The noise was starting to get on even my nerves, which was quite an achievement.

At the very least it was making my song about beer bottles sound downright eloquent.

"Boss—" Mickey's face appeared in the door frame. His hair was shaggy and knotted, his beady eyes bouncing between me and Jameson as he bent over at the knees. He nodded towards the hall, even though Jameson hadn't bothered to look up at him. "They're really struggling down the hall. I don't think there's going to be any breaking through to that wolf—he's too far gone. You want me to put it out of its misery?" A flash of jealousy burned in his gaze as he watched Jameson regard his tools with a cool, critical, disdain.

Mickey valued being the one to do the dirty work. He clearly didn't want to share that purpose. If he wasn't needed for a job most didn't want, what reason did anyone have to keep him around?

My brows lifted as I studied him, almost impressed with his ability to understand how this world worked. He was a miserable sort of creature, but he understood his place, understood how to ensure his survival. That suggested more intelligence than I'd given him credit for initially.

Without acknowledging the weasel, Jameson threw another blade, smaller this time, that landed about an inch from my heart. He had power behind his throw, that much was clear. And while I was certain that he was enjoying his lazy game of darts, I had no intention of playing his game for long. The pain didn't bother me much, but I had more pressing concerns to deal with.

"Boss?" Mickey's voice was so small, inconsequential, and he looked so much *less* standing there, huddled and crumpled next to his much more impressive-looking leader.

"Leave it alone, Mickey. I want to learn why a wolf is traveling alone in my territory, attacking my people, before I put it out of its misery."

"Sir—"

"I can't kill Nash." Jameson ignored his underling, unsheathed a blade at his thigh, much weightier and better-maintained than the ones in Mickey's carnival of horrors, and took a few steps towards me. "But something tells me that since you're on his side of the curtain, your value has diminished considerably." He pointed the blade at my abdomen so that the tip pierced my skin, clean and enticing. If it had been someone else on the other side of the blade, I'd have almost found the feeling pleasurable. "So maybe I just kill you instead?"

I arched my brow, looking down at the man as he carved a thin, lazy line down my torso, his eyes burning with the sort of hatred that was earned. What had I done to this man to burn so strongly in his memory?

Maybe I ate one of his friends.

"I've always wanted payback for what you did to Shirin." His thick, well-groomed brows were pressed in a thin line, the muscles in his jaw ticking as he tried to keep his composure.

Shirin? Who the fuck was Shirin?

I sighed. "You can't honestly expect me to remember every woman I've wronged and left wanting, Jamey. No one's memory is that good. And my mind has been tampered with for years while I played a long game of lab rat with The Guild. You've got to give me more than that."

I could actually hear his teeth strain together as he tried to keep his emotions back.

"Oh yeah," Nash let out a soft chuckle, "Jesus, I'd almost forgotten about Shirin." My silence was enough to signal that I had too, drawing another laugh and low whistle from Nash. "Really? Of course you don't. Your mind instantly lets go of anything that's lost your interest, that isn't an immediate threat." There was a bite to his words now, the amusement trickling away. "Shirin was the wolf you fucked way back when, let you take a bite out of her every now and again."

A low growl rumbled in Jameson's chest, the vibrations of it almost lapping against my skin.

"One of yours, I take it?" The memory of the girl still hadn't solidified, but it was taboo for a wolf to give blood to a vampire willingly. That had been part of the excitement of it for me. Blood was a sacred, powerful source in this world. It was one of the reasons vampires were so powerful—those of us who were able to maintain a steady diet anyway. "Probably explains why she wasn't very memorable—" I swallowed a groan as his fist collided with my jaw.

Thankfully, because I was dangling above him a few feet, he wasn't at the best angle for strong impact.

"You never did know when to keep your mouth shut," Nash's words were clipped, but I could hear the war of amusement and — fear, maybe?—leaking out from his voice.

"You get one more chance," Jameson bit out, his teeth gnashing together with fury, "the girl you came with, where is she?"

"Not here, not with me." I was surprised by the peculiar wave of sadness that was climbing its way up my neck.

I saw it in Jameson's eyes, he was at his fill. He really was going to kill me. All that trouble, all that excitement, just to end up dead in this obnoxiously rank hovel. The sheer mediocrity of it made me want to howl with laughter.

He pulled back his arm, blade gripped in his long fingers as his dark eyes met mine.

My stomach dipped as I saw the truth—I'd pushed him too far. I'd been dancing along the edge, toying with him like he was nothing more than my prey. But sometimes it was all too easy to slip a toe over the cliff—and once that happened, there'd be no coming back, no one to pull me up over the side.

This was it. Hopefully the others would find Max, rescue her, then get the fuck out of hell. Something big was coming for her, and if I couldn't protect her, I had to hope that the others could. The thought of her no longer existing was worse than anything I could imagine in that moment, worse even than death.

"Stop!" A sharp, breathy voice echoed around us as the pretty girl from earlier came running into the room. Her heart was racing so fast I could see her pulse dancing against the smooth skin of her neck. "Jameson, you can't—" she paused, glancing briefly at her leader, then back to me, "please, don't kill him. This whole thing is more complicated than we imagined."

Her bright eyes were pinched at the sides, like she wasn't sure whether she'd just made things better or worse. But I saw the tightness in Jameson's shoulders, the way he craned his neck slightly so that he could study her.

He was listening.

And when I breathed an audible sigh of relief that things weren't ending just yet, my gaze caught on a familiar mop of dark brown hair and a pair of brown eyes that were looking at me with the strangest combination of anger and fear.

"Useless One," I crooned, watching the tirade unfold in his eyes. Anger that I was here, fear that I'd be dead, frustration that he needed me alive—he was becoming a fairly easy creature to read. "I see you've met my new friends."

He ignored me, scanning the room, the strange tapestry of emotions melting away until all that was left was fear. "Max. Where's Max? We thought she'd be with you."

The accusation pierced deeper than when Jamey stabbed me

in the gut—the truth of the whole thing laid bare. I'd taken Max from the group, left them high and dry, only to go and get grabbed up myself. And now—who knew where she was?

"She's not here." My voice sounded hollow, even though I didn't want her here, not really. I didn't want this slimy pack of wolves to get their hands on her, to get ahold of her power. But at least if she was here, I'd be able to formulate a plan for getting her out. Especially with Eli and Nash to help. Instead, we were left with nothing—no clues, no direction.

"What the hell is going on?" Jameson barked out, neck straining with tension, though he dropped the weapon to his side, the angle no longer threatening my heart. His eyes softened as he met the girl's. Another weakness, then. "Sarah, you have two seconds to explain. My patience is not high today."

She glanced at Eli, weighing something for a long moment. "He's a member of my old team, one of my best friends—" then, slowly, she lifted his shirt a few inches, until a thin, carved line of red stood out against his clammy skin, "and he's blood-bonded to that vampire."

Nash hissed air through his teeth, the chains above him rattling with his shock at the big reveal. I tried to keep from rolling my eyes, but I was only so strong. Dude could be so damn dramatic.

Jameson's interest was piqued, however, and he took several slow steps towards Eli. I could see the disbelief slowly turn to shock as he took in the mirrored carvings on Eli's chest and abdomen. I had a few cuts that hadn't seemed to travel through the bond, but, for the most part, it was undeniably true.

"You fucking jackass," Nash barked from behind me, betraying the first iota of emotion since we'd been captured. "A fucking protector? What were you thinking? This—this is what you do with your goddamn stolen freedom."

Well, truthfully, I hadn't been thinking. But I owed Max, and something told me that if I'd let Eli die, some vital piece of her would be destroyed as a result. And while I didn't fully understand my investment in keeping her whole, I couldn't deny its stronghold over me.

My jaw clenched, as I focused on the reality of what everyone was seeing. It was easy to ignore my brother's ire over the connection, almost fun if I was being honest, but seeing the judgment and confusion on everyone else's face in the room, made me hyper aware of the fact that I was powerless here. Made me aware of the fact that, when it came to Max, I was powerless. A shadow of who I'd been before—pliant, full of weaknesses. Hell was no place for that kind of vulnerability.

Jameson gripped Eli's chin, pinching as he tilted his face from side to side, as if the answers he was looking for were written across his features. "Interesting." Then, he said the one thing that made my stomach drop. "And who is this Max you're asking about?"

Eli's nostrils flared, eyes glassy with anger as he looked into Jameson's eyes. Surprisingly, he didn't look as badly as I thought he might—like he'd only gotten a small fraction of the injuries I'd obtained during my captivity with the Scooby Squad. Despite the fact that he was surrounded by wolves, he stood strong, not uttering a single word. Maybe there was hope for him yet.

Jameson let out a soft chuckle at his silence, turning to Sarah instead. "Do you really expect me to keep a protector alive, Sarah? You know what they'd do if the situation was reversed."

She dropped her eyes, nodding once. "He's my family, Jameson" She straightened up, posture relaxed but confident, "and he might be useful."

Jameson arched a brow, dropping his fingers from Eli's face as he stood back, assessing, thoughtful.

"He came through the portal with the girl. They all did." She clenched her fingers into a small fist, like she needed somewhere for her frustration and fear to travel, to solidify. The movement was subtle, but I caught it. "And they might prove useful for taking down The Guild, for infiltrating the North American Headquarters." Her lips bent into a thin, small frown as she nodded towards Eli, her eyes focused only on Jameson. "His father heads the field teams there. The information we could get from him would be invaluable and—" she ignored the flash of betrayal that crossed Eli's face, meeting my gaze instead, "it can't be for nothing that a vampire of his caliber would bond to him."

I tried not to preen at the comment about my caliber. Tried. It was nice being recognized sometimes. Valued.

"Boss, you can't actually be considering this. First you take in a stray that attacked two of our own, now you want to give them the benefit of the doubt too? People are going to think you're going soft, they'll start taking advantage." Mickey squared his shoulders, stood tall, like he was trying to make himself appear more imposing and confident than he was. "She's just trying to protect her friends. You can't trust them." His beady eyes shot to Sarah, both of them locked in a silent war I could tell they'd been fighting for a while. Both of them vying for Jameson's attention, both desperately in need of his protection. That made them enemies of each other. Another weakness I could use. "You can't trust her. I knew the moment you brought her into the fold, that it was a bad idea. She's nothing but a warm body and pretty face—that'll blow over soon. Once a protector, you're always a protector. The wolf is nothing but a shadow in her."

Something unreadable flashed across her face, something that made Eli's stiffness loosen a bit, like he better understood the nuances of her emotions than I did, of her fears.

"Are you questioning my judgment?" Jameson turned to Mickey, gripping the front of his shirt until the two were close enough to kiss.

Mickey mouthed "no," but all that came out was a squeak as he vehemently shook his head.

Without letting go, Jameson turned towards Sarah, "I'm trusting you on this, Sarah. I'll keep your friends alive for the night, but it's under the explicit condition that you make them useful to me—and that you find a way to get me that girl. Our pack depends on that leverage." The last sentence was little more than a breath, like he hadn't meant for the words to slip out in our company. "And the other girl, your cousin. The second she's awake I want word of it."

Her expression was impassive. Her only response was a slight tilt of her chin in acknowledgment—the movement slight, like she was afraid one wrong word or movement would cause the tenuous hold she had on the situation to go tumbling to the ground.

He reached his hand forward until it was a few inches from her cheek, before he cleared his throat and dropped his arm, his eyes flashing back to me, like he'd forgotten I was here, hanging about like a gutted pig.

For the first time, I noticed that the hard angles of his face, the shadow in his eyes, were more than the remnants of an acknowledged grudge. There was something more going on here. Jameson was scared.

And while it would have been nothing for the Jameson I knew before to be frightened—something told me that whatever ghosts were haunting him now were the sort that would make any man's legs tremble.

It was the same tangible fear I'd felt the moment I dropped into this realm, the strange static of unpredictable magic that laced the air, coating us all like a thick fog.

Hell was not the place it once was—not even the demons on the top of the pyramid were secure in their standing, impervious to the fall.

Most disturbing of all, was the question that kept dissolving and reforming in my mind: what the hell did Max have to do with any of this?

Because I could no longer pretend that she wasn't at the very center of it all—that she wasn't herself the eye of the storm.

13

MAX

I was tired. But I was also hopeful. Not only had I found my way back from Wade's room with success, but I'd managed to shift to the inside of my tomb when I did.

It had taken me a solid twenty minutes—time that I spent trying to feel the pull of my body from one place to the next, to replicate that particular tingling sensation, the emotional foundation that seemed to push me over the edge, all while trying not to hyperventilate with panic that Cloaky or his equally-creepy friend would find me first.

I hadn't seen a soul on my way back—no hellhound, no man. I wasn't sure whether that was a good thing or not.

Now that I knew where Wade was, knew beyond a shadow of a doubt that the dreams were real—that he was alive and only a long, meandering walk away—it changed everything.

We had a plan. But in order for that plan to work, I needed to maintain my energy, needed to slowly and carefully strengthen the new muscles—to test the limits of my new powers until I could turn them into something useful, use them to get us the fuck out of here. One thing was certain—I was fucking sick of hell and I wanted us home.

I hugged my arms around myself, almost giddy with excitement at the possibility. I wasn't sure how long it would take—hours, days, weeks—but I had a plan to get back to Cy and Ro.

Palms held up, I stared at my long fingers, seeing them with new eyes as I slowly recalled that feeling of fire. As soon as the flames licked against my skin, I felt a smile carve across my face. This was the sparkly new trick I had the best grasp of, probably because it was the one I associated most with feelings of fear, anxiety, anger—and there was no end to those feelings in this realm. My body was almost always humming with the lingering anxiety, adrenaline constantly coursing through my veins as I looked behind every corner, never sure who to trust or what might attack us next.

Us.

I sat back on the platform bed as a sharp pang went through my chest. The rest of Six. Darius. I couldn't trust them either, but I knew that regardless of my feelings, I didn't want them dead.

I needed to find them, the sooner the better. Hell was a dangerous place, and I wasn't sure how much longer we had before one of us was picked off permanently. I was still angry with Six. Especially Eli.

But so much of that anger was also directed at myself—the frustration I felt at not understanding who—or what—I was, felt like a constant needle poking at me. I refused to let myself linger in that frustration for too long, as tempting as that slippery slide into anger was—because when I dissected it too much, it meant one thing: I didn't belong anywhere.

Not with The Guild, not with humans, not even with demons. I wasn't a vampire or werewolf, and while I was part succubus, I had no idea where the fire or teleportation came from. I didn't fit into any box I tried to squish myself into.

Suddenly a wave of exhaustion washed over me and I pressed my head against my makeshift pillow of rags. I tried breathing through my mouth, the musty smells emanating from the fabric enough to make my stomach turn. My very empty stomach.

For a moment, I let myself dream of the cafeteria at Guild Headquarters. Unlimited food, piles of pizza and steak and potatoes. How had I let myself take that for granted? I could almost smell the salty char.

The hunger pangs hit with a vengeance as I wiped the drool from my lips.

Shifting from one place to another was draining, my body weary and sore, like I'd been hit with some awful human flu. Even breathing felt cumbersome, the subtle lift of my chest with each breath as exhausting as a marathon.

I needed to practice, needed to get stronger when it came to using these powers, but I also needed to conserve my energy. It was such a strange Catch-22, and I followed the lulling loop of the chicken-egg scenario as if it were a lullaby, until my lids grew too heavy to lift, my thoughts too jumbled to follow.

When I opened my eyes and saw her lying in front of me, an arm's reach away, my stomach flipped. I stopped breathing altogether.

"Wh—" My eyes trailed from the bruises slowly turning purple along her arms, to the ribbons left of her shirt, where deep claw marks were trenched along her belly, down to the deep gnarled, bloody mess of her leg. My vision blurred when my gaze reached her eyes—wide, filled with a fragile disbelief and fear. "Declan? What happened to you?"

Silence.

Her face was pale, lips trembling like she'd seen a ghost, eyes unblinking.

I grabbed her hand, lacing her fingers through mine, suddenly desperately in need of feeling the warmth of her skin against me. She felt so fragile, the quiet strength I'd grown so used to over the last few months, now just an echo.

"Decl—"

Her name tumbled into a grunt as she pressed herself to me, arms wrapping around my chest so tight that breath struggled to fill my lungs. I felt her nose press into my hair until it grazed the side of my neck, her fingers digging into my back like I was a life raft and she was lost at sea.

"Is this—is this one of *those* dreams?" she whispered, her breath ghosting against the shell of my ear and sending chills down my spine, the desperation in her voice palpable enough to make my stomach ache with empathy. "Please tell me that it is, please tell me that you're here, that you're okay—that you're alive."

Her words were mumbled and marled and my brain stuttered, trying to catch up to the sensory overload—warm breath that left tingles in its wake, the soft, fresh scent of her that I could only avoid by holding my breath. She smelled better than food right now. She was hugging me so hard it felt like she was afraid I'd shatter into a million pieces if she let go, the pressure alone enough to cloud my eyes with liquid.

For a moment, I let myself sink into her, to rest my head against her shoulder and breathe her in—to forget, for one minute, that she thought I was a monster, that she'd been keeping things from me with the rest of them. Being in her arms made all the bad temporarily disappear, until all that was left was a low, comforting...rightness.

"Dec—" I cleared my throat, pulling away from her. I needed some distance to keep my brain from going fuzzy at the nearness of her. I never knew where I stood with Declan—even before I'd overheard her talking to Eli. She was almost as hot and cold as Atlas. "Where are you, what happened? Are you okay?" My throat clogged with emotion and I blinked back tears, as horrible visions blew through my mind. What had happened to them while I was gone? "The others, are they okay?"

Her eyes narrowed, like she was trying to focus on the conversation, but her thoughts kept slipping somewhere else. Every muscle in my body froze as her gaze consumed me, inch by inch, drinking me up like she still couldn't believe that I was here.

"Are you with Wade, Max? Did you find him?" There was a

soft accusation in her voice as the words that she left unsaid lingered in the air: *Did you find him after you left us all without a word?*

I nodded, my breath stuttering at the slight flare of her nostrils, the hardness in her eyes. She was mad, that much was clear. But there was something softer mixed in there too—hurt, a bone-deep sort of pain. And the thought that I could cause someone like Declan pain of that magnitude sent a jolt of shame through my stomach.

I shouldn't have left them, not like I did. I hadn't exactly planned on getting attacked by a pack of werewolves and then being swept away into a dungeon by my strange new powers and a magical dagger—but I had chosen to leave them behind in a dangerous world out of anger and betrayal. Deep down, I knew that my reasons didn't really matter, not in the grand scheme of things.

That was the strange thing I was learning. Intention mattered, but so did the reality of the situation. And the reality was, that while I was angry at them all and needed space, my ditching Six the way I had left us all separated and vulnerable.

Two wrongs didn't make a right, and all that other annoying garbage that 30-minute specials liked to harp on about.

Steeling myself, I took a deep breath in, trying to calm the storm of emotions raging through my chest. "I'm with Wade. He's okay." My voice cracked as her eyes widened with hope, an emotion I knew she rarely allowed herself to feel. "At least he's okay for now anyway."

Her brows bent in question as she pressed her finger to my chin, forcing me to meet her eyes. "Max, where?"

The point of contact between her finger and my face sent a wave of something startling down my spine. Yearning, maybe? I wasn't sure. But I nibbled on my lip and tried to force myself to focus, to not buckle under her scrutiny. Declan was a force, she'd always sent my stomach into a forest of knots—mottled and complex and thick as metal.

I needed to find a balance between myself and the members of Six. The whole lot of them turned things upside down, made it difficult to see straight. I wouldn't be their punching bag, just some person they kept on hand to push around and bark orders at, a ticking time bomb they were just waiting to go off. But I also wouldn't make things more difficult than they already were.

As much as they infuriated me, I couldn't deny that I was drawn to them—that whenever I walked into a room, my eyes instantly sought them all out, pulling me towards them like magnets.

"I'm not sure exactly. The place I've been seeing in my dreams is real, and I'm being kept in a separate room from him." I closed my eyes, trying to push the hope in her eyes from my vision—when Dec let her walls down like that, when she let her real emotions shine through, it was enough to make my knees wobble. I needed to focus. "I haven't been able to look out of any windows, so it's hard to know for sure where we are, but there's something briny about the atmosphere. Almost like we're near a body of water or something." An image flashed through my memory, of running for miles over terrain with Darius. "There's a river in this place. At least one. Darius showed me."

She let out a soft grumble at that, no doubt more pissed by the fact that I'd left with him than that I'd left altogether. She'd been warming up to Darius. I'd noticed how the harsh edges of her features when she looked at him had begun to gradually soften. Something told me that softening angered her almost as much as his vampiric nature did in the first place.

"I think it was the River Styx. It's the only water I've seen. I could be wrong, but maybe we're near there?"

Her stern expression broke for a moment, making way for something more subdued, a childish wonder. "That place is real?"

I nodded, relaxing slightly. "I guess so."

"And the vamp," she said, though the word didn't drip with venom like it usually did, "is he with you there too?"

"No."

Something in my expression caused her posture to straighten. She gripped my hand in hers, drawing a slow circle in my palm with her thumb. Tingles shot all the way down my spine. "We'll get you out, Max. Both of you. I promise. I'm just —" she paused, shook her head, took a deep breath, "Right now I'm just so fucking relieved that you're alive. I thought for sure that—" her words melted into the air as her eyes met mine.

Guilt boiled low in my belly again as another flash of pain eclipsed her gaze. "And you? What happened?"

She looked down at herself, like she'd almost forgotten that she was hurt. Maybe here, in this dream-walk, the pain was gone? I wasn't sure how any of it worked, not really. "Were-wolves." Her eyes widened as they turned back to me, and I knew what she was going through, knew that panic of suddenly remembering memories that had been just out of reach a moment before. "Oh my god, Eli. He was in bad shape. Like really bad shape. I need to get back to him, need to make sure they don't get to him—"

I pressed my palm to her shoulder, trying to quell her panic, even as my own resurfaced. "I dream-walked with him not long ago. I think—" I paused for a moment, my stomach dipping at the look in her eyes, like she was lost in a wave of uncertainty and fear, looking to me to keep her grounded, afraid I'd deliver the sort of news that made your stomach drop. It felt strange, being the one with more answers between the two of us. I was so used to always being the one left in the dark where things with Six were concerned. "I think—I think I healed him. Like I did back at Claude's." A grin split my face as a realization took hold. "Let me—Declan, let me try to heal you."

She opened her mouth like she wanted to argue. She was always so resistant to giving up power, to admitting to her weak-nesses, to letting people in—always so determined to keep people at as far of a distance as possible. I saw the indecision war across her features, the tension in her shoulders, the hitch of her breath, and then, surprisingly, she relaxed, her expression going soft, warm even. "Yeah, okay."

My lips lifted in a small, tentative smile and I nodded, not wanting to speak a word in case it encouraged her to push back again, to redon her familiar, impenetrable mask. Carefully, I placed one hand at her stomach, the other on her ankle, focusing all of my attention on the wounds, envisioning them slowly closing back up, knitting back together, as Khali had guided me to do before. I felt the familiar hum along my skin, could almost feel that thread between us that I'd held onto when healing Eli.

Something inside of me was reaching for something inside of her, but it was impossible to grasp hold of, like ships passing in the night—there but not quite within reach of each other. It hadn't been easy, healing Eli. Neither through my dream-walk nor with Khali's help, but it had been easier than this. I felt my brow dampen with sweat as I poured all of my energy into trying to latch onto my power, into feeling for that strange life force of hers that I knew would be there if I just reached a bit further, just pushed myself a little harder.

"Max," she whispered, though her voice sounded far away. Why was she always so far away?

Declan had been a closed book since the moment I'd met her. Every time I thought I'd broken through, earned her trust or her friendship, something would happen to change the dynamic between us instantly—two steps forward, one step back.

But two steps forward, one step back was still one step ahead of where we'd started. I latched onto that, onto those moments where I could see that spark of connection, where I could see the real her shining through—the version of her that wasn't shadowed by fear or distrust or pain.

The movie night she'd joined with me, Izzy, and Ro—the way she slowly let herself melt into the couch that night, joining in on our meaningless banter and debates. I remembered the way her posture went from rigid to relaxed after the first hour or two, the soft smile in her eyes when she'd teased me and Ro.

The time she came to see me after Wade had been taken. She'd protected Ralph, brought him to a safe house, even though I knew that the idea of letting an unpredictable supernatural creature loose set all of her warning bells on high. And she did it anyway, because she knew how much his safety meant to me, knew what I'd sacrificed to obtain it.

The way she constantly tried to protect me, even when doing so forced her to wall herself off a little bit more, like she was afraid of growing too attached to anything or anyone that might not last. She was always pulling me back from danger, trying to stand between me and whatever force we were facing.

The look in her eyes when she told me about how her parents had been killed by vampires in a Guild lab—and then her uncle soon after—about how she'd found Atlas and her team and tried to rebuild a semblance of family.

It was there, in those moments, that the connection between us flared most brightly, and I clung to that connection like my life depended on it.

Because hers did.

And as difficult as Declan could be, as often as I didn't know where I stood with her, I couldn't lose her. Something inside of her called to me, like we were always meant to be in each other's orbit, we just had to find some way to stop resisting physics. To let it be, to let ourselves collide into each other.

My eyes were pinched together so tightly that my head was starting to ache. I felt my heartbeat gallop against my ribs, hard and clunky, my breaths coming out in short, hurried gasps. For a moment, it felt like I was drowning, floating away into an infinite aether. And then slowly, I felt that tether between us start to solidify, felt my breath meld with hers, my heartbeat steady to keep pace with her pulse as it pounded against my palm.

I wasn't sure how I knew, but I knew all the same that whatever I was doing, it was working. I could feel the limits of my energy ram against a wall, warning me to stop, telling me to pull myself back before I went too far. But there was something so intoxicating about that connection, about feeling her against me, with me, that it took all of my focus and willpower to resist.

With a deep breath, I tried grounding myself, forcing myself to disconnect, and once I did, I opened my eyes. Her wounds weren't completely healed, but they'd healed enough that some of the color had come back to her complexion—her eyes wide with some heavy emotion I couldn't name as they stared into mine.

I felt the heat between my palms and her skin, tried desperately to ignore the way touching her seemed to make my belly dip with nerves. Briefly, my thoughts flashed back to the last time I'd been this close to her—in the hotel before we were attacked by the vampires from Claude's bar. It was the most open she'd been, our bodies so close they were almost touching as we talked, and it had almost seemed like she'd wanted them to be even closer, like keeping the distance between us was like keeping air from our lungs. Was I imagining that then? Or had she felt the fire between us as strongly as I had?

Heat flared low in my stomach as I moved my hand up, just a fraction of an inch, subtle enough that I wasn't sure whether it was intentional or not, but my finger grazed the lower curve of her breast.

She gasped, the sound almost inaudible, her full lips parted as she froze, her eyes locked on mine. Like me, she was holding her breath, both of us on the edge of the moment, standing at a cliff, not entirely sure whether to pull back or dive headfirst into the abyss.

Slowly, my other hand moved up her calf, inching slowly—to the side of her knee, to her outer thigh—her skin pebbling as my fingers grazed over the holes in the fabric. I felt her breath quicken against my cheek, warm and airy, my own lungs matching each inhale and exhale as a familiar feeling prickled at my skin.

The air around us felt charged, almost alive somehow, like the anticipation of an inflating balloon, both of us waiting for it to fill too much, for it to burst. My brain went fuzzy as I focused on her bottom lip, full and smooth, feeling my own dampen as my tongue swept against it.

Her breath caught again, sounding almost like a moan, and just as much as things had felt frozen and paused before, now the room was fast-forwarding, my body dizzy with anticipation as things started to unfold at a pace my foggy brain couldn't keep up with.

She leaned forward, her lips brushing against mine in one tentative touch. The movement was so quick, so soft that I wasn't even sure if our lips had really met at all, before she was pulling away just slightly, so that our mouths were a breath apart, both of us waiting for the other to process.

We were frozen for a long moment, my eyes focused on the curves of her lips, each breath that I inhaled cutting the distance between us in half, until it felt like it would go on forever—me getting closer and closer, but never reaching her at all. We could stop here, brush this off as a fever dream, pretend that it was nothing more than an accidental touch.

The thought filled me with a deep ache, and my eyes darted to hers. I saw the same need that was tugging at my stomach, pulling me towards her, reflected back in her eyes. And then, in a frenzy, I pressed my mouth against hers again, this time hard and certain so that there'd be no mistaking my intent. One fraction of a second and I was already drunk on the taste of her.

Slowly, like she was just as afraid the moment would dissolve as I was, she sucked on my bottom lip, the sensation sending a wave of heat rolling through my body, until I was pulsing with anticipation.

Her hand swept up my cheek, threading through my hair to the back of my neck, as she pulled me closer, somehow both strong and gentle all in one motion. She slipped her tongue into my mouth, slowly, like she wanted to give me enough time to pull away if I wanted to.

I didn't. The second her tongue touched mine, I felt my heart-rate pick up into a feverish dance. I wanted her licking and kissing me everywhere, the brief thought of her tongue between my legs had me throbbing.

She moaned into my mouth as her other hand gripped my ass and pulled me forward, until she was leaning us both back, our legs threaded together, her thigh pressing against my core.

I ground against her, once and then twice, the sensations convulsing through my body as she deepened the kiss. Her kiss was teasing and slow, like she was trying to savor each touch, drawing each moment out until I felt every inch where she touched me light on fire. My hand slid up her body, gently grazing the smooth plane of her abs, her peaked nipple, before winding into her long, luxurious waves. I pulled gently on her hair as I bit her bottom lip, grinning as her chest arched against mine.

I swallowed the breathy gasp and grinned, suddenly feeling more powerful than I ever had. Knowing that I had the power to make Declan Connolly make that noise, mold herself against me like putty—it was enough to make my head swim.

Kissing Declan was intoxicating, every atom in my body felt high on the feeling, impatient and greedy.

She pulled back slightly, her bright eyes wide and glistening with an openness and vulnerability I hadn't seen in them before. There was lust radiating from her like heat waves, that much was obvious, but there was something else, something softer, unfolding in her expression as her chest pressed against mine with each heavy breath.

My throat tightened at the sight of her, below me and vulnerable, my stomach filled with nervous flutters as her hand gently swept a few stray hands of hair from my face. The feel of her skin on mine, such a simple gesture, sent a bolt of electricity through my body. I knew that I was soaked, almost embarrassingly so. To want someone so much, so badly, from just a few seconds of kissing. I felt somehow both pliant and powerful against her, waiting for her lips to meet mine again, to see what would happen if she came even more undone for me.

And I wanted more. So much more. Not just one quick kiss, one test of the waters. I'd never really let myself think about being with her in this way before, not really, but now that I'd felt my mouth against hers, my body molded to hers just so, I knew I wouldn't be able to think about her in any platonic sort of way again.

I wanted all of her—wanted to trace every inch of her skin with my tongue, wanted to watch the walls she'd always kept so strong and tall crumble away as she let herself give in to the moment. Something told me that a completely free and relaxed Declan would set the world on fire. My world, anyway. She was a ridiculously good kisser, teasing and unpredictable, and my thighs tightened around hers as I thought again about what it would feel like to have her mouth in other places.

As if she could feel it, as if the energy in me was calling her to, she leaned in, closing the distance between us again—the look in her eyes hungry this time, feverish almost, as her tongue swept her bottom lip, leaving it glistening, inviting.

I stopped breathing as I recognized what this was, could feel my vision blurring slightly as I pulled away just as her lips met mine, the touch light and slight and so not nearly enough. But I pulled away anyway, untangled our legs and crawled backwards, my limbs bumbling awkwardly, not even daring to breathe as panic flooded my body.

"Max?" her brows dipped as she leaned towards me, her shoulder lifting slightly and sagging, like she wanted to reach out to me but thought better of it.

How did I keep doing this? First Darius, then Eli, and now—Declan? What the hell was I doing? I needed to get these dream-walking powers on lock before I ruined every fucking relationship I had. It was like I'd climbed into hell and suddenly my solution to every problem was to hump it.

"Sorry," I stammered as I got to my feet. I could feel the blood rushing to my head, could feel my cheeks burning with shame, my eyes blurring with a layer of tears. "We shouldn't have —I shouldn't have done that."

When I glanced down at Declan, the look in her eyes almost cracked me in half. Any openness that had been there a moment before was bolted behind an iron wall, stronger than before, the green in her eyes sharp and unforgiving.

"Right." The word sounded metallic on her lips as she dropped her gaze, like she couldn't stand to look at me anymore.

Guilt boiled low in my belly, painful and ruthless, and my knees went wobbly as I tried to keep all of my emotions from leaking all over me.

Could she understand now? Did she see the succubus peering at her from beneath my skin, could she recognize the unfamiliar magic that seemed to pull between us, threading us together until all reason was pushed away? Could she recognize that I had the power to hurt her? To turn every fleeting attraction into something so much larger, something she might not have really wanted at all.

"I—" I wasn't sure what I was going to say, but whatever it was, evaporated from my lips as I glanced at hers. Pulling myself away from her had been agonizing, and the temptation to straddle her and pick up where we'd just left off was so strong it made my skin itch with anticipation, like the succubus was pushing against my skin, stretching it taut and thin, desperate to break out.

Declan shook her head, her long hair cascading over her shoulders, disguising half her face from view, covering the rest in shadow. Hair that was silky and soft, and that I wanted my fingers entwined in again.

My stomach dipped as I imagined pulling that hair back, exposing the long column of her neck, while I licked and nipped, eagerly pulling out reluctant and low moans from her lips, until she went wild and feverish with desire again—until the expression on her face was replaced with the one from a few moments ago.

I wanted to peel her clothes off and touch every inch of her, wanted to dip my fingers between her legs, to taste her and see what she looked like when she gave into that feeling I was slowly beginning to associate with sex—freedom, power, and something almost like floating.

Instead, I cleared my throat, glanced slowly and aimlessly around the sparse room. I wasn't sure exactly where she was right now, but I could tell that she wasn't in the warehouse I'd left them all in. Even so, it looked like most of the places I'd encountered in hell—dark, abandoned, in desperate need of a first-rate cleaning service. "I should go."

I couldn't look her in the eyes as she nodded, the small movement somehow enough to send a chill through my body. Her expression was impassive, except for some slight tension in her lips, like she was fighting to keep whatever words she wasn't saying swallowed down.

"Dec—"

"We'll come find you, Max. Just stay alive until we do." There was neither warmth nor anger in her voice, just a tired, steely indifference and a slight rush to end the conversation as quickly as possible. Like she was simply reading a report back to Seamus before she could start unwinding from a particularly taxing mission. Somehow that apathy pierced sharper than a blade.

And then, because there was nothing else for me to do or say without royally fucking things up even more, I left—leaving a small, fractured piece of myself behind.

❧ 14 ❧

DECLAN

The walls were gray and cold—like all of hell's rooms seemed to be. I found myself almost missing the mythology of fire and brimstone and torture. At least that visual came with a personality, expectations. Instead, everything here felt empty, morose, and drained of life. Utterly unpredictable.

"You're awake." Eli was hovering over me, his brows pinched in the middle as his eyes scanned me head-to-toe. It wasn't the sort of perusal I was used to from Eli, there was no teasing flirtation in the way his gaze moved from my chest to my bare stomach. He took a step back, an audible breath escaping his lips. "Thank fucking god. You're healing. I don't think it was a bite. You scared the absolute shit out of me, Dec. Seriously, you do that again and I'll kill you myself."

"Why are you whispering?" I kept my voice down low as I sat up, my head dizzy from the sudden movement as I clocked the small room, the closed door, the complete lack of surrounding decor. This was not where I'd fallen asleep, of that much I was certain. "Where the fuck are we?"

Eli's shoulders sank as he sat next to me, his arm pressed against mine. He wasn't normally the touchy feely type, but it

262

was almost like he needed the connection right now, needed the warmth. "The pack that attacked you," his nose scrunched slightly, "we're in their headquarters."

"What?" I stood up, my heartbeat pounding as I scanned the room for a weapon. The sudden movement had my head swimming, but my hand caught the wall before I fell on my ass. I wasn't dying, but I also wasn't exactly ready to run a marathon either. "What the hell happened?"

He stood, grabbed me by my shoulders, and gently but forcibly pushed me back down on the bed. Once I was seated, his hands cupped my face as his warm brown eyes, wide with worry, came into focus, so very close to mine that I almost flinched away. I could tell he was checking me for a concussion from the way his eyes darted between mine, tilting my head softly in each direction so that he could get a better look. But I knew that, like his, my face would be cast in shadow—the room's lighting was impressively dim.

"You have to keep your voice down. We don't want them to know you're awake, not yet. You're the one they're interested in."

I shoved his hands away, panic squeezing my chest as I tried to calm my breathing. We were trapped in a tiny room, alone, in enemy territory. And I wasn't getting nearly enough information from Eli's partial explanations. But above all of the panic, was a healthy dose of confusion.

"Eli," I stared back into his eyes, blown wide and jittery. I almost felt bad that I'd been unconscious and left him alone with his fear. I wasn't used to seeing him like this. "Why are we alive?"

His jaw tightened, his eyes hardening slightly as he sat back on the concrete floor and rested his arms on his knees. "I don't really know. They're looking for someone—one of us."

"Us?"

"A protector. I don't know why, but the leader—he seems to think it's a girl. It's why she was able to get us in, how she kept them from disemboweling us out there. Honestly, it's the first bit of luck we've had since stumbling into this hellhole—" he paused, a soft grin momentarily lifting the corner of his mouth, "pun intended."

"She?" I brushed off his joke, even as the familiarity of his humor settled some of my own concern. My stomach tightened as a hollow memory started to resurface. Me, clinging to a tree, a girl emerging from the forest, a fierce expression on her face as she took in the scene.

My breath hitched as the girl's features grew clearer in my watery memory.

Was it—was it possible?

A loud snap, and the door started to push its way inside the room.

A figure followed it, bathed in a soft glow of light from outside. My throat ached at the sight and I tried to swallow back the wave of emotion threatening to choke me.

Even through the shadows, I knew what I was looking at— who I was looking at.

Greenish-blue eyes that were so similar to mine it had occasionally felt like looking into a mirror, a tall, curvy frame, lined with lean muscles. Dark hair that looked like it was in desperate need of a brush.

I felt the breath pull from my lungs as my vision clouded over. Then I closed my eyes tight and opened them again, just in case I was seeing things. Did hell serve us visions? Hallucinations concocted to give us hope, only to make the misery that much more acute when they dissolved? It was one hell of a way to torture someone.

"You're awake." Her voice was just as I remembered it— confident and just a little raspy, the way mine got when I woke from a deep sleep. "I was getting worried."

"Sarah?" I stood again, shoving Eli's hands away when he made to guide me back down to the bed. "Is this—are you —real?"

Before I could lift a foot in her direction, she'd closed the distance between us, burying my face in her neck as she squeezed me to her, holding me so tight my ribs started to hurt. But a good kind of hurt, if there was such a thing. I breathed in her scent—fresh and clean, but a little more earthy than I'd remembered—the familiarity washing over me as a sob pulled through my body.

Sarah had been home to me when I needed one most. Her and Atlas, together, had saved my life growing up, given me a family, something to fight for.

I held onto her, unable to support my own bodyweight from the shock of it. My fingers dug into the flesh of her back, probably hard enough to leave marks, but I was petrified that if I gave even an inch, she'd disappear—transition from the solid, breathing force that she was, into something ethereal, like air.

"How?" The word was garbled and nonsensical, and I realized as her hair stuck to my cheek that I was full-on ugly crying against her. I never cried. In some ways, hope was more punishing than grief.

She let out a long exhale, like she was weighing something. But then she responded with one word. "Wolf."

I squeezed her even tighter, if that was possible. We'd never needed many words between the two of us, most of the time we could communicate with little more than eye contact and a well-timed eyebrow raise. That hadn't changed.

One word that explained everything. Strangely, I found myself relieved, and I sank against her. That meant she was strong, that she could take care of herself better, that she didn't need me to protect her. Most importantly, it meant that she was alive. I wasn't sure when I'd started seeing the transition as a positive thing, but I could feel something inside of me shifting, growing. I'd accumulated so many demons over the last few weeks, that I almost saw through the fear now. Wade, Atlas, Max, and now Sarah—they were all alive because they had something else inside of them, something that protected them when most protectors would fall.

I didn't think I could hate those parts of them anymore, even if Guild doctrine swore it made them agents of hell.

Wolf. She'd been turned into a wolf and taken to hell. My stomach clenched thinking about what she must have gone through—and all by herself. Atlas hadn't had to give up his life, he'd had Eli, Wade and I to protect his secret, to watch over him.

Who did Sarah have? Anyone? Or had she had to go through this transformation alone?

"Sorry," I mumbled, unable to get much more than single syllables out. My head and body ached as she clung to me, but I didn't care. I'd take all the pain in the world if it meant this was real. That she was here. That she was alive.

I knew that I missed her. She was my best friend—my blood. But seeing her made me abundantly aware of how much I'd missed her—like I was seeing a giant hole carved through my chest for the first time, wondering how it got there, how long it had been there. A wave of needing to tell her everything—about Atlas, and Wade, about Darius, and, most importantly, about Max—rolled over me. She'd been the one person I'd ever opened up to about relationships, and even though it seemed like such a trivial conversation to have right now, the giddiness that came with the realization that I'd have those conversations back made my chest ache.

"You need to quiet down," she whispered, her breath cooling the tears on my skin. "No one can know you're awake yet. Your injuries were bad. Like *bad*, bad, Dec." She pulled away from me slightly, hands on my shoulders as she scanned me much in the same way Eli just had, relief and disbelief all in one. "How are you awake already? Standing? Talking? I was expecting at least a few more hours before you'd regain consciousness with those injuries—and much longer before I'd see you moving about, standing even."

I swiped a few strands of hair from my face, wiping my cheeks on the back of my hand as I studied her right back. She looked just as I remembered, but maybe a little harder now than she had before—there was a shadow coating her eyes, a sadness lodged deep. What had her life been like since I'd seen her— what unspeakable atrocities had she gone through?

"Was it Max?" Eli's hushed voice made me jump. I'd almost forgotten that he was here. I'd almost forgotten that we were holed up in the heart of a pack of wolves, like a couple of defenseless sitting ducks.

Max.

The dream. The singularly most intoxicating and disappointing dream I'd ever had in my entire life.

I nodded.

I touched a finger to my lips, the memory of hers so strong I could almost still taste them. Kissing her had set my body on fire, in a way that no kiss ever had, like every touch was magnified until I almost couldn't bear it, until I felt like I would shatter into a million jagged pieces.

And her face when she'd pulled away from me—the disgust in her eyes, the downward curve of her lips. The image of her expression was burned in my memory, just as hard as her touch.

Regret.

My stomach hurt all over again as I tried desperately to blink that image away, but it was stuck, permanently glued, and I knew I'd never be able to erase it.

I couldn't deny it anymore though—I was attracted to her, and I wanted her more than just physically. Something about that girl spun my world upside down, challenged me, made me want things I'd never thought I'd have.

Things she'd made clear that I couldn't have, not with her.

And while it hurt like hell that she didn't want me in all the ways that I so obviously wanted her, one thing was certain: I was done pushing her away because of my own fear.

That fear had been realized. And rejection hurt. But, surprisingly, I still wanted to follow her to the end of the realms, protect her and fight alongside her for as long as she'd allow me to, even if only as a friend, a team member. If she'd have me. I wouldn't betray her again.

The fact that I'd been pushing her away for so long, out of fear of the strange connection we all had to her, it made my stomach tie up in painful knots. She deserved better. She was important—whatever was going on in our world, she was at the center of it—and we'd only made her already difficult life so much worse.

But now, one thing was clear, she belonged with us. She'd proven herself over and over, and it was time we did the same. We needed to save her, even if it got us all killed in the process.

I'd tuck my growing feelings back down, ignore them as much as I could until they shrank into something less painful. Judging by how much the thought of never kissing her again made me want to curl into a ball inside of a dark cave, I knew it would take a long time for that pain to dissipate completely. But it wouldn't kill me.

There were more important things guiding me forward—she was in trouble.

"Don't know what that girl is, but she sure as hell comes in handy," he chuckled. The sound was hollow. I could hear the same regret and fear in his voice that I felt in my gut.

The truth was, *that girl* did the one thing that scared protectors shitless. She took away our control. And without control, we were exposed, in danger. Walls were our mechanisms for survival — in a world where survival was often the only thing that mattered.

I turned back towards him, remembering the state he'd been in when I'd drawn the wolves away—about two inches from death's doorstep. For a moment, I'd thought I'd truly lost him. Another family member, gone, just like that.

He still didn't look like his typical rakish self, the bags under his eyes were darker than usual, his resting snark face nowhere in sight. But he was walking, talking, moving about like his injuries were little more than a slight nuisance.

"You too?" I tried not to think about the fact that he'd slept with Max, that she very clearly wanted him in a way that she didn't want me. Eli was my brother in all but blood. He deserved good things, even though he did his damndest to push those good things away. Emotional pain, fear—they did wild things to a person.

His jaw clenched and I saw a flash of something cross his face, but it was gone almost as suddenly as it appeared. Too fast for me to read him.

"I look forward to meeting this girl," Sarah said, her hand gently holding my arm, like she was worried I might fall over at any second. She narrowed her eyes as she studied me, a knowing grin touching her lips as she read whatever emotion was drawn across my face. She was the only one who could read me, often understanding my thoughts before I even did. "She's saved the life of two of my favorite people in the past twenty-four hours. That makes her good people in my book." She guided me over to the makeshift bed. "You should sit. Get your bearings. Tonight isn't going to be easy."

"Tonight?" I looked up at her, my eyes taking in every inch, like they still couldn't quite believe what they were seeing. I was still waiting for her figure to disappear into nothing, for me to shoot up in bed, eyes wide and bleary, like this had all just been a dream within a dream.

Sarah stiffened. She glanced at Eli, something sullen passing between them before she leaned her ear towards the door, like she was trying to pick something up. It struck me then, that if there was something to hear, she'd be the first to hear it. Like Atlas, she was operating on a different sensory level than we were now.

What would that be like? To exist in the world one way for your entire life, and then to see the entire thing from a completely amplified perspective. I'd never really asked Atlas before. He hated talking about it, and we spent most of our time ignoring the presence of his wolf unless we needed to use him for a mission. No wonder their relationship was so contentious —the wolf never allowed to just be.

Something about Sarah seemed different though, heightened; like she'd taken on the properties of the wolf, folded them into herself until she was something new, something better. She seemed stronger, mentally and physically, the way her eyes moved about the room more intentional and observant, her stance and posture more lithe.

For a moment, I almost wondered if we'd done Atlas a disservice, treating his wolf as an adversary, something leeching onto his body like a parasite. I'd spent less than a minute in front of Sarah, and I could already tell that she had the power, stamina, and confidence to take the world by storm if she wanted to.

Apparently satisfied that any eavesdropping ears were out of the service area, she turned back to me, a soft, not exactly happy grin on her face. "I'm getting you out of here now. Jame—" she closed her eyes, pinched her nose, "the leader here isn't going to let either of you get out of here alive. He's agreed to let you stay until he can squeeze everything he can out of you. But it wouldn't go well for him, keeping two protectors alive in this place, on happy and healthy terms. That sort of thing is breeding ground for mutiny or a coup and there are already whispers around here that some of his followers are starting to doubt his methods. It's a dangerous time, and for as long as you're here, you'll be a target. I've guaranteed your survival through the night, but I don't trust anyone's word beyond that."

"Do you know how to get us out of hell?" For a moment, a beautiful, happy future went traipsing through my thoughts. Me, the boys, Max, and Sarah, all making it back home, alive and ready to take on the next big bad we were assigned to go after. Together. It was rare, me letting myself hope, but the image of that future resulted in the deepest breath of air I'd taken in months.

Her typically rosey cheeks lost their color. "Leaving this realm is not an easy thing to do. Most of the people stuck here would choose to be elsewhere if they could. Hell is a prison, and one with a complex system of locks and bolts. But I will see what I can do. Right now, I'm just going to focus on keeping you two alive long enough to escape from my pack."

Her pack. It was strange, hearing her claim another group as hers, one that wasn't us. And I couldn't help but think that part of her wanted to stay here, with them—that when she said she'd help us escape, she wasn't including herself in that equation.

Eli snorted. "You're coming with us, Sarah. I've met Jameson. He's not going to let you get away with jailbreaking us. And if he does, the other wolves will come for you both." He paused, and I felt the truth of his words. Because the same thing would happen in our own world—protectors who betrayed The Guild were not treated warmly. Why would betrayal be handled differently amongst wolves? "You know there's no future here for you."

Her eyes narrowed, a world of emotions that I couldn't decipher filtering through them. After a long, tense moment, her face softened and she nodded.

Was coming back to us—to Atlas, Wade—was that suddenly such a bad future?

Everyone would be so excited to see—

A knot formed in my stomach. *Would* everyone be excited? *We* were thrilled that she was alive, of course. But we couldn't bring a wolf back to Headquarters. Not if we wanted her to stay alive. And while I might have thought it could work a few months, or even weeks ago, I didn't trust The Guild the way I once did. The world was not divided as I once thought—the lines between heaven and hell more complex and nuanced than we'd ever been taught.

"Look, the details don't matter now. There'll hopefully be time to argue tomorrow. But we've got to go." She turned back to me, expression stern. "Now. Something happened, about ten miles out. Jameson sent most of his muscle to check on it. We take territory breaches very seriously here."

"What happened?" Eli's arm pressed against mine as he

spoke. I could feel every muscle in his body tense. Territory breaches, infighting—this was our language. We'd spent years of our lives chasing down unexpected activity in the human world.

His tension made sense.

It was the same tension I felt rolling through my body. Max and Atlas were out there somewhere. What if the pack was going after them?

"It's not Max," I said, "She's locked up in the same place as Wade. They're together, but I don't know where Atlas is. We have to find her, we have to get them both back."

"What?" Eli took a step forward, like he wasn't sure what to do, just knew that he needed to do something. "Where?"

He didn't ask how exactly I knew—like me, he'd been visited by her recently in his dreams, knew the power that she had. It hadn't escaped my notice that she'd dream-walked to me without the assistance of Wade—it was her own power, carrying her to us.

"I don't know." I dug my fingernails into my palm. Why did this place feel like it was always two steps forward and one step back. Every time there was a small inkling of hope, it was like this realm just rubbed it right out. "But she said it was like a dungeon—stone and cold and maybe near the water. She mentioned the River Styx. Whoever has her has to be someone with a lot of power. The group that took Wade that night—it wasn't small."

"Styx?" Sarah's eyes danced between the two of us, confusion slowly making way for some sort of flustered realization. But whatever that realization was, something told me it wasn't good. She dropped her head back, like the answers to the world's mysteries were written on the grimy ceiling. "Fuck."

"You know where she might be?" There was so much goddamn hope in Eli's voice it felt like a knife to the gut.

Judging by the pallor of Sarah's skin, the way her eyes dropped down from mine when I tried to look into them, I knew that wherever Max was, it wasn't good.

"Maybe." She glanced up at him, her eyes hard, focused. "Y'all brought a whole bucket of complicated with you when you dumped yourselves into this realm. First, we need to get you out of here. And now."

I nodded, moving towards the door, my skin still crawling with the fact that we were locked in a room, weaponless, surrounded by wolves who would happily tear us limb from limb.

"Wait."

I turned back towards Eli. "What?"

He cursed as he ran his hand through his hair and dragged it down his face, muffling a low groan. "I can't believe I'm saying this, but we can't leave without the vampire."

"Vamp—" I closed my eyes as I caught his meaning. "You've got to be fucking kidding me. Darius? He's here?"

"Yeah," Sarah answered, her lips lifting slightly. "He's pretty easy on the eyes for a bloodsucker." Her small grin curled into disgust, "but he's probably the most annoying creature I've ever encountered in my life. Does he ever shut up?"

Ah, so she had met him.

I groaned, stretching my arm out for Sarah to lead the way. "Let's go get the fucker, then."

He may be annoying as hell, but there was no denying that we were stuck with him now—at least until we found a way to break the bond. And even then—

I shook my head, felt my lips tug up a little, he had a way of worming his way in, didn't he?

The halls were mostly empty, and Sarah led us through the complex labyrinth, pulling us into empty rooms here and there whenever she thought she heard something—or someone—in the distance.

Between her ability to weave through the shadows, dragging us through back halls with the ease and familiarity of someone who'd spent a lifetime walking them, and whatever situation had pulled most of the wolves away, we made it to Darius's room with surprisingly little trouble. It was the first thing that had been reasonably easy since arriving in hell.

She pulled a heavy-looking ring of iron keys from her back pocket, rifling through one and then another until she finally got to a large skeleton key. With a satisfied grin, she opened the door.

Darius was hung up to the ceiling by his arms, his body rocking slightly from side-to-side, like he was swinging casually in the park. When his mismatched eyes latched on me, his face split into a giant smile.

"The Moody One! You're not dead. That's good. You've always been my favorite," his tone was taunting but there was something sincere in his eyes.

Surprisingly, I found my shoulders dropping in relief at the sight of him. Had I been...worried about him? About a vampire who'd committed who knew how many unspeakable horrors?

But the truth was, he hadn't only done harm.

He was also a vampire who'd saved my life. And the lives of my teammates. On more than one occasion.

"We're getting you out of here," I said, stepping confidently in the room. "Now."

My eyes darted to the ground, where a metal box sat open, the contents covered in rust and crusted blood. My stomach dipped as I remembered Eli's throat, how close to death he'd been before Max healed him. What the hell were they doing to him here? Bile rose to my throat.

"See Nash," Darius craned his neck, trying to see the body hanging a few feet behind him. Another vampire I was guessing, though judging by the look of disgust on the creature's face, he wasn't Darius's biggest fan. Which pretty on par for the vampires I'd met over the last few days. Darius's fan club had seriously low numbers, it seemed. "I'm all about flipping the narrative. Kind of fun to be the damsel in distress for once, isn't it? We can just hang here while the girls save the day."

Eli rolled his eyes, but I didn't miss the small tug at the

corner of his lips. Maybe he didn't hate the fanghole as much as he used to either. Hell did strange things to a person, that was for damn sure. His focus darted to Sarah. "Do you have a key to unlock them?"

Sarah inhaled, stood up straight, and walked a few steps closer to Darius. Her posture was rigid and I could feel the tension encasing her body. She didn't like this. At all. "You get my friends killed," she pointed a long finger a few inches from his face, "you even so much as think about dropping one ounce of their blood," she pressed that finger into his chest, with enough force that his body swung, "and I'll have this entire pack after you faster than you can say *O-negative*," she cleared her throat, some of the bravado leaking out. "Am I understood?"

Darius clicked his heals together, expression jovial and taunting, but he held onto her eye contact. "They belong to the little protector. I wouldn't harm a hair on their heads—" he paused, brows tilting in thought, "unless she asked me to, that is."

Sarah's brows scrunched together in an echo of his. She had no idea what the fuck Darius was on about, but I saw the sincerity in his eyes, the way his lips gently curved with fondness. He was just as drawn to Max as we were. And not just because he was intrigued, not just because she was the first interesting thing to cross his path in years, to hold his attention for more than a second. Whatever draw we had to her—he had it too. Only rather than deny it, as we had all this time, he went after it, hunted it down with relish. He'd made it damn clear from the start that she was his priority, had even made her promise that she wouldn't return to The Guild right away when all of this was finished.

"Plus they're all kind of growing on me in their own right," he added, nose curling in disgust as if the revelation was as surprising to him as it was to us. "Captivity does strange things to a man's mind, apparently."

Sarah pinched the bridge of her nose, let out a long breath of air, and pushed a step stool up next to Darius. "I cannot believe that this is the path my life has taken."

She went on muttering, a sharp curse word piercing the silence here and there, though I couldn't catch everything she said.

With a loud metallic clang, he dropped to his feet. "Could've had a small pillow there to cushion my fall, love, but I appreciate the rescue all the same."

He stood, stretching like a cat as he let out a loud, satisfied groan.

"Shut up before they find out you're down here." Eli glanced at me before turning to the door. "Let's go, we need to get out of here and find Max."

"Honestly," Sarah's brow arched, "the racket he's been making, they'd be more suspicious if there was silence coming from this room."

"You know where she is then?" Darius stood still, all humor melting from his face. "She's okay? Alive? You're certain?" He closed the distance between us, moved towards the door, jaw clenched and determination in his eyes. "Well, let's go get her then." As soon as he reached the door, his hand pressed to the frame, he paused and turned around. He ran a hand through his disheveled hair as his shoulders slumped slightly. "Wait, I can't leave Nash dangling like a slaughtered cow. As amusing as it is to see him strung up like that, we need to get him down too. If they kill him—" Darius paused, jaw muscles tightening, "it would be bad. For everyone."

"Nash?" I studied the second man more closely. His eyes were narrowed, pure hatred leaking from him as he stared at Darius. His...friend?

"I need no favors from you," he barked.

"Does anyone you meet actually like you?" I studied the blond vampire, mentally clocking every demon we'd met that had seemed interested in chopping him into a million pieces. I was losing count.

Darius just chuckled, grabbed the keys from Sarah, who simply shrugged and muttered something about how we might as well make our escape a full demon parade, before climbing up to Nash.

"Pride is one of the deadly sins, old friend," he said, as Nash dropped to the ground. "Forgiveness, a virtue."

His graceful landing confirmed that he was a vampire more than anything else about his person. He stood tall, eyes calculating as he glanced at the rest of us. He was a difficult person to read, but I could see there was a dark intelligence in his eyes—the same kind of power I'd seen when I looked at Claude. It sent a shiver of fear down my spine. Hopefully Darius could keep him on a leash. We didn't have time for another battle of the titans.

"Fuck your forgiveness," he muttered, as he walked towards the door. With a reluctant glance back to the rest of us, he added, "You'd be wise not to invest much trust in him. He's not worthy of it and it's the fastest way to get yourself killed. Especially here."

And then, without another lingering glance or word, he left.

"Always a party pooper, that one." Darius clapped his hands together, a wide smile on his face, like a kid at an amusement park. "Well, at least there's never a dull moment. Shall we be off then?"

We were fewer than twenty feet down the hall, when a loud howl reverberated down the empty corridor—the sound filled with such rage and agony that it pebbled my flesh with chills, the vibration from the noise ricocheting through my bones. This place had the atmospheric vibes of a haunted house—the sort that had even the most stoic of visitors wetting their pants.

"What the hell was that?" Eli's eyes were wide as he looked around, his fingers instinctively moving for the blade on his leg that wasn't there. He cursed. "We need to get some fucking weapons if we're going to have any chance of making it out of here alive. Your people took ours."

Sarah's posture was stiff as she glanced at a door a few feet from us. "There's a feral wolf that some of the guys brought in not long ago. Heard mention of it earlier. A loner. It's rare, in this realm."

"To not belong to a pack?" I flexed my hands, missing my own dagger as much as Eli was missing his. I felt naked. After a lifetime of training to fight creatures far more powerful than us, it was impossible not to feel even more vulnerable than usual without protection. And we weren't exactly in friendly territory.

"To be alone in this realm and still alive," Darius responded.

The way he spoke about hell—the way everyone did, really, set my body on edge, like we'd only hit the tip of the iceberg with this place. I sure as hell didn't want to know what other atrocities there were in store. We'd been here less than a day or two and we'd already been split up, kidnapped, and nearly killed multiple times between the lot of us.

The howl sounded again, lower this time. A pang of familiarity shot through me and I felt my body running towards the door Sarah had indicated before my brain understood why.

My hands clasped the handle, jiggling it with a desperate impatience, but it wouldn't budge.

Sarah walked silently to my side, her teeth nibbling at her bottom lip as they often did when she was nervous. "What are you doing? We don't have time for this?"

"Can you open this door? Will one of your keys work?"

"Dec, come on—"

"Now." The demand came out more forcefully than I'd intended, and I scrunched my nose in apology. "Please, it's important."

She took a deep breath, eyes meeting mine for a long moment, before she nodded. With a quick rattle of metal, she pushed the door open.

There were thick iron cages stacked against the wall. They looked like the heavy-duty version of what you might find at a low-budget animal shelter—rusted and tarnished, but sturdy enough to keep a werewolf inside.

At the far end, thrashing against the sides like a pinball, was a large tawny wolf. Startled by the sound of us all spilling into the room, the creature's eyes met mine.

Familiar bright yellow orbs, filled with a whirlwind of emotions, each equally strong so that it was impossible to tell exactly which feeling took center stage. He'd never looked at me like that before—anger directed at me. I saw what Sarah meant by feral now, there was a wildness about him that hadn't been there when he left us.

My stomach tightened at the sight of him. I ran over and crouched down low, my fingers gripping the bars as I studied him. A few tufts of hair were missing here and there, like he'd had a few skirmishes during his time away, and there were several splotches of fur that were darker than the rest. I assumed it was blood, but hopefully not all of it was his.

"Atlas," I whispered, as he slowly made his way over to me, posture somehow both tentative and coiled with tension.

Atlas's wolf and I didn't have an abundantly loving relationship, but he'd often tolerated me in the past, generally responding to my attempts to calm him better than the others'. I was usually the one to help pull Atlas back to the driver's seat, to settle the wolf down when emotions and instincts were running too high. But something in his eyes now, the way his lips curled back into a snarl, the low growl so deep I could feel it more than I could hear it, told me that Atlas wasn't anywhere near running the show right now—he might as well have been in a completely separate car, on a completely separate road.

Fuck. This was bad. I didn't understand what had happened to him, but the lack of connection, the lack of excitement when he'd seen us, made my blood run cold.

"Are you alright? Has anyone hurt you?" I felt a bit ridiculous asking a creature questions when I knew it couldn't respond, but the more I spoke, the less angry he seemed to be, like he was listening even if he didn't want to be.

"Atlas?" Sarah kneeled next to me, her fingers shaking as she reached them gingerly through the bars. "Is it really you?" And then, in a breathy whisper that seemed to be more to herself than to him, "You really have transitioned. You're like me."

My chest squeezed at the yearning in her voice. I knew her well enough to hear her fighting back tears, in the way her voice deepened, the irregular inhale like she was trying to suppress a sob.

The wolf tilted his head as her hand inched closer, his nostrils flaring slightly as he sniffed. The transformation was subtle, but I could tell by the doggish sneeze, and the shift of his ears that there was recognition there, that he understood, at least in part, that Sarah was important to the man who shared his body, if not to him.

Just before her fingers touched his fur, his teeth snapped together—a growl, much louder this time, rolling through him. I didn't think he would really bite her, it was more warning than anything, an acknowledgment that while Atlas might know her, the wolf did not—not in the same way, anyway.

And she probably smelled like the pack that had attacked and caged him. I couldn't blame his wariness.

"Sorry," she muttered, the words rushed and filled with a delicate sadness. She pulled her hand back and quickly swiped a tear from her cheek.

She was hurt. She'd loved Atlas so much, ever since we were kids. If he was ever in the same room, that's where her focus was always drawn, like a homing beacon. The day of their bonding ceremony, I thought she'd crack with excitement, all of her dreams laid out, before the people she loved most, hers to keep —forever. And then again, much later, I remember thinking that she'd crack from the sadness of the truth—the realization that he'd never looked at her the same way that she did him, that he'd never quite loved her with as much force as she did him.

To see the wolf hardly recognize that bond, whatever lingering vestiges were left—my heart squeezed for her. It was a difficult thing, loving someone who didn't love you back.

"We need to get him out of there. Now." Eli's jaw was clenched as he spoke, his words tinny with anger.

I knew that some of that anger was reserved for himself. We'd come so close to almost leaving one of our own behind in this place. And something told me that if we had actually left as intended, Atlas wouldn't have been kept alive for very long.

Sarah sniffed, nodded, and riffled through her ring of keys, her movements shaky and clumsy. "I-I don't think I have the keys for this cage. I don't ever come into this room, if I can help it." She looked up at me, her eyes wide and brimming with liquid, like I might have whatever answers she sought. She looked so childlike in that moment, all the strength and confidence I'd admired just a few moments ago shriveled and hushed. "I don't know where—whoever was in charge of taming him—of breaking him."

She hiccuped over the word 'taming' and I tasted bile. What the hell had they done to him?

And what the hell had they done to *her.* The shadows eclipsing her eyes told me all that I needed to know—that it wasn't just stray wolves they *tamed* and *broke.* They'd tortured Sarah too, hurried along the melding process between her and her wolf.

I knew from my experiences with Atlas that turned wolves went through a difficult period, a transitioning season where they had to figure out where they ended and their wolf began and how to interact with that boundary while maintaining a semblance of control.

Born wolves were different—they were never not at peace with the demon beneath their skin, because that demon was never not present. Turned wolves had to parse through two different selves—marrying together the mind of the original person with that of something else, something other.

I reached my hand to her shoulder, squeezing softly. As much as I didn't want to hear the details of her pain, I'd be an open ear when she was ready to talk. There was so much built up emotion in her expression that I couldn't fully read, not the way I used to be able to read her. Sarah had always been an open book to me. But now—now she might as well have been a book written in a lost language for all I could intuit.

"Turned wolves are rare." Darius's voice was softer than usual, like he was just as aware of Sarah's pain as I was.

Moments like that, when his humanity started to shine through, it was difficult to hate him. Honestly, I couldn't remember the last time that I'd hated him. For taking Max, maybe. But that had less to do with him being a demon and more to do with him making me panic needlessly—making me drown in the guilt of how we'd all treated her. That she'd choose a vampire's company over ours, feel safer and more welcome with the very creature she'd spent a lifetime learning to fear.

He shifted awkwardly, shrugging one shoulder. "Packs don't often have protocol for dealing with them." He glanced sheepishly at Sarah, not quite holding eye contact, like he didn't want to look at her pain directly. "You and Atlas are probably two of the only transitioned wolves to make it to hell in many, many years. Although it does seem some packs have found a way to easily hop between this realm and yours—so there may be others that they've brought back. Hell has never been a place where people come and go, not until the last year." He sighed, ran a hand through his hair, frowning when a poof of dust enveloped him like a cloud. "I need a shower." He shook his head, looking more wolf-like in that moment than Sarah. "Anyway, my point is that born packs don't understand turned wolves very well—it's not a process anyone really knows how to handle, because it's rare. I'm honestly surprised that they kept you at all, that they took that risk."

"That doesn't justify what they—"

"I know," Darius said simply, cutting Eli's anger off before it carried him away. "It doesn't."

Eli's hard angles softened slightly as he studied Darius. I saw my realization reflected between them—that our people had done something equally reprehensible to the demons we kept locked in the lab. For a long, tense moment, they stared at each other, and then Eli nodded once before walking up to Atlas. "How do we get him out? You've got vamp strength, can—"

"What the fuck are you doing?" A harsh, nasally voice echoed through the room.

I felt my heart drop to my stomach, and searched uselessly, once again, for a dagger that wasn't there. The intruder was thin, his hair long and matted together in stringy waves. His shirt was rolled up to his elbows and what looked like dark smudges of blood coated his forearms. Something told me that it wasn't his.

"Mickey." Sarah's eyes darted to me, then back to him. Any vulnerability that had been on her face moments before melted away in an instant. She tilted her chin up until she looked strong, confident, and maybe even a little bit arrogant. Was that what was necessary to survive here? Were all of these demons posturing and acting out dominance until the lines between performance and reality blurred? "I thought you were out." She arched a brow before adding, "then again, I guess Jameson only needed his top dogs for the breach."

"I fucking told Jameson that he couldn't trust a protector. Doesn't matter if the bitch has a wolf sharing her skin, she's still a traitor, an enemy." His lip curled as he met her eyes, then surveyed the room, his beady eyes darkening as they moved from me to Eli, to Darius. He was the sort of guy who looked so stereotypically slimy and evil, that I was almost a little disappointed that he glomped on to the cliche with such relish. "But he refused to listen because you hypnotized him with your cunt. Wait until he hears what you've done." His eyes landed back on hers, narrowed and seething. "He'll have your head for this. I can't wait to watch."

My heartbeat picked up loud and fast at his threat.

Sarah's jaw clenched, the lines of her face becoming more angular has her eyes focused on him. They weren't the bluish-green shade I was used to seeing. They were a vibrant, piercing yellow.

My breath hitched at the strangeness of seeing her that way, at seeing her wolf casually rise to the surface, as if it had never not been there, peering out at us.

"Where are the keys, Mickey?" Her voice was cold, her posture rigid as she stared him down.

We were so close, so goddamn close to getting out of this place, with all of us—well, most of us—together again. I forced myself to breathe, to focus on taking down the last creature in our way. Something in that grin unsettled me, forecasted his seething hatred—like I could read his desire to rip Sarah apart, limb-from-limb, with as much clarity as if he'd announced it.

Mickey grinned, his dark eyes sparkling with delight as his hand slid in his pocket. "Like I'd tell you, you traitorous bitch. I should do Jameson a favor and kill you right now, before he lets his dick override his brain. Again."

His unconscious gesture had told me more than he'd intended—and there was no way in hell I was letting him get even a single step closer to my cousin. With a deep, steadying breath, I dove for him, not allowing myself a chance to second guess it. It was reckless, but I'd just gotten her back, I wouldn't lose her again. I was so fucking over losing the people I loved.

His arms gripped mine, as we each fought for control in the violent embrace.

He was stronger, and I felt my arms bruise under the pressure of his fingers as they dug into me, could feel his long, thick nails pierce my skin. A sharp prick pinched my neck, and I knew with the sort of certainty that was born from living a life coated with violence and death, that he had a blade pressed against my jugular. One well-placed push of pressure and I'd be bleeding out on the floor. Gone, just like that.

I heard the rest of the room come alive during our skirmish, as everyone moved closer, no one wanting to get too close, to spook him into ending my life with the slightest shift of the blade. Atlas's low, familiar growl grew louder and louder until it was all that I could hear.

My teeth gnashed together as my eyes met Sarah's. What the fuck had I been thinking. I was the weakest one in the room. I should've thought, should've focused. I inhaled sharply, jaw clenching with frustration at myself, guilt at the fear in my friends' eyes eating at my insides.

My nose curled when the scent of the man stole my focus, his body odor surrounding me like a cloying cloud. I hadn't seen any showers in hell, but this guy gave a whole new meaning to the word pungent.

"You're barely more than human," he said, his breath rancid and warm against my neck, My stomach sank at his reminder of my powerlessness. For the first time, I almost wished that I was like Atlas or Sarah. Hell, I'd even be grateful for Darius's powers right now. Instead, I felt useless. "I'll snap you like a tw—"

As if someone had flipped a switch and turned him off, he shut up, his words evaporating in the air, his body collapsing against me, on its way to the ground.

The shock of his weight started to pull me down. With one firm shove, I pushed him off me, tripping awkwardly as I tried to regain my footing. The round ring of keys that Sarah had been carrying dangled from his back, one long skeleton key pierced through his back like his ribs encaged a macabre lock.

His heart, it'd pierced his heart.

My gaze traveled to Darius, his eyes light with mirth as he swept his hands together as if just completing a full and honest day's work. "I've been fantasizing about doing that for ages. Would've preferred to draw it out longer, to languish in his misery and pain as he had mine, but we are on a deadline, aren't we, so I'll settle for quick and resourceful."

Of course.

Darius was strong, so much stronger than all of us, so I knew I shouldn't be surprised that he could turn such an innocuous tool like a key into a deadly weapon, but I still found my brain trying to catch up and parse the ease and speed with which he'd managed it.

I rubbed my neck, smearing the small line of blood there as I started to cough. "Th—"

He waved his hands at me. "Don't thank me. I would've killed him whether he was threatening you or not. Your position just added a bit of an edge, and I've got a flair for the dramatic." He turned his attention to Sarah, arching a playful brow. "Hope he wasn't too dear of a friend, but I'm going to assume that since he was threatening you less than thirty seconds ago that you won't mourn his passing too deeply."

She shook her head, mouth still rounded in surprise.

Without waiting for more theatrics, I bent down and fished through Mickey's pocket, scrunching my nose as my finger accidentally grazed the outline of his flaccid dick. With a quick tug, I grabbed a new ring of keys, this one significantly smaller than Sarah's, the keys more familiar in size and shape, like they were crafted in this century, not last.

Quickly, I moved to Atlas, trying each key in turn as my fingers shook with the fear of more wolves walking in on us, of us getting ambushed while I worked through each key.

The last one. Why was it always the last one? It seemed like a cruel trick the universe liked to play.

With a small shift, the gate opened, and Atlas leapt out. He shook his head like a dog, his hair poofing out as he stretched.

His hackles were raised, and the low growl that had been emanating from him had been so consistent that I almost didn't hear it now, like it had become part of the background noise, the soundtrack to our escape.

Eli stepped forward, but Atlas only bared his teeth in response.

He'd never reacted to us this way before, had never directed any of his wolfy animosity against us, as if we were the enemy. I wasn't sure what had happened to him between the moment he left us in those woods and now, but whatever it was, it wasn't good.

And why hadn't he shifted back?

"Don't touch him," Sarah said, her head cocked to the side as she studied him. "I don't think he'll attack, but he's operating completely on instinct right now, pure emotion. His wolf is one-hundred-percent in charge. Atlas is in there, but he's not calling any of the shots right now. Best we can do is leave and hope that he follows with—"

Atlas crouched low before leaping through the air and landing on Darius, the two collapsing in a ball of fur, skin, and torn clothing.

"Atlas!" I took a step forward, ready to interject, but Sarah's arm pulled me back until I was flush against her chest.

"Don't even think about it, Declan." Her voice was calm, like she was simply watching a boring golf match, and not my best friend's final moments.

"So much for not attacking," Darius grunted as he wrestled to stabilize himself.

Darius was stronger, so much stronger than Atlas, and I knew that he could kill him with little more than a flick of his wrist if he really wanted to.

And why wouldn't he? Atlas initiated the attack, so long as he didn't kill Eli, Darius would survive the altercation just fine—the rest of us were just fodder to him, nothing but barriers standing between him and Max.

Almost as soon as they'd fallen, Darius regained his footing.

Atlas went sailing through the air until he crashed with a yelp into the very cage he'd just emerged from.

Darius stared back, a malicious amusement carving across his lips.

Atlas growled, his shoulder blades contracting until they almost touched, like he was preparing to attack the vampire again, not even slightly deterred by the fanghole's power and strength.

With a frustrated groan, Sarah stood between them, her eyes unblinking as they reached for Atlas's. His teeth bared as she edged closer, one step at a time. She held her hands up in the universal sign for 'I mean you no harm, you twat,' and inched closer.

My fingers were curled into fists, every muscle in my body frozen as fear and adrenaline coursed through me. I sent up silent prayers to a god I didn't believe in, begging for Atlas not to attack Sarah, and for Darius not to pull Atlas's spine from his skeleton just because he could.

Atlas's body was coiled, ready to pounce, and Darius just stared, the small curve in his lips daring him to strike again.

As if suddenly changing his mind, the vampire shook his head, annoyed resolve cannibalizing his expression. He inhaled long and slow, pinching the bridge of his nose. "She's alive, you mutt. And of all of us here, I'm the best weapon you have. Which makes me the best chance you have at finding her at all." He pointed to his palm, for extra emphasis, "and we all know that I could detach your furry head from your body in less than two seconds flat if I really wanted to. The thought need only cross my mind and stick there once. But lucky for you, my clothes are already a mess and, right now, I'd rather not add another layer of unappetizing blood to the ensemble. I only drink from wolves out of desperation. So can we just be on with it and save the pissing contest for a time when I can properly enjoy beating you?"

A breath I hadn't realized I'd been holding released from my lungs. And just as quickly, my own anger flared.

Atlas was pissed at Darius. *Of course* he was fucking pissed at Darius. In all the chaos of the last hour, I'd almost forgotten that the fanghole had taken Max from us—that we were all separated and in this mess in the first place because he tried to run off with her like some grotesque knight in shining armor. And now Rapunzel was locked up in some mystery dungeon, facing an unknown monster that we were probably ill-equipped to defeat.

But instead of the rage that was currently coursing through Atlas, I'd only felt...relief when I found out that the vampire was nearby. Relief that he hadn't gotten himself killed or ditched our cause completely, leaving us all here to rot in hell forever.

"You took her," I whispered, the words like a soft curse on my lips. "We're in this mess because of you. Atlas—" I glanced at the feral wolf who hardly seemed to recognize us, yellow eyes shining with a quiet fury, "he's like this because of you."

Darius's sharp gaze cut to me, his eyes narrowing and lip quirking up in that insufferable way of his. I could never tell whether he was mocking me with that smirk or if the small twitch was his body's only tell that he was two seconds away from snapping my neck—the only sign of his restraint. Either way, it wasn't good.

"Let's not play the blame game tonight, my little band of misfit protectors. She needed a reason to run from you all. That was not on me. I merely offered her company if she wanted it. You handed her a reason to leave on a large, shiny silver platter." He shrugged, examining the dirt under his fingernails with clear distaste. "You can hardly blame me for taking advantage of the situation."

"You fuc—"

"Enough!" Eli stepped between us, his back facing me as he stared the vampire down. I could see the muscles in his back tense through his shirt. He was shaking slightly, like he was dealing with his own battle—his own silent war.

Sarah was frozen in front of Atlas, lips parted as her eyes darted from person to person. I could see her trying to piece the dynamics together, to make sense of all the nonsense filling this room.

No one moved, no one spoke, all of us waiting for the first person to step out of line, to initiate a fight. The air was so thick with tension that the pressure of it made it almost impossible to breathe, like moving one centimeter in the wrong direction would make all hell break loose.

Eli's shoulders slumped, and though I couldn't see his expression, I knew him well enough to know what I'd see if I could—dejection, guilt, a haunted look in his dark eyes that only came out when no one was watching. A look I'd been witness to far more frequently than I'd have liked. Disappointment. Shame.

"You're right." The admission was little more than a breath given shape. I could feel the pain dripping from him as if it were my own. "I fucked up. This is on me. All of it."

"*We* fucked up," I corrected, reaching toward him. I squeezed his shoulder gently, before letting my hand fall awkwardly back to my side. Neither of us could be described as touchy-feely. That small act—it was enough to get the sentiment across. "All of us."

"*I* didn't fuck up," Darius countered, brow lifting as his gaze traveled from Eli to Atlas, and then over to me.

"No offense," Sarah cleared her throat and raised a slim finger in the air, as if asking for permission to speak, "I don't know the details of this whole twisted family drama you've all got going on, though to be clear, I'm definitely invested in catching up at the earliest convenience—" she cleared her throat, eyes locked on Darius, "but if you ran off with the girl, got yourself captured, and left her who knows where, I'm guessing you could have handled things a bit better as well."

For a long moment, the room was silent again. My heart raced against my ribs as Darius studied Sarah, all emotion emptied from his face. I'd seen him snap before, seen him turn inside of himself and explode with rage. Would he attack Sarah with as much force as he'd leveled against his own brother? I took a step towards her, as if my body could offer her protection should that happen.

Like a predator, he clocked the small movement, his impenetrable gaze on me as I held my breath. Then, eyes softening just slightly, he turned back to Sarah, giving her a reluctant nod. "Touché. I stand corrected. We *all* fucked up."

"Exactly," Eli continued, as if he hadn't been interrupted by tense, nonsensical babble in the middle of a wolf prison. Atlas's growly soundtrack had even abated slightly, like he was hanging on every word in the room, trying to make sense of things as much as the rabid wolf controlling his body was able to. "We all fucked up. And we know that Max is with Wade and that she needs us. So maybe right now, let's just shut the fuck up with the fighting and blame game, and get to the whole finding and rescuing her part." His words were strained, like he was fighting to keep the pain and guilt from seeping into his voice. "Before we're too late."

Without waiting for everyone to chime in with agreement, he turned towards Sarah and nodded to the door, a silent encouragement for her to lead the way.

With a single nod, she straightened her posture and did just that.

I loved her so much in that moment—for her willingness to go along with a half-assed plan that she knew only small snippets of, for helping us even if she didn't understand the series of clusterfucks that had brought us all to this moment.

Darius trickled out after them, leaving me alone with Atlas. The wolf showed no signs of receding into him, of letting the man out of the furry cage.

"Be all Cujo if you must, but do me a favor and try not to attack Darius until we can find her," I muttered before following the rest of the group into the hall. "He's linked to Eli."

It felt strange, showing my back to the wolf, to trust him not to kill me when Atlas clearly had little to no control over him in this state. Rage pulsed out of him, lapping against my skin, and I knew without an ounce of doubt that every instinct was telling him to attack, to protect himself, to run. But I refused to turn around, to make certain that he wasn't lunging to attack, to abandon the trust that I'd always reserved for Atlas.

Because maybe we'd had this all wrong. Maybe, like Sarah, Atlas could find a way to meet his wolf in the middle, to fold the demon into himself as she had done, to become both creatures at once: stronger, smarter...more.

Soft steps echoed behind me, the pace tentative but calm, like I was being followed by a stray dog deciding whether or not to trust the human holding out a handful of food.

Even as my heart raced with fear—fear of the wolf, fear that we'd run into more of Sarah's packmates as we wound through their headquarters, fear of what could possibly be happening to Max and Wade, fear of everything that was to come—I smiled.

The wolf was willing to work with us. To trust us.

At least for now. And for now, that would be enough.

❧ 15 ❧

DARIUS

Leaving the compound was less difficult than I'd imagined. The building felt like a ghost town, and between me and the wolves, it was easy enough to carve a relatively peaceful path to freedom. If there could be such a thing as freedom in this place. I still couldn't quite believe that I'd found myself back in this realm, after all that I'd done to leave it in the first place.

I couldn't blame Claude for his anger, for his disbelief at my decision. And honestly, I was starting to think that I'd follow the little protector into the void if that's where she was determined to go.

A chill ran through me at the thought. I wasn't used to a creature having so much control over my decisions, over my life. What the hell was happening to me? I was starting to wonder if the researchers in the lab had done something more permanent to my brain.

I could feel the tension rolling through the group, like a giant, glitchy wave that none of us could escape. They were all as tense and lost as I was, just on different paths.

No one spoke as we moved, other than when the girl, Sarah, had mumbled a brief, hushed "try not to kill any more of my packmates," when I'd walked by her. But there was no bite to her words. Something told me that she'd miss Mickey about as much as I would. Which was to say she'd probably have killed him herself if given the opportunity.

I saw the way she had looked at that cage, saw the empathy radiating from her when she'd met Atlas's eyes. She knew what it was to be captured by this pack. She might be partially attached to a few of them—finding friends in this realm was a necessity for survival—but her position here, her relationship with the wolves, was a fragile one at best.

Even after we'd made it beyond the pack boundaries, weaving our way through the forest at Sarah's whims, no one spoke. It was like we'd all silently agreed that the moment one of us uttered a word, the relatively peaceful escape would dissolve, making way for an ambush. It had been easy, escaping. Far easier than I would've thought. Sarah had executed things impressively well, considering she was born of protectors.

But something hanging in the air made my blood run cold. The woods were too still, too silent, and that scared me more than anything—far more than a wolf attack, anyway.

"What's happened to this place?" I whispered, suddenly no longer able to stand the heavy anticipation on my own. A pair of wolves and protectors wasn't exactly my ideal version of company, but right now, they were all I had to keep the chill of this place at bay. I could feel the darkness eating away at my thoughts, slowly blotting out the world, making way for my demons to emerge. "When I left, things weren't like this," I continued, waving my arms around, not exactly sure what I was gesturing towards, but maybe that was part of the point. "This realm has always been strange, unpredictable even, but never like...this."

Sarah's eyes darted to mine briefly, but she didn't pause, just continued moving forward, muscles coiled like she expected something to jump out at us at any moment. "I don't know. I've only been living in this realm since my transition a while back. I can't speak to what it was like before that."

She was silent for a few long moments, as Eli and Declan glanced at each other, speaking in that obnoxious, silent way of theirs, the only sound that of the leaves crumbling in our wake. I knew the girl didn't trust me, and could see her very carefully weighing the decision of whether or not to tell me anything more. She might be a wolf now, but she'd lived her life as a protector—which meant she had the same prejudices as the rest of Max's friends. Not that I really blamed her. If I didn't have these surly fucks policing my every move, and if I wasn't reliant on her guiding us to Max, I probably would've ripped her head off and drained her dry for her part in my capture. I almost thought less of her for taking Declan and Eli at their word that I was some sort of harmless vampire with safety restraints on.

Then again, maybe they were right. My bloodlust hadn't been as strong as it once was—all of my focus was lasered in on one thing. Finding her. Hopefully, once I did, I'd feel more like myself again.

Sarah shook her head and let out a low sigh, losing whatever tedious battle she'd been waging within herself. "But people talk of things being different. Resources are more limited, food almost impossible to come by. The factions have grown more dangerous, more territorial. And Jameson—he often spoke of the magic feeling off. Like he could taste it in the air, and that it had grown bitter. People have been panicking for years, everyone growing desperate to get to the bottom of it, to lift whatever veil has darkened this place." She swept some branches back, guiding us all through the brush. The way she moved through this place, it was as if she'd been born here. It was almost impressive how much more in-tune with this place she was than me. "Truthfully, I'm not sure that anyone really understands what's going on. But even I, a stranger to this place, can feel something building up— something with the power to destroy us all. Sometimes if I focus on it, try to feel the magic Jameson always speaks of, it rips the breath from my lungs."

I grunted in response, letting her words filter through me. I couldn't taste the magic, not literally, but I think I understood what Jameson meant. The air was static with it, like the calm before a storm. It was impossible to feel anything but on edge in this place, and I hated how jumpy it was making me, like my muscles were permanently tense, permanently waiting for the shoe to drop.

Something had happened to this place—was happening. Something big.

"And the girls," Eli slowed, scrunching his brows together as he closed the distance between us, until his steps matched alongside my own, like some warped, distorted mirror, "why did he want Dec? You said he's been collecting girls."

Right, that had been mentioned. I was almost embarrassed that I'd let that thread drop. Because of course he didn't want Declan, not really. He wanted Max and thought that Declan might be her. I just wasn't sure why. Where did the little protector fit into all of this? None of it made sense. She was a succubus—a rare creature in comparison to wolves or vampires, sure, even rarer still since she was part protector, but they weren't exactly notable otherwise. The shifting, the fire conjuring—that was unaccounted for. What else was she? I could feel my mind pushing, trying desperately to connect the pieces quickly and efficiently, the threads familiar and terrifying. But no matter how much I tried to make the picture fit, I couldn't—it was impossible.

Sarah took a deep breath, but still, she kept walking. "There are rumors. Rumors that some important players are looking for a girl, a female protector specifically. It's why there's been an increase in attacks near Guild boundaries over the last few years, why so many of the women specifically have been taken. They're looking for her."

"Why *you* were taken, you mean? Why they didn't kill you,

and why they stole you away when you survived the initial attack." Declan clenched her jaw, her tone steely.

I'd gathered they all knew each other, picked up on the little introductions during the escape, but I didn't quite understand how they'd all come to be separated. Not yet, anyway. To be fair, I wasn't sure I really gave a shit. The interpersonal dynamics of protectors was tiring and boring—there were far more interesting things afoot.

She nodded. "Whoever finds her, they'll be in a strong bargaining position."

"What would demons need to bargain for?" Eli asked, glancing briefly out of the side of his eyes at the wolf.

He'd been keeping his distance from us all, but he'd followed us nonetheless, creeping silently behind. I could still feel the anger radiating from him like a beacon, but even stronger than the prick's rage was his fear.

I'd warned the alpha asshat that this would happen if he didn't learn to work with his wolf, to see himself and the demon as one and the same. I understood better than most how difficult and necessary it was to keep two halves of yourself together as one, but I doubted anyone would find an 'I told you so' as amusing as I would right now.

"The same thing protectors, humans, and anyone else would bargain for. Power, protection—the things necessary for a chance at surviving in this place." Sarah's voice was light and airy, but I could see the slight tremble of her lips, the way her eyes shot around as we walked, like she was constantly expecting company. She was scared. Absolutely and completely petrified of this realm and the creatures in it. Good. That meant she was intelligent. And that sort of perception would be necessary if she had any hope of staying alive. "None of us really understand who this girl is. There's very little information about her. Some believe she's not really a protector at all, but has some mysterious power, some think she's stolen something—a solution to fix this place maybe, to put it back as it was. But it's all speculation

—at least among those I've spoken to anyway. I'm about as low on the ladder as you can get down here. Like, I'm honestly lucky to have even found a spot in my pack to begin with. But I've been given no description of her, no concrete image. Just that she's among protectors and that someone very important is looking for."

"And when someone important in this realm needs something," I continued, as Max's face flashed through my mind, bright and beautiful and terrifying in her own way, "whoever possesses it—or destroys it—holds great power."

Sarah's lips thinned into a straight line, as she nodded in agreement.

"Everyone is after her, then? This girl?" Eli asked, his voice hitching slightly as he scanned the woods, fist clenched around his blade, ready to take on the invisible forces if they made themselves known to us.

I'd give the kid one thing, he sure as hell wasn't one to run away from a fight.

It would get me killed, one of these days.

Sarah nodded as Declan's eyes shot to mine—cold realization dawning on her features.

We all knew that Max was different, special. And wherever she was, it sounded like she was under the possession of a powerful player in this fucked up game. For now, we just had to hope that whoever that player was, they were one of the ones who wanted to use her, not destroy her.

I bristled at a soft scratching sound.

When I searched for the culprit, I saw only my hand, covered in blood as my fingers dug into the bark of a nearby tree. I wiped my hand against my leg before anyone noticed, trying to rein in my thoughts before the demon beneath my skin unleashed any real damage.

In that moment, I couldn't think of anything worse than Max being destroyed, of her presence no longer being in my life. And neither could my darker half. She'd added so many layers and colors and complexities to my world—I wasn't ready to let that go, even if I didn't fully understand it.

All this time I knew that a bigger game was being played, that the pieces were being slowly manipulated around the board, ready to play their part when given the sign. And I knew that there was something about Max, that she had a role to play in all of it.

I'd just always assumed that Max would be one small pawn, a tiny piece no one would miss if I stole her away and kept her safe, protected. A source of amusement, mine to do with as I pleased.

I'd forgotten that all pawns had the power to become something more, something pivotal.

Somehow, while the rest of us were getting kidnapped and beaten up, deciding whether to destroy each other or pool our strengths together, Max had crossed the board all on her own.

I was so focused on staying one step ahead in the game, that I didn't realize until it was too late—she'd become a queen. There was no untangling her from this mess anymore, whatever this mess actually was. She was woven into it, tethered and fused.

Our walk was mostly silent after that, all of us too tired and hungry and terrified for Max to discuss much of anything else. At one point, the wolf caught a pair of rabbits and brought them back to us, tentatively dropping them at my feet before darting away again in the woods. I quickly drained one dry, then cooked the meat up, while we all tried to pretend that the few bites of gamey meat we were each able to force down were enough to satiate our empty bellies.

We didn't come across any creatures, at least not any that wanted to be noticed anyway, as Sarah carved a path.

She paused frequently, listening carefully, touching a twig or tree here and there, like she wasn't entirely sure she knew where she was going, not completely trusting her instincts as she might in her other form.

I imagined it was because she'd spent most of her time traveling as her wolf. That's how her pack would have wanted to see her after recently transitioning—in the body of her wolf more than in that of the protector, at least until they could trust that she was one of them. Judging by the way that Jameson had devoured her with his eyes, and the fact that Mickey's lip curled with jealousy whenever she was around, she'd found her place amongst the group eventually, carved out a niche all her own. She was valuable to them, and hopefully that meant she would be valuable to us—our own pawn to use as we made our way to Max.

She frequently shot furtive looks at Declan, and though I didn't know her well at all, I saw the fear in her eyes, the shame. Almost as if she'd thought about shifting, allowing her wolf to run free with Atlas's, but didn't out of respect for her.

And the other two—Declan and Eli—kept almost completely silent, both lost in their own thoughts, trying with every step forward to stay standing. Hell was a formidable realm for the strongest of us. For two protectors who'd already taken a series of brutal beatings, it was like walking through a field of landmines. Together, they looked crumpled and weary, one obstacle away from collapsing altogether. Still, something about them was sturdy, stronger than most protectors, like they were morphing into something else, something better before my very eyes.

"Should we pause for the night?" Sarah's voice was little more than a whisper, but it carried on the wind.

Strangely, I found myself liking her. Maybe it was because she was part wolf. She didn't seem to have quite the same hangups about sharing a body with a demon as the others had. When we first escaped, she seemed filled with a quiet terror, the sort that broke most people, made them fragile. But the more I studied her, the more I realized that she used her fear to empower her, to protect herself like a shield, to fuel her forward. She'd abandoned and betrayed the one group in hell who had offered her a place, protection. She gave it up without a thought for her new packmates. All to save her friends from another life.

Protection and safety were not the sort of things people let go of lightly. And yet she had—for them.

I wasn't sure where she'd go from here, once we got wherever we were going, if we even survived this place at all, but I found myself strangely hoping that she found safety somehow, somewhere.

I glanced at the other two, seeing them through her empathetic eyes, the limp in Declan's step yielding a double take. I clenched my jaw. The last thing I wanted to do was leave Max for another night. A night was a long time—anything could happen to her. Her captor could decide she was of no more use, could move her somewhere else, could do something worse.

"Maybe you should," I said, settling for a compromise, "just tell me where to go and I can try to find her tonight. We'll come back for you all once I've got her."

The wolf growled from a few feet away, his eyes lasered on mine, ears pressed flat against his head as the leaves crunched beneath his flexing paws.

Declan froze, her nostrils flaring slightly as she looked past me to Sarah. "No. We keep going. We are getting them back as soon as we can. This isn't up for a discussion."

Something softened in my chest as I watched resolve straighten her posture, flatten out the limp in her step. She was very good at masking her injuries and vulnerabilities, when she knew someone was looking for them. Less so when she didn't. Still, something like pride swelled through me, maybe even a little gratitude.

Wherever Max was, our odds of breaking her out increased as our numbers did. There was no denying that.

Sarah opened her mouth, closed it again, then finally turned towards Declan. "Are you sure—'

"We do as she said. We continue." Eli's fingers flexed and relaxed, flexed and relaxed over the blade in his hand, almost like the repetitive motion lulled his anxiety and anger into something softer. Since Sarah had collected our weapons and distributed them back to us, he'd been unconsciously keeping a hand on his at all times, clearly terrified it'd be taken away again, that he'd be defenseless once more.

I didn't blame him. This wasn't the place to be caught unarmed. And protectors didn't exactly have the built-in tools that most of us here had. Honestly, I was kind of surprised he'd made it this far.

As soon as that thought hit me, a shudder ran through me—not for the first time, I found myself regretting my decision to tie my life to his.

"Alright," Sarah said, exhaling so sharply that the hair framing her face started to dance around her. "We continue." She glanced once more at Declan, her eyes betraying only a transient look of worry before they walled back up to the confidence she donned like an armor. "But if you change your mind—if you get even a little bit tired—you tell me and we stop. You'll be no help to the girl where she is if you wear yourselves out before we even arrive."

"Promise, cuz," Declan said, a small grin tilting her lips.

I could hear the lie, see it painted across her face in every micro expression she made.

But I wouldn't press. I was getting to Max. If the others dropped like flies in the process, let them.

"Where exactly is it that you think she's being kept?" I asked again. I'd asked a variation of the same question a handful of times since leaving the pack's headquarters, but each time, the girl had acted like she couldn't hear, the only sign that she had, a slight stiffening in her posture, her lips thinning into a flat line.

"You're like a broken record," she said, at least deigning to give me a response this time. "I'm beginning to understand why that other vamp was almost excited by the prospect of your death."

Nash. There'd been no sign of him since leaving our prison,

and I didn't expect I'd see him again. He wasn't the sort to stick around and deal with someone else's problems. Still, I couldn't deny that his departure stung—not sharp and loud like a knife wound, but lingering and frustrating like a papercut. We'd been friends once, and I doubted I'd ever learn the truth about his sister, Nika, now that he was gone.

"It's nothing personal. Nash enjoys being the most interesting, powerful man in the room," I said, grinning at Sarah. She blushed slightly before breaking eye contact. In another life, I'd take this as an opportunity to flirt. She was a pretty girl, smart, entertaining. But I had no interest in her beyond her ability to take me to Max. "And he knows that if I'm around," I continued lazily, "he doesn't stand a chance."

"Jesus, quit preening." Eli nodded ahead of us to where a small stream split the forest. "Is that drinkable?"

When Sarah nodded, he and Declan hurried over, gulping down handfuls of water like they'd been in a long, tumultuous war with dehydration.

"Humans are so fragile," I muttered.

"They're not human," Sarah said, though her brows bent with concern as she studied them.

Was she noticing the rift gradually shaping between them, now that she had the power of a demon inside of her? Was her awareness of protector fragility heightened?

I shrugged. "Close enough. Protectors don't carry the sort of power that they once did. They are mere echoes of what they were, no real danger to us unless they have numbers."

She arched a brow, walking towards the water herself now. "I don't know, leech. From what I hear, seems they're powerful enough to have captured you and locked you away for a few years."

My jaw clenched, my teeth creaking under the strain. I opened my mouth to argue, to explain what had really happened when I'd been locked up, how one small moment of weakness, compassion, years ago had almost gotten me killed, but then I closed my lips, joined them at the water, and took a few long, deep sips. I almost groaned as the first drop hit my tongue, a wave of nostalgia washing over me at the earthy sweetness.

I didn't miss living in this place. When I was here, I'd spent all of my time and energy on finding a way out. But I'd spent most of my life wandering this terrain. It was where some of my fonder memories had taken place—and as much as I hated the claustrophobia of this realm, the constant, exhausting fight to survive, it had been home.

A soft, peaceful silence fell over us as we took a minute to collect ourselves. Even the wolf joined in for a few sips, though he was sure to stand a good fifty feet ahead of us.

Eli sat down, his arms propped on his knees, expression stern as he studied Sarah. "Where is she? You've avoided the question every time it's been asked. I can't tell if it's because the fanghole is the one asking it or because something else is eating away at you."

Sarah ran her hands over her face, and when her eyes made their appearance again, there was a haunted look in them. "There's a place about half a day's walk from here. No one steps foot on that territory—not even Jameson." She paused, shaking her head, "and I know you guys don't know much about Jameson, but he's big time. He has a lot of power here, a lot of respect. For even him to be afraid—"

"Whose territory is it?" I asked, dropping the stick I'd been absentmindedly carving pictures in the dirt with. When I glanced down, I saw the silhouette of a girl's body drawn into the ground. It looked suspiciously like Max's, which made my stomach flip with embarrassment. Maybe the protectors really had broken me. I was not some teenage girl, lovesick and carving a name inside a heart on a tree. I swept my foot over the image, erasing the likeness before anyone else saw it.

"I don't know."

"You don't know?" Declan's voice held a note of urgency, and she gripped the blade at her side as if whoever had Sarah shaken up so badly was in the woods amongst us now.

"There are rumors. That a powerful group has emerged. They call them the ancients. No one's heard from them in recent memory, but some believe that they are back. That they're secretly running things here, controlling the different factions and hiring them out to do their bidding. Whoever lives in that territory—" she paused, dug her nails into her fists, "Jameson's worked for or with—I don't really know the details—them a few times, but he won't speak of it, not even to me. Each time I asked, his face would get drawn and pasty and he'd change the subject." There was an undertone of hurt in her voice, and I wondered if she actually cared for that asshat, worried about whether or not he lived or died. He'd kept her alive, so maybe she was just grateful. "He wouldn't let me near the boundary. It is understood amongst my people—the wolves, I mean," her cheeks reddened as she stumbled over her words, "that no one crosses into that territory without invitation. Not if they value their lives."

"And you think this is where she is?" Eli asked, like the absolute fuckwad he is.

I resisted the urge to roll my eyes. Of course that's where Max was, did everything need to be spelled out for him. When danger was involved, Max was like a goddamn magnet, heading straight for it.

"Obviously, you twat," Declan answered, though there was no bite to her words, just a lazy amusement, like she was talking to an obtuse younger brother.

I didn't bother hiding the grin that spread across my face.

"The boundary," Sarah continued, "it's near water."

"Then that's where we go." I stretched my arms above my head, letting the muscles in my body tense and relax. Wherever this was, it sounded ominous. But I knew Jameson, and while he'd clearly grown up since I'd last seen him, he wasn't the big bad that Sarah seemed to think that he was. He might be frightened of whoever existed beyond this boundary, but that didn't mean I needed to be.

With a quick sweep of my hands, I glanced at the others: the wolf sulking near a lopsided tree, body tensed and ready for a fight like some hormonal teenager whose emotions swung in competing directions, an indecisive pendulum; the girl awkwardly caught in her family drama, deciding whether she fit best with her old pack or her new one; the moody protector who despised everything about the hell realm, but secretly harbored resentment that she didn't hold as much power or strength as the creatures she hated; and the fuckboy who seemed to get himself almost killed every five minutes, but who occasionally provided some useful insight or comedic relief.

For a moment, I wished I had a bit more of an impressive army. They didn't inspire much hope when charging into unknown territory led by some mysterious entity. If I weren't so completely obsessed with keeping Max around, I'd ditch them all here and watch as hell had its way with them, picking them off one by one. But that moment passed as quickly as it came, until I realized that while I disliked them all intensely in theory, I also found myself increasingly enjoying their company. Almost like they were...friends.

So into the fray we'd go, and all I could do was pray that we weren't met with death. I'd certainly made do with worse.

WE WALKED FOR HOURS, STOPPING BRIEFLY, ONCE OR TWICE, for the two protectors to catch their breath. I knew that if the wolves and I ditched them, we could have cut the time in half, but as agreed, we stuck together. It was strange. I'd spent so much time not killing them and draining them dry one-by-one that I was growing almost accustomed to the company—even the annoying one was proving more entertaining than tiresome.

Most of the time was spent in silence, each of us focusing all of our attention on making sure that we weren't followed, on carving paths through the forest that kept us hidden. The girls would whisper together whenever we'd stop to quickly share a few gulps of water or a bite of rabbit, both of them shredding meat casually from the bone as if they were catching up over chicken wings at an Applebee's. The wolf kept his distance, but as the hours wore on, I could feel him growing more restless, constantly torn between staying with us and voyaging after her on his own.

"How much longer?" I could feel my own restless energy stirring beneath my skin and almost wanted to join him, to tear off through the trees and be done with the suspense and anticipation.

Sarah rolled her eyes, cursing under her breath before she walked up to a large hedge, running her hand smoothly along the leaves, admiring but not touching. "It's here." She took a step back, her posture stiffening. "Once we cross to the other side, we'll be there. But like I said, before, be sure you want to do that. No one who crosses uninvited ever comes out."

"Ominous." Eli stretched his arms in the air and rolled his neck from side to side. Then, with a bright smile and soft clap, he moved towards the hedge and started to climb. "Let's get at the dying then."

The rest of us followed, half climbing, half falling through the twigs and leaves, until we were all standing on the other side.

Eli stood first, then pulled Declan to her feet. He looked around, his lips turning down in a slight frown as he scanned the woods and path that looked no different than where we'd just stood. "That was kind of anticlimactic. I was expecting some fiery pit, or at the very least a dragon or something to come and devour us alive."

Ignoring him, I walked towards the base of a large hill. A huge wave of power hit me just as I reached it, running through me until it was lacing my veins, wrapping my bones. I shuddered, fighting the impulse to drop to my knees.

Judging by the collective grunts behind me, like a strangled or garbled echo, the others felt it too.

"Jesus," Eli gasped, his teeth grinding together as his wild eyes darted between the rest of us, desperately searching for one of us to have an answer.

I didn't. I'd never felt anything like this, had never encountered this kind of magic before. It felt like we were on a fault line between worlds, the magic seeping through us, not unlike it did in portals.

It wasn't painful, not in the traditional sense anyway. But it was a heavy sort of power—pure and raw and hungry. And just as I could feel it fighting me back, warning me away, something about it enchanted me, pulling me forward if I just dared to push myself a little.

I took one slow, steady step, and then another until, eventually, I reached the top. My brow was covered in sweat, my legs shaky as I tried to keep myself steady.

When I turned around, I was surprised to find that Eli wasn't too far behind me, his jaw clenched, face ashen, but, like me, he seemed to have made it through the worst of it.

Atlas was behind him, teeth bared and head bowed as he fought his way to the top.

I was surprised to see Declan clawing her way up after him, her hands digging into the dirt as she pulled herself up, unable to rely on just her feet to keep her steady. Sarah was still at the bottom, her face pinched in pain as she pushed forward, inch by measly inch, trying to catch up with us.

How was Eli stronger than a werewolf in this moment—was he changing, morphing into something...more? Because of my blood?

I shook my head. No. Declan didn't have my blood streaming in her veins, but she was fighting this resistance off better than the other girl was.

"What the hell is this?" Eli breathed out, his hands pressing into his knees as he tried to catch his breath—it was as if he'd just run a double marathon, not walked slowly up a small hill.

And I got it, because while my body didn't look quite as strained as his seemed to be, I sure as hell felt it.

I said nothing, having no other response. Slowly, with each inhale and exhale, I felt my body start to adjust to the power, to find a way to move within it, between the cracks. Judging by the way the wolf shook his head, his hackles relaxing slightly, I wasn't the only one.

After what felt like an hour, but could have been nothing more than a minute or two, Declan reached us, landing on her back with a soft thud. Her eyes opened to the sky, her irises like a mirror, reflecting the swirling atmosphere in them. Each breath looked excruciating as her body fought to calm itself, to regulate with the magic instead of against it.

But, eventually, like us, she succeeded—the strain in her face melting away into an exhaustion, uncomfortable, but manageable.

And then we could do nothing but wait for the second wolf. When she reached about a quarter of the way up the hill, she peeled off her shirt, and then her pants, the striptease awkward and disjointed in her discomfort. With a pain-filled groan, her bones snapped and reformed.

I turned away, for some reason compelled to give her the semblance of privacy, watching her cousin's expression instead. Declan's eyes were wild with too many emotions for me to read, though fear and curiosity seemed to take center stage, as she watched the girl turn from a woman into a wolf. Surprisingly, there was little animosity in that storm—the reactive emotions slowly slipped away, until all that I could see was a soft compassion. She didn't hate her cousin for transitioning, the anger held in the line of her jaw, the bend between her brows, appeared more internalized than anything.

I averted my gaze, suddenly uncomfortable reading her like this, her thoughts all but etched in her skin as she recovered her body from whatever the fuck we'd just pushed through. The wolf was halfway up now, her fur black as night, threaded through with highlights of brown. She was larger than I would've pictured, her yellow eyes bright and hungry as she fought her way towards us.

Transitioned wolves were often weaker than the others, but there was a quiet strength in this wolf, just as there had been in the girl.

We all watched silently as she made her way towards us, each step forward feeling like it took an eternity of effort to accomplish. Why was this so much more difficult for her?

Just as I was getting ready to leave her to her struggle, a sudden desperate urge to find Max rolling through me until my toes curled, she made her way over the hill, standing closer to Atlas than the rest of us. Her yellow eyes looked everywhere but at Declan for a long moment, until Declan stood in the path of the demon's stare, crouching down until they were at eye level.

"I see you," Declan breathed out, the words little more than a whisper along the wind. She raised a shaky hand up, though something about the tremble seemed to be more a result of her body's exhaustion than fear.

As if that was all it needed, the wolf walked forward on shaky legs, nudging its head against Declan's hand. The tension dissolved immediately and, as one, we all turned towards the other side of the hill.

Nothing but a long, winding path, the trees covering most of it in shadow, but in the distance, I heard the soft murmur of the river, and my shoulders relaxed. I'd never been to this part of the shore before, but the River Styx was my place of calm—and though I couldn't see it yet, I could feel it as I breathed in, searching for the familiar scent.

"Let's go," I said, stepping in the direction of that familiar brine, the sense of detachment I associated with the river washing over me in a steady gulp—no other place had ever made me feel small and large at once, powerful and insignificant. We were nothing against this river. But that meant that whoever had Max was nothing against it either.

I felt my body slowly recover from whatever strange magic stood at the barrier of this territory, my legs feeling less and less wobbly. In all of my years in this realm, I'd never once experienced anything like it—the magic felt old and powerful, but it wasn't the same unfamiliar magic that had been lingering in the air. They both stemmed from the same place, maybe, but they weren't the same.

The others seemed to grow stronger slowly as well, though the female wolf hadn't quite adjusted as we had. I wasn't sure why it seemed to affect her so much more. Perhaps because she'd been living here longer than we had, the power had more influence over her body. She stayed in wolf form, her eyes constantly darting towards Atlas, though he seemed to have very little interest in her. His focus was steady and forward, like he felt the same strange tug towards the river that I did.

We climbed hill after hill, each time a similar wave of power knocking us to our knees, but the recovery time reduced with each threshold we pushed past. For all of us, that is, except for Sarah.

"Maybe you should turn back," I whispered to her quietly as the others carved their way, slowly and begrudgingly up the nearest hill in front of us.

She growled in response.

"Can I carry you at least?" The power dipped into my belly, until my limbs felt like jelly again, but it was a tolerable pressure, like my body was slowly growing accustomed to the feeling, making room for it.

She growled again.

I walked slowly by her side, watching her body tremble with pain as she fought against the source. Midway up, she collapsed to the ground.

"Fuck it," I whispered, scooping her into my arms against my chest. Her weight added little difficulty to my climb and I was feet away from the others in moments.

A low growl vibrated against my chest, like she was pressing her frustration into me.

"Don't be so dramatic, we're almost to the top."

Eli clutched his knees as he reached the peak, his breaths much steadier with this climb than they had been with the last one. It was like he was growing stronger the further we pushed. I was almost impressed with the stamina. Maybe a life attached to his would be longer than I'd given him credit for.

"Oh my god," he whispered. His tone always had a trace of teasing to it, but the sarcastic lilt was drained dry this time.

I set Sarah down as I closed the distance between us and traced his gaze with my own. "Fuck."

On the other side of our hill, in a long row, stood what appeared to be at least fifty creatures. I couldn't identify them all by appearance alone, but most seemed to be either wolves or vampires. It was the line behind them that made my breath stutter in my chest.

Declan's arm brushed beside mine as she moved to stand between me and Eli. "Those can't be...are those—" her question trailed off, like if she didn't give words to our completely fucked situation, we might be able to escape it somehow.

"Hellhounds," I answered, a wave of dread hitting me like a sharp wave, "more than I've ever seen in my life. More than I knew even existed."

There had to be at least fifteen there, lined up with teeth bared as they watched us, waiting. Other than Max's hound, I'd only ever come across the creatures two or three times. And the overgrown dogs below us made Ralph look like an absolute runt, like a goddamn puppy in comparison.

"Fuck," Eli repeated, like a soft chant or prayer.

For a long moment, we stared at the row of creatures, not one of us making a move to turn around and head back—away from this place.

Like me, they knew the truth, knew what this meant.

"She's here," Declan finally said, as she unsheathed her blade. There was a small tremble in her fingers, but she controlled it almost as soon as I'd noticed it.

"She's here," I confirmed. "And something tells me that the only way to get to her is through them."

My eyes darted to the wolves, then back to the two protectors at my side. I nodded once and they each followed suit, the reality of the situation settling over us all. As one, we turned back towards the line of creatures, hands gripping weapons, claws digging into the soft dirt—and then, we charged.

I crashed into a werewolf first, the gray fur threading through my fingers as I wrapped my hands around the creature's neck, snapping it in half just as it dug its teeth into my shoulder. The wound was shallow and I didn't give it a second look.

Chaos sounded around me, yells and clamors as bodies rammed together. I caught brief glimpses of Declan and Eli out of the corner of my eye as three vampires surrounded me, two women and a guy who looked like he'd walked straight out of a surfing magazine.

I didn't recognize them, not that I expected otherwise. Something told me that I'd never encountered any of these creatures before. There was a heavy power about them, like they were tapping into some mystical source that none of the rest of us had access to. What the hell was this place?

The guy lunged for me first, but I dodged just as his fist went soaring past my face. He turned with a grunt, the carefree look in his expression dissolving into something darker as rage seeped through.

Not waiting for him to strike again, I turned to the shorter of the two girls and dove onto her. We crashed to the ground in an awkward puddle of limbs as I hit and punched with as much force as I could muster. The man jumped on my back, scratching and beating at it, but I ignored him long enough to force my right hand through the girl's chest, squeezing her heart until the light left her eyes.

With a loud roar, I unsheathed my hand, the warm blood running down my arms as I turned and shook my body from side to side, trying to dislodge the California asshole.

When I turned back to him, ready to attack, I saw Declan gripped by the other female vampire. Just as her fangs were about to puncture Declan's porcelain skin, she paused, her eyes wide with shock, and fell to the ground. Eli was behind her, face covered in a wash of blood. Without breaking his stride, he bent down for his blade and the two of them went off to take on the next creature.

I broke the surfer's neck, waiting until he dropped, stunned, before I turned his heart into playdough too.

That was four of these assholes down, but there were too many for us to take. It was like they were toying with us all for now, taking us on one by one, trying their skills against us.

A black and brown wolf lunged towards me, digging its claws into my back when I tried to regain my footing. I reached back and lifted it back over my head, tossing it with as much force as I could, knocking three or four other wolves down in the process, like a gorey bowling ball.

But where were *my* wolves?

I turned in a quick circle, my ears ringing with the sound of battle, a sound that was somehow filled with silence and noise all at once, until I found them a few feet away.

Atlas was entangled in a skirmish with two others, but he seemed to be holding his own. And then there was Sarah—her head clutched in the hands of a man with black hair and alarmingly blue eyes, dressed in all black. I couldn't tell what he was, but everything about him screamed pure, unbridled strength.

He held her gently, like he was studying her with the sort of curiosity and disgust one might reserve for an intentionally ugly installation in a museum. But curiosity or not, I could feel it in my bones—he was going to kill her.

Eli was closer than I was, and as I ran towards her, I kept one eye on him. He was...fast. Way faster than I'd ever given him credit for, faster than any protector I'd ever seen.

Was my blood changing him? Or was there something else in play?

I caught up to him just as he reached them.

"Stop," he screamed, his hands thoughtlessly reaching towards the man.

Could he not feel his power? He wouldn't stand a chance.

The man turned, a dark brow arched as he studied Eli with the same curious amusement he'd leveled at Sarah. But then, his eyes narrowed, curiosity turning to surprise, and he dropped Sarah to the ground.

She skittered away quickly, clawing at the dirt until she reached Eli's feet, her yellow eyes wild with fear.

"You're strong," he sniffed, his blue eyes tracing Eli from head to toe. "But I smell nothing but protector about you?" His lip curled around the word in disgust as his eyes darted to mine, "and maybe just a touch of your friend."

He could *smell* the blood bond? What the fuck kind of demon was this?

The man's gaze leveled on me and I knew that I'd have to be the one to take him down. I was stronger than the others, the only member of our pathetic group who'd have even a small chance of escaping this nightmare with my spine still attached to my skull. The only one with enough strength to try and reach Max—but even then, I knew with a certainty that pulled heavily in my stomach that I would fail.

The other demons were still crowding around us, pressing us closer, but no creatures attacked inside of our bubble with this stranger. A single glance from him had stopped an over-eager vampire charging towards us, her heart racing with adrenaline, cold in her step, shoes skidding as dirt splashed up to my knees in a cloud of dust.

Who the fuck was this man, and what the hell was this place?

He turned back towards Eli, taking another slow step towards us both. "How did you get through the barrier, protector?" he pressed, tilting his head to the side, like it would help him decipher the answer. "And how did you do so less affected by its power than a werewolf?"

There was no rage on his face, none of the bloodlust that I could feel radiating from the demons surrounding us, just a strange sort of unexpected curiosity, like the evening had suddenly become far more interesting than he'd imagined.

Atlas's wolf stalked the perimeter of our strange, slowly tightening circle. Hopefully he wouldn't attack this man as recklessly as he'd attacked me. He wasn't the brightest creature in the world, but I had a feeling that even he could read the room, could understand that he would stand no chance against a creature like this. None of us would stand a chance against him.

The man's questions washed over me as my eyes darted from person to person, tracking each member of my strange group, trying to identify a hole through the demons, a path for us to escape. But there were none.

How had Eli and Declan pushed past such a strong barrier with less effort than Sarah had?

"And why," the man continued, waving a strange, glowing dagger, "has a vampire willingly bonded to a protector?" His eyes landed back on me again, but my focus was on that blade. There was something familiar about it, though I couldn't place where I'd last seen an instrument like that. The mere sight of it sent the darkness within me ramming against the wall I kept it contained behind, desperately pushing to escape, to either take this man head on or leave this place, and these people, behind for good. I couldn't tell which desire was stronger. "These bonds are so interesting, don't you think?"

And then, without another word, the movement so fast I could hardly even track it, he plunged the blade into Eli's abdomen.

My groan echoed his less than a moment later. The

mirrored wound was instantaneous, as if he'd stabbed me at the same time that Eli had—the pain sharper than anything I'd ever felt before. It dropped me to my knees, my hands running uselessly over the wound, searching for a weapon that wasn't there.

I could feel Eli writhing on the ground next to me, Atlas's whines dancing in the air around us, weaving together with Declan's screams. She was bent over Eli, and I could see the indecision in her posture, the rigidness of her spine, the strain around her eyes. Was it better to leave the blade where it was or better to pull it out?

She left it, her hands pressing down on my stomach, like she was trying to stem my bleeding.

Surprise at her action, more than the pain, stole the breath from my lungs. But it passed as soon as it came. Of course she needed me to survive. If I didn't then Eli wouldn't either.

Generally, a cut to the gut wouldn't do much to a vampire, but something about this blade had my insides flaming, like I was being burned from the inside out. A blinding, piercing light was flashing across my eyes, a deep, low whistling sound pulling through my ears. All of my senses were firing at once, and I could feel how clammy my skin was, how difficult it was to push each breath through my lungs. I was not an easy vampire to fell, not by a long shot. In fact, on a good day, at my peak, I might even stand a chance against this asshole. But whatever magic he was wielding through that weapon wasn't good. Like maybe even reaching a kill-a-vampire-without-decapitation-or-heart-piercing level of not good.

Fuck.

"Yes," the man said, crouching low so that his taunting eyes were level with mine. He almost reminded me of Eli in that moment—smug, powerful, teasing. A more nefarious version of him, anyway. "Such strange magic, isn't it? Beautiful in a way." He arched his brow, lip lifting slightly, though he was starting to seem more bored than amused now, like the game was almost over. "Let's see which of you dies first. And then, I'll kill your friends."

Great.

I felt the certainty in his voice, the realization sinking into my flesh. This was it. This was how I was going down. I'd survived literal hell, and then after that, years living as a glorified lab rat. And my ultimate demise was going to be this? Charging into a horde of demons with a fucking B-team, like an obnoxious tool? Maybe Claude was right to despise me as much as he did. Clearly, something really had been irreparably damaged during my captivity.

A small whimper pulled through my lips. If I was in less agony, I might even be embarrassed by the fact that I'd let such vulnerability slip through when surrounded by so many enemies. Were they all just going to sit here and watch?

Declan was whispering something, eyes darting wildly between Atlas and Sarah, like she was reaching for anything, any option to keep us alive. She even turned to the man, fell down to her knees, lips moving a mile a minute. When he only grinned, she stood up and started beating her fists against his chest. He merely laughed as she broke down in tears, the exertion pushing her back down to the floor.

Max. Suddenly a wave of fear, so much more acute than the agony, pierced through me. What would happen to Max with none of us there to save her? Would she die, alone and abandoned in the prison she was trapped inside? The thought of her no longer walking this world, or the human one, hit me with a wave of pain that made the man's blade feel downright fun and flirty.

A shimmer in the air surrounded us, a small disruption in which there was nothing there and then, all of a sudden...something.

And not just any kind of something, something goddamn beautiful. Dark hair, clothes in tatters, limbs wobbly from whatever the fuck had just happened, but there all the same.

Max.

It was like my mind was carving out a final, perfect hallucination, something tender to guide me into the afterlife, a hand to hold as I went.

But when her dark eyes met mine, wide with worry and laced with fear, I knew that she wasn't a hallucination. No magic in the world could conjure her with such vivid clarity, every curve, every hair, every impossible-to-separate emotion flitting across her features.

She was always simultaneously an open book and impossible to read, all in one—just one of the many things that made her so intriguing. The invitation was always there, I just didn't always have the tools to translate.

I chuckled, in spite of it all, my vision going in and out as I felt my lips split into a smile. How did I keep making this mistake? Why did I keep underestimating her?

It was so fucking obvious to me now.

We were never going to be the ones to rescue her from the dungeon, like a pack of misguided fairytale heroes, desperate for a redemption arc.

It was Max.

She was the hero of this story.

Max was always going to be the one to rescue us. She'd already done so more times than I could count.

16

ATLAS

H^{er.}

🜨 17 🜩

MAX

pparently, this was my life now.

One minute I was practicing the whole flame conjuring thing, trying not to be weirded out by the fact that snapping my fingers turned me into a living chemistry experiment, and the next my body was being pulled through space like I was little more than a genie being summoned through a lamp.

But the pain, holy shit the pain.

I clutched my stomach as my body recreated itself in this new landscape, trying to swallow back the bile rising towards the back of my throat. My feet pressed firm into the ground as my eyes adjusted, my vision swimming with lights and colors as I tried to make sense of what I was seeing.

It was the smell that hit me hardest, cluing me in to where I was, just a few moments before my eyes could take everything in: cool, fresh air, the briny salt of the ocean.

Were there oceans in hell? I shook my head, trying to focus on what really mattered, my hands trembling with a strange mixture of relief and fear.

I was *outside*.

Not just outside of my tiny prison cell, but outside of the dungeon-castle altogether.

A brief flare of joy pushed past the sharp pain in my stomach, the exhaustion in my limbs. I took a deep breath, savoring all of the different scents competing for my attention, relishing the feel of the breeze and light against my skin.

And then I peeled my eyelids back open and looked—really looked.

Any relief I'd felt moments before, evaporated in an instant.

This was not some peaceful scene. I was not standing, toes in the sand, as waves of water splashed on my toes. I'd landed in the middle of something dark, something tinged with the aftertaste of death and destruction.

My breath skipped as my gaze dropped to a man. It wasn't just any man, of course. My luck didn't work out like that. Instead, I was face-to-face with the terrifying man with piercing blue eyes, who I'd narrowly escaped as I ran through the halls of the dungeon, awkwardly shifting in and out of space as I'd made my way to Wade. His eyes were wide with surprise as he studied me, fixating on where my hands pressed against my stomach.

I dropped my fingers slowly, expecting to find a bloody wound, but my skin was unblemished, the pain I was feeling invisible.

He took a quick step closer to me, fingers twitching like he wasn't quite sure what to do with his hands. Something in his face softened slightly, as if he was deciding whether he wanted to finish the job of killing me, or protect me from the invisible wound carving its path through my body.

Instead, he cleared his throat and settled on one word: "How?"

It was only a breath, that word, but I felt the wonder in it all the same. Whatever I'd done had shaken him to his core.

I parted my lips, ready to shoot the same question back at him, when I dropped my gaze to my left. My chest squeezed at the figure kneeling there, battered and bruised, but breathing. Alive. "Darius?"

His eyes met mine, but there was so much shadow hidden in their depths that a wave of fear trickled down my spine. Every muscle was tense with pain. He looked like he was holding onto his life by a bare thread, worse off even than when he was locked up in The Guild research lab. I took a step forward, arms stretched out to touch him, to feel and process the fact that he was really there. Suddenly, I was desperate to prove he wasn't an illusion, some mirage conjured up by the demon hovering beside us, watching our every move.

But as I shifted towards Darius, I noticed Eli—dark hair clinging to his forehead, his entire body slick with sweat. My gaze dropped to his abdomen, where he held his stomach, hands unsure of whether to pull out the glowing blade that pierced him or not.

That blade.

I clenched my teeth at the sight of it, the memory of the last time I'd seen one like it rushing back with crystal clarity. It was the same as the one the cloaked man had used on Wade when he'd drawn me here. Or, at the very least, it was an identical match to it.

My fingers lightly pressed to my stomach again, the fading pain there an exact mirror to his. "What?"

My voice trickled away as I turned back to the blue-eyed man, desperate for answers. As I did, I noticed Declan, her clothes ripped to shreds, the typical illusive mask she wore nowhere in sight—pure fear and wonder were painted in the light of her eyes, the line of her lips, as she watched me. And then, next to her, tawny fur darkened with patches of blood, stood Atlas, yellow eyes locked on mine, unblinking.

My breath caught at the sight of them all here, my momentary gratitude cannibalized by a sharp fear. They were alive, all of them here, with me. But we were surrounded. And they all looked like they'd only barely just survived the fight of their lives.

A wall of demons, deep and terrifying, circled us all. And behind them, like a final sentinel, stood a row of hellhounds—most of them twice the size of Ralph and not one pair of eyes looking down on us with even a shadow of friendliness. Instead of the puppy-like joy and compassion I always found when I looked at Ralph, I saw instead a wall of bared teeth and raised hackles.

How the hell were we going to get out of this? I wasn't sure I had enough energy left to transport myself through space, let alone four others.

"You might be more interesting than I've given you credit for," the blue-eyed man tilted his head, studying me again, stare unflinching as he took another step towards me. "I can see why he thinks you're the one now. I'll admit, I didn't quite see it before, running about the castle like a reckless child. And your control over your power—laughable at best."

"Let us go," I said, straightening my posture as I stepped between him and my friends.

He simply chuckled in response, the sound deep and raspy.

My stomach dipped. I knew it was a futile demand, that I had nothing to give him in return, nothing to offer. And we were all cornered, surrounded by too many demons for me to even count at the moment. Even Darius, the strongest of us all, was wavering in and out of consciousness, a strangely amused grin on his face as he stared at me, like his mind was lost in some distant place, oblivious to the dangers threatening us all.

My fingers instinctively reached for my blade, determined to fight, even to the end. But of course it wasn't there. I'd lost it when—

"Looking for this?" The man held a dagger in front of my eyes, pinched between his thumb and pointer finger, swaying softly like a pendulum. "It's a nice piece. I've taken to carrying it around on the off chance you were let off your leash again. You can have it back if you'd like."

I held my breath as my eyes latched onto the familiar sapphire blue handle. It had been a gift from Cyrus and Ro when I turned nineteen. My fingers itched as I kept every muscle in my body still, trying with all of my willpower not to swipe it back from the man and carve that smug grin from his face. I'd lost it, last time I encountered him, the blade sinking into his neck as I took off running.

He shrugged, brow arching as his eyes met mine again. "I have no use for it." He grinned, but there was no humor in the gesture, only a sort of darkness that raised the hair on my arms. "Here."

He threw the blade like a dart, the handle and blade cart-wheeling through the air as it came bowling towards me, heading straight for my face at a speed no protector could leverage.

With a quick flick of my wrist, I plucked it from the sky, the swiftness and grace of my move startling even me. The muscle memory of my fingers latched around the sturdy handle like my hand was a glove, perfectly designed to fit to the piece. I held it at my side, eyes darting from the man to Darius and the members of Six, as I desperately tried to think up a plan to get us out of this situation.

I knew that I was powerful—I couldn't deny that any longer —but something told me that I was no match for the man in front of me, not while my powers sputtered in and out of control like a candle in the wind.

"Quick reflexes," the man said, voice a lazy drawl. The curiosity and wonder that had slipped from beneath his mask upon my arrival were nowhere to be seen. Instead, he looked suddenly bored and restless with the situation, like my friends and I weren't two inches away from being slaughtered by a horde of demons. "Let's put them further to the test, shall we? See what exactly all the hype is about." His bright eyes left mine briefly as he nodded to someone behind me, the gesture fluid and subtle, an entire conversation with no words.

"What do—" I spun around, just as a large wolf crossed the invisible barrier encasing us, diving straight for my chest.

I heard the chaos of the moment, as the creatures around us started to shift and bristle, but the noise reached me like an echo —near me, but also not. It was the grumbling of a warning, of what we would be met with once the blue-eyed man was tired of his games. The promise of death.

The wolf took me down with a heavy thud, my lungs deflating on impact. Its fur was a shiny white threaded through with shades of gray. I would've found it beautiful under any other circumstance. But the sharp teeth heading straight for my jugular pushed back any appreciation that might have lingered deep in my thoughts.

I heard the others start to protest, Declan's yell, Atlas's growl, the sound of shuffling feet and groans my clue that they were trying to intervene, to help. But without so much as a word from the man, a line of hellhounds appeared from nowhere, a new circle forming where the other was before, cutting me off from my team like a border of shaggy-furred sentinels.

The wolf's fur stuck to my lips as I grunted under its weight, trying to regroup, to focus. I slid my blade into the animal's abdomen, unable to reach anything more pivotal from my precarious position underneath it.

A low whine whimpered in my ear, cannibalized by a growl as I shoved the creature off of me. I grabbed its head between my hands and a heavy snap rang through my bones as the wolf fell, temporarily stunned. I yanked my blade from it's abdomen, wiping the crimson liquid off on my pants.

The air was heavy with tension though, and I knew that this win would be nothing to the man—he was only just getting started.

Just as I got back to my feet, three other demons circled me —another wolf and, judging by the quick flash of fang, two vampires. One reminded me of an older version of Eli, dark hair and eyes, the smirk lazy and plastered against his face. The other looked young, a small teenage girl, but with a feral glare that made my blood run cold. Something about the hardness of her jawline, the subtle flare of her nostrils, made it abundantly clear that this was no game to her—this was life and death and she would be sure that in the end, she was the victor.

Not hesitating a moment, I pulled my arm back and punched the vamp who looked like Eli in the mouth. The impact sent him flying backward and me forward as a loud crack echoed around us. My hand hurt, but it was still mobile, so I was assuming his jaw was the unlucky one in that encounter.

Fingernails dug into my shoulders as the girl jumped on my back. I wrestled the man to the ground, trying to shake her off in the process, hitting and clawing at whatever my hands could reach. My breath came in heavy pants as adrenaline coursed through my body.

Despite it all, I felt a small grin pull at my lips from the exertion, from the chance to vent out all of my frustration of the last few days.

But that momentary was reprieve and appreciation was just that—momentary.

I felt something sharp pierce the back of my neck just as the blue-eyed man yelled a hurried and harsh 'no,' and I knew with a vivid certainty that she'd bitten me. Warm blood spread down my back and shoulder as she took in long, feverish drags.

Fear clamped my ribs and I took a deep breath, visualizing my fire as I slipped my dagger into the other vampire's chest cavity, relaxing slightly when he stopped thrashing at my chest, teeth clattering shut a millisecond before they bit into my other shoulder, ready to join his partner in the feast.

Blinding light flared around me and I heard the girl's high-pitched screams of agony echoing and distant, before I fully understood what was happening.

The flames were strong, dancing with a hurried tremor in

shades of purple and orange, until the vision of them eclipsed the girl altogether. Her body crumpled to the ground in a series of low wails, and I tried to call the fire back, wanting to keep her from attacking me, but not end her life entirely.

But the flames wouldn't listen, they were growing and flaring tall, like they were responding to the adrenaline coursing through my veins, and before I could spare another second on the matter, two of the hellhounds from the strange line stepped forward, teeth bared and dripping with lines of drool.

They walked through the flames, unscathed, growls so low and powerful that the ground itself felt like it was shaking from the vibrations. They circled me slowly, red and green eyes latched onto me as they grew closer with each lap.

I gripped my blade in my fingers, searching for a sign of the hellhound I'd met while walking in the corridor, hoping that it would intercept its friends. The hound I'd encountered had looked at me with curiosity, not hunger—a realization made clear by the animosity dripping from the two hounds in front of me now.

Could I strike one of them? Could I bring myself to hurt a creature like Ralph?

A sharp wave of longing went through me as I thought of the hellhound—my hellhound. I wanted to wrap my arms around his neck, wanted to curl up in the den we'd created months ago and read a book while the sun set around us.

I took a deep breath, taking in the dozens, maybe hundreds, of demons surrounding us—watching us closely, ready to act on the whims and orders of a single man. A man impervious to my strongest weapon.

A fatigue like nothing I'd ever felt rolled through me, weighing me down with a sudden, strange emptiness. I would never go back there, never see him again, never see any of them again. This mission had failed, and we were naive to think there was ever going to be another possible outcome.

I was so tired of the death and destruction, the senseless

fighting and killing. There was no end to it in this place, and I was finally understanding that the boundaries between good and evil, between heaven and hell, were warped and fluid. Each time I wrestled with a creature, it became an act of my life or theirs, but I didn't want that anymore.

My gaze shifted to my friends, shimmering in and out of focus through the wall of flames, trying to reach me. Declan, Atlas, and a wolf I didn't recognize, were fighting against the barrier of bodies that separated us, though the creatures they were clashing with seemed more focused on keeping away from the fire than on harming them. Darius and Eli crawled towards them, fighting to regain their strength, to reach me.

The hounds were less than a foot from me now, the warmth of their breath heating my cheeks as I lifted the blade a bit and then dropped it back down.

How would we get out of this? What was the point?

"Please," I said, the word a whisper pulled without consent from my lips.

And then, I saw the blue-eyed man.

His brow arched as he walked towards us, the light-filled blade dangling casually from his fingers. The hounds separated as he reached us, making way for him to close the distance. He took the blade, and sliced it against my cheek.

I felt the warmth of my blood run down my face, like a thick tear.

"You're not what I thought you'd be," he said, as he studied his blade, where my blood coated it. It was as if he was looking at a whole universe in that crimson pool.

And then, a heaviness pulled through me, like my body was reaching for something, searching. One moment, I was staring into the icy-blue depths of the man's eyes, the next I was met with a pair of familiar, warm brown ones.

I dropped to my knees, equal parts fear and relief warring for focus. A wet nose pressed into my cheek, a soft chirping bark, sending the first wave of comfort I'd felt in so long through my bones.

"Ralph."

He shouldn't be here, I knew that whatever was happening here, was no place for him, but I wrapped my arms around his neck, letting him pull me back up anyway. My face buried into his fur, as I used his strength to ground myself.

A low chuckle reverberated around us and I looked past Ralph to the man, his face lit up with the first real smile I'd ever seen from him. It was blinding.

"That's what you named him? One of the most powerful creatures hell has to offer, sent to you for protection, to be your champion, a warrior. And you call him Ralph?"

I stepped back from Ralph as his words sank into me. I opened my mouth to respond, then shut it again.

Sent to you for your protection.

Ralph hadn't just happened upon me by chance, hadn't just bonded to me out of luck. He'd been sent to protect me. By who?

"This confirms it at least, that dickwad has finally found the right girl. Ralph," he said the name with a bemused wonder, "wouldn't have bonded to anyone else. I'd half thought he'd died out there, in the other realm, that he'd been captured by protectors, didn't really expect him to fulfill his duty."

My fingers felt numb, my head swimming with a low, buzzing hum.

The blue-eyed man slapped Ralph's shoulder, his expression softening around the edges with a warmth I hadn't seen there before. "Good to see you, runt." He turned to me again, white teeth flashing in a quick smile, "he's a bit of a goofball, but he's the smallest one I had. Figured that would help him fit in as much as possible, terrify you the least, maybe." His eyes narrowed slightly, a knowing look that I couldn't completely decipher. "Then again, it seems even when you're faced with the strongest hound I have to offer, you've misplaced your fear for affection. Strange girl."

I shook my head slightly, trying to process the small movement enough to pull my focus to the flames that were melting away, until all I could see was a band of confused expressions—both on my team and the demons surrounding them. Eli still looked half a breath away from unconsciousness, but Darius seemed to be gaining some of his strength back. I wondered, briefly, if some of that strength would seep into Eli, if the bond could protect in the same way that it harmed. Darius had made it to his feet, his wild eyes studying the man with a clear, cold focus. I could see his mind running a million miles a minute, could see the darkness that lingered within him pushing against the walls, begging for escape.

"Why?" It was the only question I could pose, the only word I could form my tongue around and taste. What did it mean to have a demon like this, in the pit of hell, sending me a hellhound for protection? And if he wanted to protect me, why had he attacked?

Had he attacked me? Or had I just assumed?

I thought back to our first meeting, after I'd met the hellhound in the corridor. He'd been toying with me, chased me, even, but he hadn't harmed me. Not really. I'd left the encounter anxious and afraid, but unscathed.

I looked around at the demons, noticing that they only attacked under his direction, his word. The vampires, the hounds—it had been a test. He'd been upset when the girl sank her teeth into me, when she'd done something that could cause potentially irrevocable harm.

And I'd killed her.

The others hadn't been touched since my arrival, not one of them harmed.

"Why?" I felt like a broken toy, stuck in a single loop, a broken record. I wanted so badly to see the big picture, but I felt like I was stuck riding on top of a single puzzle piece, perspective limited.

The man's gaze met mine, but just as he opened his mouth to speak, another figure appeared beside him.

Tall, golden skinned, bearded face.

Cloaky.

"I see you've been having fun while I've been away, Sam." His voice was cold, eyes hard as they landed on me. He clocked the blood on my shoulder, the cut on my cheek. "I'd hate to have to kill you after such a long...fruitful friendship."

The blue-eyed man, Sam, snorted. His face darkened slightly, like a shadow had fallen as soon as Cloaky showed up. "Death would be welcome at this point. The Troops were rallied when they," he nodded towards Six and Darius, "crossed the threshold. They made it all the way here. Somehow." He drew 'somehow' out long and taunting, as his focus moved back to me, his lips curling almost imperceptibly. "Seems she's got more secrets than even you're aware of, old...friend."

Cloaky's nostrils flared slightly, the lines of his jaw sharp and hard. "She's bleeding, but alive. I suppose no harm done in the grand scheme of things."

Sam shrugged, dark brow arching in challenge as he nodded once, the hounds backing away, out of the circle. Ralph followed suit, but not before swiping his tongue along my cheek, where the blade had punctured. "I only wanted to have some fun. Keeping me here has left me...without much entertainment. She's a better fighter than I'd originally given her credit for, but her control over her gifts leaves little to be impressed by."

Cloaky's eyes met mine, irises so dark I couldn't even see a pupil. "Leave us."

At first, I thought he was talking to me, or maybe even Sam, but suddenly we were surrounded by echoes of shuffling as the multitude of feet and paws withdrew.

The vampires, werewolves, and whatever other demons had been in Six's welcoming committee, departed without a word.

Ice ran through my veins. Cloaky had even more power than I'd realized. This many demons? All of them unflinching in their hurry to respond to his demand. Not one of them even bothered to point out that Sam's little game had cost several of their friends' lives.

My stomach churned, my posture stiffening as I realized that I'd killed two vampires because Sam wanted a bit of *entertainment?*

Who the fuck were these men?

I was done. Done being a pawn, a punching bag. Done letting everyone else use and abuse me to suit their whims.

No more.

I clutched my dagger, flames engulfing the blade as my hand lit up. Without another word, I sprinted towards both of the men. Neither moved so much as a muscle as I shoved the dagger forward, puncturing skin and thick cartilage, until I reached his heart.

I froze as Sam's blue eyes met mine, noticed the mirth dancing in the blue pools as my fire licked at his friend's skin.

I'd hit true, I was sure of it.

But Cloaky didn't drop.

Instead, he just sighed, swept his hands together as if he were swiping away crumbs, then pulled my dagger from his chest, dropping it with a soft clatter at my feet.

"No." Darius shook his head, his lips parted softly as he stared from the man to my blade. "It can't be."

The others were staring at Cloaky, expressions hard with fear and confusion, but they didn't have the flash of recognition and terror that I saw written plain as day on Darius's face.

He stepped forward, movements unsure, like he was going to reach for me, but one quick glance from Cloaky had him in a dead stop, his hand twitching forward like he wanted to pull me to him, shield me from the two men surveying us.

Instead of hiding behind him, I stepped in front of Darius, putting myself between the two men and my team. I turned all of my focus towards Cloaky. "I'm done with this, Cloaky." Sam sputtered out a laugh in my pause, but I pressed forward, "I'm sick of this drawn out, tacky and fabricated shroud of mystery. What the hell is this? Why are we here? And more importantly, what the fuck are you?"

His face twisted into a dark grin, eyes sparkling, though whether with humor or malice, I couldn't quite tell. "Better question, girl, is who—who am I."

"Then who?"

Beside him, Sam shook his head, mouthing the word, 'Cloaky,' eyes wide with mirth.

"I understand that I go by many names in your world." Cloaky took a step closer to me, his lips peaked in a sharp smirk, "Prince of Darkness, Father of Lies, Beelzebub, The Morning Star, or my personal favorite" he paused, arching a dark brow, "Satan." My stomach dipped as he circled me slowly, my throat tightening as I processed each word. "They're all a bit dramatic for my taste, conjured by humans with imaginations that outstrip their intelligence, but I suppose it's nice to be respected nonetheless." He stopped moving—dark, unblinking eyes meeting mine. "Those who address me in this world simply call me Lucifer." He arched his brow, lips lifting slightly at the corner. "Though I suppose I could add Cloaky to the mix."

I heard Declan's small gasp, saw all of them look at each other in quick, darting glances, their silent communication filled with tension and fear that I could see and understand, but didn't quite feel.

I knew we were in danger. I understood that if this man decided he wanted it that way, that in the blink of an eye, we'd all be dead in a puddle on the ground. But something about the absurdity of his claim outstripped my fear, shifted something in me. And then, as if a bubble inside of me finally reached its breaking point, I did the unthinkable: burst into loud, echoing peals of laughter, until the force of it almost brought me to my knees.

My eyes darted back to Declan, her lips parted in surprise, no other expression evident on her face as she watched me; to Eli, his skin suddenly an ashy gray-green shade like he was holding back a burgeoning desire to vomit; to Darius, his eyes wide with shock and a healthy dose of fear and recognition that made the trailing, breathy laughs dry up slowly on my lips.

I straightened, my stomach tightening at the heavy silence in the air as I studied the cloaked man.

I saw it then, suddenly surprised that it had taken me so long to piece it together—the dark depths of his eyes, pooling with a silent strength and knowingness that was unmatched in any creature I'd encountered before, the power emanating from in droves so intense that I often found simply being in his presence enough to send chills down my spine. I'd been living with the actual epitome of evil—the literal fucking Morning Star—naively brainstorming ways to take him down during our escape.

Not only had I underestimated how absolutely royally screwed we all were, I'd gone and nicknamed...the devil himself...Cloaky.

We were fucked.

18

MAX

All that I felt was...nothing. Like all the emotions had been sucked out of me, the sound of that name ringing through my ears on repeat until it was all that I could hear.

Lucifer.

Satan.

The original evil dude.

Straight-up biblical shit. Literally.

He wasn't even supposed to be real. Sure, hell existed, and protectors were born from angels centuries ago, but all of the intricately-woven details beyond that—the people in those stories—they weren't supposed to be real. They were there to give humans meaning, purpose. Give protectors a reason to fight, confirmation that good and bad were clearly drawn lines between heaven and hell.

But the devil? That was nothing but a dark and twisted mythology fabricated to make people behave, to keep them in line—a fictional social contract. At least that's what Cyrus always told me and Ro growing up, anyway.

"Heaven?" I wasn't sure I'd even said the word out loud, my jaw felt locked, frozen shut.

But the man chuckled, suggesting that if I hadn't voiced the question, someone had—and probably many before me. "Don't go spiraling into dramatics, girl. I don't have time for it. Suffice to say you know nothing of the truth of things. Like humans, protectors have most things wrong."

I focused my attention back on the present, but suddenly everyone was gone, until I stood there, standing with only Atlas and...Lucifer, in the middle of nowhere. I spun in a slow circle, the movement clumsy and awkward, as I tried to breathe movement back into my limbs. My legs felt like jelly, like entities separate from me.

"I don't have any use for feral wolves," he said, his dark eyes studying Atlas with a leveled disdain.

Atlas's growl deepened as he moved towards me, inching closer and closer until the tip of his furry tail brushed against my leg, standing between me and Lucifer like my final sentinel.

But we both knew that was meaningless—there was no sentinel, no protection from someone like him.

Lucifer reached for the glowing dagger at his waist, the movement lazy and slow, but the threat clear all the same.

"No," I whispered, the word rough against my dry lips as I tried to find my voice. "Please."

Sam materialized in front of us, hair slightly disheveled as he took in the scene. "The others are squared away, what do you want to do with him?" He nodded casually to Atlas before cocking his head to the side, eyes narrowed. "Put him down?"

I took a step forward, the fog slowly lifting with each moment that passed. I was ready to defend Atlas to my dying breath, even though I knew that neither of us stood a chance against either of the creatures before us.

Sam's lips quirked up slightly, but the rest of his expression remained impassive. He let out a low sigh, like he was weighing something before going against his better judgment. "Maybe give him one night? He did make it through the barrier after all, so you know what that likely means. Maybe he'll push through, come back to himself. Prove useful." He turned his focus towards me, eyes narrowed and a cocky smirk dimpling his cheek. "Then again, maybe not. Who am I to say?"

Lucifer's nostrils flared, his eyes unblinking as they stared into mine. "Fine. I can wait one night before I end his misery—give her time to come to terms with things. Keep him separate from the others. If he kills them all, I'll have no leverage over her."

Sam nodded, stepped forward, and wrapped his arms around Atlas's chest, lifting him as if he were nothing more than an oversized, stuffed dog. He was completely oblivious to the fact that Atlas's teeth and claws were burying deep into his skin as he thrashed about, the howls that reverberated from him sharp and desperate. They sent chills down my spine.

And then, just as Sam had arrived, he disappeared, taking the wolf with him until the growls were nothing more than a distorted echo in their wake.

Had he taken them all like that? Just lifted them from one place to the next? Had I watched him take them all? Did I stand there and do nothing? Say nothing?

I blinked; my hands trembled at my sides as I tried to focus. My fingers felt numb, stiff. Time felt like it was slipping, like I'd fast forwarded through the events, the moments skipping randomly, so that the entire picture was blurry.

"You're weak." His voice was deep and echoed around me. "And likely in shock. It's to be expected. You've pushed your powers too far, with little control. I thought," he shook his head, nose lifting slightly with disgust, "I didn't think you'd be this weak—undeveloped—once I found you." He sighed, ran a hand through his hair in a gesture that seemed too human to belong to a creature of such stature. If even the devil himself could feel this fatigued, this drained, what chance did the rest of us have? There was a weariness in the downward slant of his eyes, the tightness of his mouth—a small flash of exhaustion. "You're barely stronger than a protector in this state, your emotions and bonds are draining you instead of filling you. You have too many, all of them too nascent. You're hardly the champion I'd expected."

Emotions? Was he doing the biblical equivalent of calling me a weak female right now?

And that word—bonds.

Ignoring him, I glanced around, a wave of nausea pulling at me as my head spun. I felt my heartbeat everywhere, the steady hum like a metronome, focusing me. It was like the anxiety pulsing through my veins was a living, breathing thing—more in control and clear than anything else. "Where have you taken my friends?"

I moved my fingers to reach for the blade at my hip, until I realized that I'd been holding the handle this entire time—my fingers numb from gripping it so tightly, my hand almost stuck like that, in a claw-like formation.

He straightened, scratching the stubble on his chin as his eyes darted to the side, like he was trying to see this place from my perspective. The soft scrunch of his nose suggested it was lacking, even to him—there was almost a small flash of shame on his face, like someone had entered, unannounced, into his home before he could properly clean. "They're alive. And they'll stay that way so long as you remain amenable."

"Is that a threat?"

He shrugged. "I prefer to think of it more as a compromise, but call it what you want. I have no desire to argue semantics at present."

"What do you want from me?"

"Right now?" His brow lifted slightly as he took a step towards me. I flinched, embarrassment pooling in my belly that I'd shown my fear so openly. His hand reached forward anyway, gripping my bicep. It wasn't hard enough to bruise, but I felt powerless in that moment, watching his fingers wrap so possessively around my arm which looked so insignificant in comparison. "I want you to rest. To heal. You're no use to me like this, dazed and drained. And if you want your friends to live through the week, you'll find a way to prove your use."

The world tightened and expanded all at once, every atom in my body tensed and condensed, like I was trying to squeeze my entire body through a mouse-sized hole. A familiar wind brushed against my skin, as a thick darkness coated my vision—the sort of darkness that was speckled with colorful lights, like hues were trying to form but couldn't quite find their shape.

And then, when the force of the feeling subsided, I opened my eyes.

Familiar stone walls met my glare, firm and unyielding, the cloying stench of stale air choking me as I took a deep breath.

My cell.

I spun around, to say...something. To demand more answers.

But I was alone.

The Devil—Lucifer—whatever the hell he went by—was gone.

And, once again, I was alone.

Panic temporarily flooded my system as I spun in a slow circle, the turn of events tunneling through my mind as I tried to process...everything.

Six, Darius—they were all here. For the first time since Wade's disappearance, we were all in the same place. But rather than inspire calm and hope, it filled me with a spiny, carving dread.

Because we were all in the same place, but that same place happened to be the humble abode of the goddamn Prince of Darkness.

What the actual fuck?

My butt fell until I hit the joke of a bed I'd spent who knew how long sleeping on. I forced myself to take deep breaths. There was so much to consider, so much to untangle and plan for.

I didn't know where to start.

A deep, uncomfortable churning was tightening my belly,

drawing me to something, begging me to pay attention to it, but I didn't understand what it was—not even my body made sense to me anymore.

Slowly, I ran through everything that had happened since I was pulled through these walls—the battle, the blade in Eli's gut, Lucifer's words that seemed filled with a specific ambiguity, but doomy all the same—all of it. Until my thoughts caught and latched onto one phrase—*one night.*

Our problems were too many to count, but there was one that was more pressing and immediate than the others.

I closed my eyes and focused, ignored the exhaustion and anxiety fighting for centerstage in my chest, and found myself strangely leaning into that churning sensation. I stayed like that, no idea for how long, breathing into the discomfort, trying to trace it, to follow it, until that familiar wave of tightness and pain made every molecule of my body stand to attention, the pain and discomfort too extreme to ignore.

I shook my head, took a deep, steadying breath in, and opened my eyes. They took in my altered surroundings—stone walls, but not the same as the ones before—before latching on to a familiar pair of yellow-gold orbs, buried deep in a landscape of tawny fur.

I'd teleported again, with more ease and control than I had before.

"Atlas." I took a step forward, arm outstretched, but every muscle in my body was shaky, unsteady. It was taking less and less time to reorient myself each time I flexed these powers, but it still took time.

The wolf growled low and deep, head ducked down slightly, as it studied me, inching forward moment by moment, circling me like it was preparing to attack.

I saw the creature then, in that moment, and understood that word now—feral.

I didn't see Atlas anywhere in his eyes, couldn't even be sure if the wolf recognized me or not. It was probably a thoughtless thing to do—enter a cage with a rabid wolf, with nothing but a blade and my hands to protect myself. Not that I'd be able to hurt Atlas, even if he did try to attack me.

Still, I'd need to stay here for a bit, to rest and gain the energy I'd need to make it back to my own small cage.

But I couldn't leave him, couldn't sit and do nothing knowing that he was very much on Lucifer's death row here. Given nothing but one night to conquer himself, to fold the demon back, to merge.

"Come back," I whispered, the words so needy and filled with grief that I almost didn't recognize my voice through the quivering sound. I held my hands up, the sign for universal surrender, hoping that it was universal enough for even were-wolves to understand, and tried desperately to push back the fear threatening to eclipse everything else. "Atlas, please."

The wolf stopped moving, its posture straightening slightly, eyes wide and filled with so many emotions that I couldn't begin to untangle one from the other.

A loud crack echoed around the room. I jumped, scanning the walls to figure out where it was coming from.

And then another. And another. And another.

I turned back to Atlas, and saw his body shifting slowly, his limbs bending at awkward angles, his face compressed in agony as his body turned against him. His bones were breaking and reforming, the lines of his legs thickening and lengthening, his paws elongating into thin, fur-coated fingers.

He was shifting. But I knew from the small whimpers he was biting back, from the fear in his yellow eyes—eyes that were warring with shades of brown, creating intricate Rorschach plots as they leered at me—that this wasn't a normal shift. There was something drawn out and unnatural about it.

I felt each bone that broke ricochet through my own, every nerve of my body hyper-aware of the pain coursing through his.

Loud, chilling wails and groans pulled from his snout as his body simultaneously resisted and gave in to the transformation.

Quickly, I closed the distance between us, no longer concerned about whether or not he'd try to sink his teeth into me, too focused on the pain ripping through him. It almost seemed unsurvivable.

I crouched down beside him, resting my palms gently against his shoulder, his back, pulling them away the second I felt his bones shift below me. The last thing I wanted to do was cause him any further pain.

"What can I do? What can I do?" I murmured softly, afraid even the volume of my voice would add to the war waging inside of his body.

Yellow eyes pierced mine, and I saw the fear so clear there, incandescent and bright. I pressed my fingers gently against his face, the fur soft against my skin and held his gaze, desperately trying not to jump with sympathy at each crack that sounded from him.

I straightened my spine, focused all of my attention on holding eye contact, on lending him what little strength I already had. And then, with a deep breath, I went inside of myself. I searched as I had with Declan and, before her, Eli, feeling aimlessly inside myself for that strange strand I'd seemed to find with them—that tether of connection.

For a long, insufferable moment, I didn't think I'd find it. But then, like I was staring at one of those old Where's Waldo portraits, I scanned and scanned, stuttered with recognition, and retraced my focus until I latched on to something both familiar and not. I breathed deeply at first, and then the air was pulling through my lungs in fast, breathy gasps, until the pace matched Atlas's perfectly.

Closing my eyes, I tried to calm my racing heart, to focus all of my attention on that spark of recognition, to imagine his body transitioning seamlessly from wolf to man and back again —to mending the pain and difficulty by taking it into myself.

It didn't work as it had with the others, I couldn't feel him in the way that I could them, couldn't fold my energy into his or visualize a path to success with any ease.

But, slowly, I felt a heavy strain in my body, a slow, lazy push of force that sent a wave of exhaustion and exhilaration through me, each battling for center stage.

The face between my hands grew more smooth, the lift and fall of his breath less labored. Until, after a long, impossible moment, I opened my eyes.

My palm was pressed against Atlas's cheeks, his face sweaty and pale, eyes still a yellow so fierce and bright I glanced down, as if the sight alone could burn me where I knelt.

But when I looked down, I was met with an eyeful of smooth, lean muscles, skin clammy with sweat, chest stuttering with quick breaths. And below that—

Well, when werewolves transitioned, they didn't exactly come with a fresh change of clothes.

I cleared my throat and drew my eyes back up, until they latched briefly on Atlas's full lips. They twitched, the movement so small I wasn't even certain that I caught it.

"I'm sorry, uh—" I licked my lips, trying to draw moisture back to my suddenly dry mouth. I met his eyes, and whatever else I was going to say simply dried away.

Gold and brown, the colors weaving and bleeding together until I couldn't tell where one hue ended and another began. But it was the look, the steady focus in those eyes that had my heartbeat stumbling about chaotically in my chest.

There was a heavy heat in that gaze that sent a bolt of electricity through my body. I dropped my hands, realizing that I was still basically caressing his face, and stood up, suddenly in need of as much space as possible between us.

I stumbled slightly from the fast movement, still disoriented from a combination of teleporting, healing, and whatever other lingering chaos was raging through my mind.

Atlas stood too, his head tilting to the side slightly as he continued studying me, the lines of his face sharp, expression predatory.

He took a step towards me, and I took a mirrored step away, until my back was pressed against the cool stone of the wall. His eyes narrowed slightly, head still tilted, posture coiled like he was deciding whether to move towards me or away. Something unfamiliar flashed in his expression, his jaw ticking as he took a deep breath—and suddenly I was far more terrified than I'd been when his wolf had growled at me. Adrenaline had my heart racing in overtime now.

"Atlas, I—"

As if the sound of his name alone decided his actions for him, he closed the distance between us in two quick steps, until his body was pressed against my chest, pinning me against the wall.

Before I could make sense of the hurried motion, his lips pressed down against mine, breath hot against my mouth, pressure bruising as he kissed me—long and deep enough to make my toes curl uncomfortably in my shoes.

Atlas was...kissing me. It took an embarrassingly long moment for my brain to catch up with my body, and by the time that it did, I realized that my lips were very much kissing him back—with just as much anger and need. It wasn't gentle, wasn't soft and sensuous or even hurried and hot.

Kissing Atlas felt much like fighting with him did—an adrenaline rush that filled me with equal parts rage and excitement.

My lips parted as his tongue slipped in, sweeping feverishly against mine until one—or both, I couldn't tell in the moment—of us groaned, the sound uncurling something low in my belly.

I scraped my teeth against his full bottom lip, drunk on the taste of him, and suddenly couldn't remember why we hadn't been doing this all along.

Every nerve in my body was on fire as his fingers dug into my sides, hard enough that I knew he'd leave marks. But somehow the idea of his fingers leaving small scrapes and bruises on my body sent a spark of excitement through me—I'd have proof that this was real, that this had happened. It wasn't just a dream or some misplaced, lazy fantasy that I had as I'd fallen asleep.

Every sweep of his skin against mine sent a new wave of chills through me, like every atom in my body was filled with a feverish anticipation of something more—something bigger.

I knew in that moment that I'd always wanted him, had always wanted to feel the scratch of his stubble scrape against my chin, had always wanted to test the way his body fit when pressed against mine, had always wanted to taste the mouth that was always tight and slightly frowning, filled with disapproval and supernatural restraint. All the anger and distrust that had pooled between us acted as fuel now, each of our movements hurried and harsh as my mouth battled for control over his.

I was absurdly wet from just a few moments of kissing him, and knew that if his hand so much as swept against the seam of my pants where my legs met, that he'd be able to feel me soaking through the fabric.

The hard stone dug into my shoulders as I raked my fingernails through his hair, even the feel of his soft hair against my skin enough to send a fresh pulse of need through me. My lips were starting to throb from the punishing battle between us, but it was a strange sort of soft pain that had my stomach flipping over itself for more.

His hands dug into my hips in response, lifting until my legs wrapped around his waist as he pulled me closer to him.

It was then that I remembered that he was completely naked —and, judging by the pressure at my core, very, very aroused.

"Atlas—" the sound came out as a pant, need so evident in my voice that I'd be embarrassed if I wasn't so fucking desperate for him to touch me everywhere, all at once, right now.

A low groan rumbled in his chest as he took advantage of my open mouth and shoved his tongue against mine again, the movements strangely slow and languid as we met, despite the rage pulsing from him, and hot enough to pull another needy groan from my throat.

He slid one hand up my shirt in the back, the feel of his fingers ghosting over my flesh the most delicious fire I'd ever felt. In a quick, hurried manoeuvre, he peeled my shirt off, pressing his lips back to mine as soon as the fabric was out of his way, as if he couldn't wait another moment for his mouth to be fused back to mine. His teeth pressed softly into my lip, pulling gently, before he started making his way down my neck in small bites and bruising kisses. I was vaguely aware of strange mewling pants and moans, before I realized that they were coming from me.

Every touch was harsh and filled with an intoxicating dance between pain and pleasure, and my entire body throbbed as he undid the latch of my bra, pulling the material away with an erratic, hurried movement.

When the peak of my nipples pressed against his bare chest, a tingling pulse shot to my core, every inch of my body electric with the feel of him. The strange fire that I conjured had nothing on the heat pulsing between us, and despite the fact that I was literally pressed up against him, I wanted to be closer, to feel him on every inch of me, to feel him in me.

As if sensing my thoughts as I thought them, I felt his fingers dig into the waistband of my pants. He tugged them down roughly, his body still pressing into mine hard enough to keep me pinned up between him and the wall.

With an impatient groan, I unwrapped my legs from his waist, missing the feel of him against my clit as soon as I did. With quick, clumsy movements, I slid down the wall and helped him peel the fabric from my legs, until the cool air of the stoney room seared some of the heat radiating from my skin, like a balm.

For a moment, both of us stilled, our chests heaving with deep, panting breaths, as we stared at each other. He was a good foot taller than me, his presence towering over me and somehow making me feel both trapped and safe. His dark eyes, struck through with flashes of yellow, glared down at me, lids narrowed and heavy—and I could see the battle raging inside of him in that moment.

This wasn't a sweet, romantic encounter. This was surrender —neither of us able to pretend we didn't want the other for a moment longer. I could see it in the hard line of his jaw, the slight flare of his nostrils—he still didn't trust me...or himself. He still wanted to keep me as far away as he could.

Atlas didn't want to want me. But he did. It was, perhaps, the thing that frustrated him more than anything.

And I wanted him just as much.

His fingers ghosted up the length of my arm, and it felt like a spark was igniting through my entire body.

I studied him, my lips parted as I tried to keep from crawling up him like a tree and fusing my mouth to his. He still hadn't said a single word to me since I'd shown up, and I could see the wolf lingering behind his eyes—there and also not.

The depths of his eyes sent a flash of fear—and excitement— burrowing into my chest. He looked like the Atlas I'd met months ago, but his edges were frayed, shot through. The walls around him were still standing tall and sound, but I suddenly realized that the careful control that had always emanated from him, the absolute steadiness I'd always associated with him—it was nothing but an illusion, an attempt to disguise the raging storm battling within him.

As if he couldn't control that battle for one more second, his hands gripped my hips, lifting me back around him, and sheathed himself inside of me, in one smooth, punishing thrust.

The feel of him inside of me, my core tightening and adjusting around him, was almost enough to undo me right there. He wasn't quite kissing me, but his lips brushed lightly against mine with each inhale, our breaths mingling together as my eyes lifted towards his.

As soon as our gazes met, he closed the distance between us, kissing me harshly as he threaded his fingers roughly through my hair. I bit his bottom lip, tugging roughly as he lifted my hips up and down, the soft sound of my skin slapping against his the only thing louder than our heavy, panting breaths.

I could feel the sharp edges of some of the stones slicing and scraping against my back, but something about the small inter-jections of pain, cut with the mind-numbing waves of pleasure, did nothing but increase the tightness building in my stomach.

A familiar feeling unfurled low in my belly—a heady excite-ment clouding my senses as I tightened around him. His answering gasp made me grin against his skin, and I loved having this power over him—could feel myself growing drunk on the feel of him inside of me, on the war for power we were both fighting and losing.

Our clammy skin was salty and slick as we slid against each other. He gripped my hair at the base of my skull, tugging until my neck was more exposed so he could nip and lick my earlobe, the column of my throat—each touch—whether feather-light or hard and demanding—was like fuel to the fire growing beneath my skin. His movements grew more rigid and forceful as he lifted me up and down, both of us grinding into the wall as we dove deeper into the sensations, any illusion of resistance too far gone to reclaim.

My fingernails scraped down his back, and I grinned as I felt the indentations groove into his skin. I wouldn't be the only one leaving this encounter unscathed—I wanted to make sure that there would be no denying what we'd done tomorrow. He could shift back into his removed, sullen self as I was certain he would do, but I would make sure to leave my mark. He wouldn't control every element of this moment—I'd make sure of it.

He growled deep and low, his thrusts growing more and more fierce as he burrowed his head into my neck, teeth scraping along my neck and clavicle.

Suddenly, things shifted—the harsh, angry movements

started to transition into something different, something almost soft.

His eyes met mine again, and all that I saw was the familiar dark, impenetrable brown. There was no golden yellow in sight. There was a storm in those eyes, an entire world—and while I couldn't unweave every emotion pooling in their depths, I was certain that there was a flash of fear, and maybe even of awe.

I pressed my lips back to his, the kiss soft and deep now as I swept my tongue against his, the tension low in my stomach so tight and hungry that it was almost painful.

"Atlas," I whispered, my voice nothing but a breathy moan against his lips.

He groaned, his hand coming up to rest gently against my cheek, the rage and anger seeping out of him, like he no longer had the energy or room to hold it. His other hand gripped my hip as he thrust into me.

I let out a low moan as I came, a low hum growing in my ears from the intensity. His teeth bit into my neck as he followed me over.

Neither of us moved, still tangled in each other against the cold stone wall, now slick with our sweat, both of us silent as we reveled in the quiet ecstasy flowing through and between us.

He pressed his lips softly over the bite, the movement so quick and gentle that I wasn't even sure it could be called a kiss. He stepped back, pulling out of me as I slid against the wall. My legs were like jelly and I found myself grateful for the sturdy stone at my back.

The silence between us was deafening, so I quickly scooped up my clothes and slid back into the worn fabric. I wasn't sure what this was, what it meant.

When I glanced back at him, I saw him leaning against the wall on the opposite side of the cell, dark eyes studying me.

"Um," I said, awkwardly twisting my hands together as I tried to think of something to say—but my thoughts dried up and whatever words were forming on my tongue died where they started.

He exhaled a long, deep breath, turned away from me with his eyes pressed shut, and rolled his forehead against the hard stone wall.

From the harsh, tense lines in his back, the heavy exhaustion that was making his muscles tremor, I knew that there'd be no pillow talk or afterglow cuddle with Atlas. I wasn't sure how long he'd been stuck inside of the wolf, but I could tell that he had some shit he needed to work through and that my presence wouldn't further the process along in any helpful way.

I rolled my shoulders, stretching slightly, relishing the sore muscles and skin along my back. I felt better than I had before I'd come here, like I'd found a vital source of energy I'd been missing, yearning for. It was probably the succubus, happy and placated after being sated.

And, more importantly, Atlas was back. Lucifer's threat pierced through any awkwardness I was feeling and I knew that I needed to leave, needed to follow whatever instructions that man gave me—if I had any hope of keeping us all alive through the night.

"Your wolf," I said, taking a soft step forward, but pausing before I was within arm's reach of him. "You need to find a way to work with it, to share yourself. The cloaked man—Lucifer I guess—he won't let you live if he thinks you're a danger, if he thinks you're more work than you're worth." Atlas's shoulders tightened as he listened. "I'll do everything I can to keep him away from you and the others, I promise."

He turned around, eyes wide. I saw his lips start to form the shape and sound of my name, but I was gone before I could hear what else he said, the sudden rush of energy making it easier to call on my power.

The air of my cell was growing too familiar for comfort and I recognized the musty scent of the bedding before I even opened my eyes. I let myself adjust to the strange feeling of having my body disappear and be remade again in a new location. I wasn't sure it was a power that would ever feel natural or normal.

"That's not exactly what I meant by rest and heal." A cold voice echoed behind me.

I spun around, head swimming from the movement as my gaze landed on the cloaked man, his face darkened by shadow. He was always an intimidating figure, but now that I knew who he was—who he really was—the harsh lines of his face, the haunted look in his dark eyes, made my blood go cold.

He shrugged, examining his nail beds as if bored by my presence. "But," he continued, the word harsh and gravelly, assessing, "I suppose it ultimately accomplished what it needed to, giving you a much needed boost of power, so who am I to complain? It's also promising to see that your shifting skills are getting stronger. You can't go very far yet, and you drain too quickly, but it is progress. We'll need to hurry that process along if we're to get any use out of you."

"What do you want with me?"

"Not to be dramatic, but," he arched his brow in the antithesis of his statement, "you're here to save us all."

I opened my mouth to retort, but closed it again, his words like a language that I couldn't completely translate.

"It's a shock to me, as well. Apologies that I'm less than impressed with," he waved his hand in my direction, "well, this. I was expecting someone a bit...more?"

"Why me?" I crossed my arms over my chest, hating myself for the diminutive gesture, but it was impossible to feel anything but powerless in his presence. The dude *was* the fucking devil himself.

His lips pulled into a caricature of a grin, but it looked terrifying and cruel on his features. "Hasn't any of it made you curious? Or have you just been hiding behind ignorance because you're afraid of the truth? You're a succubus, yes, but you're so much more than that." I narrowed my eyes, confused. He exhaled sharply and pressed on, as if he was tasked with the tedium of explaining calculus to a toddler. "You arrived here with the etchings of a wolf's tooth in your skin." He leaned against the wall, the movement somehow making him look even more menacing, rather than relaxed. "And you healed almost instantly. You've survived vampire bites as if they were nothing more than a scratch. You can dream-walk, shift from one place to another, and summon hellfire in the palm of your hands. You have creatures from all walks of life revolving around you, as if you are the sun."

"So?" I croaked out. My tongue dried up in my mouth as he laid out all of the things I'd more or less ignored, afraid of learning the true depth of their meaning.

But now, everything that I'd tried to ignore was suddenly unavoidable, staring me head-on, taunting, and I felt childish for wishing that he'd stuff them back into his mouth and swallow his words before uttering them, before shifting the world out from under me.

"Don't you realize yet that you are different? That you're so much more than what you've always thought you were? You've been spending so much time floating in shame and confusion, when you should've been reveling in your power—owning and harnessing it." He shook his head, exhaling softly, "and now, we're so behind."

"But—why? Why can I do all of these things?" I was vaguely aware of the light buzzing in my ears, the hard squeeze around my chest that was making it almost impossible to breathe a full breath of air.

"Your body absorbs the magic of others because you're directly from one of the lines that created it."

"It?

"Magic. Power."

The buzzing grew louder, and I sat down on my makeshift bed. There was an odd sensation rolling through me, like my body understood where this was going before my mind did. "I don't understand. What line? Do you know who my parents are?"

His eyes crinkled softly in the corners, pleased that I was finally asking the questions he wanted me to ask. "Your mother was a protector, who came from the line of a succubus. It wasn't particularly strong in her blood, but that power has emerged stronger in yours."

I licked my lips, but my mouth was too dry to offer relief. "And my father?"

He grinned, dark eyes narrowing as they pierced mine—sharper than any blade. "Guilty."

FASHIONED BY FLAMES

Grab Book Six in The Protector Guild series:

Everything Max thought she knew is wrong. Now, she must figure out who she can trust before the world as she knows it crumbles down around them all...

ACKNOWLEDGMENTS

This book wouldn't be possible without the support of my family and friends. You know who you are, and I couldn't be luckier to have you in my life. Thanks for always encouraging and pushing me to chase after my writing worlds.

Special thank you to my editor, Kath, and my cover designer, Michelle. This book is so much better because you've all contributed a piece to it. Thank you.

And to my very own 'Ralph,' thanks for keeping me company while I wrote this series for hours and months on end.

ABOUT THE AUTHOR

I'm a teacher by day and a writer by night (and, occasionally, I moonlight as a bartender as well). Most of my time is happily spent hanging out with my cartoonish dog (who is spoiled to the core, as he should be), going for meandering walks around the city, and reading everything I can get my hands on. I drink way too much coffee, binge-watch obsessively with the best of them, and love playing board games or kayaking with friends.

Want to know more about me and the fictional worlds I spend my time in? Come follow me on social media! I'm particularly active in my FB reader group and on instagram.

Printed in Great Britain
by Amazon

28602789R00205